# ROSALIE HAM

# THERE SHOULD BE
# MORE DANCING

*fi*

# PART ONE

*'Everyone's got plans ... until they get hit.'*

Mike Tyson

# ROOM 4321

I'm not going. And I'm not living with her.

I'd sooner die.

Last week, they moved Florence into my home. The second I laid eyes on her standing there in my doorway, with her Ava Gardner hair and Lana Turner bust, I said to myself, 'This isn't going to work.'

She's not my type at all. For a start, she's a common barmaid. And, in the end, she turned out to be nothing less than a thief, a liar and an adulteress.

One week we lasted together, and then the truth came out.

You see, there's been a conspiracy. I found out on Sunday that for almost sixty years the entire neighbourhood, everyone in fact, knew things that I didn't know, things I should have known. And there have been plots against me. Shockingly, Walter, my firstborn, was in on them as well. He says he wasn't. But how can I trust what Walter says now? How can I trust what anyone says?

Today my heart is aching. I can feel it. It's gasping, like a fish on a beach, because my own children have broken it.

In fact, everyone I've known for the last sixty years has betrayed me.

So, this is my final day. I've come here to throw myself to my death. I know what will happen to my body, my hands and my head. I know it'll be quick, but I can't jump yet because at present there's too many people in the foyer, so I've had to book in for the night. I must say, it is a lovely room, though beige and brown aren't my colours. I'm right up on the top floor and I can see all the way across to the war memorial.

But, if the truth be known, since you died I've been a bit ambivalent about life anyway. So this morning when I realised I was left with no option but to kill myself, I decided to swallow thallium, but you can't get it anymore. The chemist didn't even know what I was talking about when I asked for some. 'It was popular in the fifties,' I said, though she didn't look as if she was born until nineteen eighty so I don't suppose she would know.

So then I went to the railway station, but there were too many people waiting on the platform. I decided to throw myself under a tram instead, but the first driver to come along was very young, and I didn't want him to have me on his mind for the rest of his life because of *them,* because *they've* betrayed me.

It all started about five weeks ago. It was my birthday. *Our* birthday.

Judith said, 'We're having an eightieth birthday party just for you!'

As you know, it was actually our seventy-ninth birthday, but I just let them be a year early and got on with enjoying my day out. Lovely lunch. I had a prawn cocktail and a slice of cheese-cake. The cream wasn't real, but it was still nice. Mrs Parsons had poached fillet of fish and a slice of lemon tart. She said hers was lovely too, but she couldn't get her spoon through the pastry so she wrapped it in her serviette and popped it in her handbag for later.

It was a lovely day, then they dropped me back home and it all went to mud. Judith told me I had to go to a home. I said, 'I've got a home,' but she meant a home in a retirement village. That's when I knew I'd have to be careful about you. I didn't want to be put away just because I talk to you. If Judith heard me, she'd say, 'She talks to herself, she's demented.'

These past weeks have been truly dreadful. As I say, it all started on my birthday, and then they moved Florence in, and, well,
it ended last Sunday. It was the last straw, so here I am.

It's obvious that, together, the very people who are meant to
care about me planned the whole conspiracy. As the saying
goes, 'Crows everywhere are equally black.'

Why? That's what I want to know. Why would they do that
to me?

# DAY 1

Walter told them to be dressed and ready for the surprise birthday party by eleven. So, on Sunday, Margery inched out of bed especially early to eat her breakfast. After she'd been in to see Mrs Parsons, she showered, ran a wet comb through what was left of her curls, dressed in her best frock, coat and hat—a squat, felt hat she'd bought in 1949—and was waiting at the gate by ten, peering down Gold Street.

Eventually, Walter came kicking along the footpath, smiling just for Margery, a sixty-ish ex-boxer, balding yet hirsute, a shiny Elvis curl on his forehead and the remnants of a ducktail carefully constructed at his nape. Because it was his mother's birthday, he carried his purple suit folded over his arm, and as always, Walter was jaunty, victorious, draped in silk, his opponent prone on the canvas, his boxing gloves bloodied, triumph obliterating the pain in his battered ribs, not a sleek black hair on his head out of place and his entourage behind him. All around, the spectators pulsed, 'Bull, Bull, Brunswick Bull!' At the sight of her son, Margery's stern, slightly bewildered expression warmed.

'Nine hundred and eighty days,' she said, her distorted image looming back at her from Walter's chrome lens sunglasses.

'Nine hundred and eighty days without one single drink,' he said and kissed her on the cheek.

'How are you, Walter dear?'

'Never better.' He gave her a plastic supermarket bag. 'You look pretty.'

Margery blushed, 'It's just an old thing,' and looked into the plastic bag. 'Oh my! Walter ... chocolates and flowers!'

'Carnations,' Walter said, pleased with himself. 'Happy birthday, Mumsy.'

Just then, the Boyles arrived. As Barry eased his almost-

new, second-hand Mercedes-Benz M-Class four-wheel drive to
the kerb, Judith observed her eroded family standing there on
the footpath: a plain old woman contracting into her distorted
shoes, mauve hair squirting out from under her aged hat, and
a punctured and pulverised bloke with black-dyed sideburns
and bleach-white footy shorts, which were tight enough to be
confronting. Behind them, the family home was crumbling, its
once grass-parrot-green paint lying in pale flakes on the ground,
the splintered rails of a picket fence rotting on a dry patch of
couch grass. 'Christ, it's like a scene from an old horror film.'

'You can't pick your family,' Barry said, and in the back seat
Pudding said, 'Pity about that.'

'Right, listen,' Barry said, checking his image in the rear-vision
mirror. 'It's Marge's eightieth birthday. It's in our best interest to
keep it nice, no matter what, for the next few hours, alright?'

'You just want her house,' Pudding said and got out of the car.
She strolled across the narrow street to speak to Tyson, who'd
known her since the day she was born. These neighbours, Tyson
and his housemates, were a bunch of unkempt twenty-some-
things, aged teenagers lost between genres. As usual, they sat in
the wreck of a modified 1998 Holden Commodore. The wheels
were missing and the car itself was rusting into the overgrown
front lawn beneath the broken front windows of the house, but
the leather seats remained and the in-car entertainment system
boasted stinger wiring, custom sub-enclosure, clarion head unit,
sound processor, tweeters, sub-woofers, amplifier and speakers.

Judith smiled tightly at her mother and puckered to give her a
birthday kiss, but Margery said, 'Hello, Judith. Goodness, you've
put on weight since Christmas.'

'You're not much chop yourself, Marge,' Judith said evenly.
'You could have at least worn your pearls, that's what they're
for—to wear.' Judith had coveted the pearls for thirty years.
On the occasion of her twenty-first birthday she assumed her
mother had actually gifted her the pearls but was stunned when,
at the stroke of midnight, Margery asked for them back.

Over her mother's shoulder, Judith spotted the For Sale sign on Mrs Bist's house. 'Renovator's delight. Expect the unexpected in this delightful cottage in a prime location.'

'You didn't tell me that house was for sale, Barry! Why didn't you tell me that house was for sale?'

'The sign's been up since Christmas, Judif,' Walter said, and Barry raised his hands in surrender. Barry worked in real estate, but his patch was Reservoir, a suburb to the north of Melbourne not yet quite noticed by restorers and opportunists.

'Kevin from over the road wanted to buy it,' Margery said, 'but a young couple ended up getting it.'

'That'll be nice for you, Mumsy,' Walter said. 'A nice young couple next door.'

'Renovators.' Margery sniffed. 'They take all the parking spots in the street, have a baby—think they're the first people in the world to have one—then take up all the room on the footpath with those ruddy great prams. You can't get around them with a shopping cart.'

'Modernise the suburb,' Barry said, throwing his arms wide. 'Your house price will skyrocket, Marge, and they'll plant nice gardens and trees.'

'That's right,' Margery declared. 'They plant trees, the roots ruin the footpaths, block out the views and the birds drop all over the cars, and then they complain.'

Walter suggested at least yuppies would be a change from Tyson and his mates, but Margery just screwed her nose at the house opposite. 'Wretched ruddy so-and-sos they are.'

'*Progress,* Marge. This is where the boom is,' Barry said, reaching inside his beige leather bomber jacket to take out his Black-Berry. 'There's thirty-six renovations in a three-kilometre radius of this street as we speak. A real boom. This one went for six fifty.'

Judith's face lit up. '*Six hundred and fifty thousand dollars,* for a smelly little cave like that?'

Barry ran his finger over his BlackBerry. 'I've been telling you for months, Judith, these little workers' cottages are going off.'

'My little home can't be worth much,' Margery said. 'Lance's parents only paid ninety-five pounds for it.'

'Free-standing, single-fronted terraces are very in demand. A boom, right here in this street.' Barry slapped his brother-in-law on the shoulder. 'Aged care and real estate, that's where the future is, eh, Walter?'

'You shouldn't wear those shorts, Walter,' Judith said. 'They're obscene.'

'Better get changed,' Walter said, and went inside. Margery leaned on the car. She was longing to sit down, but Judith was poking her mobile phone with her long, filigreed fingernails, and Barry had gone to peer through Mrs Bist's front window. Soon Walter bounced out onto the street in his purple suit, trying to stretch his jacket over his paunch. His mother beamed at him. 'I remember when you got that lovely suit, Walter. Lance called you a lair, but you were never a lair. You were a champion.'

Pud wandered back to the car and Judith snapped her phone shut. 'Purple matches the colour of your skin tone, Walter.' His proud smile fell away and he stepped from one foot to the other, rubbing his nose with the palm of his hand.

Pudding stroked his lapel. 'I think you look cool, Uncle Walter. Seriously retro.'

'I'm the one here that's trained in "Colours",' Judith said, and it was true, the Certificate Three in Beauty Services class of 1995 did spend one entire lesson on matching colours with skin tone. 'My gift with style, DeeAndra, is precisely why I am an unqualified success.'

'That's true,' Pud said brightly. 'You are an *unqualified* success … especially with women who want to look like Middle Eastern dictators' wives.'

Barry rubbed his hands together. 'Ready for your big day out, Marge?'

'My word,' she said, tugging at the doorhandle.

'I'll get the special guest,' Walter said.

Pudding opened the car door, 'Hop in, Gran.' Margery started to climb into the car but Judith called, 'No!' She retrieved a towel from the back and spread it on the seat for her mother and Mrs Parsons to sit on. Pudding eased Marge into the car, and Walter arrived with Mrs Parsons, a small, nut-coloured old woman clinging to his purple suit, her little brown legs coming out of the bottom of her coat like in a kiddie's drawing. Walter placed her on the back seat as though she was a new moth and squeezed in beside her. Pudding strapped the two old ladies and her uncle in, made herself comfortable in the dickie seat, and off they went in Barry's almost-new Mercedes to the Tropic Hotel, an establishment renowned for its succulent tropical decor.

On the short trip, Mrs Parsons and Margery stared wondrously at the Elms along Royal Parade, the stately terrace houses, the taut joggers and fubsy city workers toiling around Princes Park, and the portentous stone buildings of Melbourne University.

'It's all changed,' Mrs Parsons said, and Walter concurred, 'Fings do change, don't they?'

In the city, Margery stared at the shoppers and bankers, shop assistants and office workers, the milling students and the tourists. 'These days it's like we're in another country,' she sniffed, and Pudding rolled her eyes. 'They're just people, Gran, like you and me.'

In the underground car park Barry waited patiently while Walter helped the aged birthday girl and her decrepit friend from the car. Pudding walked her grandmother and, behind them, Walter came slowly with Mrs Parsons curled at his elbow. Judith, feeling pleased and important to be going out to a posh hotel with her husband, caught Barry's arm as he rushed purposefully towards the lift. 'It's like taking a couple of raisins out, isn't it?'

'Yeah.'

'You're right about the old people's home,' she said, struggling to keep up in her new high heels. 'I mean, if Mrs Bist's house got six hundred grand ... and Pud will be at uni next year, and I'll have expanded into counselling ... Well, it is a good time for you to go into a business.'

'Yeah,' he said and removed her hand from his arm. He hurried to press the lift button.

'There's never going to be a shortage of old people, is there?' she called.

He missed the lift, so again, Barry had to wait. The old ladies faltered at the small gap between the floor and the lift, but stepped gamely over it and moved to the back, clinging to the handrail, and were soundlessly transported to the foyer. By the time the lift stopped, Barry had managed to distance himself from his wife again. Stepping into the foyer, he glanced around and made a beeline for the restaurant, but he was spotted by a concerned young man with an indoor complexion. 'Mr Boyle! Were we expecting you? I'm sorry—'

'No, mate,' Barry said, cutting him off. 'The in-laws.' He jerked his head and the concierge turned to see a large, heavily made-up woman with big hair lumbering towards him in a diamanté-studded, knee-length kite dress. 'Mrs Boyle?' he said, astonished, but Judith had stopped to squint up into the atrium. Creeping across the foyer behind her was a withered little Islander woman and a sunken old lady wearing glasses that didn't sit well on her old face. Both ladies carried at least two handbags each and were dressed for winter. With them was a dilapidated, oversized bodgie in an undersized purple suit and a strapping, stylish young woman typing on a mobile phone as she walked.

'Got a booking,' Barry said. It took a moment, but the concierge's arm shot up, his fingers clicked and a waiter arrived and led the group to a table in a corner behind an imitation rubber plant. The Blandons sat, looking up at the plastic potted palm fronds peeping from all forty-three balconies, and the indoor rainforest bathed in sky-lit air, colourful plastic parrots dotting its branches. In keeping with the ambiance, the furniture was cane and the carpet a busy pattern of hibiscus and lyrebirds.

'It's real nice here, Barry,' Judith said, taking a bottle of sparkling wine from her bag. She ripped the cork out effortlessly and filled her water tumbler, and as she drank Pudding took the bottle from her and poured some for Margery and Mrs Parsons. When a waiter arrived with a scotch and Coke for Barry, Judith asked for an ice bucket and 'a list of the sorts of champagnes you've got', and Pudding asked for a vodka and red cordial. Walter wiped his sweaty brow with his table napkin and told the waiter he'd happily kill anyone for a beer but the doctor would kill him, so he'd better have dry ginger ale, 'in a seven-ounce beer glass, if you don't mind, thanks, bud'.

Barry's mobile phone rang, and Pudding reached across and snatched it from the table before her father could. 'Hello?' Then she smirked at her father and said, 'Wow, Dad, what a surprise, it's your secretary ... again!'

Judith poured herself more sparkling wine and Barry grabbed the phone, walking away with it. 'Yes, Charmaine, what's the problem?'

Pudding looked around the hotel and said, 'This is very special for you, isn't it, Gran?'

'Very special,' Margery replied, and everyone smiled and raised their glasses, but before they could say 'happy birthday' Margery added, 'Though armrests on dining table chairs are uncalled for.'

Judith pointed out to everyone that the Tropic was a skyscraper hotel, 'It's got an opening that goes all the way up to the sky, see? And there's an indoor forest and waterfall right there in the foyer.'

'It's called a water feature,' Pudding corrected. 'Let's go for a ride to the top, Gran.' Margery hesitated, but Mrs Parsons moved about between the armrests, so Walter pulled her chair out and Margery gathered her courage and followed. 'Coming?' Pudding called back, but Walter was staring at the waitress at the next table and Barry was still talking to Charmaine.

When Judith stepped into the lift, Margery patted Mrs Parsons' arm reassuringly. 'It's quite safe. The sign there says it can take five hundred kilograms.'

At the top a man's voice said, 'Level forty-three,' and Mrs Parsons asked, 'How does he know?'

'It's pre-recorded,' Pudding said. Margery and Mrs Parsons nodded, though they were no wiser.

Judith and Pudding went to the high balustrade and looked down to the carpet forty-three floors below. Margery stayed by the lift. There were no chairs to sit on, so she perched on the edge of the potted palm and watched a family try to get into their room. A girl, aged about ten, swiped the key card and opened the door for her mother, while her brother and father struggled with their luggage. Mrs Parsons wasn't tall enough to see over the balustrade, so she came back and stood next to Margery. 'I went in an aeroplane once.'

'What does it look like from up there?' Margery asked.

'I had the aisle seat.'

After a short time they descended in the lift, Mrs Parsons grabbing her beret, and made their way across the foyer, satisfied that they'd been all the way to the top. As they settled again at the table, Barry said, 'Top suicide spot, this place. Take it from me, it can kill a lovely meal when someone lands.'

Pudding looked at the busy carpet and said, 'The floor's the right colour.'

Barry explained that all the chairs had been removed from the balconies so people couldn't use them to climb onto the balustrade to jump off.

'Occupational health and safety,' Walter said importantly. 'We keep the balcony door locked at the hostel too.'

'That's because all the residents are drunks,' Judith said, pouring the last of the champagne into her water tumbler.

Walter ignored her. 'We're converting the lodging house into a hostel for international travellers.'

'You mean backpackers,' Pud said.

Walter lifted his chin and jerked his head to loosen his neck. 'Job'll be right.'

The waiter appeared again and asked if they were ready to

order. Judith asked for another bottle of champagne and the others turned their attention to the menu.

Things were still relatively pleasant, even after the dessert dishes were cleared. Barry toyed with his nine-carat rolled gold cufflinks—the right cuff read 'Sell' and the left 'Buy'—and talked at length about some of the houses he'd sold, how he was set to make a fortune when the Brunswick boom reached Reservoir. Walter related to them again, blow by blow, how he'd won the 1983 middleweight championship fight against Archie the Annihilator. Pudding drank three vodka and red cordials, and on her way back from the ladies' missed a step, fell into a potted palm but was righted again by Justin, the maître d', before anyone noticed. Judith placed her palm on Mrs Parsons' red beret and watched it disappear into her fuzzy Islander hair, explaining loudly and in great detail the process required to straighten it. Margery dropped a prawn and wasn't able to retrieve it from the colourful fern fronds in the carpet. When she tapped the side of her glass with her bread knife to say a few words the waiter started tidying dishes. 'Anyone require anything more?' He leaned down to take Judith's plate. 'Coffee, perhaps, Mrs Boyle?'

Judith said she'd 'loveanothabottleashampers, thanks,' and Barry said, 'Just the bill, mate.'

When it came Barry told Walter he could pay for his mother and Mrs Parsons, but Walter had only brought twenty dollars so Mrs Parsons gave him a five-dollar note and Margery paid the balance. They were standing to leave, Mrs Parsons turning from side to side between the armrests, when Walter said, 'The watch, Judif.'

'Oh, yes!' Pudding pulled back her mother's sleeve and there, pressing into the flesh of her wrist, was Margery's watch: delicate, pink-gold and ancient. Pudding unlatched it and Judith said, 'You'll love this, Marge. I got it fixed.'

'I paid half,' Walter added.

Margery took the watch gently in her soft fingers and was taken back to the dim, rarely used front parlour in her childhood home—and Cecily. They sat side by side on the couch, wearing their Sunday-best dresses, bows in their hair. Their mother was there, proud and pleased, their brothers and sisters squirming with suppressed excitement, and their father came slowly into the room in his dark, immaculate railway station uniform and stood ceremoniously in front of them. Margery thought she saw tears in his eyes. 'You're thirteen now,' he said, and their mother dabbed her tears with a hanky. 'Teenagers!' he said, and from behind his back brought two flat, satin-covered boxes and held them out to the girls. Cecily wrenched the box from its pretty wrapping immediately, while Margery untied the ribbon and rolled it neatly around her fingers. Then she carefully peeled away the wrapping paper and folded it, smoothing it to an even square. Cecily snapped the clasp closed on her wrist—'It's three o'clock!'—just as Margery opened her box.

'We got a watch each,' Margery said. 'Exactly the same.' She showed the watch to Mrs Parsons.

'Marge had a twin sister,' Judith said. 'Did I tell you that, DeeAndra?'

'About fifty times.'

'She died,' Judith said, and drained the last of her champagne.

'Hold it up to your ear,' Walter said, so Margery held it up to her ear.

'Oh my, it's ticking! Thank you, Walter.' She slid it onto her wrist.

Judith said, 'I took it all the way to the city, Marge, especially. To a specialist old-time jeweller Barry knows.'

Margery was trying to fasten the latch on the wristband, but her fingers were no longer agile. She said, 'I'll have to get a new band.'

'Tell us the time, Marge,' Judith said, but Margery couldn't see the hands, so Judith reached over and took the watch from her mother. 'Well, that was a waste of my well-earned time and money.' She dropped it into her handbag. 'Let's go.'

'That's Mumsy's watch, Judif,' Walter protested, but his

mother waved his concern away, pressed her hat into place, gathered up her handbag and turned to the waiter.

'Thank you, son,' she said. 'It was good of you to try and make it special.'

Behind her, Judith protested, 'I organised it,' and Walter added, 'It was my idea.'

It all went completely to mud when they dropped Margery back at home. As they pulled up outside 253 Gold Street, Mrs Parsons was already trying to locate the doorhandle. 'Thank you for a lovely outing, you're very kind, now I really must say goodbye.'

'The party's not over yet,' Walter said. He opened the door for her and lifted her out of the car, placing her gently on the road. 'Come in for a cuppa.'

'I really should get home,' she said, but it was no use. Although her little brown legs reached towards her house, Walter steered her straight through Margery's gateway and into the house. He eased her coat from her small bony shoulders, folded it neatly over the arm of the couch and settled her in Lance's old chair next to Margery. Pudding put the kettle on. Then Walter got Margery's slippers and, just as Judith came in from the lavatory, turned the ceiling fan on. Four blades of fluff, dust and crusty flies dislodged and landed on her special hair. Barry laughed, and that's when Judith said—shouted, actually, though Margery wasn't deaf—'You should be in a nice air-conditioned home, Marge.'

Barry told her to pipe down.

'No, Barry. You're right. She should be in a retirement home.' Mrs Parsons tried to nudge herself forwards in her chair.

Barry glared at his wife. 'You could have waited until after her birthday.'

Mrs Parsons raised her creaky little arm for Walter to help her get up. 'I really should get going,' but Walter was busy stepping from one foot to the other, rubbing his nose with his palm.

Judith kept on, 'You have to admit, she hasn't got as much

dexteritiveness these days, have you, Marge?'

Margery said, 'I dropped the prawn because the chairs were too far from the table,' but Judith just said, 'I'm talking about the fall you had,' and lifted up Margery's foot by the toe of her slipper. She pointed to the gauze held to her cigarette-paper-thin skin with blue bandaids.

Walter stopped stepping from foot to foot. 'Have a little fall, did you, Mumsy?'

'I tripped,' Margery said desperately. 'It's the footpath.'

It had happened the day before as she made her way back from doing up Mrs Parsons' shoelaces. She stopped to check the letterbox—sometimes there was a card from Morris—and as she moved away, sorting through the specials brochures and advertising material, the toe of her slipper caught the edge of the footpath and down she went. The sky circled and the footpath came up, and she grabbed the bin as she passed on her way down. There was a terrible crunch and Margery said, 'Oh dear,' but it was just the geranium bush. At the time, the young couple who'd purchased Mrs Bist's place, Tony and Miriana, were in their front yard talking about windows, but they didn't notice her. It was Tyson who saw her marbled, bleeding shin sticking out from under the bin. He nudged it with the toe of his boot and, while he dialled his mother on his mobile phone, failed to notice Margery had raised her hand.

'Guess what? Another crustacean's carked it. The sack of bones from 253's in the flower bush.'

'You were nice when you were a little boy,' Margery said, which wasn't strictly true. He wandered away and soon his mother, Bonita, came jogging down the street in her dressing gown, a towel around her shoulders and her hair plastered with a muddy mix of charcoal-brown permanent hair dye. She knelt beside Margery. 'Did you break anything, Mrs B?'

'The geraniums,' Margery said, thinking the dye in Bonita's hair was too dark for someone her age.

Bonita reached for her phone. 'What's Judith's number?'

'There's no need to phone her,' Margery said, scrambling onto her hands and knees with an agility she didn't know she had.

Bonita helped her up. 'You're lucky, Mrs Blandon. If you'd fallen in the backyard you could have ended up like Mrs Bist.'

'Never. Mrs Parsons would have known something was up when I didn't show up to untie her laces.'

Bonita helped her inside. She put the kettle on, stuck an adhesive bandaid to the fragile skin on Margery's torn shin and left, saying, 'Give us a hoy if you need anything urgent, eh, Mrs B?'

And now Judith was using the fall as a weapon. She put her hands on her hips, pulling the fabric of her kite dress against her tummy apron. 'We know what it means for old people when they start to fall, don't we? And, may I remind you all, she has to use a commode at night.'

'She's always had a pot,' Walter said. 'They all had them as kids. It's normal.'

'No, it's not!' Pud called from the kitchen, and Barry said knowledgably, 'It's like an *en suite*, eh, Wally, only old-fashioned?'

'I've still got most of my own teeth,' Margery said proudly, but no one heard.

'It's her feet. She should be wearing her new slippers,' said Walter.

Margery looked to Mrs Parsons for support, but Mrs Parsons, her fingers curled around the end of the armrests, was trying to lever herself out of the chair. Lance had sat in that chair for over fifty years, and his father before him, so the springs and horsehair rested on the linoleum, and Mrs Parsons had no chance of raising her small bottom from the cavity.

'She has to go to a home sooner or later,' Judith said, but Margery objected, 'I can't go to a home. Who'll do Mrs Parsons' laces?'

'Slip-ons,' Barry said, and Mrs Parsons closed her eyes, pursed her lips and pulled hard on the armrests.

Walter, stepping from foot to foot, said, 'You don't have to go,

Mumsy. You don't have to go,' and Barry said, 'Judith, why don't we wait until after we've had the dinner with our new partners?' and Pudding said, 'You're not partners yet!' and placed two mugs of weak, milky tea on the small table between Margery and Mrs Parsons. Margery looked sideways at the tea-leaves floating on the top.

Judith counted off Margery's ailments on her fingers: 'She's infirm, she's not as dexterous as she used to be, she's got bad feet and a bad heart—she's a cripple. She can't even change her sheets anymore.'

Margery said, 'Cheryl changes my sheets.'

'See? She needs a home helper *and* she's *forgotten*! Cheryl's gone, remember?'

'There's a new home help coming Tuesday,' Margery said.

'Everyone knows home helpers steal all your antique jewellery—pinch the wedding ring right off your finger and sell it at Cash Converters—but there's no need to worry about your pearls, is there, Marge? Got them well and truly hidden, eh, Marge?'

Margery looked at her ring finger, the flesh narrow where the thin gold band had rubbed for almost sixty years. 'I'm not sure where my wedding ring is,' she said absently.

Judith said, 'See? Forgetful.'

'But I don't see why I have to leave my home,' Margery declared.

Walter turned sideways, his right punching hand raised to his chin, and said to his imaginary opponent, 'On Tuesday she's getting a new home help.'

Judith nodded emphatically. 'My point is proven. She needs help, her memory's gone and her bad heart complicates her diminished mobility, and because of that she'll end up like Mrs Bist!'

'I'm just a bit stiff in the mornings!'

Judith shouted, 'That's what I mean, Marge. Diminished mobility!' And that's when Margery said quietly, '*I* can still get out of a chair.'

Mrs Parsons froze between the armrests. Walter stopped rocking. Everyone looked at Judith. She flushed deep red from her diamanté-trimmed décolletage to her cheeks.

'That's not fair, Marge.'

Pudding said, 'What does Gran mean about the chair, Mum?'

Margery examined a cross-stitch flower on the corner of her hanky, and Mrs Parsons put her arm up again. Barry pointed at the ceiling and said, 'Pressed tin. Good selling point.'

Walter started rocking, again, raised his fists and dodged an invisible left jab. 'This was s'posed to be a party, for Mumsy.'

Pudding asked again, 'What chair is Gran talking about?' but Judith just clutched her sparkling bodice and wilted, as if her mother had stabbed her.

Barry looked at his watch. 'It's time we were long gone.'

Pudding persisted, 'What is it about a chair that's upsetting you, Sajida?'

'Stop calling me that!'

'Well, stop dressing like Saddam Hussein's wife!'

'We'll go now,' Judith said, 'Come on, Wally, we'll give you a lift.' Her voice caught in her throat.

Walter said he wasn't ready to go yet, so Judith pleaded, 'We'll give you a lift,' and nudged Barry, who said with feigned nonchalance, 'Sure. No trouble to drive all the way to Collingwood for you, Wally.'

Walter stopped dead. He lowered his fists and wound his head to loosen his neck. He stepped close to Barry, put his face close. 'Job's right.'

Barry raised his hands in surrender, and Pudding prodded her mother—'Tell us about the chair?'—but Judith just played with her mother's watch on her wrist.

Mrs Parsons said, 'I really should get going.'

Finally, Barry looked down at her, smiled gallantly, 'We should all get going,' and offered her his aim. He prised her out of the sunken chair, then Walter helped her on with her coat and walked her down the side of the house to her back door. Mrs Ahmed, who lived on the other side of Mrs Parsons, stopped picking plums and turned, smiling at them from the tree, her brown face bordered by her bright headscarf, while Pudding's voice carried across the small, concrete and corrugated iron yards: 'You started the story about the chair, Gran, now you should finish it.'

When he got back, Walter found Margery calmly cross-stitching while Judith ransacked the house. Pudding followed her mother, badgering as she searched for Margery's pearls, shaking boxes and cartons in the pantry, opening all the frozen vegetable packages in the freezer.

'It's about time you gave up, Judif. You'll get the pearls when Mumsy's ready, you know that,' but Judith up-ended the peg basket into the old copper then moved to the bathroom, where she opened old denture containers and drained every bottle from the cabinet into the bath—bleach, moisturiser, disinfectant—then went through the first-aid tin before tapping the walls in search of secret compartments.

Barry was pacing around the clothesline, talking on his BlackBerry. Walter paced the lounge room, counting back from ten over and over in his mind, clenching and unclenching his fists, 'Calm like a canvas, Walter, calm like an empty venue.' He stopped, pressed his arms to his sides and said, 'The pearls belong to Mumsy.'

Next door, Mrs Parsons sat on her bed in the front room, her hands over her ears, the sound of Judith bawling on and on—'Infirm. She's infirm!'—and Pudding screeching—'The chair? Tell me!'—warbling over the back fences. Finally, the Boyles left. She watched them pile into their car, Barry saying, 'Six hundred and fifty thousand dollars. I told you, Judith, there's money in these little workers' cottages,' but even Mrs Parsons knew six hundred thousand dollars was far too much to pay for a detached, two-bedroom weatherboard cottage with kitchen and bathroom tacked onto the back and outside lavatories, even if they were situated close to the park.

# ROOM 4321

Judith's got no right to put me in a home, and no one's got the right to make me live with a so-called flatmate. They said she had nowhere to live after she came out of the hospital, but no wonder she fell and broke her hip. The heels! Open-toed wedges with flowers across the front. She's a smoker as well. You can tell because her laugh ends in a frothy cough, and she holds her long, thin fingers as if she's still holding a cigarette. One of the first things I noticed was she wasn't wearing a wedding ring, though it's clear she was once attractive enough to be married. Very fine-boned, like an ivory hatpin. I thought to myself at the time, *She could have been a model if she wasn't the barmaid type.* People notice Florence. She's got *presence,* like you had, though not for the same reasons as you. Florence isn't refined. People noticed you and, though we were the same, somehow there was more of you. You could swim all the way to the other side of the Maribyrnong River. I was only game enough to go to the end of the jetty.

Anyrate, when she showed up last week I took one look at her and thought, *I don't want you sitting on my toilet seat or washing your body in my bath any more than I want to go to a home and use towels thousands of strangers have rubbed all over their bits.* As I say, I tried to live with Florence, gave it a whole week, but we argued from the first day. Firstly, she ate the last chocolate in the box—my birthday present from Walter. Didn't ask, just took it and popped it in her mouth. 'I don't usually like sweets,' she said, 'but these are nice.'

Then she refused to do the dishes. While I eat my tea I like to watch the news on the television. So at six o'clock I sit in my chair with my cold ham salad on my stable table to watch the news. She came and sat in Lance's chair. Being hospitable, I offered her something to eat and she asked for poached egg on toast, which she ate standing at the kitchen bench. 'I ate a steak sandwich standing at the bar for fifty years,' she said. Quite reasonably, I suggested she do the dishes since I cooked her tea, but she just said, 'We'll do the dishes in the morning, eh, love?' Then she pointed her red toenail at my piano and said, 'How about a song?'

I said, 'You think life's all about singing and dancing, don't you?'

'To be truthful,' she said, 'I'm not much of a singer. Not many people are. Dancing's a different matter, it's something every-one can do.' After a while she pushed her frame out to the front verandah. I heard her harassing the innocent passers-by: 'Ya haven't got a cigarette, have ya, love?'

She got one in the end. Tyson gave her one. Then she came in and plopped down in Lance's chair, stinking like a pub, like Lance.

All night I heard her wheelie frame, heading out to the lav, *tweet-tweet-tweet,* and then back again, *tweet-tweet-tweet,* and when I got up, I found she'd strung a ball of my cross-stitch thread from the back door out to the lav. 'It'll guide me in the night,' she said, so I complained about her squeaky wheels.

'No worries,' she said, 'I'll get Walter to put a drop of oil on them.'

Then she sees me standing there with my pot to empty, so she says, 'Better still, I'll get him to get me a commode. What's his phone number?'

I said I didn't know, and I put a notepad and pencil next to the phone so she could record her phone calls but, in the week she was there, she never did.

The other thing was, while she was living with me I wasn't able to talk to you.

Walter was on Florence's side from the start. 'Think of her as a refugee,' he said. 'Mrs Bist'd be kind enough to have her.' I must say, he did have a point. You should always try and do the right thing.

'Just fink about a flatmate, Mumsy,' he said.

Just how long had they been finking about it, I wonder.

Anyrate, I thought about it for a few seconds and decided she couldn't stay, but then I looked down the hall and saw Judith pull up, and, well ... five weeks later it's come to this ...

But I'm getting ahead of the story of my treacherous children and their betrayal.

You know, just last week, Judith said to me, 'You never really cared.'

How could I not care? She's my daughter.

Now that I think about it, as I sit here, perhaps it was a bit mean to mention the Incident with the Chair at the cinema, and perhaps I should have let her keep the pearls after her twenty-first, but I didn't want to give them up just then. They were our mother's. Our sister, Shirley, got the matching earrings when Mum died. She got your watch as well. I got your hair ribbons. As I say, Judith has my watch. Stole it sixty-six years to the day after Dad gave them to us. Mind you, that watch did remind me of Pat and the Public Scalping Incident, so I really didn't mind letting it go. That's a story for another time. The Chair Incident happened during pensioners' week.

Mrs Bist popped in one day with her basket over her arm and her cardigan sleeves pressed to a straight, sharp line. She always stood over me as I sat stitching in my chair, and she always smelled like warm lavender talcum powder. 'It's pension week,' she said all hoity-toity. 'I insist you go to cinema on the council bus.'

I said I wasn't interested in going on a bus but she patted me on the shoulder and said, 'You've got to seize all opportunities in life, move with the times. You'll find it very liberating.'

But I know now I've got to be careful about advice from people who should know better. Frankly, I find cross-stitch the most liberating thing to do. It's a solitary adventure filled with nice colours and lines, but there's absolutely no danger, no risk. You can't get hurt. There's no room to think of anything else when I have that needle in my fingers. I know exactly where I'm going, how I'll get there and what will be there at the end, and if I'm careful to choose the needle that suits, it'll be a contenting and comfortable experience.

So at the time I said, 'Mrs Parsons prefers to stay at home, like me,' but Mrs Bist just sucked in her chin and heaved her bust up and declared, 'You can't pass an opportunity like this up. It'll be a nice day out for us all.' In the end she phoned Judith, who made us go. The thing was, Judith wanted to come as a volunteer helper because then it would be free for her too, and she got to hand out her business cards to all the ladies: 'Judith Boyle—mobile beauty, finesse and panache in all your needs for skin, nails and hair.'

So off we went for the first—and last—time, as it turned out.

You'll never guess, Cecily, but the film was our all-time favourite. Yes, that's right, *Mrs. Miniver*. It was still lovely. Just lovely. Greer Garson and Walter Pidgeon, a perfect couple happily married with lovely children and so stoic through all their tragic circumstances. We loved that film, didn't we? But I can say now, Cecily, it's not like that in real life. It most certainly isn't. As far as I'm concerned, there was no happy marriage or lovely children, just tragedy.

Anyrate, Judith couldn't get out of the seat when the picture ended. She was stuck. The manager was called, then a boy was sent out to buy a shifting spanner to remove the armrest. She held up the whole bus. I apologised and explained to everyone that she'd always golloped her food, but that she couldn't really help it because Lance's sisters, Faye and Joye, were big. So was his mother. Lance once said, 'You could steam-press a suit in their armpits.' I told them how Lance's mother got sugar—nowadays they call it diabetes—because she was so big, and how she lay in the second bedroom for years, fermenting to death. I had to look after her, and all I ever got for it was her commode. Lance would only ever stand at the door and wave. Said he couldn't look at her.

'She's got a face like a bunch of haemorrhoids,' he used to say.

Faye and Joye will go rotten with the diabetes, if they haven't already got it. Unfortunately, Judith takes after the Blandon side of the family.

But getting back to the day this last dreadful month started. After the Boyles left, Walter paced back and forth, back and forth, so I made us a pot of tea.

'I might lose my job, Mumsy,' he said. He was in the same anxious state that time he lost his weekend rates. Some workplaces don't have weekends, as such, anymore, Cecily. They make all the days in the week the same. And they've changed the hours in the day as well. They took one hour from the end of the day and put it at the start so the sun comes up earlier. Things are very different these days. They can even grow grapes without seeds.

Anyrate, Walter told me the council had been to his lodging house to inspect it. They made a list of changes Mrs Stapleton has to make so they come up to standard to be a hostel for international students.

'Your standards are very high,' I said, but his main concern was that he didn't have a ticket that qualified him to do the cooking and cleaning. 'Mrs Stapleton says I have to pass a food hygiene course,' he said.

Since that last bout, Walter can't hold some things in his mind for a long time. I said, 'The spare room here is yours anytime you want. This will always be your home, Walter, and you'll always have me.'

'Always be my home,' he repeated, but I know he wants to live in Collingwood with his friends. He's a man of the world, after all.

Then he settled down and we talked about Pat. We like to have a bit of a giggle about Pat. Pat Cruickshank lived opposite me for sixty years, but as I say, I've just found out she's been lying to me for most of those years. Her son, Kevin, takes me to see her in the home every Saturday. Mostly I go so I can play the piano for the old people.

Like most people around here, Pat worked at the brickworks and drank at that pub, so no wonder she's got beer dementia. A cold snap last winter followed by an unexpectedly high fatality rate from a new strain of influenza on top of rampant gastro-enteritis meant there was room at the local nursing home, but it was actually getting her there that proved difficult. Kevin got her into my car by telling her we were all off to the races. Pat always loved a day at the races. We got her as far as the foot-path before she suspected something. It was the suitcase. She attached herself to the lamppost and said, 'Since when do we need a suitcase to go to the races?'

'We've *been* to the races,' Kevin said. 'The suitcase is full of money.'

She just gripped that pole harder and said, 'I don't remem-ber that.'

Kevin asked, 'Do you know where you are now?' and she said she knew exactly where she bloody was.

'Where?'

She hugged the pole tighter, looked up and down the street and said, doubtfully, 'At the races?'

Kevin shook his head, so Pat said, 'You're right. I'd never invite Margery Blandon to the races.'

I wouldn't have gone anyway.

Kevin said, 'Mrs Blandon's kindly driving us because we've got the suitcase.'

'Where to?'

'To the races.'

Then it was like a light went on inside Pat's mind and she said, 'Liar,' and grabbed the suitcase. 'We've *been* to the races.'

'And now we're going home,' I said and smiled reassuringly.

When we got to the nursing home, Pat said, 'I can't see any horses,' and wedged herself into my car like an umbrella in a birdcage.

She always said, 'Kill me before you put me in one of those places.'

The truth is, and I'm ashamed to say it, but I was secretly gleeful when Kevin put Pat in a home, but I'm eating humble pie now. I'm not demented, and I get home help from the council, so there's absolutely no reason why I should be locked up in a home, nor do I deserve to be forced by my very own children to live with that demented adulteress Florence. I used to feel sorry for Mrs Parsons, not having any children, but it seems to me at this point that they just cause you pain. Look at Mrs Bist; she had all those foster kiddies, hundreds of do-gooder friends and even a niece, though she moved to America. Fat lot of good they all were to Mrs Bist in the end. None of them went to her funeral. Then her so-called friends came, the ladies from the Catholic Opportunity Shop—packed up her house and shot through with the lot.

And I didn't want Cheryl to leave me either, but she said, 'You'll find the new home help, Anita, is actually nice, *once you get used to her.*' I should have woken up that something was afoot, but I didn't.

There's a lot of things I didn't wake up to.

# DAY 2

The morning after her so-called birthday party, Margery was woken by an explosion. She jolted awake thinking the pub had exploded again, expected to see dust billowing out over the park and the grass glinting with sprinkles of shattered glass. But it wasn't the pub. It was a truck backing away from Mrs Bist's precise little house, *beep beep beep*. A jogger bobbed out of the dust cloud rising around a large waste-removal bin settling on the street.

Margery lay back again, her heart lurching. She watched another truck arrive and roll a small excavator off its back. It ground up the kerb, over the melaleuca sapling the council had planted and straight through Mrs Bist's small brick fence. It stopped and waved its arm at the front verandah, scraping the posts from beneath the corrugated iron roof. A second later the front of the small weatherboard cottage shuddered, black dust fell like a curtain from the eaves, then Mrs Bist's short, snub-nosed verandah roof fell with a clang. More dust billowed. The excavator flattened the pile of twisted metal and splintered wood with its tracks, scooped it all up and dumped it in the bin. The whole thing took less than ten minutes.

'Good grief,' said Margery. She was reaching for her dressing gown when a tidy woman wearing a pink suit and carrying a clipboard picked her way up Margery's short footpath and knocked cheerily on the door. Then she peered through the front window straight at Margery. She smiled, waved and called, 'Morning,' pointing at the front door. Behind her the excavator swung its arm and the walls of Mrs Bist's front bedroom crashed to the ground.

Her name tag read 'Charmaine'.

Margery said, 'I thought you were coming Tuesday, and

Cheryl never got here until at least eleven, but since you're here you can start by emptying my pot.'

Charmaine stepped past Margery into the house. 'How lovely your geranium bush is. I just *love* pink!' She walked down Margery's narrow hall, leaned into the tiny second bedroom and glanced about, smiling at the patchwork quilt and the cross-stitched wall hangings, frowning at the box of wooden embroidery frames, bunches of thread and cloth offcuts. She sidestepped the small telephone stand and stopped dead in the lounge room, overwhelmed by Margery's craftwork. Every wall was hung with cross-stitch proverbs: *I grow old ever learning many things*; *A* CROSS-STITCH *in time saves lives*; *Faithful are the wounds of a friend, but the kisses of an enemy are deceitful*; *All things good to know are difficult to learn.* The lampshade read, *The unexamined life is not worth living.*

There were cross-stitched landscapes as well: Uluru at sunset, seascapes, snow-capped mountains, horses' heads, rural scenes. Also Tom Roberts' *Shearing the Rams*, Rodin's *The Thinker*, and a huge depiction of Michelangelo's *Pietà* above the fireplace. The flat surfaces were covered with doilies, their edges embroidered with cross-stitched flowers. The antimacassars were trimmed with orderly coloured fabric patterns, as were the curtains, and the floor mat was a cross-stitched depiction of Mount Kosciusko. The cushions featured a series of bushscapes, and a calendar was illustrated with cross-stitched proverbs for each month.

'I just *love* embroidery,' she said. 'It's like being in a craft shop.' Charmaine went to the kitchen.

'It's not embroidery,' Margery said. 'It's cross-stitch. There's a difference.'

'Oh?' She wiped down a kitchen chair with a tissue and settled at the table, chatting very loudly about the weather. 'Don't you just *love* summer?'

'Embroidery patterns are a bit limiting, I find. You can't always get a nice landscape pattern, but with cross-stitch I can just count out any old picture I decide I want to do—landscapes, seascapes, proverbs. I'm not one for flowers so much. They're more for the embroiderers, though I've never seen one yet that's been able to get a snapdragon right—you know, the gaping dragon's mouth?'

'Sit down,' Charmaine said, pointing to Mrs Parsons' Sunday chair.

'That said, cross-stitch is actually quite a unique skill.'

'Interesting,' though it was clear Charmaine wasn't interested at all.

Mrs Bist's second bedroom cracked and shattered and fell into a heap next door. Margery put the kettle on to make a cup of tea. She needed one herself and Charmaine didn't look like she'd be leaving any time soon.

'You can use any old fabric as well,' she continued, 'as long as it's evenweave. And that, along with the pattern of course, influences the stitch you choose. There are more stitches than you think: marking cross-stitch, long-armed, tied cross, upright, double, even ermine. In fact, you can cross any old stitch if you know how.'

Charmaine nodded absently, noting the gaps under the windows where the frames had dropped, frowning at the wedge of daylight streaming in under the kitchen door. 'Drafty,' she said. 'You must get cold in the winter.'

'Not really,' Margery said and pointed to the gas heater in the fireplace.

'These old places don't have insulation. You must get hot in summer.'

'I've got the ceiling fan.' Margery placed a serviette in front of Charmaine, pointed to the teapots and teacups cross-stitched on its edges and said, 'Linen, no pattern, see how even it is? And small. I can't do them that small anymore.' She put her thick glasses on the kitchen table, sighing.

Charmaine looked up at the fan in the lounge room and pointed her biro at the hole in the ceiling. 'I bet the roof leaks.'

'I catch it in a bucket. Tip it on my geranium bush.'

'It'll cost at least ten thousand dollars to have the house

painted. When was the last time you had it done?'

'Lance, my husband, said his parents painted it, but that was before I came to live here.'

'The roof needs replacing and the house needs restumping.' Charmaine opened her clipboard and removed a piece of paper.

'I'm very comfortable in my home,' Margery said, circling her arm to indicate her cross-stitch cocoon.

'You'll need to spend a hundred thousand dollars to renovate.'

'As I say, you can start your duties as soon as you like, but we'll start with how to make a pot of tea properly.'

'I'm not actually the maid; I'm here to assess the house.' She placed the sheet of paper in front of Margery.

'Are you from the ACAT team?'

'No.' Then Charmaine became very crisp. 'In its current state it's an eyesore, especially now they're rebuilding next door. You could ask the builders for a quote for repairs, which will be substantial, *or,* you won't have to worry about anything like that if you sign this piece of paper.' She handed Margery a biro and pointed with her glossy fingernail to the dotted line. 'Just sign here, Mrs Blandon.'

Margery tried to pull the paper closer, but Charmaine held it fast with her spearhead finger. Her hair was very short, Margery thought, far too short for someone with such hard features.

'I'll keep it to read then post it to you,' Margery said.

'It's very straightforward,' Charmaine said, standing over her.

'I'd just feel better if I read it closely,' Margery said, and sipped her tea.

Charmaine sat down again and looked at her watch. 'I'll wait.'

Margery reached for her reading glasses but they were missing. 'I put them on the table,' she said. 'You haven't picked them up by mistake, have you?

Charmaine said, 'There's the dotted line there, see?'

'I need my glasses.'

'Just sign it.'

'I have to speak to Walter first.'

'No you don't.'

'Yes I do.'

'Do not.'

'Do so.' Margery sat on her hands. She'd had enough of smiling, fragrant estate agents telling her they'd do her a favour by selling her home from under her.

'The new maid will be here soon,' she said.

Charmaine held a biro up to Margery's face. Next door, the excavator roared and timber clattered, glass shattered and the ceiling above the women vibrated. Charmaine rolled her eyes towards the demolition sounds, 'Out with the old and in with the new.' Fine black ceiling dust fell, powdering her pink cotton shoulders.

Margery said, 'I'm happy to sit here until I die.'

Charmaine put the biro on the piece of paper next to the dotted line and said, 'Well, I might not have to sit here for very long then.' She crossed her arms and legs.

Next door, Mrs Bist's walls groaned and folded in on each other. The roof collapsed on top, then the chimney imploded and bricks crashed down onto the metal heap.

'That'll send the rats scurrying,' Margery said, lifting her feet and searching the floor for small furry creatures. Charmaine leapt up, snatched the piece of paper from the table and ran out of the house.

Margery remained where she was, calmly finishing her cup of tea, running her tongue across her teeth to remove the dust.

Judith was powdering her sliced grapefruit with artificial sweetener when Pudding strolled into the kitchen, tall and glossy in her school uniform, a backpack over her shoulder. Her mother was dressed in a plain, black shift, her hair loose and wavy. Pudding pressed her earplugs into her ears, picked up a banana, tub of yoghurt and a slice of toast with Vegemite waiting for her on the bench, kissed her mother's cheeks, 'You look very stylish today, mother,' and wandered out the back door, eating her toast.

Judith said, 'Love you, Pudding,' and sat to eat her grapefruit. She spread a paper napkin on her lap, pushed back her sleeves, washed two Fatbuster diet tablets down with sweetened black coffee and said, 'Day one, Judith. You can do this, just last three weeks without eating anything fattening and then you're off and running. *Just get obsessed!* You are *fat*, Judith. You *must* get rid of the flab.' She jabbed a wedge of grapefruit with her fork and popped it into her mouth, chewing slowly, making every bitter mouthful last.

Then she curled and teased her hair, spraying it into a firm round helmet over her head. She spread thick, creamy make-up over her face, glued on her eyelashes and ringed her eyes with black kohl, then she pinned a gold brooch to her frock, strung three gold chains around her neck, put three gold rings on three separate fingers and clipped on a pair of gold-mounted, cutglass earrings. Then she sat down at her computer, two rice crackers and two diet mints beside the desk. She logged on. The computer screen read, 'Welcome to the Diploma of Counselling. Please select your subject.'

Barry arrived bringing currents of cologne, jangling his keys. 'So, as we discussed—'

'Yes, Barry, as always, I'll do my best for you but you know Marge. She's not the most approachable or cooperative person on the planet, never has been.'

She clicked 'Parenting and Family Care'.

The front door opened. Barry called, 'See ya.'

'Will you be home for tea?' But Barry was gone and the screen had captured her interest. She studied the words, pondering what they meant. 'Aspects of child temperament and parenting style most likely to be associated with observed behavioural problems caused by possible combinations, including negative reactions with low parental warmth, low inductive reasoning, can cause low inhibition. Behavioural problems include evidence of the child hurting others, damaging objects, disobeying instructions and having temper tantrums ...'

She highlighted the words and moved the cursor to 'Copy' then pasted it in the document titled 'Judith's Diary, A Lifetime of Negative Enrichment' then read the words aloud: '*Negative reactions with low parental warmth and low inductive reasoning, and low inhibition, behavioural problem measures include evidence of the child hurting others, damaging objects, disobeying instructions* ...'

'My God,' she cried. 'This is my life!'

Sitting with her hands loose in her lap, the flurry travelling around the screen, the memories came. She was standing behind her mother, her shoulders high above in a blue cardigan. 'Mum,' she said, but the shoulders didn't turn, her mother just kept washing dishes, stacking plates neatly on the draining board. Then there was her mother's lap, a wooden frame holding her at bay, a haven that was out-of-bounds, an exclusive place only for cloth and thread, needles and scissors, yet Judith's scalp crawled deliciously as she remembered the feel of a brush pulling through her hair, the bristles scraping across her scalp. She felt a comb slice down the back of her head, the tug of her mother's firm hands parting and plaiting. 'Now go and tie your ribbons for school.'

Judith moved the cursor to iPhoto and looked at images of Pudding's happy, loving and carefully photographed life. As she sat back to eat her rice crackers, she felt reassured.

Margery rinsed her cup under the tap, left it to drain on the sink and sat in her chair with her cross-stitch. By the time Mrs Parsons' blind went up, she had come to terms with Charmaine's visit and felt calmer, so she set out for next door. On her front path, just beneath the letterbox, were her glasses. One lens was cracked and lay in three neat triangles in the rim. Next door, in the bright morning sunshine the excavator roared, Mrs Bist's carefully painted walls splintering under its iron tracks. Margery stepped cautiously towards Mrs Parsons' place and pushed the squeaky little gate open. She made her way down the side of the house to the back door, knocked, called 'Yoo-hoo,' and let herself into her neighbour's kitchen. Mrs Parsons waited in her rocking chair near the wood stove, though there had been no fire in the grate since electric heaters started appearing in summer sales catalogues in the 1950s. Only the winter before, Cheryl had replaced her two-bar electric wall heater with an upright electric oil heater on wheels. Mrs Parsons also used it to dry her rinsed cottontails and wool stockings of an evening.

Margery sat down opposite her neighbour. From the wireless, a soprano with a warm, lyrical voice sang,

> *Shepherd, the meadows are in bloom.*
> *You should graze your flock on this side,*
> *Sing baïlèro lerô.*
> *Shepherd, the water divides us and I can't cross it,*
> *Sing baïlèro lerô.*

'Good morning, how are you today, Mrs Parsons?' Mrs Parsons said she was as well as could be expected, thank you. Margery reached down and lifted Mrs Parsons' right foot, rocking the old lady's chair back. She tied her neighbour's lace, gently lowered her stiff leg and, as she picked up Mrs Parsons' left foot, apologised again, 'Sorry about the argument yesterday.' Again, Mrs Parsons said, 'Never mind.'

'Mrs Bist's house has gone.'

'Is that what all the noise is?'

'It was a perfectly good house.' Margery stood up, smoothed her skirt and, as she did every morning, asked, 'Are you alright then, Mrs Parsons?' and, as always, Mrs Parsons replied, 'Yes, thank you. You're very kind.'

'You didn't get a bossy lass called Charmaine bothering you?'

'Not today.'

At her gate, Margery paused to take in the vast space above the pile of splintered weatherboards, twisted iron, smashed window frames and blackened chimney bricks where Mrs Bist's house had stood, just an hour ago. The excavator sat bludgeoning its way through the back shed, the arms of Mrs Bist's Hills Hoist poking out from under its tracks. Feeling threatened by the destruction of certainties she had known for sixty years, Margery went inside her little house, snibbed her screen door and pulled shut the front door. She tried to close the back porch door, but it wouldn't go past a bulge where the sunken stumps had buckled a floorboard, so she closed and bolted the kitchen door instead. While the kettle boiled again, she sticky-taped her glasses together, gluing the glass triangles to the frame, and secured them with the ends of a blue bandaid. Then she flicked on her wireless. Andy Williams was just finishing 'Moon River' and the announcer on Magic Radio Best Tunes of All Time told her it was ten fifteen.

She tipped the still-warm pot of tea down the gully trap, took two slices of bread from the freezer and popped them into the toaster. While they toasted she warmed the pot again with boiling water, tipped it out, put two teaspoons of tea in, filled it with boiling water and covered the pot with a cross-stitched cosy. She opened the side doors of her little toaster, turned the bread and got the butter, marmalade, plate, knife and tea strainer organised. She took the toast from the toaster, propped it in a steeple to cool, turned the toaster off, put the strainer over her cup, turned the pot three times, poured her tea then carefully buttered her toast, making sure the butter went all the way to the crusts. She spread the marmalade sparingly and sat enjoying her breakfast while Rod Stewart sang 'Maggie May' and the excavator next door shovelled Mrs Bist's house into the dump bin, fine dust raining down from her vibrating ceiling. Then Margery removed her slippers and went back to bed until Tuesday morning.

# DAY 3

From her bed Margery could see her new neighbours, Tony and Miriana, standing on the razed block next door, Miriana's burnt-orange belly protruding from the gap between her small singlet and tracksuit pants. 'Tsk, just look at them,' Margery scoffed. 'They spray a suntan from a can these days, so everyone's the colour of a raw saveloy. And he's got hair like an echidna.'

Tony wandered to the middle of the street, mobile phone to his ear, watching down to the corner, waiting for something. 'He's probably waiting for some thunderous machine to rattle my house all day.'

Over at Tyson's, the curtains billowed through the smashed front windows. Next door, Kevin's dark, leafy house was, as usual, quiet.

'Well, I'd better get up now, Cecily. I'll have a shower, though I only just had one Sunday for my birthday party.' She reached for her dressing gown. Nat King Cole sang 'Rambling Rose' while she ate her tea and toast. In the bathroom she undressed, hanging her gown and nightie on the back of the door, then carefully covered what was left of her set with a shower cap. She removed an old shampoo bottle from the bottom of the bath, took hold of the shower taps and swung her right leg in, and was alarmed when she found she wasn't able to gain purchase. She started to slide, clinging to the taps, sinking. Her crotch came to rest on the edge of the bath, stabilising her temporarily, but her left leg lost its faint hold on the floor and she sank to lie along the edge of the bath, clinging on with her knees like a caterpillar to a stem. Then her left knee lost its hold and she rolled into the bath, tearing the bandaid from the wound on her shin. Water from the cold tap shot from the rose and, feeling her twisted arms being dragged from their sockets, Margery let go of the taps and flipped over like a sausage in hot water.

She lay in the bottom of the bath, gasping under the cold downpour, the clean water gushing down the plug hole, her water bill rising second by second. She ripped the shower curtain down, the plastic rings pinging onto the ceiling and bouncing to the floor, and she pulled it up over her head. She was still there, shivering under the torturous roar of water, when she heard someone calling, 'Yoo-hoo! Anyone home?' Then the water stopped and the shower curtain pulled back. Margery looked up into the painted face of a pantomime actress. The woman looking down at her had startling blue eyes edged with black kohl in a pale face rimmed with wild, letterbox-red hair. The actress turned the taps off.

'I'm Anita, your new carer.'

'You don't look like a carer.'

'I don't want to look like a carer. You'd be Margery.'

'Mrs Blandon to you.'

'You're alright then?'

'I'm stuck. You can help me out, if you wouldn't mind.'

Anita said, 'There might be something broken.'

'I'd certainly know if I'd a broken bone, don't you think?'

'We'd better call an ambulance just the same.'

Cheryl had warned her that the old lady could be cantankerous, but Anita saw terror in her eyes. 'Mrs Blandon, it's okay. You don't necessarily die if you go to hospital these days.'

'Now listen here, I'd know if there was anything broken, and I tell you there isn't. Just help me out.'

'You're bleeding.' Anita carefully peeled the bandaids from Margery's papery shin. 'Ouch. That's nasty. Right on your tibia.'

'Do you always state the obvious?'

'Stay there,' Anita said and winked. In the kitchen she flicked the kettle on, then collected pillows and a blanket. She propped Margery up in the bath and tucked the blanket around her. While Margery drank a cup of sweet black tea Anita sat on the back step smoking a cigarette. 'Tell me what happened, Mrs

Blandon.'

'I slid, very gracefully I must say, on spilled shampoo.'

'You're real lucky, you know. One of my other ladies, Mrs Razic down the street, slipped in the bath but she wasn't holding on. She's got stitches.'

Margery said, 'I'm perfectly alright and you can tell my daughter, Judith, that I am not going to a nursing home.'

'You should get a flatmate, an international student since you're so close to the uni. You could have been there for days.'

'A flatmate's not going to stop me from falling.'

'No, but they help around the house and they'd help you out of the bath.'

'This is the last time I'll fall in the bath, I assure you.'

'We'd better get you checked out by your doctor.'

Margery panicked. 'As I've said, I'm quite alright!'

'Okay, okay, don't give yourself a stroke. But what if something goes wrong with you later because of this fall and I get thrown in jail? I can't afford to have any sort of trouble.' Any sort of trouble was a very real threat to Anita, since she held her job on a probationary basis through her Corrective Services officer.

'That's right,' Margery said, 'just thinking of yourself. I thought you were here to help *me*.'

'I am,' Anita said, sitting on the edge of the bath. 'And you do need to see a doctor.'

'If you tell Judith,' Margery said, 'I'll phone the council and tell them you stole my pearls.'

'Yeah, right,' Anita said, 'and I'll phone the ACAT team and tell them you need to go to a home.'

'You're an appalling person.'

'You started it.' Anita got a kitchen chair and put it beside the bath, dug around in her work basket and found dressings. She tenderly cleaned Margery's bleeding shin, creased the skin back into place and covered it with a clear plastic dressing, then she got into the bath behind Margery and wrapped her arms around her chest. 'I'm going to lift you up, alright? Trust me.'

She knew that Margery had never felt so vulnerable or useless, knew that she wanted to cry but was too furious, afraid of slipping again, and didn't really trust someone the size of Anita to bear her weight. She also knew she no longer had a choice.

'One, two, three,' Anita-said and felt Margery's slight body stiffen against her, but she eased her up, rested her on the edge of the bath then slid her over to the chair. Anita was probably the only other person on the planet apart from Margery's husband who had seen Margery naked, and even then he might not have actually seen her *completely* naked. She felt humiliated sitting there like a thawing chicken, a stranger patting her bottom dry and holding panties for her to step into while she steadied herself on the handbasin like a drunk. But Margery let Anita sponge her down with warm water, and as Anita eased her knee-high stockings over her dressing, Margery said, 'Just have a look and see if Mrs Parsons' blind is up, will you? You can see through the lounge room window.'

Cheryl had also told Anita about Mrs Parsons, that she could just let herself in, if needed, since Mrs Parsons would be waiting in her chair, and since the blind was up, Anita declared she would pop in and 'say g'day'.

'No you won't. You'll give her a fright.'

'That's okay, she'll be sitting down when she sees me.'

'You don't know what to do.'

'Tie her laces. I'll tell her you'll be in later, as usual, okay? I need to meet her, introduce myself. Cheryl always popped in to see her, didn't she?' She left Margery to finish dressing, arriving back just in time to help her comb up what was left of her set and rinse. Then she buckled Margery into her car and drove to her own doctor, Doctor Kosztadinov.

'What sort of a doctor has a name like that?' Margery sniffed.

'What's his name got to do with his ability?'

'Nothing, I suppose, since they're all sorcerers and thimbleriggers.'

'Didn't you work for one for forty years?'

'Forty-four, but I never imagined he'd be able to cure me of anything.'

Doctor Kosztadinov studied Margery's skin tear through the Tegaderm, gave her a routine examination and asked a lot of questions.

'When was the last time you needed to see a doctor?'

'Fifteen years ago, I had a little turn.'

Doctor Kosztadinov prescribed new medications, told her she'd feel so much better she wouldn't know herself, said Anita would put her tablets in a dosette and all she had to do was take the tablets according to the day of the week. Anita would show her. Then he asked how long she'd lived alone.

'My husband was killed twenty years ago.'

'How was he killed?'

'He was careless,' Margery said.

'Was it a happy marriage?'

'I raised three children. Of course I was happy,' she snapped.

On the way home, Anita stopped at Union Square, and while the chemist filled Margery's prescriptions Anita smoked a cigarette, watching across to Margery, a small, unhappy woman sitting low in the front seat, scowling at the world outside. It was Anita's first week on the job, and she'd already had one near miss with Mrs Razic. This was the first job she'd ever had that didn't involve serving beer or taking orders, and she understood from her brief, accidental brush with incarceration that life was not a practice run; she was halfway through her only chance at it, and she didn't want to spend the rest of her time cleaning other people's houses, nor did she want to end up alone, a cantankerous nuisance, or in a nursing home. It was now certain that she didn't want to get to eighty and wish she'd done things another way, *better*.

She found her bankcard, slid it into the ATM and checked her savings account. *It wasn't raining when Noah built the ark,* she told herself. Then she resolved to give up smoking, save eighty dollars a week, travel—a trip to Disneyland with a stopover in Hawaii. If Skye, her twenty-one-year-old daughter, could save enough for a deposit on a house just from working in a bank, she could start a business, her own business. She knew about cleaning houses; she would set up a business cleaning other people's houses, branch out to offices, schools. Then she remembered her criminal record.

She ground out her last cigarette, paid for Margery's prescription and bought a packet of Nicorette patches. At Gold Street, she put Margery into bed, made a nice poached egg on toast and, while Margery ate it, she sat propped against the other end of the bed and filled the complimentary dosette with tablets. Monday–Sunday; Breakfast—Somac for reflux, two Panadol Osteo for arthritis pain, Coversyl anti-hypertensive, Frusemide diuretic and half an aspirin. Lunch—two Panadol Osteo, Frusemide, a multivitamin and potassium. Dinner—Temazepam to sleep and Panadol Osteo. Then she made a list of things that would make life for Margery safer, a 'Plan for Independence List'.

1. New glasses

2. Portable phone—push-button, big numbers

3. Take the bath out and put a shower base and chair in, OR, put a bench across the bath temporarily. New taps + washers

4. Move the handrails next to the shower so M can reach them

5. Replace all floor mats in the house with non-slip ones

6. Adjust the doors so that they are secure

7. Get new solid shoes with grip and better insoles

8. Smoke detectors put in

Anita studied the list then drew a line from the bottom to the top, making the smoke detectors number one. She tried to sell Margery the idea of getting a SCEM—a Safe Call Emergency Monitor telephone. 'You hang a monitor around your neck so that when you fall, you just push the button and the council comes.' But in Margery's mind she saw three council workers with reflector jackets and Stop/Slow signs standing over her as she lay naked in the bath.

'Mrs Bist wasn't able to push a button after she fell,' Margery said defiantly. 'She was unconscious.'

Anita tried guilt. 'How would your family feel if you'd fallen and had to lie there for hours before Mrs Parsons decided she didn't want to go to bed with her shoes on?'

'They'd be happy and relieved,' Margery replied.

Anita conceded defeat when she phoned the council and was told that, due to budget restraints, Margery's name would be added to the bottom of a long, needs-based SCEM waiting list.

After she'd soaked and scrubbed Margery's commode pot, cleaned the bath, dragged all the floor mats into the sun, put the chairs up then swept and mopped the floors, she stood in the bedroom doorway and asked if Margery had ever wanted to see the world.

'Those sorts of things weren't possible in our day,' she said. 'Anyrate, you can see it on the telly for free, and a lot of it isn't much chop as far as I can tell.'

'Right,' Anita said, scratching in her basket for her cigarettes, 'I'll be off now. Give us a buzz if you need anything.'

Margery said again, almost tearfully, though she wasn't sure why she felt so emotional about something she knew she wasn't going to do, 'I don't want to go to a home.'

Anita said, 'You don't have to go to a home these days. The government prefers you to stay put. It's cheaper.'

'Judith will put me in a home.'

She put a cigarette in her mouth and continued rummaging in her basket for a lighter, a tattoo peeking down from her uniform sleeve, and though they were mostly hidden under her red fringe, Anita's brilliant eyes were true when she said, 'Not if I can help it.'

'You know,' Margery said, studying her new home help in her short uniform over black, skin-tight shorts, black ankle socks and runners, 'I cleaned Doctor Woods' rooms from nineteen sixty-two until two thousand and six, and I never looked like the type of cleaner you look like.'

Anita admired herself in Margery's dressing table mirror, said, 'Well, that's a great relief to me,' and sashayed out the front door. At her car she remembered she'd given up smoking so threw the cigarette in her basket and stuck a Nicorette patch on her arm.

Margery watched her get into a low, silver car with red trim. To Margery, it sounded like a tractor, but across the road Tyson said to his flatmate, 'That's a 1970 XY GT Falcon.' Next door, both the surveyor and the bloke in the orange reflector jacket taking soil samples paused to watch the car drive away.

You can't see anything from these windows, just treetops and buildings. And the windows don't open. The colour scheme is very dull, and there's only one picture of some fruit, but the towels are soft and the bed is comfortable. Nice crisp sheets, hospital corners. Very neat. In fact, it's a bit impersonal, like the rooms at Pat's nursing home. I'll admit I was saved from the nursing home by Florence, and I suppose I'd have to include Anita in that as well, but as you can tell, a week living with Florence and I've decided I'd rather die.

To go on living with her I'd have to go against every principle I've lived by. It's beyond me how they ever expected I would do that.

As I sit here thinking about it I see there were signs. I should have woken up to those two. Like mother, like daughter. Florence and Anita Potter. Potter's an Irish name. Remember we had that girl in our class called Evelyn Potter? Pixies lived at the bottom of her garden. We asked her mother about them and she said, 'Yes, I've seen them.'

Anyrate, Anita's far too old to wear skirts that short, and all that mascara and that great mess of bright red hair sticking out all over the place. Pat would say it had 'natural body', but I think it needs a good trim. And she's a show-off: 'You've injured your *tibia.*' Tibia indeed. She isn't even a nurse. She's just a council worker, a *house* cleaner. Some call themselves home carers, but they don't care at all, like that Kate. Kate was before Cheryl. She tricked me into going to church once, but it wasn't really a church, just a bunch of babbling holyrollers running up and down like electrocuted budgerigars. And they had the hide to ask me for money. I told her, 'God, if he exists, is a fraud!' After that, I phoned the council and asked for a new carer, and that's when I got Cheryl. Surprisingly, Cheryl had very good manners. I didn't know what to expect when they said they were sending this Anita. She turned out to be something else, I tell you.

In the week between Anita's first and second visit, my life began to really unravel. Wednesday, I rested, but as I say, I wasn't injured badly after my little slip in the bath. Mind you, I still have some bruising on my ribs, even now. That day a big backhoe dug a hole where Mrs Bist's laundry once stood, and what with all the shuddering and the noise of that thing and the workmen bellowing all day in other languages ... Anyone could tell they were swearing.

I was able to get up Thursday, pension day, and do my shopping with Mrs Parsons. Pension week we do our Big Shop, so we take the car and go down to Barkly Square. Mrs Parsons always enjoyed her ride in the car, and I drive a mile or two out of our way but it means I can get all the way to the shopping centre with only one right turn against the traffic.

The first thing Mrs Parsons and I did was go to the ATM. You get money from a machine now, Cecily. Or from the lass at the cash register, and when I booked into this hotel I gave the receptionist the same little plastic card and she just' took money from my account. These days you put in a code or sign a little ticket to let authorised people take money out of your account. Cheryl said everyone is on a police checklist, so no one steals. The receptionist let me sit down while she did it all, and I told her my code because I was exhausted when I got to this hotel. Public transport takes a lot out of you as you get older.

As I say, things have changed. You can also gamble at the newsagent, which is usually a post office as well these days. Cheryl brought Mrs Parsons and me up to date. She taught us how to use the plastic card and the ATM. She wrote the instructions out for us, so now, every pension Thursday, we park the car and go straight to the ATM machine then pop into the newsagent to pay our bills. Then we do our shopping before taking advantage of the 'Coffee and Cake for Five Dollars' special at the coffee shop. I order tea for Mrs Parsons because that's what she prefers, but the shop assistant knows us and always gives Mrs Parsons the five-dollar deal anyway. I bought cross-stitch thread from Kmart that day because I'd designed a cross-stitch for Anita's work basket, a William Blake. I remember reading it as I turned the desk calendar, and I thought it was very inspirational. It turned out to be one of my best, an upright cross-stitch, red thread of course, on a nice blue Aida, elastic-edged to fit snugly over the top of the basket. William Blake was a poet, so his sayings were very good, popular on the desk calendars year after year. Another of my favourites of his is, *As a man is, so he sees.*

Anyrate, then we used the public lavatory and set off for home. As usual, I said cheerio to Mrs Parsons, unpacked my groceries and had another cup of tea and a little rest. I suppose Mrs Parsons did the same. That was our last Big Shop before the Incident with the Motorcycle. But I'll get to that. The next disappointment was Glen, my podiatrist, and then Angela, my hairdresser. Very upsetting. Oh, and Pat made a nuisance of herself as well.

# DAY 6

Every second Friday of the month Margery set off at nine o'clock
for her permanent ten o'clock appointment with Glen, her podiatrist. When Glen's new shopfront opened on Dawson Street,
Margery was the first to make an appointment, the first to sit on
the new couch in the waiting room and one of the first to walk
on the new carpet Glen put down a year later. Over the years
she'd seen several pot plants live, thrive and die, and several re-
ceptionists start, get engaged, married, pregnant and disappear
from behind the varnished chipboard counter. And when Glen
married, she waited at the church fence, eager to see him emerge
with his new bride. She knitted booties for his newborn son and
even came to terms with his cheerless wife when she took command of the receptionist's chair. But it was still a shock that Friday to find Glen had gone. She placed a small wot-not jar—an
empty jam jar with an embroidered pincushion lid—on top of
the counter. 'It's a koala,' she said. 'Twenty-eight count linen.'

'Thanks,' Glen's wife said, and popped it under the counter
with the embroidered picture frames, handtowels, tea-cosies and
soft-top trinket jars. 'It's only half past nine, you're way too early.'

Margery took her cross-stitch from her bag, '*Great things are
done when men and mountains meet.*'

'May as well tell you, Glen's gone to Queensland.'

'He didn't mention it to me,' Margery replied. 'Why would he
rush off like that?'

'He didn't have much choice, really.' Glen's wife pointed to the
couch with her pen. 'Have a seat.'

'Will he be back?'

'Na,' she said, smiling.

It was upsetting, but Margery was entirely devastated when
she met Glen's replacement. He was excessively young, nineteen

if he was a day, it seemed.

'My name is Blaine,' he said. 'How are you today, Margery?'

'Mrs Blandon to you, son.' Margery unlaced and kicked off her shoes, rolled her knee-high stockings down and draped them over the arm of the chair. 'I wasn't told Glen was going to Queensland.'

'Things change.' He came out from behind his computer. 'What seems to be the problem with your feet?'

'They're getting old,' Margery snapped, settling herself on the podiatrist's chair. 'Up we go,' she said and pressed the button. The chair rose with a faint hum. She indicated the stool near her feet. 'You sit there, Blaze.'

Regular monthly appointments meant Margery's feet were in relatively good condition, so Blaine trimmed her nails, checked her corn, scraped some skin off her bunion and suggested she get slip-on shoes 'since you're pretty much past bending down to look after your feet'. He pressed the button to lower the chair, dropped his nail clippers into the steriliser and said, 'You also need to get orthotic support insoles to stabilise your gait and help prevent falls.'

'Glen never made me get them.'

Blaine removed his yellow gloves and chucked them in the bin, already puffed with discarded disposable gloves. 'I can see that.'

'How much do they cost?'

'Four hundred dollars. They last a lifetime.'

'I've just had my eightieth birthday party.'

Blaine picked up his little vacuum cleaner. 'We don't want you to fall again, do we? Especially with that very nasty wound on your shin—'

'If I fall again it'll be because of the footpaths, not because of me.'

'With orthotics, you won't need to spend money on monthly appointments—you could leave it for six months, even longer.'

'But I've got a regular appointment every month,' Margery said.

'Well, now you can spend the money you save on sturdy shoes instead.' He turned the vacuum cleaner on and started running it over the carpet beneath the chair.

Just thinking about those lovely monthly foot massages made the follicles on Margery's arms rise, and she felt bereft knowing she'd never experience Glen's warm, assured grasp, that sleepy, *caressed* feeling again. But at least there was Angela, her fingers pressing into Margery's scalp as she lathered the shampoo, the comb slicing across her scalp, the nuzzling noise when she poked the cotton balls into her ears and the release on her scalp when Angela took the rollers out. She walked home despondent, her eyes on the footpath, her handbags hanging limply from her arm.

At home, she drank a cup of tea and took her tablets, then poured herself a nip of cooking sherry and turned on the television. The six-thirty shows always made her feel much better. Other people's battles with their obesity, brutal landlords or children kidnapped by angry fathers gave Margery licence to impart wisdom: 'All he has to do is stop eating rubbish ... Why don't they just find somewhere else to live ... If she hadn't married the wrong man in the first place, silly girl ...'

# DAY 7

Because it was the Saturday after pension day, Margery set off at 9 again, this time for her usual ten o'clock appointment at the hairdresser. Every fortnight she had a wash, blue-tint and set. At her front gate she found Kevin perched on his flimsy racing pushbike, watching the excavator dig a hole. Saturday was his riding day, and at about 9 o'clock Kevin—dressed in his anatomically fitted lycra tri-suit, high-visibility vest, Lance Armstrong signature helmet and carbon-soled, caliper-buckled bike shoes—rode to the café opposite the Brunswick Touring Bicycle Club clubrooms.

'A cellar,' Margery said, pointing to the excavator.

Kevin smoothed his lustrous moustache with his finger and thumb. 'Nar, it'll be a hot spa, Mrs B. That's their culture. They'll build a house around it, you'll find.' He lowered his anti-pollution mask over his face and rode away.

'It's a cellar,' Margery said.

Angela was combing her hair, dividing it into neat, pale-blue slices when Margery noticed something sparkling on the third finger of her left hand.

'Oh, dear,' she said. 'You're not engaged, are you?'

'Yes,' Angela said, pausing to smile lovingly at the insubstantial diamond chips sprinkled across the thin gold band.

'I should congratulate you then,' Margery said. 'I'll have to train another hairdresser now.'

'You'll get Toula. She's good.'

'No doubt you'll have a six-month honeymoon in Italy and come back pregnant.'

'Hopefully.'

Margery dragged herself home again, limping slightly

because of the raw tightness of her injured shin, her eyes on the footpath beneath her sensible shoes, her mind consumed by both Glen and Angela's betrayal. She stopped briefly outside the pub to scowl at the door, and again in the park to stare hatefully at the young mothers, designer types, expensively dressed in badly finished inside-out clothes, chatting by the safety swings with their babies called Rupert or Maude. Golden retrievers and heeler–kelpie crosses tore across the grass, yapping. At home she sat at the kitchen table staring at her good shoes, her cross-stitch and her sheet music in bags at her side, waiting for Kevin.

Kevin was spying on riders from behind a newspaper in the café opposite the Brunswick Touring Bicycle Club clubrooms. On occasion, he'd done the 'hell ride' with them to Mt Eliza, but a misunderstanding with the club saw him ostracised. After several mediation sessions, a quorum used rule 6.1c to declare that Kevin had 'conducted himself in a manner which, in the opinion of the Committee, was prejudicial to the good order or name of the Association', and although his natural state was that of outcast, he was still crushed. The dispute was over a lost reflector cuff. Kevin felt the club should replace it since it vanished during an exhibition ride as part of the Brunswick Street Festival, but the club didn't agree. The same thing had happened when he was a member of the local tree planting club and lost a trowel during a Regeneration Day exercise.

The cyclists set off for Beach Road, a river of bobbing reflective green and yellow flashing red and white moving down Sydney Road, and Kevin set off for the three-block ride to take his elderly neighbour to see his demented mother.

At three-thirty, he arrived at Margery's house, showered and shaved, with a bag of Pat's clean washing, some cans of beer and Fifi, Pat's Pomeranian—a small, decrepit dog, stained and matted, with flatulence, yellow teeth and halitosis. He took the car keys from the nail behind the kitchen door and went to the shed where he warmed up Margery's car, an apple-green Hillman Minx that Lance bought brand-new in 1961. Margery ducked into the lavatory one last time then hopped into the back seat with Fifi, gathering her bags to her side—handbag, cross-stitch bag, the bag containing sheet music and her spare bag—fencing Pat's putrid, rotting dog against the door.

As he backed out into the lane, Kevin said, 'I'd like to borrow this car, Mrs B, join the vintage car society,' but before he could conclude his request, Margery said, 'This car belongs to Morris.'

'It's no use to him where he is, I assure you,' Kevin said, eyeing her via the rear-vision mirror, but she kept her gaze straight ahead. It was Morris's car, as written in Lance's Last Will and Testament. Her second-born son was to inherit the car, and one day he would come home from Thailand, so that was that.

The nursing home was a modern square building surrounding a central garden. Kevin punched in the code, the doors slid open, and they were embraced by pastel-hued ambiance permeated by a faint humid stench of effervescent, urine-soaked carpet squares and perfumed oil burners. Margery presented her latest lot of cross-stitched pillow covers and face washers to the loud, cheery carers, then went to the day room to play piano for the residents, an assortment of distorted figures slumped in cushiony chairs like discarded frocks. Some men crowded around the fridge. They'd been there, asleep in their wheelchairs, since lunchtime because Happy Hour started at four o'clock and they longed for their one free glass of beer. If Nurse Graham or Nurse Garry was on, they always got two. Christmas and St Patrick's Day, three.

Kevin pulled a chair up next to his mother's armchair and put Fifi in her lap. Pat screwed her nose up and said, 'That dog stinks,' so he put her on someone else's lap. Generally the old ladies loved to goo at her and pet her, though Fifi preferred to lick the carpet squares. Kevin looked sideways along the line of frayed grey hair standing out from the wing-back chairs, and said, 'Hello ladies,' switching the TV to the sports channel.

'Mrs Bist's place sold for $650,000,' he said to his mother. Kevin had desperately wanted to buy Mrs Bist's house. He'd haunted the estate agent and lobbied Mrs Bist's fellow volunteers at the opportunity shop, but Mrs Bist's niece sent word from America that the house was to go to auction. So Kevin was first at the auction, eyeballing the auctioneer, his raised hand visible from the very back of the crowd. As soon as the bidding started, a surly bloke—Tony, as it turns out—and his substantial accomplice, Dennis, a short, thick man with stiff white hair and colourless skin, arrived to flank him. 'I've got nine hundred thousand dollars to spend on this place, mate. Cash. But I'd prefer not to spend that much, if you know what I mean.'

Kevin's bidding paused, and Dennis took up the lull. But Kevin tentatively raised his hand for six hundred and thirty-nine thousand nine hundred dollars. Then Tony leaned in and said in his ear, 'You live over the road, don't you, Kevin? Ride a *pushbike* to the city every day, eh?'

Kevin looked into Tony's eyes, and brought his hand swiftly down.

Suddenly, Pat turned her dull, blue eyes to Kevin and said, 'Mrs Bist? She got a prolapse from all those babies.'

Margery said, 'Mrs Bist didn't have any babies.'

Pat focussed on Margery, her expression defiant. 'Well, who did all those children belong to?'

'She got them from St Joseph's,' Kevin said.

She turned on Kevin, 'You're not suggesting that the priests—'

'No!' he said. 'St Joseph's ... the orphanage.'

Kevin brought the conversation back to Mrs Bist's house. 'They knocked Mrs Bist's house down, Mum. They're building a new one—architect-designed. I wish I could have bought that house. I could renovate it, put a tenant in, retire. It's my greatest wish to retire, Mum.' Forty-five years as a salesman at a menswear store in the city had taken its toll on Kevin, especially since he had never possessed a name tag declaring anything more important than 'Relieving Manager'.

Pat wasn't listening, so Margery filled the silence with an old

English proverb, 'If wishes were horses, beggars would ride,' just as a kitchen attendant, a long-nosed woman with prominent teeth, her dark hair caught up in a ponytail, wheeled the tea trolley in and started up-ending cups and sploshing milk into them from the two-litre carton. Then she spooned two sugars into each cup, held a giant teapot over the lines of cups and ran it up and down without lifting the spout. Tea ran off the side of the cart and disappeared into the carpet squares.

Pat pointed to the trolley and said, 'There's a horse.'

The attendant, rattling the spoon around the teacups, rolled her eyes and said in a broad Irish accent, 'There's no horse here, Pat.'

'Yes there is,' Pat said. 'I can see it.'

The attendant dumped an arrowroot biscuit and a plastic cup half-filled with beige tea on the table in front Pat. 'There's no horse in this room.'

Margery, thinking of pixies in Irish gardens, imaginary gods on clouds in the sky, and acknowledging her habit of talking to Cecily, said, 'It might be an invisible horse.'

The attendant said, 'Then its poo is invisible, so no one will see it and they'll walk it all over and I'd be all day cleaning it up.'

The male nurse who was pouring the beer for Mr McNickle checked the soles of his shoes and winked at Margery.

Margery declined an offer of a cup of tea and played a few tunes. A couple of nurses got one or two of the residents up onto their feet for a dance, and just when everyone was having a lovely time, Kevin said it was time they were off, and they left.

The last time Margery saw her, Pat was busy shoving the tea-soaked paper serviette down the spout of her feeding mug with a plastic straw.

Back in the womb of her cosseted fabric-and-cotton walls, Margery took the frozen chicken from the freezer and left it to thaw in the sink. She had just flicked on the television and settled with her Sao biscuits with cheese and sliced tomato to watch

David Attenborough's *Tiger—Spy in the Jungle* program when Kevin came striding down her passage, his helmet light flashing and his bicycle shoes clattering on her linoleum. He walked straight past her, down her back steps and into the shed. Margery made a mental note to remember to keep the screen door snibbed. He came back and stood in her lounge room, the exaggerated crotch of his reflective orange lycra bodysuit blocking Margery's view of the tigers on the television. 'Mum's gone. She ran away just after dinner.'

Margery said, 'At least she'd had something to eat. She'll have her strength.'

'Well, that's just it,' Kevin said. 'She'll have enough strength to walk straight under a tram.' He tugged his cycling gloves on and said, 'She's not in your yard, or the shed. I'm going to search for her,' and clacked down the passage again. David Attenborough said he was going to use elephants equipped with cameras to enter the world of the tiger for an intimate look into their lives.

'Fancy ...' said Margery, and bit into her Sao biscuit.

Saturday night passed like any other Saturday night at 253 Gold Street. Margery ate her dinner, took her tablets, careful to drop the sleeping pill down the plughole, and went to bed early with her transistor radio on Magic Radio Best Tunes of All Time. She reclined in the dark, watching out to the street, the streetlight opposite illuminating the passers-by. She dozed and woke, dozed and woke, and through the disjointed night she saw Tyson and his mates kicking a football up and down the street. It bounced onto Kevin's front verandah and broke his wind chime. He burst through the front door, objecting strongly, so the boys kicked it through his front window. Waves of harmonica and you-done-me-wrong music floated to her from the pub, and then she heard the patrons singing as they spilled onto the street and lurched past her front window. A slip of a girl stood swaying outside her gate, her dress, the smallest dress Margery had ever seen, sparkled in the lamplight while her friend, a smart-looking chap in a striped suit, tried to break into a car. The girl looked up and down the footpath, then she opened her little purse and was about to vomit into it when she saw Margery's letterbox, so she flipped up the top and vomited into it instead.

'Got it,' her friend said, opening the car door, then he grabbed her and kissed her passionately.

'Tsk,' said Margery and hopped out of bed to bang on her front window, but it was too late. The hoodlums drove off, scraping the side of Mr Ahmed's parked taxi. Kevin's light went on and a little while later a police car cruised by.

Margery woke early Sunday morning to that particular stillness streets have after a busy Saturday night, and more palings
from her front fence were missing. 'Wretched so-and-sos,' she
snarled. Tyson and his flatmates used her fence to light fires.
They also tore branches from the trees in the park to cook sausages on sticks or to burn.

She moved her legs to the edge of her bed, sat while her
blood oriented itself to her upright position and, when she felt
stable, she stood. Again, she paused while her feet adjusted to
the weight of her body, and her tarsals and phalanges clicked
into position. She rotated her shoulders, loosening her verte-
brae, and then rolled her head as much as she could to free her
neck. Blood had found its way to her feet; her fingers started
to tingle and her heart seemed to be coping so she moved off,
best foot first—in this case, her left foot, because her right foot
supported a particularly sensitive bunion—sliding her feet into
her slippers.

She gathered her dressing gown about her and made her way
cautiously out to the lav with her commode pot, and that's when
she found Pat. The noise, a snort, drew her to the shed. It went
through her mind to phone the police, or go to Mrs Parsons',
but Mrs Parsons' blind wasn't up. She told herself it must be
a sick pussycat or a possum and went to investigate, arming
herself with the copper stick from the laundry. She shuffled to
the shed door and opened it—'Here, kitty-kitty-kitty'—but then
she noticed that the travelling rug was not folded on the back
dash of Morris's car, and the passenger door was slightly open,
the small yellow ceiling light burning. Someone was in the car.
Margery tightened the belt of her dressing gown, secured her
feet in her old slippers and approached the car, squint-eyed and

determined. The snoring person was under the travelling rug on the back seat, a hand poking out, and gathered across the knotty, speckled fingers were dress rings, familiar dress rings—a fake black pearl on a silver-coloured band, a plastic cameo, an apex of glass diamonds. And the fingernails—Pat's signature burnt-orange—lit by a shaft of morning light from the gap between the iron roof and the wall. It was definitely her. Margery gasped, her hands went to her cheeks and she said gleefully, 'She's dead!'

For sixty-one years Margery had watched her neighbour skipping off to Saturday-night ballroom dancing in her stiff, twinkling skirts of many petticoats, and several times a week Pat passed on her way to the pub to have the time of her life with all her hilarious good-fun friends, over-dressed and over-happy. Often Pat would just pose in her front garden in her nylon slacks and matching colour-coded blouses, pressing her nose to her precious ruddy Baronne Prévost rose. Year after year Margery had endured Pat's backhanded compliments about her knitting and sewing, her love of polishing and her colourful cross-stitching; 'I suppose it's nice ... if you like that sort of thing.'

Once, back in the 1960s, Pat had said to her, 'You'd learn a lot if you ever bothered to get off your bed and participate rather than watching the world pass by your front window, Margery Blandon.' But Margery had gathered in her irritation and replied, 'You've never been much further than the pub yourself! You think life's just one big party, that you're here just to make a spectacle of yourself.'

'Life's too short to go unnoticed,' Pat retorted, lifting her apron and shaking it like a cancan dancer in the street. 'I know exactly what you need, Margery. I bet you've never had an orgasm.'

Margery was indignant. 'Certainly not,' she said, knowing she was telling a lie, that she and her children had been victim of organisms—nits—from school.

And so Margery felt a sort of soaring disappointment as she noticed the rug rise and fall, felt her stomach turn with churlish malice when the rug fell away to reveal Pat, alive and breath-

ing, crunched up on the back seat, clutching the street directory. There were twigs in her hair, or what was left of it, and she
looked like she'd been eating dirt. But she was alive. She opened
her eyes, looked at Margery and said, 'Are we there yet?'

Margery was wondering what to do when she sensed her toe
was unusually cold. Looking down, she saw a dark circle in the
dirt. A puddle. Pat had emptied her bladder, and Margery's big
toe, protruding from a hole at the tip of her worn slipper, was
resting in it.

'You always said to kill you rather than put you in a home, Pat,'
Margery said, calculating that it was a full twelve days until she'd
need to use the car again, twelve full days until the next pension
Thursday, the day she and Mrs Parsons would do their Big Shop.

She bolted the shed door behind her, dropped her slippers
in hot, soapy water in the laundry trough and went inside for
breakfast.

After tea and toast Margery reluctantly decided to do the
right thing. Kevin seemed concerned, so she would tell him.
Then Mrs Parsons' blind went up, so she made her way up to
her room and got her new slippers out of their box. Walter gave
her a brand-new pair every Christmas, but as she squeezed her
right foot into one slipper she found it antagonised her bunion.
The other slipper crushed her com. Her indignation growing,
Margery carefully negotiated the undulating cement squares
of her garden path in the stiff-soled slippers, holding the front
fence as she travelled over the unrelenting footpath to Mrs
Parsons. She knocked and called 'Yoo-hoo', and let herself in
to Mrs Parsons' kitchen. Her neighbour was waiting in her old
rocking chair, tending the rinsed cottontails and wool stockings
draped over the upright electric oil heater. Margery sat opposite
her, said, 'Good morning, how are you today, Mrs Parsons?' and
Mrs Parsons said she was as well as could be expected, thank
you. Margery reached down and lifted her right foot, and as Mrs
Parsons rocked back in her chair, Margery said, 'Sorry I took so
long. I had trouble getting my feet into these new slippers. The

trip here today was quite painful.'

'I'm very sorry.'

'It's not your fault. You haven't seen Pat, have you?'

'No. Kevin's been in to ask.'

'Are you alright then, Mrs Parsons?'

'Yes, thank you, you're very kind.'

'See you later.'

'If it's not too much trouble,' Mrs Parsons said.

Back in her own kitchen, Margery kicked off her painful slippers, put her apron on over her dressing gown and turned up the radio. Buddy Holly was singing, '*My lonely heart grows cold and old.*' She stuffed her thawed chicken and popped it in the oven, peeled the potatoes and carrots and put them in with the chook. She washed, dressed, dabbed some face powder on her nose and chin, admired her fresh blue set in the mirror, then sluiced out the letterbox. The lass in the small sparkly dress had obviously been drinking something with orange juice. Over at Tyson's, noise thumped through the front window. She stayed waiting at the gate, and soon Walter came striding down the street, thick and hairy in his shorts and black-and-white guernsey, waving like a super star. Under one arm he carried a frozen chook and a newspaper, and his thongs flicked at his imaginary rhinestone cuffs.

'Nine hundred and eighty-seven days, Mumsy. Nine hundred and eighty-seven days since my last drink.'

'Nine hundred and eighty-seven days,' Margery said. 'How are you, Walter dear?'

'Never better.' He kissed her at the gate and said, 'Cracked your glasses.'

'Yes.'

'Mrs Bist's house has gone.'

'They shovelled the whole house into a truck and drove it away last Wednesday,' she said.

'Progress.'

'Then they dug a big hole.'

'A pool, maybe,' Walter said.

'A cellar,' Margery said, and they gazed at the striped reflective ribbon that fenced off the hole in the centre.

'Quick workers.'

'Very noisy.' Margery moved to her front door, Walter following. He paused on her verandah to rip an extension cord from a power outlet where the sleep-out once was. Across at Tyson's, the music ceased immediately, and the front window filled with pale, pierced faces. Walter pulled on the extension cord violently, and there was a crash, then loud profanities.

Margery put the frozen chook in the freezer for next week. She didn't mention Charmaine, Angela's engagement or her disappointment with Blaine, or Pat, though she did mention again to her son that it had been a very, very noisy week. As she turned the potatoes and pumpkin Walter set the table, then, while Margery shelled the peas, Walter read the paper. 'See Pat yesterday?'

'Yes,' she said, turning on the peas. 'How's the hygiene course going, Walter dear?'

'Good!' he cried and added, over-confidently, 'Yep-see-dep-see, job's right.'

'What's the teacher like?'

'Nice legs, spiky hair, up herself.'

'Have you got a pen and paper?'

'Red and blue, and a pencil case.'

They did the crossword. Walter read out the questions and Margery answered as many as she could.

When she turned the peas off, Walter made the gravy and went to get Mrs Parsons. They came back, Mrs Parsons clinging to Walter's arm. He helped her out of her big wool coat and high red beret and draped them carefully over the cross-stitched antimacassars on the couch. He sat her down on her chair and pushed her up to the table. 'Would you care for a small glass of sherry, Mrs Parsons?' He'd been asking the same question for fifteen years, but today she replied, 'Just a little one, if it's not too much bother.'

Confused, Walter looked to his mother, who had stalled, a basting spoon in her hand. 'Well, Walter, get Mrs Parsons a nice glass.'

He got the smallest tumbler from Margery's precious crockery collection in her mirror-backed crystal cabinet and declared it to be Mrs Parsons' Special Glass.

Margery served the vegetables and Walter carved the chook and they sat down, as usual, said, 'Cheers,' had a sip of sherry and a mouthful of food and Mrs Parsons complimented Walter on his gravy and Margery agreed and, as always, Walter said, 'Special gravy for special ladies,' to which Mrs Parsons replied, 'You're very kind.' Then Mrs Parsons said, 'It's a shame about Mrs Cruickshank,' and so Margery had to explain to Walter that Pat had run away from the home. 'She always said to me, "Kill me before you put me in one of those places."'

'Should we take a look?' Walter said, concerned, but Margery said, 'Nar, she'll turn up, and anyrate, the police are out looking.' She removed Pat from his mind completely by breaking the news to Walter about the Plan for Independence List. Walter put down his spoon, wiped his hand on the serviette tucked into the neck of his guernsey and looked at the list. 'Job's right,' but Margery knew he didn't understand what was written on the note, so she read out the things Anita said needed fixing. When she got to 'take the bath out and put a shower base and chair in, OR, put a bench across the bath temporarily,' Walter rubbed his nose. He jerked his head on his neck when she read out number five and six—'move the handrails next to the shower so M can reach them' and 'adjust the doors so that they are secure'—he stood up and turned circles in the small kitchen. Mrs Parsons put her knife and fork down and placed her hands on the edge of the table, glanced at her coat and beret on the couch.

'She also wants you to put smoke detectors on the ceilings.'

'On the ceiling?' He circled, clenched and unclenched his

fists, and Mrs Parsons pushed at the table, trying to shove her chair back, but Walter settled at the table again when Margery stressed that it was for her own safety, 'So I can stay at home.'

He picked up his knife and spoon and said, 'I'll drop in, have a word with this bossy-britches Anita.' He laughed, his false teeth perfect under his dyed moustache, '*Anita the Hun,* ha-har, how's that, eh? *Anita the Hun?*' and Margery laughed and Mrs Parsons stopped turning from side to side in her chair, and they went on to enjoy their lovely lunch and Walter went on his way, as he did, when he'd finished his pudding, dried the knives and forks and delivered Mrs Parsons back to the sanctuary of her silent little house.

Sunday afternoon, Margery put things in order in her kitchen, had another nice cup of tea, started another cross-stitch— *Cursed be he that removeth his neighbour's landmark*—then ran a polishing cloth over some of Walter's trophies: Junior Featherweight, Junior Welterweight, Super Middleweight. Before she went to untie Mrs Parsons' laces she checked on Pat, found her wide awake but occupied reading the Street directory, so she handed her a vegemite sandwich through the half-open window. 'Thanks,' Pat said.

She made herself a cold chicken-and-lettuce sandwich for tea and ate it while she watched the news, but there were no missing-persons reports. Before going to bed she peeped into the garage. Pat was sitting in the passenger seat, head tipped back and mouth open, snoring. Margery left a glass of water on the bonnet of the car, bolted the shed door and fell off to sleep in her cosy bed with Matt Monro singing, '*Born free, and life is worth living, but only worth living because you're born free,*' through the pillow. After she'd slept on the situation, Margery decided to do the right thing concerning Pat, mainly because during the night her disappearance had been announced on the Magic Radio, Best Tunes of All Time. 'Anyone seeing an elderly woman ... last sighted in the Sydney Road vicinity ... possibly suffering hypothermia from exposure.'

It took a long time for Kevin to open his door. In the morning light his eyes were bloodshot and his moustache unkempt. 'Mrs B,' he said, looking apprehensive.

'Pat's in my car.'

'Right.' He thought for a moment. 'Is she dead?'

'Asleep.'

'Are you sure she's not dead?'

'Quite sure.'

'Right.' He ran his hands over his crew cut. 'I'll be over soon, okay?'

Margery tottered back, woke Pat and quickly gave her a biscuit and glass of cordial.

'I usually have porridge,' she said.

An ambulance took Pat to hospital, and Margery spent the day watching a huge mixing truck vomiting liquid grey all over Mrs Bist's bald, suburban block.

The glaziers replaced Kevin's smashed window that afternoon, and that night Kevin dropped in. 'Lucky she had that travelling rug, Mrs B,' he said. 'It probably saved her life.'

As soon as it was dark, Margery ducked back out to the shed and removed the rug from the car.

# ROOM 4321

That was the one good thing that happened during that disappointing week. I was big enough to save Pat's life even though I'd been dismissed by Angela and Blade. He just hacked off the end of my toenails then chucked his nail clippers into the steriliser and said, 'One more fall could finish you off.' Little did he know in a matter of six short weeks I'd be sitting here on the forty-second floor very much looking forward to my final fall.

Tuesday came around and, of course, so did Anita. While she was there I worked on my second cross-stitch. I'd done *Cursed be he* and was starting on *removeth*. I must say, that one worked out well, because I edged it with roses, something I don't often do because flowers are not always successful in the cross-stitch.

I wish I'd brought my cross-stitch now that I'm here. I've made a cuppa because you get free tea bags in these hotel rooms, but it's dreadful. Tastes like water wrung from wet cardboard, and these biscuits are tough, tasteless. The milk, or whatever it is, comes in those little pods Anita used to have in her basket.

Actually, Anita asked a lot of questions that Tuesday. She'd already mentioned a flatmate, so she must have been scheming right from the start. I was watching the builders put together the new house frame next door when I saw her pull up in her loutish car. I know it's a lout's car because Tyson and his mates love to stand around it, gawping, and she opened the hood to let them look at the engine one day. They like to look at Tony's car as well, but the second they even look like they might go near it he rushes out and hunts them away.

Anyrate, she bowled straight into my house, calling, 'Knock knock, how are ya, Margery?' and I was ready for her. 'I'm very well, thank you. You can call me Mrs Blandon.'

She attempted a joke then: 'You can call me Anita.'

'Let yourself in, did you?'

'Sometimes you've got no choice with this job,' she said.

She was obviously referring to the fact that I was stuck in the bath the first time she came, so I ignored her. 'Don't presume to let yourself in ever again. My hearing is very good. I would have heard you knocking.'

'Fair enough,' she said. 'Before I get stuck into the housework I'll do your dressing for you.'

I said, 'You're not allowed to.'

'People are always saying that to me,' she said and just settled herself in front of me, on the floor of all places, didn't even suggest we go to the bathroom. She unwrapped a plastic dressing pack, so I pointed out that she wasn't a trained nurse.

'No,' she said, 'but I'm a big fan of *General Hospital*.'

It's a show on the telly. I don't watch it.

Then she peeled the plastic off, washed the wound, dabbed it with some sort of ointment and covered it with another piece of plastic. She's got a light touch for someone so hard-looking, and she mentioned that if the wound ulcerated 'we'd really be in trouble'.

She put my washing on, swept, dusted and put clean sheets on my bed, all the while asking the usual questions: had I taken my tablets?

'I take them every other morning; why would I not take them today?'

'Do you have any problems getting in and out of bed?'

'I'm up, aren't I?'

'Trouble getting on and off the toilet or the commode?'

'Certainly not.'

'Would you like meals delivered three times a week?'

'Would you?'

'Certainly not,' she said. 'It'd be like eating fishing net.' Then she made a pot of tea and I was very surprised because she made it properly—found everything herself, warmed the pot and popped the cosy on it and left it to draw. Then she put her nose to the milk carton and promptly poured it down the sink.

'That was Cheryl's milk,' I said.

'I'll mention it next time I see her,' brisk little thing that she is, digging into her basket and bringing out a little pod of long-life milk. She asked if I needed any shopping done.

'I'm quite capable of doing my own, thank you, and anyrate, I don't take milk.'

'Milk's good for your bones.' Then she squeezed her calci-um-enriched, long-life milk into her cup, turned the pot three times and poured the tea, even pausing to tilt the pot as she poured, but the most remarkable thing to me was, she used a strainer! I nearly fell out of my chair. Who'd have thought some-one who looked like her could make tea properly? Cheryl's tea tasted like dishwater. No love in it.

Anita said her mother taught her how to make tea.

I can see now that it was a clue as to who she really was, and I remember thinking at the time, 'It was as if I'd taught her myself.' If only I'd had my wits about me.

She sat on the stoop with her tea, smoking a cigarette, and asked me more questions. 'I can see you like cross-stitch, Mrs Blandon,' she said, 'but what else floats your boat?'

I almost said, 'Minding my own business,' but I told her that I enjoyed cross-stitch more than anything. 'I've always got a few on the go. I like the proverbs best, but you can always get a nice landscape pattern with cross-stitch. I'm not one for flowers so much, or birds. They're more for the embroiderers, though I've never seen one yet that's been able to get the curve of a petal right, you know, and the exact colour. I also enjoy cleaning the house, especially the polishing.'

'You're the only person I've ever met who likes polishing,' she said, so I explained that I started my job with Doctor Woods when Judith started school. For forty-four years I cleaned that practice from six o'clock in the evening until seven-thirty, and that's where I developed my love of polishing, because I made

THERE SHOULD BE MORE DANCING

that brass plaque on Doctor Woods' door glow, and then I got to work on his doorknobs and they shone right up until the day I left, and this of course led to my other hobby—looking after Walter's trophies. And, every evening, I turned the page on Doctor Woods' desk calendar: *You are never fully dressed until you wear a smile, Health is not simply the absence of sickness,* hence my passion for wise sayings, which have been such a comfort and guide to me.

It's a pity more doctors didn't take note of their desk calendar quotes. *No doctor is better than three.*

Doctor Woods retired two years ago, so I had to retire as well, though I was down to one day a week by then. 'And of course,' I said to this Anita, 'I'm musical. Every Saturday I visit Pat and play the piano for the old people. Pat lived across the road from me for sixty years, and on Monday I saved her life.'

'Is that right?'

I could tell she didn't believe me. 'I found her in my car.'

'That's a good safe spot.'

'She's in the hospital at the moment.'

'That's not so safe.'

I was pleased for Kevin's sake that I'd saved Pat, though I will admit that when he rode away to go searching for her that Saturday night all I could think of was Pat tumbling along under the metal wheels of a tram, her sand-covered intestines flopping in the tracks with her wig, her orange eyelids and paste pearls scattered along the bluestones. Well ... if I can't be myself with you, Cecily, I'd have to pretend to be nice *all* the time, and besides, not once, never ever, did Pat attempt to include me, one of her oldest neighbours, in her Grand Final parties in the park or St Patrick's Day barbecues or Melbourne Cup Day at the pub. I sat on my bed in my front room for years and years watching them all coming and going with their big, stupid hats and plates of sandwiches, bottles of Green Ginger Wine, the laughter and hilarity wafting over to me like waves from a distant wireless.

Of course, I know why I wasn't asked *now*, but at the time Pat was in my car, all I knew was that Lance went to those parties and I never was included.

As I say, I wouldn't have gone, but it would have been nice to have been asked. Pat even went to Walter's fights when Lance could get cheap tickets. I wouldn't go, even when I was asked to go that one time. I'm not the type that enjoys violence.

And Pat bragged about that ruddy rosebush, the Barrone Prévost. 'It was Grandmother's rose,' she used to say, her nose tilting to the ceiling. 'The original one come all the way from *In-glnd* in eighteen *fordy-two*.' I think that's a bit of an inflated description, really. '*Bew-di-ful,* isn't it?' she'd say, so I'd say, 'Yes, it's beautiful,' and she'd say, 'You don't have to tell anyone a Baronne Prévost rose is *bew-di-ful.*'

She was just a blatherskite, but I got her back with the Public Scalping Incident. That's what Lance called it. *Heaven has no rage like love to hatred turned, Nor hell a fury like a woman scorned.*

# THE PUBLIC SCALPING INCIDENT

It happened at the 1976 Ladies' Legacy Luncheon. Pat and Bill were big in Legacy, and for Ladies' Luncheon, Pat was allowed to take a guest since it was her turn to give the address. As she was rehearsing her address one last time, articulating and emphasising her words to her assembled Ballroom Dancing Frocks, the phone rang. She was disappointed to hear her guest, Betty, say her car had broken down. 'I know it's a long way, Pat, but we could go halves in the price of a taxi.'

After she put the phone down Pat gazed out the front window, wondering how she could get all that way to the Legacy Hall in time. Who drove a car? Across the road Mrs Bist was bustling off down the street with her cane basket brimming with goods for the needy, her cardigan pulled tightly over her large bosom and her arms crossed supportively underneath. And there was Margery, sluicing her front footpath with hot, soapy water.

Pat turned and went to the kitchen, where her husband, Bill, sat at the table hunched over his form guide. The wireless blared above the noise of his nebuliser, chugging away on the table beside his cigarettes, ashtray and lighter.

'I'm off,' Pat yelled, and Bill looked up at her, his face beyond the green ventilator mask was cyanosed, the trim of his ears necrosis-white.

'Don't forget to turn that machine off when the Ventriloquin runs out.' Her husband raised one finger, and Pat gathered her speech, purse and cardigan and left, stopping to check her hair one last time in the hall mirror.

'I'll just get ready,' Margery said, and Pat told her to get a wriggle on.

She stood next to Lance, who was watching *The Mike Walsh*

*Show,* his cigarettes and ashtray on the small imitation-teak table next to his oxygen cylinder, a longneck bottle of beer on the floor beside him.

Pat checked the oxygen level in his cylinder. Margery maintained them, changing them when Lance asked her to, easing the taps with generous amounts of oil when they were stiff, but it wasn't uncommon for Margery to leave the tap loose or even attach him to an empty cylinder, so Lance would end up red-faced and twitching, breathing carbon dioxide. 'One of these days you'll blow us all to buggery,' Pat shouted above the sound of the telly, which made Lance smile and cough. He worked a ball of phlegm into his mouth, pulled the oxygen tube in his nose to the side and expectorated into his mug.

'A day out might do Marge good,' she said, and Lance gave her the thumbs-up.

When Margery emerged a minute later wearing her good shoes, white cardigan, her precious pearls, a smear of pink on her lips and an armful of sheet music, Pat said, 'Marge, there isn't a person within earshot who doesn't know you play the piano, but that doesn't mean everyone wants to hear you actually play the piano.'

'Good,' Margery lied. 'I'd prefer not to have to play.' She popped her sheet music back in the piano seat.

They'd been gone less than five minutes before Lance and Bill tottered down to the pub—Bill, short, round and breathless in a vinyl bomber jacket and Kmart jeans beside Lance, a tall and immaculately turned out man in a mustard-coloured cardigan and grey turn-up trousers. His mouth was open, sucking in air, a green tube reached to the oxygen cylinder rattling behind him, the little trolley wheels going *tweet tweet tweet.*

So Margery found herself at the top table, the Legacy leaders' table, a dignitary to her right and Pat on her left, before her a sea of soft brown and blue curls, ample-bosomed ladies, floral and pastel with fleshy earlobes, wattle and dewlaps, all maintained by step-ins and various prosthetics.

Before her, propped against a saucer of geranium petals surrounding a floating Chrysanthemum, was a white card advising the day's proceedings. First on the program was the local choir, who sang 'God Save the Queen'. The assembled ladies then sat through number two, 'Welcome Speech by the Chairwoman'. Number three, 'The main meal will be served', was either chicken or ham salad, followed by number four, the choir singing 'Morning Has Broken' while the ladies enjoyed a fruit compote with custard. For number five, a lass from St Joseph's school read a composition titled 'The Effects of War on Those Left Behind'. Her story was based on the life of her great-grandmother, who had grown her own vegetables and milked her cow and ploughed her own fields during the war with the help of the Land Army. And then it was Pat's turn. The MC said, 'I give you Pat Cruickshank and this month's address, titled "The Unseen Effects of War on Women".'

Pat bared her teeth to Margery and said, 'Any fruit seeds stuck to my dentures?'

'No,' said Margery, and Pat turned to stand up. At that moment, Margery noticed the tag poking out the neck of Pat's cardigan. 'Hang on,' she said and reached up to tuck it in, when the catch on her wristwatch caught one of Pat's curls as she rose.

Margery had no idea Pat wore a wig, no idea her hair had snapped off and fallen out after years and years of peroxide and perming fluid, and so Pat stood frozen before the room of fellow legatees, her rival addressees, past and future, the thin tufts of her brittle hair flattened against her shiny, damp pate and her wig dangling from Margery's wristwatch.

Finally, someone started clapping. Pat had turned deep, deep red and the audience, moved by her brave humility, started to applaud thunderously.

Pat replaced her wig to present her speech, her nasal, bandsaw timbre uncharacteristically subdued, and the chairwoman then gave a moving address about being brave and the silent

effects of war, relating how, because there were no dentists and
no money, a lot of women lost their teeth, and a lot of women
suffered back injuries and prolapses from labouring work, and
this, coupled with nervous conditions caused by the hardships
of war, meant they had fertility and hormonal problems, which
of course, in many cases, led to hair loss. She asked for a show of
hands from everyone in the room who'd lost hair because of the
war. No one owned up to hair loss but everyone put their hand
up for loss of teeth, most owned up to nervous complaints, one
for a bowel prolapse and two for uterine prolapse.

Afterwards, Margery pulled up outside Pat's house and turned
to apologise again, but Pat slammed the passenger door so hard
the window popped out of its runners and fell into the door.
Lance had the window fixed, but it was never the same. Even
after so many years had passed, each Saturday and every second Thursday, at every bump the window rattled and Margery
grinned at Pat's bittersweet humiliation.

But Pat had her revenge. At the time Margery outwardly
dismissed the spiteful words Pat delivered to her as just that—
vengeful—yet they caused a chasm that took two decades to
bridge. In those twenty years there were further minor rifts—
short, violent skirmishes that took place in the supermarket or
at Mrs Bist's front gate over principles and opinions. But eventually the vitality in the women began to wane with waxing age,
and they found themselves one day watching despondently as
yet another strange couple moved in and demolished a perfectly
good home that had taken someone they had known well a lifetime to build. Margery shook her head and said, 'Tsk,' and Pat
said, 'What's past help should be past grief,' and this signalled
a start to breach the chasm.

# ROOM 4321

You'll come to understand why I have good reason to dislike Anita, but at the time I was impressed that she took an interest in me. On that second visit, she was dusting the photos on top of the telly when she got to the personal questions. 'How old are the kids?'

'Walter Miniver Blandon is my first-born. He's sixty now,' I said. 'The talented one. A champion athlete and very musical. Then there's Morris Lancelot Blandon who's fifty-eight, and Judith's fifty in November, though she tends to celebrate six weeks later because she was premature. You can't tell now. She looks quite normal, though she's overweight.' I was working on a tapestry at the time for Pat, and I remember starting the second 'gossip' in *Who gossips to you will gossip of you* and saying to Anita as I threaded the needle—it was double thread, one of my favourite reds, number 817—'My husband worked at the brickworks for thirty-five years, but my children have all done wonderfully well.' At the time I truly believed they were all successful. They all had jobs, and if you passed them in the street you'd see they were neat and clean. But cast in the glare of betrayal, I see now that they're not much chop at all, and I'm really trying to understand why.

I bet Pat would have something to say on the subject.

I know for sure Walter's a sweet boy at heart, easily led, especially by loose women, but you don't want to upset him these days. He was always an affable sort of chap but after that last fight Morris started saying, 'His fists'll go up and you'll go down.' He's broken a jaw or two over the years, but only when he's provoked.

'Judith, well, she wasn't planned,' I continued. 'She bawled every day until she went to school. Lance used to put beer in her bottle to shut her up. She and Kevin from over the road were friends with little Sylvia in the wheelchair from around the corner. Sadly, she's dead now. They used to take her to the park, and one day she fell off the swings and landed awkwardly over on the cement path. Kevin and Judith told the policeman they were playing on the slippery-dip at the time and didn't see it happen. The family moved to Queensland after the funeral. These days Judith's very successful. She has a mobile business, a beauty shop.'

Anita stopped dusting then and looked closely at the photo of Judith. '*She's* a beautician?'

'And she's expanding into psychiatric counselling as well,' I said. 'At the moment, though, she drives to people's places and does their hair and make-up. She got top marks for nail enhancement at the beauty school and her little pink-and-green van says "Judith Boyle—mobile beauty, finesse and panache in all your needs for skin, nails and hair". Walter says it looks like it's advertising a knackery. When Walter retired from boxing he became a manager of a lodging house and now he's studying as well. He's going to be a chef. And Morris, my second boy, runs a big hotel in Thailand. He lives there. Morris was a boxer as well but Walter was the one with talent, so Lance stopped Morris doing the boxing. "Better to find something you can do," he said, so Morris decided to be a businessman and that decision has taken him to where he is today.'

Like Walter, Morris had some lost years. I've only just found that out, but I'll get to that.

I didn't tell Anita that selling cigarettes at school was Morris's first business venture, nor did I say that I hadn't actually set eyes on my second-born son since his father's funeral twenty years ago, but at the time I wasn't about to share the family secrets with the likes of someone of her calibre. Nor did I tell her that, if the truth be known, Judith's never really had friends since little Sylvia. There were no bridesmaids at her wedding. Nor mine, now that I think about it ...

You know, Cecily, I was so excited when I saw I'd given birth to a little girl that I gave her your name, Cecily Judith. Then it became apparent that Judith wasn't going to be anything like you, so I swapped her name to Judith Cecily. When she left school and got a job as the driveway attendant at the local garage, she said, 'I'm the face of the petrol station,' and Morris called from the sleep-out, 'That's because you look like a petrol pump.'

Morris was always a bit cheeky, always had a gang of kids following him. He was the first to move out of home, my most independent child. Now that I think about it, I hardly noticed him. Even so, twenty-four years is a long time to hold a grudge over one little fight. I'm talking about the fight he had with Walter at Lance's funeral service. It took me years to pay off the funeral director. They broke the leadlight picture window of Mary with dead Jesus on her lap, *Pietà,* and a few chairs, which may seem remarkable since the entire skirmish was over in less than two minutes, but Morris had been drinking and Walter still held the Middleweight Champion title, though he was not long out of rehab. Poor Walter. He took up the drink around the time of the funeral. I didn't see him for almost ten years and I haven't seen Morris since, and it pains me. At first I thought, 'It's normal, they grow up and move away,' but twenty-four years is a long time to be away.

I know why now. Everything's fallen into place.

I nearly lost Walter completely because of the Incident in the Ring, and as I understand it I may never see Morris again, but somehow I've managed to hold on to you.

Nothing was the way I thought it would be, like we planned.

# THE INCIDENT IN THE RING

Walter's final championship opponent happened to be a south-paw, which suited Walter's explosive right. But this southpaw, Rocky Wrecker, was five pounds heavier. Even worse, he had a longer reach.

The trainer held Walter's face in his hands, looked him in the eyes. 'He'll torment you, Walter.'

'I'm the bull,' Walter said.

'His right glove is a red rag, he's tryin' to make you fight dirty, lose points. Stay clean, stay calm.'

'I'm a bull, I'm *strong*.'

Walter stayed strong. He won the first three rounds on points, though his opponent held him with his beady, unwavering gaze, dancing around him, reaching out to the Brunswick Bull, gently touching Walter's brilliant black coiffure.

'Steady as she goes,' Lance called, hoping his warning words would reach his son through the din.

The comer man pleaded, 'Ignore the left ... He's teasing.'

'Bull, Bull, Brunswick Bull,' the crowd chanted. It was early in round four when Walter was distracted by the right glove hover-ing at his carefully curled forelock. Rage erased the fight plan in his brain and his explosive right shot out, his left shoulder dropped, and Rocky Wrecker's hair-trigger left swung, catch-ing him hard in the right temple. Walter fell flat, unconscious before he hit the canvas, landing like a dead man on the side of his head. The ringside crowd erupted—booing, hissing, women screaming—and Festival Hall sounded like the inside of a bass drum on Saturday night.

At the pub, the crowd craning up at the TV above the bar fell silent when they witnessed Rocky Wrecker's first KO, and Walter's last. A sinking dread filled Pat, as though she had swallowed a shoebox-sized iceblock. Things would never be as good again. The scene before her in the pub was like a photograph from a *National Geographic,* everyone so still, so captured. She left her bar stool and went straight to Margery, whom she still hated with a burning fury, hoping she had not yet turned on her wireless.

It was a depressed skull fracture. Walter was kept in hospital almost a year and the pictures he retains from that time remain vivid: the dust building on the air-conditioning vent above his bed, the light around him made pale green by the bedside curtains, and the screeching sound that wrenched him from uneasy slumber every morning when the nurse ripped them back. He liked to see how many millilitres of water the domestic put in the plastic jug on his bedside table each day before she came back the next and threw it out. The repetitive, tortuous beeping of machines made him tense and combative, as did the whine of the floor polishers and the noises made by pain. Before he could speak he longed for someone to throw a doona over him; he cried inside from the cold, antiseptic air. Every evening he gagged when the smell of hot soup in plastic warmed the ward and the stench of infection stayed in his nostrils, along with the acrid odour of cigarette-saturated nurses, the nicotine on their fingers made stale by cold night air. He bristled at their hollow encouragement; their bright, cheerless voices; the upward, nasal inflection at the end of a statement: 'We're just going to give you a little injection for the pain, all-roioioiot?' He disliked the carping voices and advertising jingles trilling through the corridors from TVs and radios, but his heart lifted every time he heard the ting of the lift. Sometimes it was his mother. He depended on her voice, day in, day out, low and guiding. His mother's face was the only one he recognised when it appeared over him in the cold, white ward—'I wasn't prepared to let you go, son, especially on your own'—but he knew things were missing from his mind. But what? Occasionally, in the physiotherapy ward, stretching and flexing on the low vinyl mattress, a wall of lights, flashbulbs and microphones suddenly appeared. He remembered skipping and sparring, sweat and noise, *ding-ding,* roaring crowds, *thwack, thwack. Thwack-thwack.*

The rehabilitation centre was better, things were more straightforward, though at times he found people holding him, tying him down—'Steady, steady, calm down'—but he knew he hadn't finished the fight, it was only round four. His bedroom was comfortable and he had a bedspread that seemed familiar. He recognised hot taps from cold, came to understand that doors could swing in or out, remembered green meant go and red meant stop, knew to cut up his own food and, once his legs kicked in with the command centre in his head, he was fast enough to get to the toilet in time. He stayed at the rehab centre for a further year, learned to count, learned the value of money, learned to read, care for his personal hygiene and health, establish a routine to live by, a system to fathom the tram timetables. By the time he got to the community house his mind and body were rebuilding, seemingly alone, and he was cooking simple meals, easing his way back into life. Alcohol was forbidden, but he'd been a boxer since he was ten, so he'd never been a drinker anyway.

Then, in 1986, when he was forty years old and finally living the independent life of a pensioner (with the help of weekly visits to therapists), the pub exploded and everything changed again.

As usual, Lance was at the pub that day, propped at the bar, his neighbour Bill next to him, Lance's oxygen cylinder tucked in close to his bar stools, a beer and an ashtray each in front of them. Morris was there that day as well, sitting where he always sat—within speaking distance of Lance, close to the rear exit with a clear view to the front door, his back to the wall, a muscly, glint-eyed lout either side of him. Lance called Morris's mates 'Dubious One' and 'Dubious Two', and he called his second son 'Dodgy Morry', but father and son had a trusting relationship—they both trusted each other to keep secrets from the rest of the family.

Morris was in the toilet, handing over a package to an addled customer with Dubious One on watch near the door; the barmaid had just put a fresh beer in front of Lance and Bill before descending to the cellar beneath the bar. Then both Lance and Bill reached for a cigarette. No one's sure which, but one of the men struck a match. First, there was a flash, and the pub and all its contents jumped. Lance's oxygen cylinder rocketed through the ceiling, a gas wall heater popped off its brackets, leaving a live gas hose exposed. Then the windows burst from their frames like splashed water; the glasses over the bar exploded from their shelves, splintering the air with razor-edged fragments. The walls popped out and stood an inch away from their foundations, and all the eddying ashtrays, coasters, bar mats, trinkets, trophies, stuffed animals, framed photos, TVs, chips, peanuts, light fittings, bar stools, tables, chairs and patrons were slammed against the walls or thrown through the empty doorways and windows, landing in the street, on the cars or in the park opposite, and for a moment a cloud-burst of flames filled the cavity that was once the main bar.

At 253 Gold Street Margery paused in her knitting and said aloud, 'Gracious. What was that?' In her office at the brickworks Pat stubbed out her cigarette and reached for the phone. When no one answered at the pub, she trotted off along the footpaths in her high-heeled sandals, her big plastic earrings bouncing. When she rounded the corner to Gold Street, there it was, her pub, a smoking shell, black dust billowing from the vacant window frames and flames dancing along the lovely, curved wooden bar.

When the sirens raced down Gold Street, Margery put aside the blue-and-white socks she was knitting and came out to the street, looking for the telltale smoke of a house on fire rising above the rooftops. She saw the pub smouldering, smiled and clapped her hands, then caught herself. Up and down the street, neighbours gathered at their gates, hands on mouths, mesmerised by the black cloud rising and spreading from the hundred-year-old, two-storey brick building.

Bonita came running up the street in her brunch coat, her hair in rollers. 'Mrs B! Is Lance in that pub?'

'Yes,' she said, just as Pat stumbled down the smoky street towards them, wailing. Bonita threw one arm around Margery, reaching to Pat with the other.

They say people as far away as Barry Street heard the *whoomph* and felt the ground leap beneath their feet.

Morris and Dubious One both still suffer tinnitus, and it took quite some time for the firemen to find the barmaid. Given that the explosion killed 'Lance the Lad' Blandon and William Archibald Cruickshank, as well as Dubious Two, there were post-mortems and a coroner's inquiry. After some delay, the respective families were informed the bodies were to be released for burial. Margery stayed in her bedroom, her radio to her ear, while the Blandon children gathered at her kitchen table.

Judith sat between her brothers, weeping. 'Dad's the father of a middleweight champion,' she cried. 'He should have his funeral service at St Patrick's Cathedral.'

Though her father had largely ignored her, he did include her in some things—she was a non-drinker so she often drove for Lance, Walter and the entourage. Happily, when Walter won his first professional welterweight title, Judith met Barry.

'Mumsy won't come,' Walter said. 'She doesn't believe in God, hasn't been to a funeral since her sister died.'

'Well that's just disgusting,' Judith said. 'What if there's news-paper reporters and photographers there and his wife hasn't even bothered coming?'

Dubious One said helpfully, 'You could tell everyone she's dead,' which stopped the discussion for one heartbeat. Then Barry snarled, 'Nobody's interested in us anymore, Judith.' When Walter lost that last fight, his brand-new brother-in-law, Barry, lost his brand-new career as manager–minder of the defending

Middleweight Champion of Victoria, 1983, and was forced to ask his sister's husband's cousin for a job in real estate, where, again, success had so far eluded him.

'We'll have the service at the funeral parlour,' Walter said.

Morris sat back. They eyed him, waited while he composed his words. His gold earrings were burnished like Margery's door-knobs and he rubbed his gold skull-and-crossbones ring. 'There are people who want a church service for him, people who were very important to Dad for many, many years.'

'Like who?' Walter said, genuinely intrigued. After that last fight, Lance regarded Walter a bit like a second cousin at Christmas lunch—someone you were compelled to be friendly to but had no interest in. To most people, apart from his brick-dusted mates and the sodden, addled men on their worn stools along the bar, Lance was just one of those tall, neatly maintained men with an invisible wife and a pub complexion, treading carefully along the back footpaths of working-class Brunswick.

'His sisters,' Morris said, poking his tongue up into the gap where his front tooth used to be.

'Faye and Joye? They'll be happy as long as there's food.'

'There are others.'

Judith snapped, 'It's not up to a bunch of smelly derros from the pub, Morris.'

Behind Morris, Dubious One sniffed and Walter said, 'That's harsh, Judif.'

'We should decide,' Judith continued. 'Who could a man possibly love more than his wife and kids?'

'His mistress,' Morris replied.

Walter shot up from his chair like a cork from a fizzy bottle and started swinging—arms *wooshing,* feet dancing—and everyone scattered. Judith followed Barry outside, Dubious One leapt into the bathroom and Morris dropped under the table. Walter's discharge notes stated that he was prone to 'sudden, uncontrolled rages', but his siblings had never actually seen one, until then.

Lance Blandon's funeral was delayed again until most of his

offspring could reconvene and, since a lot of people were still suffering after-effects from the explosion, Bill's send-off at the Catholic Church was a quiet affair.

Again, Margery absented herself from the second Blandon meeting, so Morris was able to explain that Lance had maintained a steady, devoted relationship with a particular woman for nearly thirty years, and he insisted his father's 'long-time, love-of-his-life soulmate' wanted a church funeral, and she deserved to sit up the front with Lance's special friends and his sisters. Walter insisted she was most likely merely a drinking companion and 'a bit on the side'—she shouldn't be there 'for the sake of Mumsy'.

Judith wanted to know where she lived and what she looked like, but Morris had promised not to reveal anything to anyone because Lance had stipulated, 'No child of mine's mother should be upset in any way.'

On the day of the funeral, the parlour attendants stood sombrely at the door. Slim Dusty sang, 'But there's nothing so lonesome, morbid or drear than to stand in the bar of a pub with no beer' from the portable tape recorder on top of the coffin, its extension cord draped across the wreath. Margery sat on one side of Lance's coffin, calmly unpicking some cheap cross-stitching thread—*Let the punishment be equal with the offence*—which had bled into her white handkerchief. Beside her, Morris sat quietly while Judith and Barry scrutinised the women on the other side of the coffin. Behind them, respectful and stoic, were Lance's mates, ruddy-nosed men with yellow teeth and smoker's fingers. Though the cuts and abrasions of some had healed, others still had bandaged limbs, and one chap's eye was taped over with a great wad of cottonwool dressing.

Finally, Walter strode into the funeral parlour. He looked at his family sitting fearfully on one side of the coffin, and then at the women opposite, Lance's sisters, Faye and Joye, and between them a thin woman with movie-star hair and lips, sitting with the bar flies sniffing and dabbing their eyes with balls of damp

tissues. He fixed on the slender blonde at the centre of the weep-
ers, then his eyes glazed and turned to Lance's coffin. After
two long seconds he walked straight up to it and punched it, a
haymaker, and it fell with a loud *thud* on its side. The lid popped
off and Lance rolled across the polished parquetry like a log.

Walter paused and looked down at his father, then he eyed the
crowd, spotted Morris, and reached for his shirt front, but Morris
sprang up, striking out like a swimmer off a starting block. Only
Margery remained where she was, the guests scattering around
her. Someone called, 'Fifty on the Brunswick Bull,' and Barry
said, 'Fifty on Dodgy Morris.' Walter and Morris fought, stagger-
ing, rolling and dragging each other from one side of the funeral
home to the other, chairs toppling and vases falling. Finally,
Morris got Walter in a clinch, 'Give in, Wally, give in—you're just
walking up Queer Street anyway.' Further enraged, Walter flung
him off like a scarf, picked him up and hurled him through the
stained-glass widow—a depiction of *Pietà*. Then he straightened
his hair and walked calmly out of the parlour, knuckles bleeding.
Behind him, the guests stayed pressed against the walls, looking
down at Lance the Lad with his arms folded stiffly across his army
uniform, his marbled ankles in his blue-and-white knitted socks,
all around him spilled flowers and shattered leadlight glass.

Faye and Joye asked for a copy of the will, but Margery told
them to ask Pat. Pat was executor; she had the will hidden somewhere. As far as Margery was concerned, they'd spoken to Pat
and everything was settled.

Morris left for Thailand the very next day. Margery doubled
her cross-stitch output, Judith took up eating in earnest—'I
thought Dad was a good bloke, but he's just like the rest of
them'—and Walter took to drink, disappearing completely.

Margery waited and waited, running to the phone when it
rang, gazing down the street, checking her letterbox several
times a day, but her sons didn't come back to her. She said to
Cecily, 'God does not exist, and those people who believe in their
invisible friend obviously don't understand that He is a cruel

menace.'

Five years on, outside the recreation room of the psychiatric wing at St Vincent's Hospital, a tram slowed, clanging its bell twice. Inside, Walter leapt from a corner, his footwork taking him around the ping-pong table, his fists pounding an imaginary opponent. An attendant said, 'Ding-ding,' and Walter retreated to his corner.

'You're the Brunswick Bull, eh?' the attendant said, and Walter leapt up again, his boxing gloves raised, his opponent lifeless on the canvas beneath him, the lights hot and the crowd chanting: 'Bull, Bull, Brunswick Bull.'

Consequently, Walter was resurrected, again, dried out and woken from a nightmare where he'd spent years fighting the sucking arms of an alcoholic octopus, swiping insatiable worms from his ears and smacking at ants under his skin, and then his mother reappeared above him again, her arms ready to hold him. He returned to things he knew—his mother, brother-in-law, sister and neighbourhood. He had no idea they had all fallen with him—once when he lost the fight and again when he lost the battle—nor did he know that they would all fall again.

# ROOM 4321

I'd like to go down for a bite to eat but I'm not confident about the door. They give you a plastic card to unlock it, and it's very heavy. But there's cheese and biscuits over there, and I'll make another cuppa, though it's only a tea bag.

Anyrate, while Anita was dusting that day, she picked up the photo of Lance. I remember it clearly. She asked, 'Did your husband ever talk about his war experience?' Those were her very words: 'Did your husband ever talk about his war experience?'

He did, but it sounded to me as if New Guinea was a terrific place, the highlight of his life. The occupying forces had a wow of a time, and he always spun Anzac Day out for a week or more, but I couldn't very well say that to the new home help, could I? So I said no.

She dusted Pudding next, so I told her the photo was taken when she won the Victorian Amateur Scottish Dancing Association Championship. Pudding gave up the Scottish dancing when she started going to the private high school, which was a pity, if you ask me. The dancing might have kept her weight down a bit. Not that she's fat, exactly, but she's inclined to be hefty, like the Blandons.

Then this Anita really shocked me. I didn't ask for her opinion, but I got it anyway. She got a chair and took the photo of our ex-Prime Minister down from above the door and sprayed him with glass cleaner, and all I said was, 'Be careful with that photo. He was the most important and influential leader of the nation we've had since Menzies.'

She said, and I'm quoting here, Cecily, 'Yes, his influence played an important role in prejudice.'

I said, 'I think he was only trying to protect us from terrorists,' and she said, 'Well, I think he was a heartless, old retrograde who wanted votes from all the bigots who think refugees should stay at home or die or both.'

'They're queue-jumpers,' I said, and I remember thinking at the time, *Well, that speaks volumes about the type of person you are, Anita Potter.*

Pat was exactly the same. During an argument about boat people one day, I'd said to her, 'At least the Prime Minister's got the economy in good shape,' and she replied, 'Yep, the rich are richer but he's gunna get booted out by the workers, if you ask me.'

I said, 'Why would I ask you anything, Pat Cruickshank?'

'You'll find out,' she said, nodding. 'You'll find out everything, Princess Margery, and then you'll know I was a careful friend to you.'

At the time I just scoffed at her, but of course I did find out. But I also know now that Pat, my oldest neighbour, didn't tell me anything because she was one of them, the conspirators.

But she was right. I do know everything now. She must have enjoyed herself so much at my expense.

A careful friend to me, indeed.

The shame of it all is that Morris knew everything as well, it seems. He was in the middle, I imagine, torn amongst his family, and so he couldn't say anything, I suppose ...

Anyrate, then Anita asked me all about my life. No one's asked me about myself since Great Aunt Fanny asked years ago what I was going to do when I left school, so I suppose it was considerate of Anita, though I imagine they're trained at the home-help school in how to conduct a respectful conversation with senior citizens.

'Well,' I said, 'I'm seventy-nine. There was a special birthday lunch for me at a very grand hotel in the city on Sunday.'

'What hotel?'

'The Tropic. It's very tall with a hollow bit in the middle—an atrium, they called it. People go there to jump off. They land in the buffet area.'

'Handy to the service entrance, I s'pose.'

'Are you Irish?' I asked.

'Not Irish. Why?'

'We had an Irish girl at school called Potter. She believed in pixies.'

'I've been away with them once or twice. Where were you born?'

'Well, Anita,' I said, and I told her all about our wonderful life and how Dad worked on the railways, how he was a station master at one stage. I told her about our brothers and sisters— Clarry, Shirley, Willy and Terrence. They're all dead now, except possibly for Shirley. Remember our family picnics and the sing-a-longs, Cecily? Our favourite picture, *Mrs. Miniver?* Remember the letters we got from Walter Pidgeon? I kept our membership of the Walter Pidgeon Fan Club until he died in 1984. I was more upset when he died than I was when Lance died two years later. Wasn't Walter Pidgeon respectable and decent? He was kind and handsome, too, a perfect husband really. 'We were happy, back then,' I said.

Anita said, 'Yes, the "good old days", when everyone was happier,' as if it wasn't true, so I said that we *were* happy. She just shrugged and said, 'I've come to understand you've got to live in the now, seize happiness now—you can't just be happy with memories and hindsight.'

At the time I thought it was a cruel thing to say. So I said to her, 'In the good old days we were thoughtful, we had manners.' She might be able to make tea, but she should have known better than to say something like that to someone whose greatest asset is their past, since there's not much future left. And everyone's gone now.

Now that I think about it, perhaps because she looked after old Mrs Razic and others she was able to see it's best to live for the now. People live for themselves these days.

Funny that I mentioned you that day, especially to a stranger.
It was nice to say your name out loud to someone after so long.
  Cecily!

Do you know that if you had meningitis now you wouldn't have
died? Ambulances come within minutes these days and save
you. Mind you, they don't hurry when they're called to bowling
clubs because they know it's just some old bloke twitching away
on the hard, perfect lawn, clutching his shirt front.
  His teammates at the bowling club told Mum that the last
word Dad ever breathed, as he lay there fading away, was your
name.

Anyrate, the truth is we *were* happier back then. These days to
feel fulfilled you have to have a lot of money; in our day we had
fun, and we had our whole life together planned, but we never
had a chance because you died. Just when we were about to
become the people we were meant to be.
  'That must have been sad,' Anita said.
  It still is.

Not only did she rehang the picture of the Prime Minister upside
down that day, she also seduced Walter. He called in after his
hygiene class, came bowling up the passage with his book, pens
and pencils in a plastic bag, intending to have it out with Anita
the Hun, but he was ambushed. Didn't stand a chance. From
the second he laid eyes on her, standing there on my kitchen
chair hanging the ex-Prime Minister, he was helpless. She got
down and stood there in front of him, shining like a lorikeet—
blue eyes and blue uniform, the thick eyeliner, hair electric and
her scent mixed with my homely roast-chicken atmosphere.
  I said, 'This is Anita, Walter, the new home help. The one
with *the list*.'

Anita held her hand out, smiling in her seductive way, but Walter was paralysed, his mouth hanging open. I wanted to put my finger under his bottom lip to prop it up. She said, 'How are ya, Walter?' and Walter wiped his hand on his footy jumper and shook her hand, saying, 'I've never been better in my life.'

At the time I thought she was better than those Diana Dors blondes, mostly card girls, who used to hang off Walter. In the newspaper photos there was always at least one buxom tart under his arm, smiling under a rigid platinum thatch, eyes like boot polish brushes. Pat used to be platinum-blonde in the sixties, and look at her now. Bald. Walter actually had a proper girlfriend once, before he got famous. Doreen was her name. She was Catholic. I asked him if she was a practising Catholic and Morris called from the sleep-out, 'It's not Catholicism she practises, that's for sure, eh, Wally?' Walter didn't think being Catholic was important. 'The important thing is that even Catholics have got the important bits,' he laughed.

I tried again because Walter was practically dribbling. 'Now listen, Anita, Walter's got something to say about that list, haven't you, Walter?'

She wriggled her hand out of his, smiling like a female trapdoor spider with her mate cornered, rubbing her fangs together. 'Just a few alterations around the house will help keep your mum at home. Hope you don't mind.'

Walter reached for my notepad on the table, letting his supermarket bag thud onto the floor. 'Just explain to me, Anita, precisely, exactly what you want me to do and I'll do it. I'll do anything you want.'

'I'll show you,' she said and led him all over the house, telling him things that needed doing: organise an electrician to replace the broken light switches, get someone to set up a seat in the shower, reposition the handrails over the bath so I could actually reach them. 'Margery's privacy and safety will be assured if you adjust all the doors, specially the front, back and bathroom doors so that they close properly,' she said, as if she was some sort of expert, and Walter, sounding like a love-struck teenager, said, 'I'll even put locks on them, and I'll patch up the hole in the lounge room ceiling.'

She smiled up into his handsome face. 'Margery's heating bills will fall in winter.'

'You're wonderful,' he said and straightened his left leg, tugging the hem of his shorts, which is a quirk of his when he's nervous or excited. I made some sort of rude noise then. I had to—I was starting to feel nauseous—and he regained his emotions. She kept on at him, told him he had to put new taps on every tap, put non-slip tread on the back step and, most importantly, smoke detectors. 'I can get an electrician if you like,' she offered, but Walter said the job was right. But it wasn't. He can't read or write very well anymore, so there were just scribbles all over my shopping list, and his memory's about as concrete as chicken wire.

'I can do all of this next week, after my uni course.'

'That right? Which uni?'

'Council of Adult Education.'

'I've been there, did tap dancing.'

'I'm doing food hygiene. The place where I work's changing to a hotel for international travellers.'

'A backpackers?'

'Yep-see-dep-see.'

'What's going to happen to the residents?'

Walter's proud smile fell way and he looked at the ceiling, thinking. 'I guess they'll find somewhere else to stay.'

'Under a bridge,' Anita said. 'If you change to a backpackers you still get drugs and drunks, and those poor old men end up in a dump bin or a doorway somewhere.' She left Walter standing in the kitchen, frowning at the ceiling. She put a little torch next to my bed, saying, 'Make sure you mind your shin.'

'She's real nice. Smart too,' Walter said dreamily, but, knowing what I know now, I bet she got into her loud, striped car, rubbed her hands together and said, 'That solves everything.'

But little did she know Barry and Judith were brewing a separate conspiracy.

Wednesday dawned bright and crisp to drag in another hot day. The joggers and power-walkers were up and about early, and so was Margery. She took her second cup of tea back to her bed to rest her aching shin. The wound, a hard, shiny gash, burned and pulled the taut, red skin around it, throbbing dully as she watched commuters hurrying in their sharp suits, square bags hanging from their shoulders. Vespas zoomed past, school kids ambled, and at exactly eight o'clock Kevin pedalled off to work. Next door, Tony supervised the installation of a stainless-steel sink that four men struggled to carry across the concrete slab, stepping over stacks of timber planks. They had a great deal more trouble fitting it into the staircase leading down to the cellar, but worse was to come. A huge stove proved too much for them, so the entire workforce—about fifteen men—were ordered to down tools, abandoning their work with plaster and plywood, insulation foil and timber planks, bricks and cement, and the neighbourhood fell silent. It filled again with shouting as the men bullied the stove through the cellar door and down the stairs. They had all just disappeared down the staircase, shadowed by a large plumber carrying a tool case and blow torch, when Barry's tall, sleek Mercedes slid into the kerb. Cars like Barry's often cruised the kerbs of Brunswick, wheels polished to a silver gleam, windows tinted dark. At least once a week there was note in Margery's letterbox: '*I may have a buyer interested in your house*'.

Margery watched her son-in-law wipe his palm across his comb-over, get out of his flash car and check his comb-over again in the tinted side window. He scratched deeply in the cleft of his bottom, then straightened his green suit and rubbed his beige slip-ons against the back of each calf. He stood in the middle

of the road, watching expectantly towards the corner. A couple
soon arrived in a low, grey car, parked and joined him on the
footpath. They were fashionable and affluent in a casino sort
of way, their soft flesh pressing against the seams of their somewhat garish attire, ready to pop through like pink beads along
the seams.

Barry, all big smiles and expansive gestures, indicated the
busy worksite that was once Mrs Bist's house and then turned
their attention to Margery's home. He swaggered down the
narrow side path, the podgy strangers trailing. Margery scram-
bled off the bed, wincing in pain from her sore leg. She limped
down the hall to the kitchen, where she listened to them as
they stood under her rusting Hills Hoist. 'A real boom,' Barry
said, and expanded on the wonders of the modern yet substantial cliff-like homes that were shooting up from postage-stamp
sized blocks all over Brunswick. Then he ushered the strangers
towards Margery's back porch, and by the time she had assumed
a natural, nonchalant position in her chair, they were inside. The
woman called, 'Knock knock.'

Barry tried to open the window over the kitchen sink. 'Archi-
tects can do anything with these little places.'

Margery stabbed the blue Aida with her needle and said, 'As
if having an architect was as special as screw-top jars. A house
is a house no matter how nifty the windows are.'

Barry jerked his thumb at Margery. 'That's Mrs Blandon,' he
said, then they circled Margery's tiny kitchen and bathroom. In
the cramped lounge room, they paused to take in the splendid
cross-stitched landscapes, seascapes and snow-capped mountains, rural scenes and *Pietà* above the gas heater in the fireplace.
The woman turned her attention to the old lady in her grubby
dressing gown cross-stitching something on a square embroidery frame in her sunken chair. Margery was working on the
word *When* of Anita's basket cover.

'I'm Amanda and that's my husband, Theo ... hope you
don't mind ...' and they wandered into Margery's small second

bedroom, paused again to absorb the cross-stitched bedspread, pillowcase and curtains. The adequate front bedroom was also over-decorated with cross-stitched bedspreads, pillowcases and curtains, the dressing table scattered with embroidered soft-backed brushes and wot-not jars. Amanda, Margery observed with great pleasure, pointed to the shiny doorknobs and fittings. 'Brass,' she said.

'Another good selling point,' Barry said and drew their attention to the pressed-tin ceilings.

'I'm not going,' Margery called as they closed the front door behind them.

Later, as she tied Mrs Parsons' left shoelace, Margery mentioned that Barry had showed a fat bloke in leather pants and his flaccid wife around her house. 'She was pretty, but those kind of looks don't age well.'

'I see,' said Mrs Parsons. Margery eased her foot to the floor and Mrs Parsons tilted forward in her rocking chair.

'Do you ever get the real estate agents bothering you?' Margery lifted the right foot.

'Yes,' Mrs Parsons said, adding apologetically, 'but I don't let them in—not even Barry when he comes.'

'I see,' Margery said. 'Are you alright then, Mrs Parsons?'

'Yes, thank you, you're very kind.'

'See you later.'

'If it's not too much trouble,' Mrs Parsons said, and Margery left her in her chair, the window glow lighting her hair and fading her brown skin yellow, her stockings and cottontails draped over the oil heater. Harpsichord music tinkled from the radio on the bench.

In the afternoon, Margery's indignation over Barry and his podgy accomplices was compounded by the activity next door. Two delivery trucks double-parked outside her house and started unloading bricks and timber, lifting plastic-wrapped squares of bricks with a clawed crane and placing them on the

nature strip where the melaleuca once grew. The swarthy builders swarmed all over them, slicing open the protective plastic
and leaving it to waft down to the park. The noise pollution
amplified, the site trembled to the sound of electric nail gun—
*shishthunk, shishthunk*—and the radio shouting out across the
neighbourhood. Then Tony and Dennis returned in a big,
white van and reversed up onto the kerb. Though the postie
didn't come until at least three that afternoon, Margery went
out to check her letterbox. The weekly specials leaflet from the
local supermarket advertised ice-cream topping on special, two
for one. She stayed at the letterbox, watching Tony and Dennis
unload a big stainless-steel table, a large box with 'Glass' written on the side, some plastic drums and various small boxes
and supermarket bags. Carefully, they carted them down into
the cellar.

'Tomatoes,' Margery informed Cecily. 'Mrs Calabria bottled
her tomatoes every summer. It's what ethnic people do.'

While a builder set about installing a hatch door over the
cellar, Tony and Dennis ambled across the site, watching, exud-
ing a mixture of authority and menace. The workers ignored
them, or tried to, and went on carting bricks in wheelbarrows,
stacking bags of cement, shovelling sand, checking doorframes,
measuring, drilling and nailing. At the end of the day, the begin-
nings of a frame for a two-storey house was in place.

Walter preferred caramel topping to any other flavour, so on
Thursday, when the workers arrived well before seven, Margery
was already washed and standing at her dressing table wearing
a blue linen shift with white neck-to-hem buttons, the 'specials'
pamphlet folded in her purse, ready for her walk to the supermarket. Because it wasn't pension week it wasn't a Big Shop day,
so Margery didn't drive. Like every morning since Charmaine's
visit, when she put her glasses on Margery was reminded again
of the provisional nature of her life and the threats she faced
from her family and an advancing modern society. She said to

her reflection, 'I don't care what I have to do, but I am not going to a home.'

While she ate her breakfast she kept one eye on the builders next door and the other on Mrs Parsons' blind. When it was time to go, the trip next door meant travelling through howling ethnic music and the fumes of idling trucks, men shouting in a language she didn't recognise. She mentioned the caramel topping as she tied Mrs Parsons' laces and they discussed cheese slices. Mrs Parsons no longer risked the fractured asphalt footpaths under the native tea trees and feral figs, and remained safely at home. She gave Margery five dollars and her list: four small tins of plain tuna in brine, one packet of Sao biscuits and one packet of cheese slices.

Back inside, Margery poked a comb at the thin blue curls under the rim of her hat and set off. Next door, Tony turned to study the concave old woman stepping cautiously off the footpath and into the path of a slow-moving truck loaded with bracing ply. The truck driver braked, and while the pensioner passed he bit into a bacon and egg roll, chewing as the old lady— clothed for winter, a dressing pad bulging under her stockings, blue bandaids holding her spectacles together, carrying three handbags and dragging a tartan shopping cart—passed in front of his idling truck, oblivious to everything except the ruptured road between her sensible white lace-ups.

At the supermarket Margery carefully selected Mrs Parsons' groceries, then her own: four bottles of caramel topping and a packet of no-brand cheese slices. She took advantage of the 'Special Offer Coffee and Cake for $5.00' at the Union Square Café before setting off home with her groceries rattling around in the bottom of her cart.

From as far away as the park she recognised the pink bag on the footpath outside Mrs Parsons'. It was a clothes recycling bag from St Vincent's, and the slippers Cheryl had so generously purchased for Mrs Parsons three years ago were sitting on top.

She stopped, picked up the slippers and turned them over. The soles were pristine, not a scratch or smudge of dirt.

Inside, Margery double-checked Mrs Parsons' shopping receipt with her, adding up the figures on the back of an old envelope, as they always did. Then Mrs Parsons turned in her rocking chair, opened the grate on her disused wood stove, reached in and retrieved her purse from the dusty, black interior. She counted out an extra four dollars and fifteen cents for Margery. As Margery left, Mrs Parsons said, 'Thank you, you're very kind.' Margery usually said, 'That's alright, I had some shopping to do anyway,' but instead she said, 'I see you've cleared out your wardrobe.'

Mrs Parsons said, 'It's time.'

'I never needed slip-ons,' Margery declared, 'and neither did you.' And Mrs Parsons said, so quietly that Margery didn't hear, 'You always came to do my laces.'

All day Margery watched passers-by stop and sort through the clothes in the pink recycling bag, but everything was too small. People held Mrs Parsons' beige button-through blouse with inset sleeves and broderie anglaise on the collar against themselves, then looked at the label inside the collar and dropped it back in the bag. Finally, Tyson came and took the bag away. Half an hour later Margery saw him march off down the street in a torn T-shirt and Mrs Parsons' red tartan kilt.

Not much happened on Friday. Margery sat on her bed in the front room hemming the wall hanging for Pat, one eye on the builders, the *whir* and *tink-tink* of the circular saw and the relentless *shishthunk-shishthunk, shishthunk-shishthunk* of the nail gun challenging her transistor radio. Things picked up briefly when Kevin rode out of his front gate on his thin, silver bike, like some phosphorescent, nocturnal creature. He stopped and took off his pollution mask and shouted at a driver to turn off his idling truck. 'There's a big enough hole in the ozone layer as it is, not to mention the carcinogenic elements of carbon monoxide saturating the air.' The driver wound his window up and turned back to his newspaper. Kevin shook his head and rode away through the dark clouds of gritty diesel exhaust. At lunchtime, the workers settled along the path on brick stacks and boxes of tiles and nails, and opened their lunch boxes. Margery listened to an Australian bloke with a serviette dangling from the bib of his overalls describe how a co-worker fell from a great height on a building site. 'Died instantly. His head and hands blew off,' he said. 'Pressure.' Then he dug his spoon into his leftover spaghetti bolognaise.

His friend added, 'At least it was quick.'

One of Tyson's mates—a glassy-eyed adolescent of obscure gender with a bleached complexion—hobbled over in bare feet and took the last of Margery's fence pickets. A short time later smoke billowed from their chimney and the smell of burnt toast wafted across the narrow street. Later, they gathered at the car embedded in the front lawn, the buffalo grass coiling around the wheels and seizing the bumper bars. For the rest of the day the car stereo *doof-doofed,* cigarette smoke wafted in the afternoon air and the lads settled all over the hood and roof, watching the construction over at Mrs Bist's.

At four o'clock precisely, the builders started packing up, winding extension cords and shoving power tools into milk crates, ready to start the weekend. Then the roof trusses arrived. The driver asked for help unloading them, but the workers kept their backs to him, loading their power tools and milk crates into their station wagons and utilities. The heated discussion between the driver and the foreman prompted the driver to yell, 'Right, I'm phonin' Tony.' He started dialling on his mobile phone; the foreman dropped his foam esky and everyone came back to work. Once they had safely guided the swinging trusses to the ground and the crane folded itself into a neat bend on the back of the truck, the workers headed to the pub, but then another truck arrived. This time they took no notice. Margery watched, intrigued, as the driver unloaded the roofing tiles without even getting out of his track, the crane placing the pallets neatly on the nature strip. By the time Tony eased his low, red car to the kerb, the worksite was deserted. He walked all over the concrete slab, Dennis following. They circled, wandering through the doorframes, stepping through the timber wall frames as if they might encounter a hard-working builder somewhere.

Over the road, Tyson and his mates imitated them, loping around in circles, stepping up to walls and bouncing off, making noises like apes. Margery's delinquent neighbours partied into the night, shouting, laughing and singing, cigarette smoke and the sound of the odd smashing bottle keeping her alert. At one stage, Kevin came out of his house, phone in hand, and stood looking at the hoodlums before going back inside, the phone to his ear. A short time later, headlights moving slowly down the street signalled the arrival of the police. The noise stopped and Margery's young neighbours scattered, vanishing into the shadows, Mrs Parsons' kilt kicking across Tyson's pale knees as he flashed past towards Margery's backyard. It was all quite entertaining, but Margery was relieved to wake up Saturday to a peaceful street—no loud music, no revving trucks, no builders. She said to Mrs Parsons as she tied her laces, 'The builders are a nuisance, aren't they?'

'They're noisy,' Mrs Parsons murmured.

At the door Margery said, 'I hope today will be uneventful.'

But it wasn't.

# PART TWO

*'No fate is worse than a life without love.'*

Mexican proverb

When she got to the nursing home, Margery made her way straight to the nurses' station, proudly handing a nurse the wall hanging—*Who gossips to you will gossip of you*—instructing her to hang it over Pat's bed. As she passed Pat on her way to the piano, she said hello.

'Bities,' Pat said, squashing a rolling pea on the table with her palm. She appeared none the worse for wear after her adventures across Brunswick and her night in hospital.

Margery started off playing 'We'll Meet Again', which always put a smile on the creased faces of the residents, though on this day, one lady started weeping, then another, until there was a wall of crumpled old ladies in cushiony cradles weeping as their minds replayed their memory tapes back to the war, their lost sons, brothers and fathers, families singing around the piano in the lounge rooms of their imaginations, so a nurse told Margery to play something cheerful.

'Oh, for pity's sake,' she sighed and moved on to 'I've Got a Lovely Bunch of Coconuts'.

The activities girl got a couple of the old folks up and they danced together into the corner where they stayed wedged, confused. Pat danced alone. Some residents left their bedside TVs to follow their frames down the long, long passage, drawn by the music. The male nurse poured a beer for the old diggers and a sherry for the old ladies, and the horse-faced kitchen attendant rolled in the tea trolley. Pat, being the party girl that she always was, seized Mr McNickle by the arm, dragging him from his wife, and started twirling around and around, singing. Margery moved smoothly into 'The Yellow Rose of Texas', a polka. Pat started kicking up her heels, but her ancient partner, dizzy from twirling and no longer possessing the cognitive

pliability required for a polka, lurched sideways. The tea girl
had just finished pouring tea into twenty-two neatly arranged
cups when they toppled. Pat grabbed the tea trolley on the way
down, bringing it crashing onto the carpet squares. The kettle
threw its hot brown fluid across the floor and the milk glugged
from the carton, eddying around the peninsula of tea-leaves
and dissolving the spilled sugar. Pat hauled herself up from the
broken crockery using the toppled tea trolley, her slacks dripping hot liquid. She stepped over Mr McNickle and carried on
dancing, though Margery had stopped playing. Mr McNickle
remained strewn where he landed, bleeding and pissing into
a pile of sodden paper serviettes. Fifi threw herself from someone's lap and started eating the spilled biscuits. Margery sighed
again and gathered her music together.

Kevin said the sherry had relaxed Pat—she obviously hadn't
broken anything. 'She'll dance again,' he said, but the staff
insisted she be sent for an X-ray, so she left for another night on
a trolley in the hospital emergency department, still singing. But
Mr McNickle was unconscious, his elbows raw where the skin
had torn, a haematoma building at his temple and his right thigh
swelling suspiciously.

When Margery got home she poured herself half a cup of
cooking sherry and drank it in one gulp.

It was astonishing to Margery that so many people stumbled
through her geraniums to urinate against the side of her house
or squat over her geraniums with their panties around their
ankles. Every Saturday and Sunday morning she flushed her
path and fence with hot, soapy water and checked her yard for
empty beer bottles or used syringes. On this Sunday, Margery
found only a pair of almost-new red stilettos in her letterbox.
She glanced up and down the street, then took them inside and
tried them on, but she couldn't force her knotty old feet into
them. She sighed and put them back in the letterbox, thinking that somewhere in Melbourne a lass was on her hands and

knees searching under a bed for her new high heels.

She stayed, watching down her street, which was reduced to one lane by the bulk of four-wheel drives and European wagons. The houses were changing too; they were either messy construction sites, modernised workers' cottages with restored period facades, or something ridiculous and soulless made of recycled refuse and which used minimal utilities. The lemon trees and grapevines shading Mrs Calabria's concrete front yard filled Margery with nostalgia. Soon she saw a flash of black-and-white stripes at the end of the street, and then Walter waved to her, like Elvis coming towards her in his imaginary white jump-suit and cape, his dark glasses glinting, stepping gracefully in his rhinestone cuffs around the Vespas parked on the footpath. 'Nine hundred and ninety-four days,' she said, and Walter said, 'Nine hundred and ninety-four days since my last drink, Mumsy.' He kissed her cheek.

'How are you, Walter dear?'

'Never better.' He handed her the frozen chook and the news-paper, jerked his head at the construction site and said, 'Frame'll be finished soon.'

'Soon,' she said.

There was no music coming from Tyson's, but Walter reached down and tugged the extension cord that ran across the street. Somewhere in Tyson's front room a sound system crashed to the floor. Walter tugged again, reeling in the cord, winding it into a coil around his elbow. Then he ripped the plug from both ends with his bare hands and threw it out into the middle of the street. Margery put the frozen chook in the freezer for next week, and while Walter set the table she turned the vegetables. She sat down to shell the peas while Walter read the paper. 'See Pat yesterday?'

'Yes,' Margery said and popped a pea into her mouth.

'Seen Anita since Tuesday?'

'No. How's the course, Walter?'

Walter put his newspaper aside and stood up, circled the

tiny kitchen rubbing his nose with his palm. He jerked his head to loosen his neck and dug into his tight pocket with his fat fingers, handed her a printed page, worn and soft from folding and unfolding. 'This is what we did,' he said, and Margery read aloud, 'Food Poisoning and Food Contamination.'

'Never put jelly under defrosting meat in the fridge,' he said with authority.

'Week Two: Handling and Storage Conditions.'

He turned another circle. 'There's a food hygiene test at the end.'

'You're a very clean boy, Walter,' Margery said. 'You just listen to what they say, then they ask you what they said, and you tell them.'

He put his hands over his ears. 'I listen, but it all leaks out.'

'When the time comes, Walter, I'll help you,' Margery said, closing the door of her old gas stove. 'Ask them if you can bring the test home.'

'Right,' he said, and his pacing slowed. 'That's a good idea, Mumsy.'

'The globe on the back porch has gone,' Margery said, taking his mind further away from his problem. After Walter changed the globe they did the crossword, Walter reading out the questions and Margery answering as many as she could while Walter filled in the squares as best he could. They never checked the answers these days. The results were disappointing. Up until that last fight Walter did the crosswords every morning, in three daily newspapers, while his porridge cooked.

When Margery turned the boiling peas off, Walter made the gravy and went and got Mrs Parsons. Walter poured them a small sherry and carved the chicken, and Margery served the vegetables. They said, 'Cheers,' and Mrs Parsons and Margery complimented Walter on his gravy, and as usual, Walter said, 'Special gravy for special ladies.'

'Big Shop this week, girls?' he continued.

'Big Shop,' Margery said, and Mrs Parsons sipped her sherry.

'What do you fink of Mumsy's new home helper, Mrs Parsons?'

'She seems like a lovely girl.'

'Some girl. She must be going on forty-five,' Margery said. 'She's not like Cheryl.'

Walter said he was sure she'd be a great help, and then Judith arrived. She was carefully attired in a smart denim skirt with silver studs lining the hem, her highlighted hair was round and stiff above her carefully spread-on face, all subtle shades of variegated beige and dusty-pink blush with frosty lipstick. Barry also looked smart, his jacket sleeves casually ruched up to his elbows and his sneakers a brilliant white. He wandered out to the back steps and gazed up at the frame next door, and Pudding spread herself along the couch, eyes on her iPod, and swung her high-heeled pink suede boots over Mrs Parsons' carefully placed coat and beret.

'We can't stay,' Judith said, and Walter said, 'Off you go, then.'

Judith scratched a welt behind her knee. 'Where's your shower curtain, Marge?'

Barry sidled back in and pinched a potato from Walter's plate, so Margery asked him if he'd like some lunch. 'Not allowed,' Barry said. 'Judith's on a diet.'

'Barry!' Judith called. 'I told you not to say anything.'

Pudding left the couch to come and dig into what was left on the chicken carcass with her long, black-painted fingernails.

'All she's allowed to eat are grapefruits. I wouldn't do it. I'm beautiful the way I am, and if no one else thinks so they can go fuck themselves,' she said, her mouth full of chicken.

Barry said, 'It's a complete waste paying for expensive schooling for you, isn't it?'

Pud raised her arms above her head in a V 'See this,' she said, rolling her eyes up towards her arms. 'It's this ...' she showed her father the up-yours V-sign with two fingers. 'Only *big*.'

Judith bent over the bath, running her hands along the bottom, the back of her podgy knees red, like they'd just been slapped. 'Where's your shower curtain, Marge?'

Barry banged the window frame, trying to open the window over the sink, and Walter told him it hadn't opened since the stumps at the back sank. 'Bathroom door doesn't shut properly either.'

Barry jigged up and down, testing the stumps, 'Wouldn't be hard to fix up, this joint. The new house next door'll block your light and depreciate the value, Marge. Sooner we get the For Sale sign up the better.' He took another spud from Walter's plate.

Margery said she wasn't going to sell her house, and Walter put down his spoonful of peas and gravy, very gently. Mrs Parsons stabbed one of her potatoes with her knife and dropped it onto Walter's plate. Walter picked up his knife and spoon again.

'Did the council send you anything, Marge?' Judith asked, scratching another patch of red, raised skin, this one in the crook of her arm.

'Well, Judith,' Margery said, 'I get my rates, and of course the newsletter from the library—'

She looked at Barry, 'See? She's deaf as a doorknob. *Marge!* Did you get anything about the building next door from the *planning* department?'

'Not in my letterbox.'

'If you do this place up a bit, Marge,' Judith said, rubbing her back on the doorjamb, 'it'll add thousands to the value. You could get a nice, warm, comfortable room in a stylish place where your every need will be catered for.'

Barry was peering in behind the light switch, which was hanging out of the wall by the electric cords. 'These light switches are collectors' items,' he said. 'Bakelite.'

'DeeAndra can put them on eBay.'

'I've got a Plan for Independence List from the home helper,' Margery said. 'She's marvellous. I can stay at home as long as I like because the government said so.'

'No, you can't,' Judith said, snatching the list from her mother. 'You can't stay here because you're deaf and you keep falling over— you fell again, didn't you? In the bath, didn't you, Marge? I can't understand how you're not dead. Is that why your shin's infected?'

'It's not infected,' Margery said, and Mrs Parsons eyed her hat and coat on the lounge.

Judith pondered the list, her long, hard fingernails sinking into her large curls, the scratching sound filling the tiny kitchen. Barry and Pudding joined her, reading over her shoulder.

'This is a good list,' Barry said, taking it from his wife.

'She cannot stay at home, Barry.'

'No,' he said firmly, 'but think about it. The stumps need doing, don't they, Wally?'

'Mumsy *can* stay at home,' Walter said.

'Let's not have a Walter-cation, Wally,' Judith said. 'She can't stay here, look at her shin.' She grabbed Margery's shin, yanked it out from under the table and started picking at the corner of the Tegaderm with her acrylic filigreed fingernails.

'Leave it,' Walter said, pointing at her with his knife.

Judith managed to lift the corner of the plastic dressing. 'This's dis-gusting.'

'*Leave it, Judif!*'

'Leave it on, Mum!' Pudding said.

'Look, there's infection.'

Mrs Parsons said, 'I think I'll get going now,' and put her hands on the table, trying to push her chair out.

Margery tried to brush Judith's hand away. 'There's a little germ war going on under the plastic and the wound will heal itself.' But it was too late. Judith ripped the plastic off and Margery jumped, wincing in pain.

'See? Pus.' The translucent square of film in Judith's fingers was smeared with a clear yellow liquid and a small spot of blood, but Margery's skin was now bleeding where she ripped the Tega-derm off, and the wound gaped at them, like an ancient crater, concave and rubbled with fetid vegetation.

Walter dropped his knife and spoon, 'You made it bleed, Judif.'

'Blood's good, takes nutrients to the site of the wound.'

Mrs Parsons started to rock in her chair, pushing against the table.

Margery screwed her face as if she'd sucked lemon, and Pudding grabbed a tea towel and wrapped it around Margery's ankle, catching the blood.

'That's one of my good tea towels,' Margery said, and Pudding went to the bathroom to search for the first-aid box.

Mrs Parsons turned sideways on her chair, tried to wedge her legs between the chair leg and the table. Barry had his head against the wall, squinting along the boards to gauge the degree of warp. 'You're going to stuff this whole thing up, Judith, the rate you're going.'

Walter stood up, nudging the table. 'You've already stuffed it up.'

'Wally, it was infected,' said Judith, looking as if she'd been caught slitting a baby's throat, but Walter said it wasn't infected, ripped his serviette out of his guernsey and slapped it on the table. He started rocking, shifting his weight on the balls of his feet.

Mrs Parsons curled back into her chair like a scared slater. Pudding said, 'He won't hurt you, Mrs Parsons,' and pressed a wad of cotton onto Margery's bleeding shin.

Barry put his hand up like a referee. 'Now, Walter, the wound's clearly infected.'

'Anita would have cleaned it up, put a new dressing on it.'

'Your mother's old and unwell. She needs caring for.'

'She is cared for.' Walter moved side-on but managed to keep his fists at his side, clenching and twitching.

'It's obvious she's not cared for very well,' Judith said. 'And, she slipped in the bath.'

Pudding secured the wad of tissues to Margery's wet wound with bandaids, Margery said, 'Ouch,' and Walter said, 'You're hurting her.' He shifted on his feet, rattling the plates in the bureau.

'Yuk,' Pudding said, 'This is so awful, I could never be a nurse.'

Mrs Parsons said, 'I really should get going.'

Barry pointed to the rattling plates. 'See what I mean about the stumps, Wally?'

Walter's head went down and the wind whistled as his fist swung through the kitchen like a flicked rope.

Margery said, 'It's all right, Walter, dear,' but Walter's elbows hugged his torso, his fists remained firmly upright and he danced, the house rocking on its uneven stumps. Bending and ducking around Walter, Pudding managed to get some tinfoil and cover Mrs Parsons' plate, then she helped her out of the chair and they crept out and down the hall while Judith, Walter and Barry shouted.

'No one's going to no home, Judif.'

'Judith's only trying to help.'

'Help herself, you mean.'

'That's a lie!'

Walter yelled, 'I've got stakes in this house too!'

Judith screamed again, 'You owe us, Wally. When you lost that fight we lost too, *big-time.*'

'A small fortune,' Barry said. 'And I lost my career.'

'And we're not the only ones—just ask Bonita Jarvis.' Margery knew Bonita lost her house—the house her father built—to gambling, that the Calabrias had bought it and Bonita had been forced to move to the commission flats with Tyson, a toddler at the time, but she had no idea Bonita had wagered her house on Walter's fight. Tyson rented the house now, and misguided revenge prompted him to destroy his old family home on behalf of his mother. It hadn't occurred to Margery yet, but eventually it would dawn on her that that was the reason he stole her water and used her fence for firewood.

Walter was walking around and around the clothesline, trying to calm himself, while Judith begged, 'Please, Wally, we want to invest in a nursing home.'

'He doesn't understand, Mum,' Pud said, so Judith explained. 'She has to sell her house to get a bond to go into a home, right? So what we'd do is, we'd sell it and buy into a nursing home, then we'd give Marge one of the allocated beds for the low-income or disadvantaged from the government. They subsidise a few beds, so it'd be free, and Marge can have one of them, only we'd give her the best room and the best treatment—and the money from this house would be invested in the home itself. Marge would have an investment.' But more importantly, if Judith could make the plan work for Barry, he'd be happy, and then so would she.

Barry said, 'A burgeoning, capital-making new venture that'll benefit your own family rather than someone else's. Your future's assured, Wally.'

'So,' Judith said, 'that's a good deal, isn't it? If we use our inheritance to buy into a nursing home? It's a better use of the money for everyone, wouldn't you say?'

Pudding put her finger to her cheek and looked at the ceiling and said, 'But, gee-whiz, I wonder if you get your value-added money back when Gran dies, Uncle Wally?'

'He can move in,' Barry said, his hand on his heart. 'Like I said, his future's *secure.*'

Walter stopped circling the clothesline. 'I'd like to remind everyone that a third of this house belongs to Morris.'

It was at this point that Judith said, 'I'm not giving anything to that criminal.'

Well, as Lance would have said, you could have heard a fly fart.

'Criminal?' Margery said.

Pudding's eyes stayed on her uncle but she placed her hand on her grandmother's arm. 'It'll be okay, Gran.'

Next door, Mrs Parsons noted the sudden silence, so she scurried inside, locking the door behind her.

Walter bounced, winding his head, his fists up, springing sideways around the clothesline and up the back steps, jabbing at the air. Barry grabbed the laundry stick. Judith shot into the bathroom. She tried to close the door, but it wouldn't move over the warped floor, so she scurried back into the kitchen and grabbed a table knife, pointed it at Walter, but he held her against the rattling kitchen bureau with his glazed gaze, his fists wheeling.

'I paid a lot of money for Judith's nose. Break it and I'll sue.'

Walter said he'd be happy to rearrange her whole face for free, 'Anytime you like, Bald Barry.'

Judith said, 'You should go back to that loony bin, Wally,' and he swung at his sister, a reaching right hook, the breeze from Walter's arm lifting Barry's comb-over. The dishes in the bureau clanked as he jabbed, back and forth. Judith cowered sideways. 'Stop it, Wally, you're scaring me,' but Walter sparred, pushing her along the wall to the corner, sweat on his brow, feeling the heat from the glaring spotlights, the smoke-filled air and the pulsing crowd: 'Bull, Bull, Brunswick Bull.'

He took another swing. It missed.

Barry moved back to the doorway, ready to bolt. 'You just had to say it, didn't you, Judith? You just had to open your big, *fat* mouth.'

Judith forgot she was pinned against the wall by a middle-weight champion and leaned forward. 'Don't call me fat, Barry. I've lost three kilos this week,' and Pud added, 'Dad's lost five.'

Walter's fist flicked, quick as a lizard's tongue, and hit the wall right where Judith's face had been a quarter of a second before, and Judith's knees went. She slid down just as Walter's right arm jabbed up, his fists *swish-swished*. Pudding cried, 'You're a winner, Uncle Walter,' and he stopped dancing, his arms shot straight up, almost to the ceiling, and he bounced again, danced around the little kitchen, the floor springing like a canvas, the plates clapping, the crowd roaring—'Bull, Bull, Brunswick Bull'—and the imaginary referee counting over Judith, a defeated puddle on the floor.

He sat back down in his seat; the glaze started to leave his eyes and he smoothed his Elvis forelock. Margery said, 'There's steamed caramel pudding for dessert, Walter dear,' and he said, 'You got ice-cream to go with that, Mumsy?'

'I have.'

Judith said, 'You should be locked up, like Morris.'

Walter just lifted up his spoon and stared at the place on the table where his bowl of pudding was going to be.

# ROOM 4321

The sun is setting, and all the city lights are coming on. It's very pretty, but boring. You can't hear anything, can't see people walking past, and it's not as if you can just stroll outside to the letterbox for some fresh air, or walk straight out the front door to the corner shop, not that I can walk far these days what with my shin the way it is. The wound on my leg started getting worse about the time Judith made her plans about the nursing home clear. Anita did her best, I must say. At the time I thought she tried so hard because it made her feel important, but it wasn't that at all. It's obvious to me now that she didn't want me to go into care because if she did she'd have no one to look out for the floozy, her so-called mother, but I'll get to that. Anyrate, Anita started dropping in any old time, just breezing down the hall, her excuse being she needed to do my dressing. She never bothered knocking.

'How are ya, Mrs Blandon?'

'It's only Monday,' I said. 'And you should knock.'

She just said, 'I should,' and dumped her square, green plastic basket with all her potions and spells on my table. 'You could snib your door.'

Then she saw my shin and said, 'Shit.' I calmly explained that the dressing had come off in the shower, but all she said was, 'Mrs Blandon, those dressings stick like shit to a blanket,' so at this point I felt I had to say something.

'I do not appreciate your language.'

She was picking off the tissues. 'Is that Mercurochrome on that wound?'

When I said yes she found the bottle and chucked it in the bin. It still had some in it.

I said, 'You're not supposed to do dressings.'

'I'm not supposed to keep secrets about clients who have falls either. It could get me into real trouble, Mrs Blandon, and trouble is the very last thing I need. This wound could ulcerate. You have to be very careful with it.'

'I am very careful with it,' I said. Well, I could hardly tell her my daughter ripped it off, could I? Looking back, I should have.

She went ahead and redid the dressing. I had to put aside my cross-stitch; I had started on a big, yellow excavator I'd designed at the time—I did double-thread, double-herringbone stitch for the tyres because they were black. They needed texture. I abandoned it in the end because I actually do prefer working on the proverbs. That day—somewhat prophetically, I see now—I was in the mood for *Deceit always returns to its master.* Anyrate, it took her a long time to do my dressing because the bandaids had to be coaxed off without tearing my skin off. Then she checked my dosette, but she found everything in order because I drop the sleeping tablets down the sink. So she did the dishes on the sink, even though I'd already rinsed them and left them to drain. That became a habit of hers, actually, re-washing all my dishes, but it wasn't nearly as annoying as the new shower curtain she put up. Awful colour, but I offered to pay for it regardless. 'Nar,' she said. 'I'll take it out of your hide.'

It's still there, that curtain. Florence likes it, but she would.

Then she stripped my bed and put the washing on, did the bathroom and swept and mopped. While the hall and lounge room floors dried she made a pot of tea and sat on the back stoop, ripped off her Nicorette patch, smoked a cigarette and told me I'd 'lose a bit of sky once that renovation goes up next door'.

'There's enough sky for everyone, though these days people don't take the time to look at the sky.'

'Too busy trying not to step in dog shit.'

'I'll remind you again that I don't appreciate your bad language.'

'Sorry,' she said. 'I forget my manners.'

I made no comment, though it was obvious she has never been taught manners. For a minute or two we drank our tea, then I told her that our honourable ex-Prime Minister, Mr John Howard, wasn't hung properly.

'Well,' she said, 'he should be.'

I reminded her again that he'd held the title of leader of a country for a very long time, and she said, 'So has Robert Mugabe,' but I said I didn't want a picture of him on my wall.

She'd finished her cigarette by now and was looking into a little mirror and pulling the hairs out of her chin with tweezers, so she asked me how my weekend was.

'I had the family over on Sunday.'

'How did it go?'

'We had a nice family day.' That wasn't exactly a fib because I'm sure we must have had nice, friendly family days in the past.

'Walter and Judith came, did they?'

'And Mrs Parsons.'

Whenever Anita came she popped in to see Mrs Parsons for a minute. Mrs Parsons avoided the council home help list, but she would have had to go on it as soon as she'd had a fall. Poor Mrs Parsons never got the chance to fall, of course.

We used to have lovely Sunday lunches, me and Mrs Parsons and Walter, but everything was starting to fester. We've had squabbles in the past. Judith's not normally a big drinker, but she tends to drink to excess at Christmas and birthdays. And last Christmas Walter got upset because Judith gave me a blow-up neck rest with Virgin Air written on it for a present. She gave me a bunch of cocktail stirrers the Christmas before, but Pud always gives me something nice ... body wash or bath salts. But I felt in my heart that Walter wouldn't actually punch Judith. *Barking dogs seldom bite.*

I don't think that operation made Judith look better anyway; it just made her look like someone put the heel of their hand on her face and pushed. I said at the time she told me she was getting it done, 'Your nose is the least of your problems.' And when she said Morris was a criminal I assumed she was talking about the business he started at school selling cigarettes. I'd heard nothing about jail, let alone hanging, until Walter explained it all to me. It still kept me awake most of that Sunday night, my shin stinging and my mind in turmoil, trying to sort things out. How anyone could plant drugs in someone else's suitcase and watch them cop the consequences is beyond me. What type of person would do such a thing? They could have hung him.

I realise now what all those blazing rows with Pat were about. We had several arguments about hanging criminals, and of course Pat knew all along about Morris.

That argument started way back in the sixties when Ronald Ryan escaped from Pentridge Jail and shot a policeman. At the time I was afraid he'd come to our house, but Lance said if he saw Ronald Ryan he'd invite him in for a beer and ask him what really happened, 'establish the real truth'.

'He's a murdering criminal,' I said. 'Hanging him is the correct thing to do!'

Then Pat weighed in, saying that capital punishment was wrong, and so we had lots of arguments about it. In fact, as I sit here, I now see just how significant this is! In 1986 we had another big row about the death penalty. It was the year Lance died. Remember I said Morris had the fight with Walter at Lance's funeral and took off to Thailand? Well, that very same year, two Australian chaps, a Mr Barlow and Mr Chambers if my memory serves me right, were hung for drug trafficking in Asia. I remember there was a lot of fuss over those hangings; they were in all the papers and on the telly. Anyrate, when I saw it on the news I went up and sat on my bed and waited, and sure enough, Pat comes storming across the road. I can still see her in my mind's eye. We had a ding-dong row that time. I said drug traffickers were bad eggs, and she said I couldn't possibly know that for certain, and I said they broke the laws and customs of the country.

She stood in my kitchen, so bothered she was red with the veins in her poor old weathered neck standing out. Her scalp must have been very hot and itchy under that wig. Anyrate, she yelled, 'Killing is wrong, full stop, in any country. Legal murder does not achieve anything.'

I insisted that Ronald Ryan, Barlow and Chambers were criminals, that they had done the wrong thing. 'Let the punishment be equal with the offence,' I said.

I'll never forget the look of triumph on her face when she said, 'That's right, Margery Blandon. "Whoever sheds man's blood, by man shall his blood be shed: for in the image of God made he man." Genesis, chapter nine, verse six. But, since you believe killing is a fitting thing, since you agree that the death penalty is right, you should therefore be prepared to hang my Kevin, or let me hang Morris, or Walter.'

Well, I'll admit now, she had me stumped at the time. All I could think to say, was, 'But my sons would never do anything wrong.'

'You don't know, Margery.' I can still see her orange fingernail in my face. 'You just don't know,' she said. 'It's the principle of the matter!'

'Well,' I said, 'if it's about principle then I could easily say that by letting those criminals stay alive you're condoning drug trafficking.'

She turned purple with rage then and shouted, 'I did not say they shouldn't be punished!'

Anyrate, at the time I could actually see her point, but I stuck to my guns because that's what you do, you stick to your principles. Given hindsight, well, you'd have to say she was right.

I suppose I'd have to say now, perhaps, that it depends on the circumstances, because I realise that, at the time, Morris was in jail in Thailand, and some overseas countries still have the death penalty.

It's dreadful to think that my son endured jail for years in Thailand because of something he didn't do. Some people just see no wrong in ruining other people's lives.

I said to Walter when he explained it all, I said, 'At least he was warm, the climate's good over there. I know that because I've seen Thailand on the telly.'

Walter said, 'He wears shorts all day and the food is very cheap. Lots of vegies.'

That's something anyway. It's not right to let people go cold or hungry.

'Have a nip of cooking sherry,' Walter said, but it didn't help. To think Pat knew about Morris all along.

If she knew, then everybody knew.

Of course, I see now that Pat was right about a few things, but I also see that she never told me things I should have known. Not one thing.

That Sunday when I found out Morris went to jail was a dreadful Sunday, worse than any Christmas squabble we've ever had, and it turned out to be the start of another shocking week. Just shocking. And things got worse as the weeks went by. For one thing, that Sunday turned out to be Mrs Parsons' last Sunday lunch.

I can hardly speak about it, just remembering what it was like sitting there waiting, then hoping her blind would go up.

On Tuesday Margery's shin felt less tight and looked a little less red, which made her feel generally better, so she settled down to a spot of polishing. She screwed the lid firmly on the bottle of Silvo and positioned Walter's championship silver trophies in the crystal cabinet, then she aligned the little cardboard squares—the year and the title written in her best hand—in front of each trophy, and then she heard shouting next door. The builders stopped nailing and stood on the roof trusses of the second storey to watch Tony argue with the architect. The architect stormed off, Tony followed, and so did Miriana, so Margery went to her bedroom, smiling at her polished door-knobs as she passed. In the front street, the architect spread his drawings on the roof of Tony's low red car, and that's when the shouting really started. Tony scraped the sheet of paper onto the ground. 'Get your fucking bullshit off my Ferrari!' The shouting intensified. It sounded to Margery as if the architect objected to a fence, so she went out to check the letterbox. The red stilettos were still there, and there was a pamphlet from the local pizza place and another advertising nasal spray for stronger, longer erections.

Tony was poking his finger at the architect, 'Youse don't know what you're talking about. I know people who could disarm that alarm in five seconds, mate. The security bars are staying—to hell with your schematic fucking minimal fucking horizontal lines.'

As he yelled yet another truck arrived and stood idling while the builders unloaded the wrought-iron gates and spiked lace-work fence. Margery watched the heartbroken architect roll up his plans and went back inside, taking the red shoes with her. She tried to get her feet into them once more but finally put them in the wardrobe in the second bedroom.

That afternoon, when Margery did Mrs Parsons' laces, she said again, 'I'm sorry my children were such a bother on Sunday,' and Mrs Parsons repeated what she'd said on Monday morning and afternoon, and again that morning— 'All children are a blessing'—though Margery decided Mrs Parsons only said that because she'd endured the pain of having none of her own. She spent the rest of the day wave-stitching the trim on Anita's basket cover.

# DAYS 18 & 19

On Wednesday Margery settled down to her tea and toast, then Judith's little van pulled up out the front. The special was Airbrush Nail Art—ten fingers or toes for the price of five.

Margery's stomach lurched, but Judith just hurried down the passage, calling, 'I'm not staying,' dumped a bag from Spotlight on the couch and kept on towards the lavatory. 'I'm on new tablets, Marge, so I might call in from time to time to use your toilet.'

Margery was pouring a cup of tea when she came back in. 'Would you like a cuppa, Judith?'

Judith squinted at the tiny hands on her mother's tiny, antique watch and sat down at the table. 'That'd be lovely. Black, no milk.'

'You should drink milk for the calcium.'

'How are you keeping, Marge?'

'Good thanks, get yourself a cup then.' Margery eased her frail body, still tender from the fall two weeks ago, down onto a chair while Judith heaved herself up to get a cup. As she poured, Margery spread jam evenly on her toast. 'Would you like a slice?'

'Can't,' Judith said. 'Diet.'

They sipped their tea.

'I've lost eight kilos.'

'That may be so, but no amount of foundation make-up will hide the rash that's creeping up your face from your throat.'

'As ever, thanks for the nurturing, caring support, *mother dear*,' said Judith. She had a few sips of tea then got up and moved through the kitchen, lounge room and hall, kicking all the floor mats into a lump by the front door. She came back scattering new mats from the Spotlight bag throughout the house. 'They're rubber-backed,' she said and held one in front of her mother.

'See? They won't slip.' They were bath mats—olive green, with looped pile.

Margery said, 'Thank you, Judith.'

'You owe me twenty-five dollars.'

It was when Margery was counting out the sum in five-dollar bills that Judith spotted the dosette in her mother's bag. 'You're sick, aren't you?'

Margery shook her head. 'Vitamins.'

'Don't underestimate me, Marge. I'm smarter than I look. I've got a Certificate Four in Skin Biology, Anatomy and Physiology of Beauty Therapy Treatments, not to mention Human Development and Helping Skills, so I know these are not vitamin tablets.'

'Then you should know what to do about that rash.'

'I do. If I'd had an attentive and nurturing upbringing, and if you were in the retirement home, Marge, I wouldn't be covered in a stress rash. You could fall and lie dying for days like Mrs Bist. You should be grateful that I care.'

'Mrs Bist knew every person in Brunswick, good and bad, *and* she had her invisible friend, *God.* Fat lot of good any of them did her.'

Judith studied the dosette. 'Who put these tablets in?'

'Anita.'

'The cleaner?' At this, Judith pulled the lid of one of the cells open, but she pulled the wrong catch, the entire lid came off and tablets ran all over the kitchen table and onto the floor.

'Stupid thing,' she said. Margery fetched her little broom and shovel and swept the tablets off the floor, then she tipped them onto the table, where Judith formed colour-coded little piles. She poured them all back into the bottles Margery kept in an ice-cream container on top of the fridge, and as Margery ate her toast Judith refilled the little cells with her long, diamanté-studded acrylic fingernails, frowning at the instructions on the side of the medicine bottles. When Judith unscrewed the lid on the big jar of dissolvable calcium tablets, Margery said, 'They don't go in the dosette—they're too big!' But it was too late. Judith cupped a string of pearls in her hand.

'Oh,' said Margery. 'You don't want those, Judith.'

Judith smiled, an insincere smile that didn't reach her blue-tinted prescription contact lenses. 'I'll just borrow them, alright?'

Margery nodded. 'Well, if you want to, but you don't want those—'

'I do. I deserve them.'

'I'm not sure you do,' but Judith was at the front door, the old mats in her arms. She turned back to her mother and called, 'See ya, Marge,' and was gone, leaving a faint smell of warm perfume and nail polish remover. Margery was left sitting at the kitchen table, anxiously twisting the top button on her frock.

She had just settled once more when Anita dropped in, again. Margery shoved the basket cover to the bottom of her cross-stitch bag and took up her new cross-stitch—*Only when we are no longer afraid do we begin to live.* Margery stitched while Anita dressed her wound, and after she'd popped in to see Mrs Parsons she picked up her work basket. 'Not having a cup of tea?'

'No. Tea makes me want to smoke.' Anita gathered all the new mats Judith had just purchased. 'These belong in Tony's dump bin,' she said. 'You'll catch your toe in the loops.'

'Those mats were expensive,' Margery called as the screen door banged shut.

That night the phone rang. 'This will be Morris,' Margery said and got out of bed as fast as she could, feeling her way along the wall, padding down the passage in her bare feet—her bunion bulbous on the cold lino, her bones not fully prepared to accept her weight—but the phone stopped ringing just as she reached for the handset. She stood in the dark looking at it. 'Bother!' She went on out to the lavatory, stopping for a little glass of cooking sherry on her way, and in the dark she caught the corner of her face on the bedroom door as she passed. It was a nasty rebuke that sounded loudly in her head and rattled her remaining teeth. The ache in the side of her face kept her awake. 'I'll need to get my rest,' she said. 'It's Big Shop today.' Near dawn she got up and had another little glass of sherry.

Mrs Parsons waited at her kitchen table with her red beret perched on top of her fuzzy head and her frangipani brooch pinned to the lapel of her blue woollen coat. Finally, she heard Margery start the car. She gathered up her bags—handbag, shopping basket, spare bag—locked the back door behind her, crept through her shed to Margery's shed and hopped into the car. Margery backed out, successfully avoided the brick garage behind hers, bumped down the bluestone lane, turned right into Watson Street, her front bumper scraping the driver's side door on a silver Golf, then swung left into Brunswick Road, bringing the number fifteen bus to a dangerous halt and dislodging three passengers. At Sydney Road she turned left through a red light, and at Barkly Street she failed to notice a motorcycle on her right. The motorbike glanced off her car with a dull thud and made a raw, scraping sound as it slid along the tram tracks before coming to rest up against the number nineteen tram, waiting for embarking passengers at stop number twenty-two. Margery looked across at Mrs Parsons, curled over in the front seat, her hands holding her beret. 'Goodness gracious.'

The motorcycle rider simply got himself up and took a few steps over to where his motorcycle rested beneath the tram. He was still inspecting his motorcycle when his pillion passenger gathered herself from the road and limped over to him. She hit him, bellowing, 'You look at your fucking bike before you even think about me!' The rider shoved her away, so she took a swing at his helmet but missed. The tram started dinging its bell, car horns tooted, so the rider stood his motorcycle up and wheeled it off the road. The commuters and shoppers watched him approach the little old lady sitting frozen behind the wheel of her apple-green Hillman Minx. The motorcyclist leaned in her window. Margery was staring ahead, her foot jumping on the accelerator. Though her hands gripped the steering wheel, her elbows shook. Next to her, Mrs Parsons was tugging at the doorhandle. The motorcyclist smiled. 'Well, well, if it isn't Mrs Blandon and little Squigglehead. I live in your street, the other side of the pub.'

Margery said, 'We don't know the people beyond Mrs Ahmed's house. Mrs Ahmed lives next to the park.'

'You've hurt your eye, broken your glasses,' he said.

'I hurt my eye last night, it's perfectly alright, and I can get another pair of glasses.'

Behind them, the tram dinged and the cars horns blared. The angry pillion passenger kicked the motorcycle and it fell over again.

The motorcyclist asked, 'Would you like me to drive your car home for you?'

Mrs Parsons turned her rheumy eyes hopefully towards him and said, 'I need to buy a card and a stamp first,' but Margery replied in a thin voice, 'It's really my son's car, and we're perfectly alright. I can drive Mrs Parsons home. I always do.'

'I see.' His girlfriend was kicking his motorbike behind him, but he persuaded Margery to let him drive them to the car park behind the mall. 'My name's Russell. I knew your husband from the pub. In fact, I was there the day it blew up.'

Margery said, 'I don't remember you from the funeral.'

'No,' he said. 'I was still in the hospital.'

'Oh, dear,' Margery said.

'No worries,' Russell said. 'Lance was always a bit of a hard case, and I liked that, and there was the payout I got, bought the house at number 223. Bloody brilliant. It's worth five times as much now.' He parked and helped the ladies out of the car. 'You have a good, strong cup of tea now, alright?'

'Yes, thank you.'

'You're very kind.'

As he handed Margery the keys, he said, 'You ever want to get rid of this little car, I'll be happy take it off your hands.'

'Morris will want it,' Margery said, but Russell said he didn't think he would.

They did their shopping, clogging the aisles with their carts. Margery chose carefully, shaking the tins and inspecting them for dents, comparing the contents of one jar against another. Mrs Parsons bought a small packet of cheese slices, the smallest jar of Vegemite and a birthday card, a picture of a small boy running across the front of it, smiling up at a kite. Margery bought an engagement card for her hairdresser at the same time. Then they took advantage of the five-dollar special cappuccino—Mrs Parsons had tea—and a muffin, though Mrs Parsons couldn't finish her muffin so she popped it in her handbag for later. Margery had a yoyo, which she bit into then left on the saucer because it was made from margarine, not butter. 'They say butter kills you these days,' she sniffed.

Judith wanted to get home. Nests of damp, itchy welts burned in her creases and she felt she was stewing in her sticky nylon pantyhose and slacks. She longed to strip off, sink into a long, cold bath and scratch herself all over with a brand-new loofah. Tears brimmed at the thought of it, and at her general discomfort: her life. She felt on the verge of tears a lot lately, sensed that she was getting to the end of something, that a great inertia was pushing her to some sort of conclusion, and she was pretty sure she could blame it all on her mother. But soon she'd be happier, surely. Barry said he'd be home for tea tonight and so she'd wanted to be there, bathed and smiling, with the pearls complementing the azure blouse that accentuated her contacts. She wanted to be poised, warm and welcoming in her linen sailor pants that held her tummy flat, backlit by the lighted exhaust canopy while she stirred the *coq au vin,* the house infused with the cosy smell of simmering seasoned chicken. The Interpersonal Skills module said to 'be there, giving', but an accident further up Sydney Road meant the Thursday afternoon traffic was gridlocked, and now she couldn't 'be there', providing that special something the marriage was missing, the special something that was lost when Walter lost. If she could provide some of the wealth her brother's last fight was meant to provide, Barry would realise how important she was to him.

Why didn't her mother just move to the home and live in comfort, or why didn't she just die in her sleep? She was miserable anyway, always had been, and it would be so much simpler for everyone, and it would certainly ease their financial constraints. Barry would get his business. There was money in aged care, surely, if it was handled right, just as there was money in counselling. Needy people were everywhere. The tears started to well again, so she checked her eyes in the rear-vision mirror. Her 'Exotic Lady' false eyelashes looked just like the picture on the packet.

She imagined herself sitting opposite Barry at the Tropic Hotel, a candle burning on the table between them. 'Barry,' she said. 'Darling, we need to progress to the next phase of our life together.' Then they were there celebrating the end of the financial year with their new partners, Amanda and Theodore, and Judith was much, much thinner, the discussion focussing on real estate trends, then moved to the latest government guidelines in aged care, then it was her turn to speak and she held them with her blue eyes and her views on psychology theory. Once they knew how informed she was, Barry would support her when she unburdened to him the tragic stories she carried from counselling. He would protect her, take her travelling, and she saw herself standing at Tullamarine like Sophia Loren, knee-deep in Louis Vuitton luggage, but then the driver in the car behind her held his hand on the car horn, the beep long and loud, and her dreams were replaced by pictures of long queues on cobblestones outside ruined churches, European heat and bad water, swollen feet and dirty public toilets, and foreign food.

Parts of life were just too hard. Most of the time Judith just wanted to kick back, succumb to stretchy clothes, treat herself to cheap pedicures and lunch at shopping-complex food halls, watch Ellen and Oprah or go to daytime movies. She always had to be so damned nice to everyone, when most of the time she was fighting an urge to eat cake or buy something to make herself feel better. And just at that moment she was trapped on Sydney Road with a full bowel and her stomach trying to process what felt like shattered windscreen. Her lunch—fermenting psyllium and grapefruit—was reacting gaseously with her new diet tablets. Just yesterday she'd felt a small, sticky viscosity when she'd passed wind, and now she wanted to fart again but was afraid of her boiling lower abdomen. She wished she could drive to her mother's breezy outdoor toilet to let go, feel safe and empty, have a cup of tea and eat her mother's slightly stale Arnott's Assorted Creams. She pressed down on her buttocks, tooted and wound down the window. 'For fuck's sake!'

Barry's shirt was discarded on the bare floor, his trousers bunched around his knees and his head rested on Charmaine's thin shoulder, his comb-over flipped like a wedge of cantaloupe on the side of his head. He was staring through the Venetians at the back of the For Sale board attached to the front fence, and Charmaine was staring at the ceiling, her blouse and bra pushed up under her armpits and her small, strangled breasts pointing at the walls. Her pink skirt was gathered around her firm brown waist and her panties hung from one waxed, tanned ankle. Beneath them the mattress cover was ruched and their gluey, tenderly sore genitals throbbed faintly.

Barry looked lovingly up into Charmaine's nose, a straight nose that ended a little too pointedly. 'I love you, Charmaine. You're warm and tender.'

'And I own *two* houses now.'

Barry raised his head, looked around the bare room. 'How much did you say you offered?'

'Two seventy-five.' Her voice ran away to somewhere in the empty house.

He whistled, long and appreciatively. 'Very smart.'

'Warm, tender, smart and hungry,' she said, rolling away. She sat up, found her iPhone, summoned the internet, typed in *Pizza* and *Campbellfield*. 'You don't have to be home?'

'No.' He stood up, wiping his groin with the bottom of his singlet.

'Hawaiian?'

'Yep. And a can of coke. Two seventy-five. Wow, bargain.'

Brandon, the Corrective Services officer, was typing on his computer while Anita watched him, her arms crossed, chewing her cheek, legs jigging. The office window was slightly open, and the strident sounds of irritated Thursday-afternoon commuters spiked into the stuffy little office.

He nodded, typing. 'How's the job?'

'No worries.'

'Ruby?'

'Splendid.'

'Still living with your mother in the flat?'

'Yes,' she said, crossing her legs and her fingers.

He typed on. 'Must be crowded.'

*Please, God,* she prayed, *don't let him announce he needs to visit.* 'We're moving soon,' she said cheerfully. 'To a house. In fact, we're moving in a week or two, so we're in a bit of a mess at the moment.'

'A house? That'll eat into your Disneyland savings.'

'I've given up smoking, save fifty dollars a week.' His typing paused. 'Alright then, eighty dollars a week.' She twisted her mouth to chew the inside of the other cheek.

He stopped typing, rested his arms on his desk, linked his fingers together and stared at her. She held his gaze, and he knew that if he looked at her long enough he could make her cry, but there was urgency in her eyes—*I'm doing my best.*

'I'll let you know when we've moved, then you can drop in,' she said, her voice soft.

'Keeping away from trouble?'

The question he was asking was to do with Raymond, her latest troublesome so-called flatmate. She laughed, grabbing the armrests. 'I'll be in trouble if I don't collect Ruby from school on time.'

He looked at his watch. Outside, a tram rang its bell, *ding ding.*

'Sorry I was late.' She jerked her head to the road outside. 'Traffic jam.'

'I heard it. Traffic backed up as far as Coburg.' She started to reach for her handbag, but stopped herself.

'See you next time,' he said, and Anita bolted from the chair. He watched her fire-truck-red hair flashing through the glass partitions as she ran for the stairs. From the window he watched her dart across Sydney Road, a cigarette in her mouth, feeling around in her work basket for a lighter. 'Please don't get a speeding ticket,' he said.

While the kettle boiled, Mrs Parsons unpacked her shopping, then took two aspirin and her cup of tea to her lounge room, where she sat under her standard lamp, running her magnifying glass over the lines in her historical romance, *The Unlocking of a Lady.* Eventually, the sound of the motorcycle colliding with the car and the scrape of metal on bitumen faded, and she was able to immerse herself in the intense passions of the free-spirited Countess Augustine Scarlette and her efforts to save her childhood friend, Lady Louisa, from a loveless marriage in a far-off county, many, many days' ride by coach from her distant home and large, loving family. Mrs Parsons read all the chapters on Lady Louisa's anguish at not being able to get home to see her dying father, and Countess Augustine's unexpected feelings of intense passion when she fell hopelessly, unexpectedly in love with Bede, the Earl of faraway Berkenshire, Lady Louisa's betrothed. Then she put her book aside, rolled her creaky little shoulders and moved carefully to the side window and pulled the blind down. When her neighbour came, Margery apologised again for the motorcyclist, and Mrs Parsons said, 'Sometimes there's nothing you can do about how things turn out.'

Margery untied her laces. 'Are you sure you're not hurt?'

'Quite sure,' she said, and to reassure her she followed Margery to the front gate, shuffling along as effortlessly as she could. It was a lovely evening, the sun low, huge and orange in the sky. 'God's provided a lovely sunset,' she said, and Margery agreed it was a lovely evening.

'Thank you for all you've done,' Mrs Parsons said. 'You're very kind.'

She watched Margery walk home, a bent old lady, careful-footed, reaching for the fence posts for reassurance, the hem of her floral shift lifted because of her stoop, like Mrs Parsons' own stoop. For an instant Mrs Parsons wanted to say she appreciated Margery being there, appreciated being included but not asked questions, not pried at like nosey Pat always did, but it might cause Margery concern, so she let the impulse go. At her kitchen table she opened her handbag and took the birthday card from her purse. After a minute sitting there with her biro poised over the card, she put it down and sat back, looking down at her folded hands in her lap. Some time later, she had a few bites from a slice of bread with jam and butter before dropping it in the backyard for the birds.

On her return from her yard, Mrs Parsons opened the grate on her stove and placed her purse in the thin layer of grey ash next to a little tin of her precious memorabilia, then made her way slowly towards her bedroom. It was then that she heard her front gate squeak open. She stopped, her eyes wide, then, like falling rocks—*bang, bang, bang*—three sharp strikes of the doorknocker, the thud of metal on wood rattling the windows and shaking the landscape print on her passage wall. She hurried to the front door, her laces clicking on the linoleum, stumbling to fall against the wall on her way. When she finally wrenched the door open, there was no one there, so she hurried across her narrow verandah, eased herself down her front steps and tottered out through her gate, but there was no one. The street was empty, quiet except for Fifi yapping hoarsely in Kevin's arms across the street.

'It's kids from the commission flats,' he called. 'They were in the park earlier. I've phoned the police.'

Mrs Parsons went back inside, leaned against the door, her breath shaky and inadequate, tears wetting the soft brown crinkles under her eyes. It was her second fright of the day. From the wireless, Dame Janet Baker sang to her, *'Yes, press my eyelids close, 'tis well, Yes, press my eyelids close, 'tis well, But far the rapid fancies fly, The rolling worlds of wave and shell, And all the lands where corals lie,'* and Mrs Parsons sighed again, and saw in her mind a palm tree reaching across a white beach towards rolling green waves and her family as they were when she left them more than sixty years ago; a staircase of brothers and sisters, cousins and aunts, uncles and nieces, nephews and neighbours, and her parents, gathered together at the edge of the airstrip, their brown arms waving goodbye. With the birthday card in her hand, she dismissed any hopes of a visitor and turned instead into the second bedroom where she sat on the narrow, blue bedspread. In the kitchen Janet Baker sang, *'Thy lips are like a sunset glow, Thy smile is like a morning sky, Yet leave me, leave me, let me go, And see the land where corals lie.'*

At nine-thirty that night Pud rounded the corner to see her mother's van—Free Skin Biology Test to Every New Customer—alone at the kerb. In front was a vacant space where her father's Mercedes should be. Blue television light flickered behind the curtain, and she knew that inside, her mother was lying on the couch with a glass of wine in one hand, the almost-empty bottle on the floor beside her, and the remote control in the other, weeping into a wad of damp tissues.

'Hello, darling. How was the film?'

'Good.'

'Did your friends like it?'

'Johnny Depp was in it. What's to eat?'

'On the stove.'

Pud lifted the lid to the pot. 'Yum, chicken stew.'

Her mother blew her nose, sat up and sighed. Pud came in

with her bowl of *coq au vin* and sat next to her. 'Lovely stew, Mum.'

'I had two rice cakes with vegemite and a half a grapefruit.' She wiped the tears from her eyes and fanned her hot, itchy throat with the hanky.

'Let's go for a drive.'

'You just want a driving lesson, that's all.'

'So? No, you're right, it's better to sit here and watch TV than go to St Kilda and eat a low-fat yoghurt while we watch the try-hards and the dying.'

'No, *you're* right,' Judith said weakly. 'I'd actually love that.'

'You'll fit right in. You look just like a drag queen.'

'It's my Sophia Loren look, DeeAndra.'

'Same thing.'

Barry's headlights swung across the windows. They watched him come in, drop his keys in the bowl on the hall table and go through his mail. 'Kevin tells me your mum knocked a motor-cyclist off his bike in Sydney Road today.'

'Big Shop day,' Pud said.

Judith tried to smile sweetly for her husband, 'Is the car alright?'

'Apparently. Marge and Mrs P are alright as well, in case you were wondering.'

'She would have only been driving at about two kilometres an hour, Dad.'

'She is a worry,' Judith said. 'Should see all the tablets she has to take, and all those falls and bruises. What if she kills some-one in that car?'

'You can't padlock her in the house, Judith.'

'I made your favourite, Barry, *coq au vin,*' she said, still smiling, being there, warm and welcoming.

Barry said, 'I've eaten, had pizza.'

Pudding put her empty plate on the carpet beside her chair and said, 'Let's go, Mum.'

'Where are youse two going?'

Pud shrugged, 'Spend money, take drugs, *meet our lovers.*'
Barry just walked to his office, tearing open an envelope.

The next morning, Friday, Walter was counting off smoked cod
fillets and laying them carefully side by side in an oven dish
when Mrs Stapleton screamed from her office, 'Wally, ya mum's
on tha' phone.'

Walter looked at the fish in the tray, then at the defrosted
packets of fish on the table and said, 'Right, I'll finish this
when I get back.' He wiped his hands on his apron and went
to the phone, slightly rattled by the intrusion to his routine. He
assumed, rightly so, that his mother was upset. 'Now, Mumsy, I
told you, there's no point worrying about Morris, he's out of jail
now, safe and sound. Did you and Mrs Parsons have a lovely day
shopping yesterday?'

'Not especially,' Margery said and started crying.

Of course I phoned Walter straightaway after I found her. He said, 'Go over to Kevin's. I'll call the cops,' but Fifi barked and barked when I knocked so it was clear Kevin was out on his pushbike.

I would have gone to Mrs Calabria's if she was still there, and I would even have gone to sit with Mrs Bist, though I doubt she'd be home, even if she was alive. As for Mrs Ahmed, well, she's from somewhere in Africa, so I just went back in and sat on the edge of the bed with Mrs Parsons until the police came. One young policeman stayed with Mrs Parsons and the other one, a young constable with fair hair and green eyes, walked me home. He was the same one who came when we eventually found Mrs Bist, though he didn't make me a cup of tea that time.

'It was very sudden,' I said. He was understanding, saying, 'It can be at that age,' and put the kettle on.

I said Mrs Parsons had been quite well the evening before, and I asked if the chap on the motorcycle might have caused her death.

'Is that where you got your injuries?' he asked, so I explained about the little tumble at the letterbox, my shin getting grazed, then the bath being slippery with spilt shampoo, and how my glasses got dropped, how the door caught my eye in the night, and though we were only going slowly when the motorcycle hit us, I still managed to bump my forehead—that's why the other eye was black now.

The constable said he'd heard about the traffic jam the day before; he asked if he could inspect my car. 'It's an old green car, isn't it?'

'No,' I said. 'It's hardly used. Lance bought it brand-new in nineteen sixty-one, but he never drove it anywhere further than

Festival Hall.' I made a point of saying that it's a good car. 'We attract quite a bit of attention in that car,' I said. 'Lots of people wave and toot.'

'I can imagine,' he said.

I told him that the passenger's side door rattles and the handle gets stuck, but that's not my fault, it's Pat's fault. And now it's got the dent. 'Another bad incident in a bad week,' I said and explained that Angela got engaged and the new podiatrist had upset me. 'He's a handsome young man,' I said, 'and he wears aftershave, but Glen gave good service.' I started to tell him I was also upset about Morris, and Judith wanting to put me in a home, but it must have seemed trivial compared to Mrs Parsons' situation, so he said, 'Just tell me as briefly as you can all about the Incident with the Motorcycle.'

'We take the car out on Thursday because the Sydney Road footpath is narrow and you can get stuck behind a crowd of old people. Or you can get held up by a swarm of Arab women. You can't pass three Arabs abreast if you're pulling a shopping cart, and they yabber away. They can't hear because they've got the full jihad covering their head and body. The Italians are slow too because they know everyone, so they stop to chat and fling their arms about. The Asians are fastest.'

'We all have different ways,' he said. 'Now, about the accident?'

'Well, this motorcycle just shot out of nowhere, then, *bang!* Frightened the living daylights out of me. There's a fan of black marks across my driver's side fender from the tyre. Terrible scraping noise across the bitumen. If only people would take intersections seriously.'

The constable reminded me, very nicely, that I'm supposed to give way to my right, but I explained I didn't notice anyone on my right, and that's when it occurred to me that *I* might have caused Mrs Parsons to die, but he said no, that wasn't the case. And anyway, he said, she was pretty old, 'as was Mrs Bist when she died'.

'What do you think of the fortress your new neighbours are

constructing next door?' he asked.

'They seem like a nice young couple,' I said, 'though I think putting the kitchen in the cellar is unusual, but people have different ways.'

He opened the fridge and asked where the milk was. I said I don't always take milk. I only buy the little cartons because the milk in the bigger ones goes off before you get to the bottom. Apparently his grandmother gave up milk because she couldn't get through the carton before it went off either, but then she started mixing up the powdered milk, and he said she did very well on it. She's dead now. As he poured my tea he said, 'Tell me all about the neighbour's kitchen in the cellar,' so I did. He was very interested. Then he gave me a bit of a talk on the importance of calcium. He meant well, I suppose, but he can't make tea.

It's funny, you know, but when I untied Mrs Parsons' laces after shopping, the setting sun was shining through her fuzzy-wuzzy hair, making a halo. It occurred to me then that she looked just like a little brown angel. In all the years I've sat on the bed watching out that front window, I never saw or heard anyone except for estate agents and nuns pass through Mrs Parsons' squeaky front gate. When her fingers went stiff and buckled up she stopped going to church—I don't suppose she could get her purse open for the collection plate. Her feet weren't real good either, and she never waited for the postie like me. When there was a letter in her box I never denied her the pleasure of taking it out and bringing it in to open, even if it was just an electricity bill. She got a letter only last month. 'You've got a letter,' I said, and her little face lit up, so I told her it was just from an accountant; and she looked very disappointed. You wouldn't think Mrs Parsons needed an accountant. She was always keen to look at my picture postcards from Morris, I imagine because it was usually a nice photo of an exotic location with palm trees. *Dear Mummy, I hope you are well. All well here, weather good, lots of love, your son, Morris.* Then a kiss. No address.

And all that time I thought Morris was having an enjoyable time.

I *might* have heard something on the wireless about Morris Lancelot Blandon being in jail in Thailand, now that I think about it, but I didn't for a second imagine it was *my* Morris Lancelot Blandon. And no one said anything to me.

I wonder now if Mrs Parsons knew. She might have heard it on the radio. If she did she never treated me any differently despite Morris being a prisoner, which I now understand was very magnanimous of her.

Like me, Mrs Parsons was content. She didn't need to fill up her life with good deeds. We never belonged to clubs or drank at the pub. Pat decided once that we needed 'more fun' in our lives, so she dragged us off to her Saturday-night dance. Pat was always big on the Town Hall dances. Every Saturday night, off she went, all dressed up, twirling down her front path in her net skirts like a merry-go-round. It was long before the Public Scalping Incident, but it was still a disaster. Pat just wanted us to admire her arching about the dance floor in her net dress of fifty-seven petticoats, her bare shoulders glinting with glitter dust and her silver shoes flashing. Mrs Parsons declined to dance with Pat's husband, Bill, because she was happy sitting along the side, the glitter ball lights swirling through her hair, though it looked like she'd had an electric shock. Then the piano player had a turn right there on the stage, fell sideways off his stool onto the stage, but the oldies just kept on, chugging around and around under the lights, like rainbow soup. They'd only just carted the old bloke out on a stretcher, his sheet music balanced on top of his body, when they asked for a replacement over the loudspeaker. Pat nominated me. I wasn't pleased, and I let her know.

She replied, 'But there's no pleasing you, is there Princess Margery?'

I imagine Mrs Parsons would have danced at some point in her life, even if it was in her kitchen on her own. As we know, 'And those who were seen dancing were thought to be insane by those who could not hear the music.' That's a German saying.

I'd known Mrs Parsons for sixty years and she died alone on a summer evening, sitting on the edge of a single bed in her spare room with a hanky in one hand and a birthday card with a small boy and a kite in the other, only the classical radio playing on the kitchen bench next to the toaster for comfort. When her blind didn't go up that Friday morning I waited and waited, but in the end I had to go in, and as soon as I stepped into her house a shudder passed over me. Her rocking chair was empty, frozen. I called, 'Yoo-hoo,' but I knew. The kitchen air was right-to-the-bone chilly, stagnant, as if no one had passed through it in decades, and it put its cold hand around me and pressed. I knew straightaway, because it felt like it did that morning when I woke up and you had died. The underside of my arm across you was numb.

She was sitting on that little bed in the second bedroom. It was made up with blue sheets and a blue pillowcase. Of course I had no reason to look in the drawers that time, I just looked up into her lovely green eyes, staring down at the birthday card in her hand, and thought about how she'd slipped away. All by herself, just sitting there with her laces undone, Tyson's car radio pounding across the street and the builder's music blaring, their electric saws screaming. She'd been sitting there all night, suspended, just went to sit there after I untied her laces. And then she died.

A lovely tune was playing on her kitchen radio, like the sad music in *Mrs. Miniver* when Carol dies. I touched her hair. It was soft, like a tangle of satin thread, and I stroked her poor old dowager's hump. I know that hump gave her jip, especially on cold days, because mine gives me jip. I suppose we should have had more milk in our diet.

Poor Mrs Parsons lived and died all her lonely, lonely days in that house.

Then I had to go and summon the strangers to her private little world.

As I say, it was a bad week, but it got worse. Next thing, to top everything off, Ron died. The phone rang that evening, just as I sat down with my cheese and tomato sandwich. Someone said, 'Ron died.'

You know, I've watched the world pass by my front window for years, and all that's happened is that Bonita Jarvis sold her house to the Calabrias and moved to the commission flats, then Mrs Calabria went to live with one of her daughters in the suburbs. Tyson grew up to be a lout and rented his mother's house back from Mrs Calabria then proceeded to wreck it, then Kevin moved Pat out and moved back in, but in these last couple of weeks, everything's happened.

I couldn't think who Ron was. I had to ask, 'Ron who?'

'Faye's husband.'

It was Joye, one of Lance's sisters. His sisters were Faye and Joye, and when Faye married Ron and moved to his place, Joye went too. I can't abide either of them. If my memory serves me right, Ron left Faye in about nineteen forty-six, a year or so after they got married.

As I say, things had started to go downhill and, as fate would have it, the news about Ron came. At the time I didn't know it, but that phone call is one of the reasons I'm here on this balcony.

I said to Joye, 'I'm sorry to hear about Ron,' and, just to be polite, asked her where the funeral was going to be.

'Western Australia,' she said, 'so you'd better leave now if you want to get there in time.' Then she shrieked laughing.

I thought to myself, *The best reply to unseemly behaviour is patience and moderation,* and so I said, 'Where can I send a card?' She gave me an address in Reservoir and said, 'But don't send a card, send Lance's last will and testimony.'

As I said before, Pat's got that will somewhere. I remember the day Lance wrote it out. He licked the seal on the envelope and said to me, Judith gets the pearls, Morris gets the car, Walter gets the piano and the house is to go to the blood children of Lance Morris Blandon's loins, the blood offspring from my loins who rightfully should inherit an equal share each, and if anyone wants to fight about what's in this envelope, they can pay for the bloody lawyers.' He wrote on the front of it, 'To be opened at the death of Mrs Lance Blandon,' and gave it to Pat to keep safe. Fat lot of good that is since she's got a beer-soaked bar mat where her memory used to be.

It's getting late, and there aren't as many people on the street below, but all the lights are still flickering in the buildings. I imagine people are still about down in the foyer, still coming back from the theatre or wherever it is they've been, so I won't go out just yet. As I say, I'm not confident about being able to get back in with the plastic card they have instead of keys, so once I go out that door there's no coming back.

# DAY 20

Walter sat on his sagging bed in his small room, a hand on each bare knee, contemplating the worn carpet between his thongs. Downstairs, the oven door slammed and he felt better, knowing Mrs Stapleton had the smoked salmon in the oven in time. The deep-fryer was already on, heating the oil for the chips.

He checked the days on the calendar and moved his gaze to the little round mirror over the handbasin. 'Walter Miniver Blandon, Middleweight Champion of 1983 and nine hundred and ninety-nine days wifout a drink.' He held one hand up and stared at it, willing it to cease trembling. It didn't, so he rolled his shoulders, hunched into a boxing stance, threw a right jab and a left uppercut, and said, 'The Brunswick Bull,' and turned to his reflection again. He rubbed a tissue over the lens of his sunglasses and saw, looking back, the middleweight champion of 1983, a smooth-faced, dark-eyed, spruce man with a lustrous ducktail and an enchanted blonde smiling up at him. 'Champ!' he said and hurried to his mother.

He sat with Margery in her kitchen, both of them staring at the tabletop.

'Poor Mrs Parsons, it's the saddest fing,' Walter said, again and again, and Margery said, 'Oh, by the way, your Uncle Ron died too,' which made Walter put his face in the crook of his arm and cry, though he had to ask who Uncle Ron was. Then Kevin came in with Fifi and sat in Mrs Parsons' chair and stared at the table. Fifi licked the grime along the aluminium beading of the table trim.

'I know what you've been through, Mrs B,' Kevin said finally. 'I found Mrs Bist, remember? But she'd been there for days!'

'We know that,' Walter spluttered, because it hadn't escaped anyone the day Kevin lifted the pile of sheets under her clothes-line, releasing a swarm of fat, green blowflies into the summer afternoon, that they should have missed her, they should have noticed she wasn't marching purposefully up the street, her cardigan stretched neatly over her verandah-sized bosom, her shopping basket brimming with good deeds. Instead, they ate their roast chicken and enjoyed their lemon delicious with ice-cream while next door their neighbour died slowly under a pile of clean bedsheets, a clot the size of a pikelet thickening over her right occipital lobe. Constable Morgan had sat at the very same table with them, waiting for the glum neighbours to tell him something he could write down. 'It looks as though some-one's removed a watch from her wrist. Does anyone remember Mrs Bist wearing a watch? Perhaps it had her name engraved on it? Ruth Bist?'

Kevin had looked uncomfortable, and Margery said, 'It was an oval-faced watch. Mrs Bist needed her watch, what with all the committee meetings about charitable functions she organised.'

'Tyson!' Kevin said. 'It would have been Tyson, for sure.'

'You didn't hear anything out of the ordinary, Mrs Blandon? Didn't see anyone in her yard? Didn't notice anything unusual, that she was unusually quiet?'

'She was always out,' Margery had said defensively. 'And she oiled her front gate, so I never heard her come and go, not that her movements were any concern of mine.'

And now, Kevin asked, as he'd asked when Mrs Bist died, 'I suppose Mrs Parsons had a will, did she, Mrs B?'

'I suppose she did.'

'Where do you suppose it would be?'

'The nuns'd have it,' Walter said, rubbing his sunglasses on his footy guernsey. Like some bald men wore a hat, Walter wore sunglasses and Kevin saw why—his eyes were bruised and pulpy in their sockets, his eyebrows desiccated and spread wide across the ridge of his brow.

'Perhaps her accountant's got it,' Margery said.

'Accountant?' Kevin asked, suddenly alert. 'Mrs Parsons had an accountant? How do you know? What was his name? Was she was secretly rich? Perhaps she's got a will hidden in there. If you were her, where would you hide a will, Mrs B?'

'I'm not her,' Margery said.

Walter blew his pliant nose, put his sunglasses back on and pushed his hanky into the pocket of his tight shorts. 'The nuns will have her will,' he said and Margery repeated, 'The nuns will have her will.'

'Yes, you're right,' Kevin said, unconvinced. 'Can we take your car to the funeral, Mrs B?'

'Mumsy doesn't go to funerals, do you, Mumsy?'

'I'll go to Mrs Parsons',' Margery said and retied her apron bow firmly around her waist.

Kevin used Margery's phone to speak to the nuns about the funeral arrangements, and he asked if Mrs Parsons had left a will, but Sister Bernadette changed the subject back to the song Walter was going to sing. When Walter left with Kevin, Margery stayed at her gate, waving at him until he was out of sight. Over at Tyson's, everything was still except for a plastic bag waving to her from the thick ropes of buffalo grass choking the rose bushes. A curtain swelled in and out of the glassless front window. The sun was setting over the park, and a man in suit pants and a white shirt was kicking a ball with his toddler son, his briefcase propped against the swings, where his wife sat, breastfeeding. Next door, the new construction was deserted. In the letterbox Margery found a pamphlet advertising weight loss for pets (with before-and-after shots of a successful labrador) and another one offering to vacuum her central heating pipes. She stepped carefully back up her short front path, snibbed the screen door and shut the front door behind her.

Then she went through her house, took Mrs Parsons' spare key from the nail behind her door, went straight out the back door, down the three worn steps, through the shed to the lane, then quickly ducked into Mrs Parsons' backyard and into the little house—a replica of her own.

Mrs Parsons' bare house creaked when Margery stepped into the kitchen, so she paused in the chilly stillness. The Scottish terriers on all the shortbread tins stared down at her from the shelf above the stove, and Mrs Parsons' toaster, electric can opener and small electric kettle waited on the bench with her cosied teapot, cup, saucer and tea caddy. Margery was about to sit on the rocking chair when she noticed the imprint of Mrs Parsons' small, neat bottom in the cushion. A single tear gathered in the corner of her eye and seeped into the tiny creases, zig-zagging down the folds across her cheek. She dragged a kitchen chair to Mrs Parsons' old stove where she settled and opened the grate door, leaning down to peer inside. Mrs Parsons' purse was waiting on the powdery ash dust, and sitting next to it was a tin of black shoe polish. Margery assumed it was empty at first, discarded, but it was placed too precisely. The tin felt empty, but something inside rattled, so she turned the small key at the side and the lid lifted. It still smelled of shoe polish but the inside had been polished clean, leaving no trace of black paste, and there, sitting on a small bed of cotton wool, was a tiny black-and-white photo, an inch by an inch in size, of a newborn infant in someone's arms. It was a man, but Margery could only see the tip of his nose and the side of his jaw. There was also a curved lock of fine, dark baby hair. And there was an envelope, unsealed, with 'Sisters of Mercy' printed neatly on it. Inside was Mrs Parsons' bankbook. In the end, Mrs Parsons' life amounted to one small tin and a bankbook with twelve thousand three hundred and twenty-two dollars and fifty-seven cents in it. Though Margery's intention wasn't to pry, she did note that from the start of the book a hundred dollars was deposited in her bank account on the first of every month up until one month before February two thousand and eight.

Margery opened the tin again, stared at the lock of baby hair. It was definitely not crinkly. 'I wonder ...' Margery said.

When she was just eighteen years old, newly bruised by the reality of her recent marriage, Margery had stepped onto her front verandah to see Mrs Bist and Pat chatting at the front gate. She'd met Mrs Bist once when she had popped in, patted Margery's wrist and welcomed her to the neighbourhood, but she'd never even seen Pat.

'Here she is now,' Mrs Bist said, and they turned to stare at her. Pat, a slight woman holding a feather duster, her bleached permanent wave caught up in a scarf tied over her forehead, wearing a striped apron over a red dress that was far too dressy for home, said, 'At last, a face to all the stories we've heard about you.'

Since it was too late to retreat, Margery joined them and the conversation began on the topic of pregnancy.

'Hear you've been crook in the morn'ns,' Pat said and inclined her sharp chin to Margery's midriff.

It was then that Margery, naïve and bamboozled, understood the implications of her tiredness, her nausea. She turned back to the small house where she lived with her sour mother-in-law and obese sisters-in-law, Faye and Joye, to swallow the acrid toast and jam rising in her throat.

Suddenly Pat leaned in and whispered, 'Look who's appeared now.' The women turned. Mrs Parsons was standing at her front gate, her sunhat high on her hair, her feet with their pale edges spreading from cheap sandals and her purse in her string basket over her arm. She was caught. It was too late to flee inside, so she kept on with feigned purpose. Her bright-green eyes high in her face failed to meet theirs as she passed, but she managed to smile faintly and say, 'Good morning.'

It was a sunny day but she had on her cardigan, as usual, over her pretty floral shift. A mumu, it was called.

'Feel the cold, do you?' said Pat.

'Yes,' she smiled, shivering a little bit.

When she was out of earshot, Pat nodded to Margery. 'Tropical. She's got tropical blood.'

Mrs Bist leaned in. 'A war bride. *His* family didn't approve.'

Pat took up the story, 'Dash of the tar brush. Her husband shot through, left her because the night they got married he found she was brown all over under her nightie. Racist,' she huffed. 'Mind you, they do throw back, that sort. Not like the aboriginals.'

'Goodness,' Mrs Bist said, looking at her wristwatch. 'Is that the time?' and hurried off down the street.

Pat stepped close to Margery. 'You'll get to know us all, fit in with how things are. Mr Parsons, as I say, deserted Mrs Parsons, but Mrs Bist lost her husband when he bent down to tie his laces. Dropped dead, just like that. They sold out of slip-ons that week down Sydney Road.' Then she nudged Margery, 'You must be pretty happy, eh? New husband, a home and a baby on the way,' to which Margery replied truthfully, 'I'm hoping to move back to Ascot Vale to give my children a good chance.'

Pat's face fell. 'That's a good idea, since you just ruined your own chance here.' She stomped across the road to her house, and Margery decided she was very rude. And so she endured Pat, hid from Mrs Bist and, for approximately forty-five years, remained wary of Mrs Parsons before slip-ons brought her and her reclusive neighbour together. One day, when Margery was heading into her sixty-fifth year and Mrs Parsons approaching her seventy-fifth, Doctor Woods suggested Margery tie Mrs Parsons' laces.

'Has she got a bad heart?' Margery asked.

Over the years, arthritis calcified and stiffened Mrs Parsons' joints and the flesh on her limbs had atrophied, but Doctor Woods said simply, 'Just old age and a touch of osteoarthritis. Why?'

'Shoelaces killed Mr Bist, so Lance bought slip-ons. So did Bill, but slip-ons didn't save those two.'

Margery had seen them the day of the explosion, side by side in the rubble right under the stools, just as if someone had come along and lifted the men out of their shoes by the collar.

'Poor Lance. Poor Bill,' Margery sighed. 'Pat said they looked like a couple of puppets with their strings snapped. Still, whichever way you look at it, slip-ons are a signal of decline since they mean you can't get to your toes, wouldn't you agree?'

Doctor Woods frowned at Margery over his bifocals, the coiled grey strings of his untrimmed eyebrows worrying. 'I'll have to think about that,' he said.

So Margery started doing her neighbour's shoelaces. At the time, Pudding was a toddler and learned to tie bows by tying and untying Mrs Parsons' laces, but Judith had put a stop to it. 'You never know what's dripped onto them,' she'd declared.

# ROOM 4321

If I'd had the time, or my wits about me, I would have thought about the bathroom here. They're very nice. Heated towels, but I'd never be able to get out of the bath, and I didn't think to bring clean panties, not even a nightie, so I've popped myself into bed in my petticoat and I'm looking out at the sky. That's all you can see from up here—rooftops and window lights. That Friday night after Mrs Parsons died I saw Kevin sneak over to her house, the cheek of him prying into an old lady's house, but I'd locked the door. Like I said, the nuns had Mrs Parsons' last will and testament, not that she needed one since there was only one person to inherit her house and savings. The nuns said Mrs Parsons wanted me to have her watch, if I'd like to have it. I thought it would be something for Pud to have, something nice, but really, things should go to people who want them, people who are going to value them. As I say, I've got your hair ribbons, and I kept Mum's pearls.

Mrs Parsons' will was a revelation, let me tell you. The things you find out. I'd never have guessed, not in a million years, that Mrs Parsons had a son, a 'past'.

I suppose I never thought about her much, but I should have noticed something.

Life's too short to go unnoticed.

Naturally I assumed the lock of hair that was there with her purse and her bankbook was Mrs Parsons'. She'd hung onto it because it was straight when she was born, I thought, though now I realise she shouldn't have been ashamed of her hair. She couldn't help it.

There are some things we can't change about the way we are. There's nothing Mrs Parsons could have done about the way she looked, but as I sit here I realise you can be wrong about things. For one thing, I was wrong about Mrs Parsons at first. I will admit I was suspicious of her. She was different, but I know better now. The sadness that woman must have endured. Had I known about her past I wouldn't have cross-stitched that cushion cover with *An undutiful daughter will prove an unmanageable wife,* which is what I gave her this Christmas gone. The year before that I gave her *You scratch my back, I'll scratch yours,* which I felt at the time was appropriate because I helped her with her laces.

And I was wrong about Lance in lots of ways. He always meant well, I suppose. In fact, he said to me once, 'If you changed the way you saw things, Margie, you might see more things.' At the time I thought he was suggesting I get out and about more, to the pictures or shopping or something.

Wrong again.

It's natural to be inclined to see things the one way, but knowing what I know now, I see I could have 'seen more things' if I'd really looked.

Lance would have been ninety-one this year, but now he's just soggy dust and crumbly bones with his gold crown on his denture glowing down there in the dark. Mrs Parsons never mentioned her age. At least she didn't miss it, that is, the end of her life, like you do when you're asleep.

I've often wondered if you woke up to take your last breath, Cecily. Or did you lie there in my arms, looking at the stars through our window, feeling your heart peter, and stop? I wish I hadn't gone to sleep. It's my greatest regret. If you'd just woken me up and said, 'I'm dying now, Margery,' I could have stopped you from going, or at least been included. Sometimes, Cecily, I can actually feel a sort of aching, as if there's a plum lodged in my chest. I can't swallow, find it hard to speak. Oh, it does hurt so, especially when I notice something lovely or splendid. I used to have several rose bushes, like Mrs Miniver, but when they all bloomed and filled the front yard with bees and lady-birds, I found it made my heart hurt. Spring fills up with singing birds and perfumes, and they find me, even in my sleep, and it grieves me to the point of pain that you, precious love, 'hidden in death's timeless night', can't know the parts of life that are achingly beautiful. We came from the same cell, you and me. We were the same person, except you were the lighter, dancing through life with a mile-wide grin. I only danced because you made me want to dance.

The day you died you stood in front of the picture theatre with Walter Pidgeon and Greer Garson on the poster behind you, and you looked into my eyes and said, 'At least Carol in *Mrs. Miniver* didn't know she was going to die.'

Did you know? Did you feel the poison under the crown of your lovely auburn curls infecting you? There, outside the picture theatre in one moment of clarity, did you suddenly real-ise something relentless was invading you, cell by cell?

After *Mrs. Miniver,* the doctor said, 'Put your chin on your chest,' and when you couldn't, Dad flopped down in a chair and Mother left the room.

That night, while Mum and Dad prayed, I crept back into our bed and held you tight, and I prayed, then I slept, and when I woke, you didn't.

Afterwards, they watched me. At first it felt as if I was a living tribute or something, as if I held some sort of answer, but I had nothing to say, and if I crumbled it would make it worse for them, and then one day I realised that when they looked at me they were reminded that you were dead. There was nothing I could do. I just sort of went on. Mum just got more and more shriv-elled, and I went on living, though it's like living with a shard of glass in my heart. It was always possible to explain, to say, 'My sister is dead.' Many times I told the story, 'They sent me to the pub for whisky to rub on her chest then my father got the doctor, but it was meningitis,' and people always make sense of it by saying, 'Oh, well, no penicillin in those days ...' But I couldn't make sense of it.

Years later, it finally dawned on me that you were actually not here. One day I just turned to say, 'Isn't it a lovely morning,' and, *bang,* just like that, years and years later, I understood. Knew. It was vivid to me, finally. You. Are. Not. Here.

But only a year or so after you died, Dad came in and sat down on the bed next to me, patted my knee and said, 'You've got to let go, lass. You've got to move on.'

So I went to the dance, and I met Lance.

But I could never let you go, Cecily.

The week that Mrs Parsons died was shocking. Just shocking. But you've got to be stoic. My mind wouldn't stop. Even my cross-stitch didn't help. I was fretting about poor Mrs Parsons and stewing over Morris being in jail, Lance's wake kept replaying in my head and everything seemed to be accumulating.

If only, I thought, Pat's brain wasn't riddled with rotten, beery holes ... I could find out so many things. There's so much that's missing.

And now I'm thinking, as I sit here, if only I could explain things to someone, to my children, tell them what it was like living with the glass shard in my heart. Sometimes the days are very long, things I thought I'd sorted out jump around, making me feel ... *unsettled.* Usually I can settle myself by doing something nice—cross-stitching some life wisdom or polishing Walter's trophies.

When I think about our own mother, Cecily, well, she was never the same after you died. No one was, I suppose. Our mother sent me back to Lance when we found I was pregnant with Walter. I thought she was cruel, and I stayed away. I let them put her in a home. At the time there was no reason she couldn't have come here, and Shirley wrote, saying she'd asked for me. Now that I think about it, I suspect she was sorry she sent me back to Lance. If I'd acted in less of a cruel way, we could have made up for all the heartache. I've come to understand that, at first, it hurt every time she looked at me, because there I was, just getting on with life, married and having a baby, and Cecily wasn't.

And now, I'm ashamed to say that our own dear, respectable mother died alone in a home among strangers.

*Behold, on wrong, swift vengeance waits,* which brings me back to the subject of my children and, well, I may as well be down in the tight, damp dark with you. I'll go out to the balcony soon, and if no one's below I'll drag that chair over there out and fling myself over the balustrade.

But just before I do, one more thing. I do regret that I never got to see my second-born again. Once, as a little boy, after he'd run away, I went to the police station to pick him up and I said, 'It's a worry to me when you vanish,' and he looked at me and said, 'I didn't think you'd notice.' It's dreadful to think that Morris thinks I would not be there for him in his time of need, that he doesn't think that, as his mother, I will forgive him anything, even if he's done the worst thing possible. Remember Pietà? The sculpture of Mary with Jesus on her lap? We did an assignment on balance and proportion for art at school. In those days we believed in God, and we chose Michelangelo and wrote a composition saying Jesus doesn't look as if he's about to slide off Mary's lap because she had strong legs from riding donkeys, and that's why she was able to balance a grown man on her knees. If Morris had come home I would have held him and balanced him on my knees like Mary holding her boy. It took me months to pay off the glazier after the funeral, but I just assumed emotions were high. Now, twenty years later, I learned why Walter punched the coffin. Not the sort of behaviour Morris would have been expecting—his brother walking in, KOing his father's coffin, punching him in the head a few times, chucking him through a picture window and leaving. No wonder he went to Thailand the very next day. Walter says he was on his way back but someone planted the drugs in his suitcase, and he's ashamed. He probably remembered how upset I was about his cigarette business at primary school. He was charging too much for just one cigarette. It wasn't right. I love my second baby as much as I can love anything, and he doesn't even know it.

I'm the one who feels ashamed.

# THE INCIDENT IN THE PARK

It was a crisp, gold-edged morning. Morris was ten and Margery was out searching for him. She looked at the bedclothes, flung back as if he'd gotten up on a sudden impulse and fled. In the tree house behind the Earls' place, Margery found only an empty packet of Craven A Turf Filter Tip and some used matches, and on the couch on the Dowdles' front verandah she found only Bing, a black labrador renowned for his singing, and it seemed that this day she wouldn't be able to find Morris in any of his usual spots, so she headed home.

Bougainvillea bushes burned on the verandahs of the houses edging the park, the dewy air smelled of jasmine, and Mr Calabria's fat grapes hung through the trellis over his front path. Magpies chortled from the gums, and little blue-and-brown jenny wrens skipped low past Margery's hem. Cecily was there, as ever, beside her in her school dress, her pale hair held back and to the side with a white ribbon. All around her tiny insects buzzed, their wings alight. She turned and said, 'Isn't it a lovely morning,' but it wasn't Cecily. It was Morris, a freckle-faced lad in shorts and a hand-knitted jumper. Margery's knees went from under her and she folded like wet cardboard and lay in the green palm of the soft grass, gazing up. Somewhere far off, a million tiny bells were ringing, and above her streaks of faint white clouds reached across the pale morning sky, and something inside her cramped. Her body wouldn't respond to her thoughts: *stand up, walk on ...*

Then Morris's face hung over hers. 'Get up, before anyone comes,' and when she wouldn't, he went across to the other side of the park to wait, smoking cigarettes on a bench while his mother lay on the ground nearby, keening, the dewy breeze scrooping through the trees.

Later, alone on her bed with the bells echoing in her head, her chest thick with the weight of her labouring heart and a pain like tearing flesh, she finally knew Cecily could not be found in a room or a street, that these places were vacant. She knew Cecily was just white bones lying neatly on a rotten, satin mattress in a damp, black coffin, and everything in Margery's life was faded and of no consequence because Cecily had only ever had nothing. There was nothing, and everything was for nothing, and the truth pushed against the soft, sad walls of her dry, sluggish heart, and that was when Margery left her dream.

She looked at her children, waiting at the bedroom door, as if seeing them for the first time. She knew that they had not really been present to her. They were already quite independent, distant from her.

'I'll be alright now,' she said, but Morris said, 'It's too late.'

# ROOM 4321

I daresay Morris liked *her*, the floozy, since he fought for her over Lance's funeral, said she could sit up the front. She'd be in bed by now, that Florence, with her earplugs and face mask. At least I can die knowing Lance's last will had been seen to. I tried to do the right thing by her, for a whole week, but she was a nuisance from the start. The very first morning after she moved in, she came out of the bathroom with her towel and sponge bag resting on the seat of her walker. 'I like your shower curtain,' she said. How can you possibly like anything that's orange with purple flowers?

She jerked her head at the wireless, 'What's this you're listening to?'

'Magic Radio Hits of All Time.'

'It's real good.' She jigged a bit in time to the music, 'Blue Suede Shoes' it was, as if she was very modern and up with things. 'What's for brekky?'

I was ready to pour my tea. 'I always make myself toast and a cup of tea.'

'Got any more eggs?'

I pointed to the fridge.

'I'll make do with toast,' she said and sat down. She pinched a slice of toast from my plate then turned the teapot three times. She was about to pour herself a cup of tea when she stopped. 'Got any milk?'

I said, 'I use the powdered.'

'I won't bother then.'

'You should, at your age. The calcium's good for your bones.'

'There's calcium in beer,' she said. 'From the hops.'

I suppose all beer drinkers say that. Lance used to say beer was good for you, and Judith told me for years there was calcium in cream, 'From the grass,' she'd say, and up-end the bottle all over her Coco Pops.

In the interest of cooperation, I reminded Florence again that she had to do the dishes. Well, you'd have thought I'd asked her to paint the house. She did them, grudgingly, then I noticed she stacked the knives blade-up, so I explained about skin tears and how dangerous it is to stack the knives with the blades up. 'Look what a skin tear did to my shin.'

She pointed to the dish rack on the sink and said, 'Pretty slim chance I'll trip over up there,' and we had our first argument. She asserted that you get a smear on the tip of the blade if you drain knives blade down and suggested we just dry the knives and pop them in the drawer, but Walter told me that tea towels harbour bacteria.

'It's a miracle we're still alive.' She sniffed, and threw her tissue into the kitchen tidy, which provided a perfect opportunity to bring up the topic of housework.

I said, 'Feel free to empty the kitchen tidy any time you like,' but she argued about that as well.

'It's not full,' she said.

I said it'd start to smell, and she said it was a waste of bin-liners. Faye and Joye were like that. They took me to task over everything I did or said. I complained to Lance and he told me to dodge them. 'Think like a yabbie,' he said. In the end I turned into a yabbie, burrowed away for years and years beneath the murky water until conditions improved. That wasn't going to happen again because I had the trump card.

'I get plastic bags for free from the supermarket,' I said. 'Recycling.' Shut her up well and truly. Recycling's all the go now, Cecily. You have to do it or you get frowned on.

Florence, Pat and Anita. They're all the same. Argumentative. And seductresses.

Mind you, all things considered now, Florence could have had Lance. Once, I told Lance to give the boys a talk on the birds and the bees, and all he said was, 'A man needs a wife.' He said the same about a shifting spanner.

All the plots started to come together as soon as Anita got her clutches into Walter. Everyone had a plot—Anita and Walter, Judith and Barry.

I'd already started to get suspicious of them, and then we had a second so-called 'accident'. That's right. Not a motorcycle this time, but a car. Tony's low red car, in fact. And not long before that, Judith had said to me, 'You never really cared about me.'

So, you can't really blame me for thinking that Judith was actually the criminal in the family. It's going to take a bit more thought to come to terms with my daughter before I go. In the past I've blamed the Blandons because Judith possessed their character traits, but I'd never have imagined any daughter of mine would actually try to kill anyone. Not in a million years. Mind you, now that I think about it, Sylvia's mother said Judith and Kevin pushed Sylvia too high on the swing and that's why she landed so hard. But they were just kiddies, swore they weren't pushing her when she fell, and as I said at the time, 'If you didn't trust them you shouldn't have let them take her to the park.'

Mind you, there was that incident with the mice.

# THE INCIDENT WITH THE MICE

Judith didn't want to start school. Morris and Walter ran ahead while all the way to school their little sister clung to Margery's knees, bellowing, 'Please don't send me away, Mummy, I promise I'll be good ...' But when she got there she kicked Miss Fingly, who was trying to appease her by offering her a dried apricot. Judith had only been at school a few weeks when the principal's secretary phoned and asked Margery to come to collect her because there had been 'an incident.' The *incident* happened during 'pet week'. Little Kevin Cruickshank had kindly lent his pet mice to the class for the week so the kiddies could learn all about caring for animals, feeding them, making sure they had clean water, fresh straw and were safe from predators ... like pet cats.

The principal's office was spare and beige. He didn't look at Margery when she arrived; he stood at the window with his hands clasped behind his back and directed his speech to the trees outside. 'We suspect your daughter, Judith, has behavioural problems.'

Margery said, 'She doesn't misbehave at home.'

The principal explained that Miss Fingly had given the kiddies coloured cardboard, pencils and animal stencils, and told them to trace around the edge of the stencils. When they had done that, she gave them each a pair of scissors and told them to cut the shapes from the cardboard, keeping the blades as close to the pencil line as they could. 'Cut them as neatly as you can,' she said. But Judith somehow got her wires mixed up. She went to the big cardboard box at the back of the room, took Kevin's pet mice out and cut them up. Then she neatly lined up all their tails from the longest to the shortest.

'Well,' Margery explained, 'she's watched me slaughter a

chook every Sunday for the whole of her life.'

'You must explain to her the difference between that and cruelty,' the principal said and took Margery to the storeroom beside Judith's classroom where Judith waited, a wide little girl with thick glasses and prominent teeth, her legs swinging under the tall chair. The front of her little uniform was bloodied, and there was a little bit of fur stuck to her glasses.

Pat was at her gate, hand on the letterbox, watching Margery coming down the street—chin high, handbag over her arm, gloves matching her hat and her square, blank daughter lolloping along behind her.

'That kid of yours has got problems,' she cried, but Margery ignored her.

Inside, she said to her daughter, 'If you've got any problems, Judith, you know you can always tell me about them.'

For years, time after time, Judith came to her mother and told her that the boys had chased her with scissors and cut off her pigtail again, but her mother always said, 'Well, let's cut your hair short.' But Judith wanted long hair, she wanted Margery to plait it every morning like Elizabeth Taylor's hair in *National Velvet,* and whenever Margery complained to Pat about Judith's bladed pursuers, citing Kevin as one of the tormentors, Pat said, 'Look on the bright side, she's getting a bit of attention for a change.'

# DAY 21

The day after she found Mrs Parsons, Margery couldn't gather the strength to throw back the covers. Outside, life proceeded: the builders were hard at work, Kevin rode off on his bike and smoke wafted from the fire in Tyson's front yard. She'd watched the boys toast sausages and bread at three in the morning, using timber off-cuts from the building site next door.

The tightness around her eyes had eased but her face throbbed, and her shin bit when she wriggled her toes, as though she'd walked into barbed wire. 'I may as well stay here,' she said, but it was the last Saturday of the month; there was a hair appointment to keep and an engagement card to take to Angela, so she struggled out of bed to face the day. After tea and toast, she washed, dusted some powder on her forehead, nose, across her cheeks and chin, then dabbed a lot around her bruised, purpled and yellow-ringed eyes. Her cracked glasses hid a lot of the damage, and she felt better when she spread a little pink lippy across her tessellated lips and dressed in her nice shopping frock. She dragged her shopping cart from the laundry and gathered her handbags. As she closed the front door she caught herself wondering what Mrs Parsons had on her shopping list. Taking a deep, shaky breath she paused momentarily to steady herself using the busted cane divan on the verandah, then stepped carefully down to the buckled paving squares. The Ahmeds were unfolding from Mr Ahmed's taxi, their lovely robes falling around them in coloured scoops. Margery smiled and waved. They stared at her, pointing, and she realised why. 'I'm a duffer for falling, aren't I?' They smiled shyly.

Margery focussed on her feet, let go of the verandah post, assured herself she'd be at the front gate soon and set off along the uneven footpath. Someone tooted, loud and long, frightening the living daylights out of her. She wavered, lunged for the gatepost to steady herself, blood thudding in her temples. The oxygen content in her breath was somehow depleted and, to her horror, Margery felt the contents of her bladder—not much because she'd been to the toilet just before she'd put on her coat—flood the gusset of her panties. *That second cup of tea,* she thought, the warm trickle moving down the inside of her thigh. The car horn tooted again. It was Judith, and Pudding sat next to her in the passenger seat of the little van, her fingers moving over the keypad of her mobile phone. This week's specials: Bridal make-up 50% off up until Easter.

'Hop in the car, Marge. We're going for a drive.'

'I've got a hair appointment.'

'You've had an accident.'

'Just a small one,' she said, glancing down at the tell-tale wet line running past her dressing.

'You'll kill someone in that car one day.' Judith got out of the van and walked around to open the passenger's side door. 'Hop in, Marge.'

'It was the motorcycle,' Margery said, fanning herself with her gloved hand. 'Just shot out from a side street.'

'Marge, you simply cannot drive anymore, you've got a bad leg, and imagine what people must think when they see you behind the wheel. You've got blue hair, a black eye and your glasses are held together with bandaids.'

'You don't look so great yourself,' said Pudding. Judith's hand went to the rash on her throat, and the spots of raised red flesh in the crook of her arm started itching.

Margery squinted at her. 'You're eating something you shouldn't.'

'You've forgotten *again.* I told you I'm on a diet.'

'The rash—'

'I've done skin care, Marge. I know more than you about rashes. Now hop in, you're coming with me today. I want to show you our elder-age living and recreation facility.'

'A what?'

'It's a home, Gran, a big brick building in the middle of the outback.'

'Boronia, DeeAndra, is not the outback. It is very nice out there. There's trees and birds and stuff.'

'I'm having my hair done; I have my hair done every fort-night.' Margery looked at the watch on her daughter's arm—*her* watch. 'What's the time?'

Judith sighed and pushed past her mother, heading towards Margery's front door. She found it locked, so she stood with her hand on the door, eyes filling with tears. 'I need to use the toilet, and I can't see why you aren't just nice to me for once, Marge. I've given up my Saturday to try and help you.' Margery struggled back to her daughter with her shopping cart and handbags and unlocked the door for her.

'I don't want to go to the home,' Margery said.

Judith hurried down the passage. 'It's got air conditioning and heating in winter and carpet, Marge—and where are the new floor mats I bought?'

'I'm not sure, Judith, perhaps they're out in the sun.'

'They're not,' Judith called from the backyard. 'It's that Anita, isn't it? You can't even trust the home help these days.'

Margery sat in her chair in the lounge room and had just eased her stocking off when Pudding came in and flopped down on the couch. Margery shoved her damp stocking into her coat pocket. 'What are you up to today, Pud?'

'Mum's sending me to the information day at the university while you're at the "new modern, comfortable, elder-age living and recreation facility with air-conditioning and heated carpet in the peaceful ambience of a rural setting".'

'I'm not going.'

'Neither am I.'

'Your mother never wanted to go to university either. Do you want to do beauty and hairdressing?'

Her phone played a tune. 'God, no.'

'What are you going to study?'

'Event management. I'm going to be like Cynthia Plaster Caster.'

Margery noticed that Pud was wearing lace slacks, as though they'd been made from a crocheted tea cloth. 'Education's a wonderful thing, Pudding. A privilege.'

'It's just a normal, boring thing to do, Gran.'

'I used to be good at composition,' Margery said. 'I always got at least eighty per cent out of a hundred. I studied piano as well. As you know, I still play, in fact, just the other day—'

'Shush, Gran.' Pudding put the phone to her ear, lay back on the couch and crossed her legs. It didn't look as though she had any panties on under her lace slacks.

When Judith came back she put her hand on Pud's knee and said, 'My daughter's going to university next year. She's going to do medicine.'

'I'm not. I'm going to be an entrepreneur.' She winked at her grandmother, though Margery wasn't sure why.

'If she gets a degree in nursing, Marge, she can run our aged-care facility.'

'I'm going on tour.'

'If you go to medical school we'll buy you a car.'

'Uncle Wally told me I'd get Gran's car.'

'You can't have that car,' Margery said. 'It's Morris's.'

'Morris is never coming home,' Judith said. 'If he comes home he'll go to jail. Come on, Marge, get cracking, we've got an appointment to keep.'

'What about Pat?' Marge said, stalling.

'We'll leave a note for Kevin. Now come on.'

'She's in hospital, sick. Very sick.'

'She's old, Marge.' She tugged her mother's coat sleeve. 'Old people are sickly people.'

'Gran wants to visit Pat,' Pudding said, holding the phone away from her ear. Margery could hear the thin scratching sound of the person on the other end.

'I rescued Pat from dying of exposure in my car. She ran away from the home.'

Judith said, 'Well, that's dis-gusting. You couldn't get out of our facility if you tried.'

Pud said, 'It's not yours yet.'

'It will be, DeeAndra. And Marge'll be safe and secure there.'

'Sajida here will drug you and tie you to the bedrails, Gran.'

'No I won't,' she said, looking at her watch again. 'You're not allowed to do that anymore. Now come on, Marge, I need to drop DeeAndra at the university and get going.' She pulled Marge's sleeve collar, trying to get her to stand up, so Margery blurted, 'Mrs Parsons died.'

'What?' Pudding snapped her telephone closed and sat up straight.

'*Dead*?' There was dry spittle in the corners of Judith's mouth.

Pud cupped her cheeks. 'Ohmygod, that is *so* sad.'

Margery started to explain that Mrs Parsons looked as if she'd just slipped away peacefully, but Judith had her mobile phone out, acrylic fingernails dialling. 'What's going to happen to her house?'

'As I said to Kevin, I expect she'll give it to the nuns.'

Judith headed out the back, grabbing Mrs Parsons' key from behind the door as she passed. 'Or the State Trustees. I'll contact the State Trustees.'

Pudding got up to follow her mother, so Margery said, 'It's sacred, that place. It's her privacy ...' but they had gone, so Margery heaved herself out of her chair, following as fast as she could, reaching for firm objects to steady herself, gripping the handrail on the back stairs and carefully negotiating the steps.

Judith had her phone to her ear, talking to Barry. 'Mrs Parsons died, and Kevin's already trying to buy her place ... I'm in her house now.' She pushed through the shed door then into the lane and Mrs Parsons' backyard, like a wombat through thick grass, Margery tottering along behind. Inside, Margery's phone started to ring, and she paused, but she could see Mrs Ahmed over in her backyard draping a floor mat over her clothesline. She glanced across to Judith from behind her hijab, nodded hello, but Judith ignored her, so Margery said good morning, again, and called, 'It's not our place to be in there, Judith.'

Mrs Ahmed started thumping the carpet with a broom handle.

'Then don't come in, Marge,' Judith said, but Pudding was already opening Mrs Parsons' back door. With relief, Margery noticed the dark outline of panties under Pud's lace slacks. In her hallway, Margery's phone rang and rang, so finally she turned and hurried up her back steps, but it stopped ringing.

Standing in Mrs Parsons' austere little kitchen, tears welled in Pudding's eyes. 'It's so sad. Poor Mrs Parsons. She must have been so lonely!'

'Walter gave her a tin of shortbread every Christmas,' Judith said, pointing to the biscuit tins lining the walls. 'I wonder if she ate them.' She took one and shook it. 'Empty,' she said, picking up another. Pudding crept into the lounge room, her arms tight around her chest. The floor was linoleum, and either side of a standard lamp there were two vinyl lounge chairs with a small mat in front. Margery's cross-stitched cushions were placed neatly on each chair—*An undutiful daughter will prove an unmanageable wife* and *You scratch my back, I'll scratch yours.* A small coffee table supported an even stack of romance novels, and opposite the chairs was an old radiogram and wireless, but there were no records in the record compartment next to the turntable.

Pudding wept. 'Mrs Parsons was so sweet and gentle.'

'And poor.' Judith was sitting in Mrs Parsons' rocking chair, an open biscuit tin on her lap, flicking through some old savings account passbooks. The lid featuring a Scottish terrier and a West Highland terrier looking from behind a stone fence propped against the table leg at her ankles. She discarded the tin and passbooks and went to the fridge, holding the door open and staring at the contents—a full jar of honey and some opened packets of dehydrated peas and carrots, No Name Brand cheese slices, Jatz crackers, small jar Vegemite. She grabbed the Vegemite, unscrewed the lid, smelled the contents and put it on the table.

Pud walked carefully up to the front bedroom, and when she saw Mrs Parsons' bed she gasped, her hands going to her heart. It was a double bed, with two pillows, but just one small dam in one side of the mattress where Mrs Parsons had slept alone for all those decades. A scrap of paper marked her place, just a few pages from the end, in a romance novel on the bedside table. Pud opened the wardrobe door, but there was only one tiny nylon shift and a wool coat hanging there in the naphthalene air, the box of mothballs sitting on the bottom of the wardrobe next to Mrs Parsons' handbag.

Pud opened the handbag but found only the pastry from Margery's birthday lunch, solid as a teacup, and a mouldy half of a muffin in rolled-up tissues. She fell to her knees in dramatic grief, clutching the muffin, 'Oh my god! It's so, like, *sad.*' Then she remembered the second bedroom, stood up and rushed to the small room. Like the rest of the house, it was scrupulously dust-free and precise, the sheet on the narrow single bed was folded back, ready for someone. In the top drawer of the bedside bureau she poked at a folded stack of small, boy-sized singlets and underpants, and took a hanky from the square stack of washed and ironed handkerchiefs. Her phone beeped, so she blew her nose and wandered out into the kitchen, reading the message. It was Tyson. 'Wot's in there?' She typed, 'It's frozen in time.'

Tyson texted back, 'Check bathroom cabinet for drugs.'

Her mother was standing at the linen press in the bathroom. It was crammed full of face washers, tea towels, bath towels, placemats and toilet paper covers ... all cross-stitched with flowers, puppies, landscapes, and years and years of quotes from Doctor Woods' desk calendars. There was nothing in the bathroom cabinet.

Margery was in her small kitchen, clutching the doorjamb, when they came back, her sunspots gathered in a worried clump in the middle of her forehead. 'You shouldn't have gone in. It's not right.'

Judith handed her Mrs Parsons' handbag. 'Put this somewhere safe, Marge, give it to the nuns.' She started putting Mrs Parsons' groceries into Margery's pantry cupboard. 'She didn't have much, Marge, unless she's cleaned the place out.'

'It's like your place, Gran, like, a museum, except all her stuff's sort of ... unused. It's like you get frozen in the olden days, isn't it?'

'You should move with the times, Marge, love what you've got now.'

Margery said, 'You shouldn't have taken her groceries. I hope you didn't go through her personal things.'

'We're uncouth, Marge, but we're not *that* uncouth.'

Pudding said, 'I did see a few things in the drawer in the spare room. Doll's clothes. Weird.'

'Why have you got all these bottles of caramel topping, Marge?' Judith asked, her voice bouncing off the back of Margery's pantry cupboard.

'It was on special.'

'And you don't need all this fruit cordial. You should have seen how many half-empty jars of out-of-date stuff Mrs Parsons had. You can't eat it now, and it's a waste. Just buy the smallest sized things from now on, Marge.'

'I need the cordial for Christmas punch.'

'Christmas is nine whole months away—you might not even *be* here.' Judith fanned herself with the birthday card Mrs Parsons had bought.

'Mum!'

'She might be *in the home,* DeeAndra. Did Mrs Parsons have a will?'

'I don't know, Judith.'

Judith shoved the card into her handbag. 'Where did she hide her purse?'

'She never actually *told* me where she hid her purse.'

'You need to find it to give it to the nuns, see if she's left her house to anyone.'

Then Anita called, 'Anyone home?' and came briskly through the doorway, smiling, her teeth white beneath her shocking fringe, her basket on her hip, her uniform short over smooth, shapely legs and her sunny, casual energy filling the tiny room. Judith sucked her stomach in and smoothed her stiff curls. 'You'd know what happened to the new floor mats, wouldn't you?'

'Yep,' she said, studying Margery in an observational, nurse-like way. 'How are ya, Mrs Blandon?' She leaned down to look at her two black eyes.

Margery smiled, 'Triffic, thanks.'

'Good to know. The hairdresser phoned the council when you didn't show up for your appointment.'

Judith said, 'She could have phoned here.'

'She did. No one answered so I rushed straight around.' She held up her pager.

'We were distracted with the sad news of Mrs Parsons' passing,' Judith said, jerking her head in the direction of Mrs Parsons' house. 'I'm Judith, Margery's daughter, and this is my daughter, DeeAndra.'

'G'day,' Anita said, squatting to look closely at Margery's wound. She screwed up her nose. '*Tsk.*'

Pudding said, 'I'm going to see Tyson,' and left.

'So, what did happen to the mats?'

'They were lethal, too dark for Margery to see, and the loops would catch on her shoes. Trying to kill her, are you?'

'You're very bold.'

'Guess that makes us alike ... in one way.'

Judith's hands slipped from her hips. She blushed and turned sideways to minimise her bulky frontal view. 'Do you have a daughter, Anita?'

'Two.'

'Two?' She looked Anita up and down, disbelieving. 'How

old are they?'

'One's five and one's twenty.'

'Twenty? You started young.'

Anita smiled at her, ripping open a dressing pack like she was tearing up an incriminating photo. 'I was very popular.'

'Does your oldest daughter go to university?'

'She's got a job so she can pay off her car and her mortgage.'

Judith nodded, somewhat thrown by the fact that someone who looked like Anita would have a daughter who was clearly making what Judith considered a success of her life. 'I couldn't have any more babies after DeeAndra.'

Anita worked on Margery's wound, sitting on the cross-stitched footrest with Margery's gnarled foot in her lap, Margery's knuckles white as they gripped the armrests.

Judith continued, 'I spent the first six weeks of my life in a humidicrib. I nearly died, didn't I, Marge?'

Margery said, 'So did I.'

'Do your girls dance or sing?' Judith asked, putting her hand on Pudding's dance photo on top of the television.

'Depends on their mood.' Anita was gently poking the skin around the wound when she became aware that the atmosphere in the room had changed. Judith had stopped talking. A short, middle-aged man with a perfectly coiffed, brown-dyed comb-over was smiling down at her.

'This is my husband, Barry.' Judith reached for his arm, but he whipped his elbow up and dug inside his grey bomber jacket for a business card. 'Barry Boyle,' he said, handing Anita the card. 'Real estate and aged-care professional.'

'Wow,' she said deadpan, turning to Margery's wound again. Barry dropped the card in her plastic basket.

'What'd you think, Barry?' Judith asked, jerking her thumb towards Mrs Parsons' house. Barry nodded and winked, rubbed his hands together. 'The two of them together; we could do them like they're doing Mrs Bist's. Big renovations. Bathroom upstairs, two bedrooms, a balcony at the back and a Jacuzzi. All

BIRs, OSP, ROW, a *huge* cellar *and* ... a playground and park three doors down.'

'Sell them, buy a bigger share of the home. What do you say, Marge? Make enough money to invest in our elder-age recreation facility with some left over for all of us! I could pay off my Visa card. Barry'd love me even more if I paid off my Visa card.'

'Judith, I could never love you more than I already do.'

Judith smiled and pushed at the back of her hair, blushing.

'Well, Marge,' Barry said, holding his hand in front of him to block his view of his mother-in-law's gaping shin wound, 'now that Mrs Parsons is gone you're all alone, but you'll have company in the elder-age recreation village.'

'Instead of sitting in the front room talking to yourself all day,' Judith said.

Margery said she was not alone. 'There's still Kevin over the road; Angela and Anita come once a week—'

'At least.' Anita wound a roll of bandage around Margery's shin, securing a protective wad of dressing in place.

'And I've got a friend called Julien from the Green Environment Society who rings me from time to time to save the whales, and of course Mrs Ahmed.' She studied something invisible on the palm of her hand.

'Mrs Ahmed?'

'Yes, she'll be down for a cuppa sometime soon,' Margery said, adjusting the antimacassar on her armrest; *Count your age with friends but not with years. Anon.*

At the kitchen sink, Anita washed the sticky dishes Margery had rinsed and left to drain. 'There's all sorts of services Margery can have from the council. She doesn't need to go to a home.'

Judith stopped smiling. 'What she needs is for us, her family, to decide what she needs—not someone from the council.'

Barry went to the sink and stood close to Anita, reached tantalisingly into his jacket again. 'This is a good opportunity to segue to the list.' He pronounced 'segue' as if it was two separate words.

'This, Anita, is a very good list. Walter can do the restumping, give the place a coat of paint while he's at it.'

'It's me,' Kevin called, clacking down the hall in his riding shoes and an aqua bicycle jumpsuit, Fifi in his arms.

'Ah-har,' said Barry with exaggerated malice, 'the rival bidder.'

'I've had my eye on that little house for a long time,' he said, putting Fifi on Margery's lap. Margery eased the dog to the floor. 'I've got plans to renovate Mrs Parsons' place, like Mrs Bist's, rent it to some young students. I need a project.'

'That's one idea,' Barry said, rubbing his hands together. 'Want to pop in next door and have a bit of a poke about?'

'No,' Judith said, 'it's private, and it's exactly the same as this place.'

Kevin's eyes were on Anita. 'I'm Kevin,' he said, holding out his hand, but she just said, 'Hi,' and went into the bathroom, which she realised immediately was a mistake. She was cornered.

He followed her, grinning like a boy with a new slug gun. 'I know you, don't I?'

'I doubt it,' she said, rubbing a face-washer around the handbasin.

'I wouldn't forget someone who looks like you. Ride, do you?'

'No.'

'Play sport?'

'Billiards,' she said and ducked around him back into the kitchen.

'Live around here?'

'No.'

'You married?'

'Your dog's pissing on the floor.'

Kevin picked up the dog and said, 'We won't bother going to see Mum today, Mrs B. She's just got back from hospital and isn't herself yet.'

'Your mother hasn't been herself for months, which isn't such a bad thing.' She nudged the dog away with her slipper, while Anita placed a square of newspaper on its small, yellow puddle.

'My mother almost died.' Kevin ran one hand briskly over his crew cut, turned to Judith. 'You know Mr McNickle died? Your mother was playing a polka and Mr McNickle was dancing with Mum and they fell. He broke his hip, got pneumonia and *died.*'

Margery reached for her cross-stitch basket.

'Well,' Barry declared, 'there'll be no dancing in our aged-care facility, that's for sure.'

'They're not as agile as they used to be,' Margery said, threading a needle stuck into the armrest with the help of a magnifying glass. 'I'll have to stick to slow waltzes from now on, which is a shame. Spoiled it for everyone, they did. You need something lively if you've been stuck in a home.'

'And,' Kevin said, bending down to Margery, 'you had a bit of a car accident the day Mrs Parsons died?'

Judith threw her arm up. 'What did I tell you, Barry?'

'Pud'll be pleased. She wants that car,' Barry said. Across the road, Pud sat on Tyson's couch, both absorbed by a video clip on her iPhone.

Kevin said, 'But it's a Hillman Minx, a classic. In mint condition!'

'Good point,' Barry said, 'Vintage Car Association might be interested.'

'I said, "It's only a matter of time before she kills someone in that car." Didn't I say that, Barry?' Judith was scratching her throat now, her colour rising.

'It was an accident,' Anita said, rubbing the floor with disinfectant.

Barry dropped his hand onto Kevin's shoulder. 'Let's go have a look at Mrs Parsons' house.'

'Let's,' Kevin said, but it was Judith who followed Barry through the kitchen and into the backyard towards Mrs Parsons' back door. 'Don't drag Kevin through, Barry, it's Mrs Parsons' privacy.'

Kevin stepped towards Anita. 'I'm sure we'll be seeing each other again.' She placed the screwed-up, dog-piss-stained newspaper into his extended hand and turned her back. Kevin left, taking the newspaper with him.

Anita put the kettle on the gas ring and lit it. While it boiled she prepared the teapot, strainer and cups, and when she poured it she used fresh milk that she had brought along especially. She also put a yoyo on the table between Margery's and Lance's chairs, then sank into his chair with a sigh. 'I wouldn't bother painting the house if I were you.'

'It'd cost my life savings,' said Margery, reaching for the tea.

'And let's face it, you need to hang onto your savings.'

They sipped their tea, the irony of Anita's comment unnoticed by Margery. Anita idly picked up Margery's cross-stitch; *Great things are done wh ...* 'You could go for a nice holiday, Mrs Blandon. A bus trip. They have them especially for older people.'

'I don't want to be stuck in a bus with a bunch of old people. Why does everyone want to get rid of me?'

'I'm just trying to support you, show everyone you don't need to get thrown into a home, show them how independent you are.' Anita pressed her a little more. 'Unless you want to go to a home, but if you want to stay here you could get one or two of the stumps done.'

'I could.'

They sat in silence, drinking tea, looking at their reflections in the crystal cabinet opposite: two women, similar in size, patches of primary colour on their distorted reflections, sitting against a cotton wall of wisdom and cross-stitched scenery.

'A lovely cup of tea,' Margery said, which Anita knew was the closest Margery was ever going to get to being friendly. 'How's my shin looking?'

'Holding its own. It's the falls you've got to worry about, broken femurs and black eyes.'

'It was dark.'

'Don't want your bickie? It's made with butter, not margarine.'

This rare insight into Margery's preferences was the thing that started her crying. She reached for a tissue but found only her wet stocking in her pocket, and the tears rolled out of her eyes, tracked down her face and dropped from her slightly fuzzy chin into her tea.

Anita said, 'You lost your friend,' and Margery looked away, biting her bottom lip. Then she started to cry, tried to gather in her shaky sobs, tea spilling into her saucer, but they came like seizures. Anita took Margery's cup and saucer from her and rubbed her shoulders, which made Margery cry harder while trying to haul tranquillity from the air, saliva and tears and snot running off her, chin and body jerking in silent sobs. Anita got a damp face washer and Margery held it to her face, but her grief didn't stop, she spluttered on and on for the first time in decades. Anita sighed, ripped off her Nicorette patch and sat on the back step smoking until Margery's shudders stopped. When she'd assembled her steely demeanour again, Anita stubbed out her cigarette and made a fresh pot of tea. Margery was able to sip her tea, though she couldn't get her mouth to work enough to eat the yoyo. 'You're very kind,' she managed to say, and Anita smiled. 'I suppose they teach you that at home care school?'

'Yep,' Anita said, 'otherwise we'd never know.'

'Normally I don't cry,' Margery said. 'It's been a tragic week, and I missed my hair appointment.'

'What you need, apart from new glasses, is a flatmate.'

'Are you sure you're not Irish?' Margery asked.

She shook her head, 'Never seen an invisible pixie in my life. Why?'

'Well, I've got a flatmate. An invisible friend.'

Anita looked around the kitchen, past Margery, down the passage and said, 'Is he here now?'

'No, she isn't here. I only talk to her when I need to. If she was here now I wouldn't have anything to tell her when you've gone.'

Anita said, 'I see,' but it was clear she didn't.

'Mrs Parsons had one as well. She kept a bed made up for hers.'

'Right.' Anita came in and put her hand on Margery's forehead. 'I might get you checked out ... those falls ...'

'I'm perfectly alright.'

Anita held Margery's wrist. Her pulse felt regular and strong. 'Have you had enough to drink today?'

'Yes,' Margery said, but Anita topped up her cup of tea anyway. 'Mrs Blandon, did you know you've only got one stocking on?'

'Of course I do,' Margery said.

'Would you like me to make you another hair appointment?'

'I'm not useless,' she said wearily, but Anita phoned on her behalf anyway.

As she repacked her basket to go to Mrs Razic, Anita said, 'Have a nice afternoon tea with the Ahmeds. You and your invisible friend.'

She felt drained, exhausted by her tears, but she changed her stockings, sprinkled talcum powder in her damp shoe, dabbed more powder across her bruised eyes, put on her hat and coat and made the short trip to the Ahmeds' house. When the door finally opened, four brown faces—one old, one middle-aged and two young—wrapped in brilliant discordant colours looked warily at her. Margery was momentarily startled by the old lady. She wore a thick gold ring in her nose and her face bore scars, long neat gashes from her cheekbone down to her chin.

Mrs Ahmed nudged her eldest daughter, who said, 'Hello?'

'Good afternoon,' Margery said, smiling.

The women smiled back at her. She spoke slowly, 'I've been meaning to ask, would you like to come for afternoon tea?' She mimed pouring tea and drinking it.

'Come to tea?' said the oldest daughter, and then translated for her mother and grandmother. They chatted among themselves, arms moving under their coloured drapes, as though there were other people under their long dresses. Margery explained that it was an Australian custom to invite newcomers to the neighbourhood in for a cup of tea and a biscuit. 'It's called "being neighbourly",' she said.

The littlest girl said, 'We've been here two whole years,' and

Mrs Ahmed said something to her older daughter, who then informed Margery that no, they would not like to come to tea. 'We don't want to come.'

'Well,' Margery said, 'no one can say we don't try.' As she pulled the gate closed she saw them, watching her from the door, still smiling. 'You know,' she called, 'you don't need your jihads in this country, the heat's too extreme,' but they had gone, squabbling among themselves, the door slamming with finality.

Margery waved. 'Bye bye. That's "goodbye" in Australian.'

Back at home, sitting dejectedly in her chair with her cross-stitch on her lap, the Ahmeds' alarmed voices carrying across the small backyards, Margery said, 'Mrs Parsons was my best neighbour ever.'

# ROOM 4321

The kettle isn't ideal but they have four different flavours of tea bags in this room. And it's comfy—cool, and I imagine in winter it's warm. I remember Mrs Bist said to me once, 'When Pat goes into the nursing home she'll be warm in winter and cool in summer,' as if she'd be better off than me. She said I'd be better off in a 'nice, modern little unit', but had I my druthers I'd slip away in my sleep in my own bed. That little house came to be my cocoon, my refuge; it's everything I know and love. She should have realised that. Lance said Mrs Bist had tits like a bus shelter, and I had my prejudices against her. In fact, I told her once she was like a crewel needle—sharp with large eyes—but I certainly didn't want her to die, and the constable said it wasn't my fault that Mrs Parsons died. She depended on me, and I'm sure she knew I'd never let her down. She didn't *have* to die. As I say, she knew. Mrs Bist certainly didn't know she was going to die, but I believe Mrs Parsons had a premonition, because she cleared out her wardrobe. Perhaps I could have put two and two together and offered to help, asked her if she was feeling chipper or something. You knew you were going to die, Cecily, I'm certain of that.

I wonder if I let Mrs Bist down, whether I should have been more friendly, not held a grudge so much about the clothes hanger, not expressed my opinions about God. Mrs Bist was always telling us about her noble deeds, and we had to put up with all those foster children. I told her once that one of her state wards was stealing Mrs Calabria's apricots. Sitting on a branch, he was, stuffing every apricot he could reach into his mouth, two or three at a time. Mrs Bist just curled her shoulders back, pulling herself up to full height, her bust rising like an awning on a hot day, and said, 'God put the inferior on earth as a lesson to those who are privileged in order that they might appreciate their good fortune and assist those less privileged.'

As far as I was concerned she wasn't privileged, and I certainly didn't need assistance. You see, it was Mrs Bist who told the council I needed a home carer. She put the ACAT team onto me, and all because one day I met her at the gate and I happened to have the clothes hanger still looped through the zip-catch on the back of my dress. As I explained to Cheryl that first day she came, I used a wire clothes hanger to pull up my zip at the back because I can't reach, and Cheryl said, 'I use one to zip up my jeans.' Then she took me shopping and we bought the front button-through frocks, and as far as I was concerned she had done her job and could have left me alone forever, but she actually turned out to be a nice girl in the end, though she couldn't make tea. She didn't have tickets on herself. *She* didn't think she was a nurse, like that Anita.

Pat always took Mrs Bist's side. I made a simple observation one day about the latest lot of boat people who landed in Australia from Arabia or India or somewhere. All I said was, 'They say they're refugees, but I think they dress too flamboyantly to be poor.'

She said, 'They obviously still need help or else they wouldn't get in a leaky boat and we, us here in the wealthier nation, and that includes all the *racist bigots,* should give it to them.'

Well, I'm not a racist bigot. I've always done the right thing by Mrs Parsons, and I'm friendly to the Ahmeds, though they practically slammed the door in my face. You'd have thought I'd turned up with a bomb the way they reacted. How could I be a racist bigot when I have Mrs Parsons as a friend? *Each friend represents a world in us, a world possibly not born until they arrive.* You can't help being born looking the way you do, can you? And I always said good morning to Mr and Mrs Calabria. They were very well-intended but the Incident with the Pig was a bit much. It was way back when they first arrived. Pat accepted some of

Mr Calabria's bacon, but I declined because at the time I didn't think raising a pig then slaughtering it in a Brunswick backyard was civilised. 'Not much difference between a pig and a chook really,' Pat said. It's true, I did have chickens in the backyard, and yes, if chopping the head off one and cooking it meant my three children and Lance's mother were fed, then it was a necessary job well done. I don't know if Mrs Parsons got any of the bacon. She never said.

As far as I was concerned, every day I did my best.

I remember hearing on the telly once—David Attenborough, I think it was—'We all started off worshipping the same sun.'

On reflection, some people would probably say I could have said something to someone when I didn't see Mrs Bist those days before they found her. And though it was no concern of mine that Mrs Parsons threw out her clothes, I suppose it wouldn't have done any harm to ask why. Over the years I might have even asked about her life, taken an interest in her broken heart, talked to her a bit more ... been there for her.

It would be soul-destroying if I found you had struggled, if you had fought on your own to stay while I slept, Cecily.

The night Mrs Parsons died I cried a lot, and I cried the next day as well. You cry all over again for everyone that's already died. You cry for your grandparents and parents, pets and friends, and even the little children and people you see on the news who die unfairly. That's what crying's for, to remind you of all the people you've lost and how valuable they were. I suppose I may have even cried for Mrs Bist. She was only doing what she thought was right when she told the ACAT team about the clothes hanger.

It was a comfort, I must say, to have Anita there to make me a cup of tea when I was so lonely and sad.

I've always had you, Cecily. You've been the centre of my life, more or less. That said, now I think of it, I suppose that could have affected things.

Judith said, 'She won't have to spend all day sitting in the front room talking to herself,' and it's just occurred to me that you, my greatest comfort, could be my undoing.

It's just that I worry about the plain truth of it; I was not there for you. I slept while you died.

Perhaps that's why Judith said I had to 'live for the now', and I suppose it could look like I don't care about other things, the people around me …

I came to this room thinking it was *their* fault, and because of them I'm about to throw myself from the balcony, but I'm beginning to see how they could see things their way. I imagine they think things could have been done another way.

Mind you, Judith also thought I killed Mrs Parsons, so I suppose she thinks it's all right to kill me, and I suppose it is, since it seems I've let everyone down. Well, I'll save them the trouble, and then they can say I abandoned them all over again.

The phone rang in the stagnant pre-dawn hours when her mouth was wide, her breathing sparse and rattly, and her heart shoving out just enough blood every now and then to keep things ticking over. The shrill ringing ripped her straight from unconsciousness to panic—'Morris!'—and as she shuffled to get to the phone her shoulder bumped the door. Disoriented, she overbalanced and walked head-first into the wall opposite. She recovered, reaching for the telephone, but when she lifted the receiver and put it to her ear, all she could hear was the blur of vacant telephone wires.

'It was probably Faye or Joye ...' she told herself. 'After Lance's last will. Morris wouldn't hang up like that.'

Dimly aware of the ache in her face, Margery retrieved a packet of frozen peas from the freezer and headed back to bed, stopping for a swig of cooking sherry on the way. She wiped the lip of the sherry bottle with the sleeve of her dressing gown and was about to replace it when she thought better of it, held it under her arm and closed the cupboard door. She crept on towards her comfortable bed, staying there sipping sherry until the sun was well up, willing her heart to cease clapping in her breast, breathing deeply, steadily. When she finally rose from bed again, her head felt light and her heart fluttered, nausea churned her stomach, and she felt breathless. The packet of frozen peas had melted, washing blue hair tint onto her pillow. Her reflection in the wardrobe mirror told her the damage: the flesh on the side of her face was black and blue, throbbing, the skin taut like a drum head, and a neat line of dried blood ran across her cheekbone. Underneath the clear Tegaderm on her shin, blood had oozed from the wound and spread, drying like a huge ink spot. As she drank her tea and ate her toast and swallowed her tablets, Margery's body trembled.

She emptied the melted packet of peas in a pot of water and set it aside for lunch. Then she wrenched open the frosty door of her tiny, ice-choked freezer and worried a packet of frozen corn kernels from the icy womb, holding it over her ruined face as she washed and dressed, relying on the solid friendliness of fixed objects to support her. She dragged on her knee-highs, reached down into the dark wardrobe for her Sunday shoes, her head reeling and her breakfast churning in her stomach. Again, when she set the table, for two people instead of three, she stopped to cling to the chair while she wept, her face screwing so that it hurt, her foundation make-up and powder leaving dried water-courses down her creased face.

Mercifully, when she plodded carefully around her tiny front yard she found only a half-full bottle of whisky sitting in the centre of her footpath where someone had rested it to piss up against her side fence.

After Margery prepared the vegetables, she sat down at her kitchen table and, holding her broken glasses over the writing pad, wrote to Morris:

> *Dear Son, I am always pleased to get your postcards, and I am pleased that you are well. All well here.*
>
> *I'm sad to have to inform you that Mrs Parsons died and her funeral is today. You know you always have a home here and that you will always be my son, no matter what. They've knocked down Mrs Bist's house and are building a new one. Pat is in a home now and Kevin's hobby these days is bicycle riding. I had been doing Mrs Parsons' laces for fifteen years. As you know, she had arthritis. Our weather did not suit her bones. Life can be unfair, and 'every path has its puddle'. Always your loving mother, x*

It was an emotional, honest letter compared to Margery's usual cards: *All well here, the weather has been hot. Judith's new business is booming and she and Pud dropped in just last Sunday. Walter is the manager now at the hostel. That's all for now, love, Mum.* She folded the page neatly, slid it into an envelope and propped it against the salt cellar. Walter would copy out the address and post it. She sat looking at the envelope and eventually felt strong enough to go to the front gate where she stood, her old hand cupped tightly over the gatepost. Eventually, Walter came striding along the street, his best suit folded over his arm again. He carried a frozen chook, newspaper and a brand-new shirt, still in its square plastic wrap. 'One thousand and one days, Mumsy,' he said brightly, but he stepped from one foot to the other, clicking his thongs on his feet.

'One thousand and two days,' she said. 'An achievement if ever there was one. How are you, Walter dear?'

'Every day is a new day. Got another shiner?'

'Door blew in the breeze and caught the side of my face. It's nothing.'

'I've seen worse,' Walter said.

'Tell me how you are, son.'

'I've been better.' He jerked his head towards Mrs Parsons' house, and Margery patted his arm and said, 'Another sad day, son.' Inside, Margery put the frozen chook in the freezer for next week, turned the potatoes and pumpkin, and while Walter set the table she lit the flame under the peas.

'How's Pat after her fall?'

'Pat's alright, but Mr McNickle didn't recover as well. How's the course?'

He dug the syllabus out from his shorts and gave it to her. It was in limp pieces, worn through along the folds. 'We just did Cleaning and Sanitation. You must always use disinfectant strictly according to the instructions on the bottle, Mumsy. You see, it's created to have maximum effect according to the proportions scientifically calculated, and if you put too much in it diminishes that scientific effect. Builds up over time to a sort of film. Understand?'

'I do.'

'Next we do Pest Control and Waste Disposal.'

'Any notices about Mrs Parsons?'

Walter opened his newspaper to the death notices. 'The nuns have put one in.' He read out loud to Margery, '"Parsons," um ...'

Margery took the paper from him, '"Euphemia Poinciana", lovely name, "Nineteen twelve to two thousand and nine. Blessed is everyone that feared the Lord, That walketh in his ways. RIP." Mrs Parsons had no need to fear any so-called Lord. She would never have sinned. Never.'

'She came to all our concerts when we were kids.' Behind the newspaper Margery saw tears dropping down onto Walter's guernsey.

'Sent you flowers when you were in the hospital.'

'A bunch of lavender.'

'From her own hedge.'

'From her own hedge.'

Then Margery strained the peas while Walter made the gravy, and when he turned to go and get Mrs Parsons, he realised again that she wasn't there and sat at the table and put his face in his arms on the table. As he cried, his big, hairy shoulders jumped, shaking the table and making Margery's heirloom salt cellar rock alarmingly. When he'd recovered, he blew his nose and they ate lunch in silence. Once, during lunch, Margery dozed off, and Walter tapped her plate with his spoon to wake her.

Kevin watched Anita park her silver 1970 XY GT Falcon outside Mrs Ahmed's house in one reverse action. He moved across to the other side of the window to get a better view. Anita paused at Margery's gate to stub out her cigarette against the gatepost, then she took something from her pocket and rubbed it onto her arm, stepped over the remains of Margery's front fence and paused again to tuck the cigarette butt under a loose paving stone and went straight inside without knocking. He heard her call, 'Anyone home?' and then he rushed to shower, dress, and get over to Margery's.

When he heard Anita's voice, Walter froze, his spoonful of chicken and peas half way to his mouth. He wanted to be standing up, tall, dark and handsome against the white fridge, in command of the house, like a man, his strong, lovely arms folded across the black and white stripes of the best football team in Australia, but she was suddenly there, small and neat, wearing a nurse's uniform, and he was eating peas from a spoon.

She didn't even look at him, just put her plastic basket on the table next to him, focussed on Margery's face, which looked like a watercolour left out in the rain. 'Jesus! What happened to you?'

'The door swung in the breeze. Walter will put a hook on the wall for me, won't you, Walter?'

'There's not a single door in this house that swings, Mrs Blandon.'

Margery contemplated something on the back of her hand, then confessed, 'Actually, it was the phone. It rang in the night.'

'Shit, look at your shin.' She put her hands on her hips and sighed. 'You alright?'

'Perfectly,' said Margery.

Walter was still staring, and he stared at Anita for a further two full seconds until Margery said, 'Walter!'

'Job's right.'

'I know I'm not meant to be here today,' she explained. 'I'm actually on my way to see Mrs Razic, but your mum's got a bit of a shin issue going on and we don't want it to ulcerate.'

'Certainly not, Anita.' He was on his feet now, his serviette hanging from the neck of his guernsey, his adoring eyes drinking her in, moving around her face from her eyes to her lips, her hair ...

'Now, Mrs Blandon, you all set to face the funeral?' but she didn't wait for an answer. She started tidying the roasting pan and stacking lunch dishes, saying, 'Let's see if we can do some-

thing with your hair,' and, 'Perhaps we'll rustle up a hat or scarf.'
When Margery stood, she winced in pain, and Anita suggested
they cut a hole in her new slipper to release the constricted toe
and its corn, but Margery refused. Walter had given her the
slippers.

'I get her a new pair every Christmas,' Walter said. 'They're
sturdy, got the zip up the front, but if you feel you have to cut
a hole in them, Anita, if it'll help ...' So Margery's toes were set
free. Then she sat Margery on the edge of the bath and Walter
watched her tenderly remove his mother's dressing, gently swab-
bing it away, dabbing at the coagulated blood, wiping away the
slough. She basted the raw hole with saline solution, smoothed
some cream over the pink, weeping flesh, expertly applied a new
dressing and wrapped the limb, around and around, securing a
wad of soft protective bandage. Walter said. 'I'm deeply grateful
that you're caring for Mumsy in such a considerate and capable
way. It's very ... inspiring.' He straightened his left leg and tugged
the hem of his shorts.

'If this gets infected she could end up needing a skin graft.'

'Fair statement,' Walter said, and crossed his arms, pushing
his biceps out.

'I'm not going to hospital,' Margery said.

'You won't have to go with Anita looking after you,' Walter
declared, taking the opportunity to place his hand on Anita's
shoulder. She was firm and warm, and her small, female bones
moved under her skin.

'Heard from Barry about the house repairs?' she said, moving
from his touch.

'I think Barry should dig the holes for the stumps with his fat
tongue, dip his nuts in paint and crawl all over the house.'

Anita laughed, which made Walter laugh, too loudly and too
long at his own joke.

While she sat on the stoop drinking tea, longing for a cigarette, Walter leaned against the clothesline and explained he was
going to sing a song at Mrs Parsons' funeral.

'Walter's a very good singer,' Margery said

'What are you singing, "Return to Sender"?'

'"You Were Always On My Mind",' Walter said, failing to recognise Anita's joke. 'You may not know, Anita, but I'm a champion boxer.'

'An athlete,' Margery said.

'I noticed the trophies.'

'As you can see, I'm not just a pretty face.'

'I can see that.' Anita looked at her watch.

'Right,' Walter said, 'we'd better get organised,' and went to get changed.

As Anita put the finishing touches to Margery's bruises with foundation make-up, she asked if Margery was going to say a few words at her friend's service. 'Not much point since she's dead now.'

Walter came back, struggling to button up his suit jacket, the top three buttons of his shirt undone and his St Sebastian medal hanging against his singlet.

Margery told him he couldn't go to Mrs Parsons' funeral with his underwear showing, so Walter got the kitchen scissors, sliced the front of his singlet down to his navel and folded it back under his shirt. His small silver medal rested snugly in the nap of his manly chest.

'Purple suits him, don't you think?' Margery said, and Anita replied, 'It goes with his haircut.' Walter wasn't sure if it was an insult, but he said thank you anyway.

Kevin arrived dressed respectfully in black: smart black shorts and a black Polo shirt, socks and sandals, his moustache neatly combed and his crew cut glistening with some sort of perfumed product. He stood next to Anita, who was on her knees polishing Margery's shoes at the time. She turned and looked straight at the fly of his nicely ironed shorts. He stared down at her. 'That car of yours is a vintage car, did you know? If you like I can take you along to a car club and we could—'

'It's a machine that gets me from one client to the next, that's all.'

'I don't really care about cars either,' said Walter, leaning over Anita possessively.

'Christ,' Kevin said, staring at Margery, 'that's a decent shiner.' He also leaned down over Anita, pretending to watch her bandage Margery's shin. 'I think I know where I've seen you. You're an actress?'

She stood up, pointed to her letterbox-red hair and said, 'I'm often mistaken for Nicole Kidman.'

'I can see that,' Walter said earnestly. Anita started to feel hemmed in, felt the gaze of two men in the tiny space, and said to herself, *Leave now before you feel obliged to be kind to them, trouble is not in your plan.* The last stalker who presumed to insert himself into her life she found hanging from her doorknocker by his collar one day when she arrived home. The lonely stalker, his nose swollen and bleeding, thrust a bunch of flowers at her and said, 'I met your flatmate.' This led to the subsequent unanticipated, incriminating visit from the police ... which led to an assault charge and a trafficking stolen goods charge for her 'flatmate', Ray, and a handling stolen goods charge for herself, hence the probation.

'I'm off now,' Anita said, grabbing her work basket. The two bachelors followed her to the front door, drawn along as if they were attached to her with fishing line, leaving Margery in her chair. Above her, the wall hanging said, *Never morning wore To evening, but some heart did break.* She fought her jealousy as her special, precious boy shadowed the home help up the hall. She had sat next to Walter, stayed awake talking to him for days; she had not let him die alone. She'd saved him, twice.

Walter reached out and tugged the car door, but it resisted—it was locked. His fingers flipped out of the handle, sending him back a few spaces. 'Oops,' Anita said, unlocking her door and slipping into the driver's seat. She pulled it shut and started the car, but Kevin was leaning on the window, motioning her to wind it down, so she did just a bit, the engine rumbling. 'I know you from somewhere, I wouldn't forget someone like you.'

Walter leaned down, told her through the same small open-ing that Judith wanted to put Mumsy in a home, but it wasn't necessary since the government wanted old people to stay at home. 'I know,' Anita said, inching her car away from the kerb.

'We should go out for a countery some time,' Walter persisted, 'talk about the house renovations over a pot and parma. My shout.'

'I'll come too,' said Kevin, but she drove off, leaving the two ageing bachelors on the footpath watching her car until it turned the corner. They sighed, looked at the glorious world around them and wandered toward the house.

'Yep-see-dep-see,' Walter said, and Kevin mentioned she was 'a bit of alright'. 'I saw her first,' Walter said.

They were sitting in the front pew looking at Mrs Parsons' tiny coffin, Margery dozing under her hat, Walter humming the tune to 'You Were Always On My Mind,' Kevin gazing open-mouthed at the majestic ceiling beams tainted pink, blue and golden in the candlelit leadlight. Beside him, Pat stared at the coffin, confused. She scratched her head, skewing her wig, just as the priest emerged from his vestiary. He recognised Pat im-mediately. 'Welcome, Mrs Cruickshank, how nice to see you.'

Pat turned to Kevin, 'Am I dead?'

'Not quite,' he said, and his mother turned again to the coffin.

The priest had only just started the first prayer when Pat nudged Kevin, 'Why did you bring me to this place?'

'Shush, Mum.'

'I don't want to be *here*.' She grabbed her walking stick and marched out, calling, 'I know why you've brought me *here* and I'm not going.'

Kevin locked her in the car and arrived back just as Sister Bernadette signalled Walter to get up and sing his song. He stood next to Mrs Parsons' coffin, closed his eyes, raised his arm, adjusting the imaginary gemstone rings on his fingers, opened his mouth to sing, and outside the car horn blared, *Tooot.*

*Toooooooot.*

'Oh, for Christ's sake!' Kevin said and stomped out, only to come back in and announce that Pat needed to go to the toilet, so the nuns went to get her but she refused to go, clinging to the inside doorhandle and shouting through the windscreen, 'I know what you're up to, but I'm not going yet!'

Kevin said he'd had enough, but Walter wanted to sing, so he sang 'You Were Always On My Mind' in his lovely nut-and-honey baritone to Mrs Parsons' tidy little pine coffin, and the priest said it was as good as, if not better than, Elvis would have sung it.

In the car Pat said, 'Where are we going now?'

'Home.'

'Liar.'

'Let's have a nice cuppa,' Walter said.

'Bugger the bloody cuppa,' Pat said. 'I'll have beer.'

# ROOM 4321

I must have dozed off. It's after midnight according to the electric clock over there. We were up to Mrs Parsons' funeral, weren't we? Pat wore floral, but she's always been the blowzy type. She thinks she's glamorous. Walter got really serious about Anita that day. I went to my room for something, I've forgotten what, and I happened to overhear him ask her out for a counter meal. At the time I was pleased for him, told myself he needed a nice *friend*. She's not my type, as I say, but Walter's fond of her so I thought, *Well, we'll just work with what we've got*, because it's proved impossible for him to find lasting affection. Morris once told him he looked like he'd walked into a bookshelf. He had a beautiful face before the boxing, and even though he's put on a bit of condition he still looks terrific. He reminds me of Lance before the drink got him.

Of course, if the truth be known, the drink got them all. It's that pub. Grog got Pat's Bill too. Kevin said it was the war that got him, but I watched people walk to that pub and stagger home for sixty years, and you can't tell me it was the war that got them all. Lance and Bill were good mates. Right up to the end, and I mean the very end, when they tottered off to the pub with Lance's little oxygen cart squeaking along behind them.

Anyrate, it was a very plain coffin, and small, like Mrs Parsons. I hoped the nuns had got her hair right, and I hoped they'd dressed her in something warm. Pat was right about the tropical blood. With a name like Poinciana Euphemia, you'd have to be foreign.

Mrs Parsons believed in God. She obviously didn't think he was unjust, even with all that business of her confiscated child.

And given the number of unnecessary and cruel deaths in the world, personally, I can't see how anyone wouldn't see that God was unjust. I suppose it's a shocking thing for someone like me, someone upright, decent and honest, to come right out and say I don't believe in God. Why would I? He took you. And what had you done?

Nothing,

We never went to church again.

That first Sunday after you died we got up, dressed in our Sunday best, as usual, me and little Shirley in our patent leather shoes, white socks and white cardigans. Clarry combed Billy's hair flat and put clean bandaids on his knees, and I tied Terry in his pram. Dad was in his Sunday suit, and we came into the kitchen after breakfast but Mum was still in her dressing gown. The breakfast bowls were piled in the sink. When she saw us she just turned and stared out the window at the clouds. Dad sat down at the kitchen table, rested his hat on his knee and looked at it, so we went back to our room and sat on our beds. When the church bells rang out across Moonee Ponds, Mother started moaning, like wind through telegraph wires.

*Once bitten by a snake you're always afraid of rope.*

After Pat's scene at the church we drove to Kevin's place for a cuppa. My word he's let the place go, Kevin has. The roses along the fence are positively dangerous. You could lose an eye going through his front gate because the rose arch is so overgrown.

Anyrate, Pat just walked in the front door, out the back door, down the side of the house and out the front gate again. We didn't notice she'd gone for a few minutes, but I did notice her wigs are still there on their false heads, poking up from the top of the wardrobe like corpses in the cupboard, but all her sparkling net dancing dresses are gone. The entire second bedroom was always used exclusively for Pat's ball dresses and shoes, and shelves full of dance trophies her and Bill had won. Poor old

Kevin had to sleep on the back porch. The dancing trophies are in a box on the back porch now. They've turned black from lack of polishing.

Naturally, we found Pat at the pub. I'd been to the hotel on occasion with Lance when we were first married but I was never comfortable, and Lance always came home beered-up with a head full of all sorts of rot and nonsense. 'One day,' he said, 'we'll be absorbed into Asia and the black man will run the world.'

I hadn't been inside that pub for at least forty years. It's been completely rebuilt since the explosion, but it still stinks, and I'm telling the truth when I say there was a fight in progress when we stepped through the door, but Pat just moved through all the swinging pool cues and flying profanities to the bar as if she was invisible. But I will say I did find out things I didn't know that day. My word I did. For one thing, I know why Tyson feels he can steal my water and run an extension cord across the street and burn my fence. He was there, still wearing Mrs Parsons' kilt, with his flatmates, thirty-year-old teenagers who all look like they've just crawled out from under a greasy car. Anyrate, Tyson tried to pick a fight with Walter, bouncing around him with his fists up, but Walter just ignored him. But then he said, 'If you hadn't lost that fight my mum would still have her house.'

Kevin added something then: 'It's not Walter's fault that your mother's got a gambling addiction,' and one of Tyson's mates, a lad with a swastika sprayed onto his shaved head, stood on Kevin's feet and put his fingers on his neat moustache and messed it up. I've never seen Kevin angry. He actually turned white.

Meantime, Tyson was still taking swings at Walter, so the barmaid grabbed him by the ear, led him to the door and shoved him out, but he bounced straight back in, so Walter lifted him by his waistband and collar and threw him out again like he was chucking water from a bucket.

Someone called out, *'Ding-ding.'* Walter's feet got into position and he bounced around as if he was just out of his corner again, a big smile on his face, and everyone clapped. They all seemed to know who we were and they all seemed to know who little Squigglehead was. Someone put money in the juke box but the noise that came out wasn't exactly music. Pat sat perched up at the bar like she'd been sitting there for fifty years, and the barmaid put a glass of beer in front of her without even asking what she wanted. She had a wow of a time but I couldn't hear what anyone was saying because of the jukebox, not that anyone was speaking to me. As I say, I was never invited to the pub, not that I'd have gone.

Walter and Kevin had a few laughs about when they were kids. They sang a song they'd made up: 'Mrs Bist made poo stew, and put it in a pot, Mr Bist warmed it up, and ate it with hot green snot.' I remember Lance gave them a clip over the ears for singing that.

Then I found out about Mrs Parsons' stolen child.

Kevin said, 'Who do you think'll end up with Mrs Parsons' house?' and that's when Pat said, 'Her son.'

No one said anything at first, but you could see Walter and Kevin thinking, the film winding back to their childhood. Then Kevin put down his glass of orange juice and said, 'I've heard a story about that.'

Walter said, 'I remember something ...'

My memory started to rewind, though I'm sure I'd never heard anyone mention that Mrs Parsons had a son. 'What son?'

'Where is he, Mum?'

'Who?' said Pat.

'Mrs Parsons' son,' but Pat just got up and went to the toilet.

'They took him away,' Walter said. 'Something wrong with him,' but Kevin said Pat never mentioned there was anything wrong with him. In fact, he seemed to think something was wrong with Mrs Parsons.

'What son?' I said, again.

'He might be dead!' Kevin said, his eyes narrowing shrewdly, but I remembered about the clothes Pud said were in Mrs Parsons' second bedroom. 'I never heard about any son,' I said.

Kevin just said, 'You didn't hear a lot of things, Mrs B,' but Walter reckoned, 'You can find out anything at this pub, if you know who to ask'.

Oh! How true that turned out to be.

At the same time it was a shock to me, and I just assumed it was most likely Pat spreading rumours about a missing son, but no one ever said anything to me. Anyrate, the day ended when some man brought Pat out of the gents. 'At least she didn't squat on the carpet again,' Kevin said, and he and Walter fell about laughing. Then Pat didn't want to leave. Kevin and Walter had to carry her out on her stool because she wouldn't let go of it. I saw him carrying it back the next morning.

It was like sitting in the middle of a toothache, the whole thing. We hadn't seen Mrs Parsons off in the way she'd have wished at all, so I was glad I'd had a quiet moment with her on that little bed when I found her.

I felt uncharacteristically weary the whole day because I couldn't sleep at night. It was the diuretics. I understand now that my tablets were sabotaged, that it was part of Judith's plot to kill me, but at the time all I knew was that it was enormously distressing, up and down, up and down on the potty all night.

She was always very reserved, Mrs Parsons, and of course it's none of my concern what she did or didn't do, but a child? A son? It just simply never occurred to me. I knew she was lonely, but that's to be expected for someone who doesn't have anyone, and I never noticed anything.

Perhaps I should have.

# PART THREE

*'When it is ripe, the apple will fall.'*

An Irish proverb

At dusk, Margery crept across her porch and down the three back steps, crossed her tiny yard and went through her shed into the back lane. She stopped there on the bluestones to listen; it was quiet and there was no one in the Ahmeds' backyard.

When Mrs Parsons' creaky little back door swung open a swell of icy air pressed against Margery. She stood in the passage looking at the second bedroom. The bed was narrow, the pillow smoothed, ready. She tiptoed in and gently pulled back the blue bedspread. A pair of brand-new striped pyjamas were folded under the pillow and, as Pud had mentioned, piled neatly in the top drawer of the bedside chest was a set of clothes: shirt, socks, singlet, little Y-fronts, a pair of shorts, a small jumper with a donkey on the front and a neat stack of blue handkerchiefs.

Margery sat for some time, rubbing her thumb over the clean hanky folded in her palm. 'Dear oh dear,' she finally said. When she left, she backed out of the little house, pulling the door firmly shut. She locked it and put the key in a new hiding spot ... the cistern of her toilet.

She couldn't sleep again that night, though she felt weary to the bones, and so she lay in her bed, eyes fixed on the street with the transistor fizzing in her ear. She played a story in her head, a film, her and Cecily playing at a dance hall, Cecily out front singing and Margery on piano, because Margery had kept up her piano study and Cecily had perfected her soprano, and Margery was there beside her, safe behind the piano. 'And we would have married a nice man like Walter Pidgeon,' she said to her dead sister, 'and lived next door to each other ... but that didn't happen.'

Mrs Parsons had gone on living too, waiting. 'She lived for the past, I suppose you could say. Makes you think, doesn't it?'

The phone rang again that night. 'Morris,' she said, then decided it probably wasn't Morris and stayed in bed. When the phone stopped ringing, she started going over her life, but had only got as far as the registry office with Lance before she was distracted by Kevin slinking across the street with a box in his arms. He stopped at Mrs Bist's dump bin, glanced up and down the street, like a fox with someone's pet rabbit, and dropped the box into the bin. *Metal,* Margery thought, recognising the sound as trophies clanging together. Pat's passionate life of championship dancing so swiftly and noisily chucked into the bottom of a dump bin by her only offspring in the middle of the night. She smiled.

For dinner, Walter prepared, cooked and served three kilograms of grilled sausages, five kilograms of boiled potatoes, and a two-kilo bag of frozen mixed vegetables, which the lodgers ate hungrily. Then he sat at the large kitchen table with his hands over his ears to read *Legislation, Codes and Responsibilities Relating to Food Hygiene,* while a slimy-haired, medicated tenant, who went by the name of Judas, methodically collected the tomato sauce bottles from the tables and wiped them down, then washed and dried the dishes, stacking them precisely in equal piles at regular intervals along the table beside Walter.

Mrs Stapleton scraped in, nodded to Judas and stood in the open back doorway. She lit a cigarette and blew the smoke into the gritty Collingwood sunset. 'How's it goin', Wal?'

'Job's right,' he said, but when Mrs Stapleton didn't say anything further he confessed, 'A bit confusing, actually.'

Mrs Stapleton ran her nose along her forearm and sniffed. She dragged on her cigarette and said, 'Don't sweat too much on it. I gotta get fire-escapes and smoke detectors yet, cost me a fortune.'

Walter jerked his head towards the dining room, where a few of the men still sat in their places, staring at the institution-green walls. 'What happens to the blokes?'

Mrs Stapleton shrugged, dragged on her cigarette. 'They'll find somewhere.'

'Under a bridge,' Walter said. 'If we change to backpackers we get the same fing: drugs and drunks.'

'You can keep your job, Wal. You gotta finish the course, but.'

'No worries,' he said and put his hands over his ears again. Judas set about topping up the salt shakers on all the tables.

# DAY 23

At times in the night, Margery slept quite soundly, but she still woke very early Monday, and she knew even before she raised her head from the pillow that things weren't right. She was not at all reassured when the floorboards buckled, rising and sinking beneath her feet, as if she was walking on a mattress. Nor was she happy about the walls that shrunk back when she reached for them, or the chairs that cowered when she presented her bottom to them. The kitchen table moved back into the corner, and cascading water, somewhere close, drowned out the sound of the television. Eventually, she crawled back into her bed, and that was where she was when Judith's little van pulled up outside. The specials were 'Eyelash Tinting, Lip and Eyebrow Waxing, 25% Off'. Judith barged in and went straight to the lavatory, and when she got back she stood over her sick mother, red-faced and shaking, the pearls in her clenched fist. 'Plastic. Your mother gave you fake pearls, Marge.'

'My mother gave me Mikimotos.'

'These are fake. Amanda showed me, and she'd know. This is how you tell.' She ran them across her teeth, 'Not rough. They have to be rough on your teeth.' Then she scraped the paint off one with her artificial fingernail. 'See?' she said and ripped Margery's gold watch from her wrist. 'I bet this is fake as well.' She threw the watch and the plastic necklace onto the bed.

'The watch isn't plastic, Judith. Keep it, dear, and I do have my mother's Mikimotos.'

'You're nuts. I don't want your bloody watch, or your pearls.' Tears were streaming down her face. She left, slamming the door behind her. In the street she turned and screamed, 'Fake!'

Mr Ahmed paused as he got into his taxi and frowned at Judith.

# ROOM 4321

Thinking back, it has occurred to me that perhaps I was being selfish about the pearls, the real ones I mean, since I really don't go out anywhere to wear them. If I knew I'd run into Pat somewhere I'd wear them, but she's demented now, so there's no need to show them off. When I did go out I was usually with Judith—I never wore pearls, the real ones or the plastic ones. Judith would've taken them. I should have given the Mikimotos to her and been done with them, but I truly valued those pearls. Dad gave them to Mother. I remember the very day. Do you? We were hanging out the washing, and he snuck up behind her and hung them on the line. When she hung his shirts up she came across them dangling from a peg. There they were. They were the only thing I had left of my mother.

I realise now it must have been upsetting for Judith to be told the pearls were fake by her new friend, but she's got the real ones now, so she's happy. The watch brought Pat back to me, or, more accurately, her revenge after the Public Scalping Incident. I'll admit now, as I'm sitting here, that I quite enjoyed the Public Scalping Incident, and I'm not terribly upset that the passenger car door rattles or that the handle gets stuck either—it was her revenge that was the thing that really split our neighbourly relations, if you could call them that.

I didn't speak to her for decades.

# PAT'S REVENGE

Following the Public Scalping Incident, no one saw Pat for a week. She paced the worn carpet behind her nylon net curtains, smoking cigarettes, watching through her front window to Margery's peeling front door. Fortified by the shelves of shining dancing trophies and the rack of twinkling sequinned dresses behind her, she festered with loathing for the uptight, up-her-self old wowser across the road. 'You're always there, watching; you're like a splinter in my heel. We can't be free because of you! Who do you think you are? Sneering at us from behind your champion son's silver trophies and your linen napkins and your bloody Ascot Vale non-drinking family and their superior opinions. If only you knew, Princess Margery, if only you knew!'

What Margery did know was that across the road, Pat was seething in a cloud of smoky hate, and so only when she had seen the postie actually put a letter in her letterbox did Margery leave the house. She was careful not to hurry, careful to pause and feign casual interest in her neglected geranium even though her heart was racing. For the rest of the time, Margery sat on her bed, rubbing Walter's trophies with flannel rags, waiting.

Finally, Pat came, travelling rapidly towards Margery, her eyes squinting with the intensity of her savage intentions, menacing vengeance propelling her so that the stiff curls across her forehead parted, the large, plastic aqua loops in her ears swung back and her nylon aqua stretch slacks and paisley, psychedelic tank top pressed against her thin body. She flung the screen door back, slapping it against the wall, and stood over her nemesis on her bed. Margery looked back at her, her sense of defiance soaring at the sight of Pat—pale, perspiring and shaking with tearful humiliation.

Her voice wavering, Pat said, 'What would you say if I told

you your husband's having an affair?' to which Margery replied, calmly, 'You're not Lance's type: he says you dress as if you're off to open day at the local rub and tug.'

Pat was speechless, but only for a second. 'You don't know, do you? How could you not know?'

'Well,' Margery said, 'I didn't know you were bald.'

Pat's head jerked back, as if to avoid a passing hornet, then she said, 'You've got no reason on God's earth to think you're so smart, Margery Blandon!'

'I'm smart enough to know that there's no such thing as God, and I'm not stupid enough to believe that he made the earth in six ruddy days.'

'It's called faith, Marge. It's about hope.'

'False hope.'

'Hope and faith, and you've got neither.' Pat left, satisfied but not triumphant. 'Let her mull it over for a day or two, then she'll come asking.'

But she never did. A few days later, Margery was digging Lance's singlets and long johns from the writhing, soapy water of her agitating washing machine and feeding them into the wringer when she said, 'Oh, bother!' It was time to face up to things, something she dreaded more than life itself. She went to the second bedroom and stood in the doorway staring at her husband, who was, like his mother before him, supine in the spare bed, wheezing away, eyeing the little red ball hovering at number five in the gauge on the side of his oxygen bottle. Margery poked him with the laundry stick. 'Pat told me you're having an affair.'

He didn't even look at her. He just reached over and held up a cross-stitched bed cushion. *No sword bites so fiercely as an evil tongue,* and Margery turned on her heel and left. The matter was never mentioned again.

For years Margery only ever encountered Pat at the supermarket or in the street, where they clashed openly, then moved on again from their brief but nasty spats, and every week, Margery watched her neighbour walking to and from the pub, laughing and talking with all her less-than-respectable accomplices.

# DAY 24

On Tuesday Margery found she was nauseous again, and too dizzy to carry her pot to empty it, so she crept down the back steps sideways then lurched to the clothesline for safe harbour. She made it to the lavatory and sat clasping the sides of the toilet seat with the door open, held upright by watching the almost-level back steps.

'It's my shin,' she said. 'I've got septicaemia, Cecily.'

She made it back to her chair and slept soundly over her cross-stitch but spent most of the night on her commode pot, humming tunes, willing her pulse to throb rhythmically, urging her bladder to stop summoning her, wishing sleep would come. She stayed in bed day and night, staring at the window ledge, a surface she was sure was straight, stationary, the sides of the pillow bunched against her ears to block the dreadful waterfall outside, though the cascade was actually blood pumping past her ears. Next door, the builders—more than any she'd ever seen—nailed sheets of plywood to the frame while others laid bricks.

Every now and then she started in her bed, thinking she must check Mrs Parsons' blind, then she remembered and settled back to watch the comings and goings next door. When someone arrived in a van and rolled out a clothes rack with a chandelier hanging from it, Margery said, 'I bet that's not crystal,' and when Tony wheeled in two white lions, seated like guard dogs at a gate, she said, 'Sculpture. Nice.'

Another van pulled up—'Your Security is Our Business'—and four men spent the entire day installing wiring for a security alarm system. Margery watched them screw cameras to the eaves, and they left many, many bunches of white, blue and red wires hung from the timber frame. Miriana arrived in a see-through maternity top and shorts, her pregnant belly sticking out like a football stuck to a banana. She carried a tray that Margery assumed—rightly—was food. Behind her, an older woman, perhaps her mother, carried two more trays. Then a four-wheel drive zoomed into the gap at the kerb, and Margery's interest was captured by the driver, a girl, a cigarette between her fingers on the steering wheel and her other hand holding a mobile phone to her ear. Her head and shoulders were covered by a firmly tied shayla, but when she got out of the car—still smoking, still talking on her phone—Margery noted her tight jeans and high-heeled sandals and said, 'Goodness me.' Two dark-eyed, curly-haired girls, identically dressed like flower girls, climbed from the back seat and followed their mother, who also carried a plastic container filled with food, into Tony and Miriana's.

'At least they can cook.' More cars arrived, more women with food, and men, lots of men, not carrying anything. Miriana conducted a tour of the almost-complete structure, up and down the stairs, trailed by her dark-eyed girlfriends, some wearing headscarves, others with striped hair, and all wearing what Margery considered unsuitably high shoes. Miriana made squares and circles with her hands where tables, mirrors and cupboards would be placed, and out on the balcony she pointed to the brickworks' chimneys on the skyline and said, 'Noice, eh?'

The afternoon wore on, and Margery watched the gathering next door, noting that while the women worked at serving food and caring for the kids, the men did nothing. 'They're the same all over the world,' Margery sniffed. She scowled at the young men—more swarthy types—crawling all over the house and sitting in Tony's Ferrari, beeping the horn, having their photo taken standing next to it. Tony even drove some of the men and kids around the block.

At one point, Kevin wandered over from his house, his hands in his shorts, baggy about his thin, bald legs. He stood close to the group surrounding the Ferrari, bouncing on the balls of his feet in his socks and sandals, and eventually moved to merge with them. They didn't acknowledge him, but he fixed his smile and circled the crowd anyway, trying to get close to the beautiful red machine. But he was still ignored, so he finally looked sideways, pretended to see something he needed to attend to and left.

By late afternoon, Margery felt better and was able to get up and eat some bread and butter with jam.

Anita was scrubbing the laundry trough, and her companion and flatmate, Ray, was standing behind her, watching appreciatively. She was applying all her determination and frustration to the task of cleaning the trough, which was brand, sparkling new. Everything was new, just unwrapped and screwed or glued into place—most of the appliances were still on the factory floor just one week ago. Since the fire, the entire house had been gutted, rebuilt and refurbished. Outside, state-of-the-art surveillance cameras peeped out from under the eaves, so new that they weren't even available in retail stores yet, and they were there especially for Brandon, Anita's Corrective Services officer, and for Ray's parole officer, should either decide to visit, unannounced. That's why there was also a handy new side gate, cleverly disguised as a plain corrugated iron fence: an escape route.

Ray was tempted to sneak up and pinch Anita's bottom, but he knew by the way her arm was moving so fiercely against the stainless steel that to do so would be to risk being struck by a wet glove. Then there would be a scene and she would cry and he would have to apologise again for the charge of handling stolen goods that she was lumbered with because of him, because of *his* stolen goods, so he crept back, stood at the front door and called, 'Hi, honey, I'm home,' in an exaggerated American accent.

Anita met him in the kitchen, her face glowing with perspiration. Ray kissed her cheek. 'How'd it go with the Brunswick Steer?'

She pushed away from him. 'Don't call him that. He's a nice guy.'

Ray shrugged. 'Sorry.'

She nodded. 'He said yes, he thinks a live-in companion's a good idea. He can see the benefits to his mother of a boarder, and he seems to think Mrs Blandon will agree, but I don't think she will.' She bit her bottom lip.

'It's just temporary, anyway.' He lifted the green shopping bag to the kitchen table and took out the box containing a new telephone.

Anita looked at the picture on the box and said, 'Perfect,' and Ray said he'd install it that afternoon. 'I can get smoke detectors too, if you like. For free.'

She sighed, turned and went back to the trough.

'Who's gunna ask a little old lady for receipts? Just tell Walter to consider it a gift from the taxpayers and shareholders of the nation in partnership with our magnificent Prime Minister.' She said nothing.

'You are doing *good* things for them,' he continued, following her back to the laundry. 'It's the right thing for Mrs Blandon to have some company for a while ... and a decent phone. It means her daughter will back off, and the Brunswick Bull will renovate her house.'

She nodded, but it was the fact that she knew in her heart that Walter was keen on her, that he thought that he loved her, and she felt that at some level she must be encouraging him. It could only mean trouble.

'Just make absolutely sure that he puts the smoke detectors in properly, and tell the guy across the road who looks like a tamperer to watch for smoke or flames.'

'Kevin?'

'Yeah.'

# ROOM 4321

It wouldn't have mattered to Pat that we didn't speak for all those years—gosh, years and years it was. She had lots of friends, and her dancing. I know now she was very friendly with *her*, Florence, the thieving, lying adulteress. Like Pat, she was trouble from the start, that woman.

The first Sunday after her arrival, we were sitting out on the verandah when she turned to me and said, 'Have we been to mass?'

My victory over how to drain knives and forks and the bin-liner issue still hung in the air, so I didn't hesitate. 'Certainly not,' I said. 'I've got the day-by-day wisdom of learned men to guide me if I need them. All I have to do is consult my cross-stitch, though it's perfectly obvious to *me* what's right, wrong or otherwise.'

'Whatever you think's a fair thing,' she said and gestured at the tree outside Tyson's, my geranium bush and the lass walking past with her baby in an oversized pram. 'But whoever's responsible for all of this did a fair sort of a job, I reckon.'

There was nothing I could say to that since I'm a believer in Mother Nature.

Our next dispute, our third in three days, was over the issue of the toilet paper. She'd used almost a whole roll. I had to use a tissue from my sleeve when I got there, so I placed a notepad and pencil on the table to list things that we shared, like detergent and toothpaste, soap and talcum powder.

'I never use talcum powder,' she said. 'It sticks in all the creases.'

I said there was no need to be crude; the point was that she used twice as much toilet paper as me.

'The war's over,' she informed me. 'Rationing's finished.'

So I reminded her about the trees, and what Julien says about recycling paper, but she cut me off. 'You leave a drip on the seat,' she said. I had a saucepan in my hand, you know. I nearly crowned her, but instead I told her that the sooner she found somewhere else to live, the better.

'You're darn right,' she said, but I didn't see her stand up and rush to pack.

She was also contrary about the butter. Butter must be kept in the fridge so it doesn't go rancid. 'You call that butter?' she said. 'It's margarine, kerosene and yellow paint.'

'It's easy to spread,' I said. I'd raised the matter of a cooking roster on the first day, but she said I should cook unless I wanted to eat eggs on toast three times a day.

'It's quite understandable that no one ever wanted marry you,' I said. Little wonder she was left like a used beer glass on the bar at closing time.

'Someone did want to many me,' she spat, 'but his mingy wife wouldn't give him a divorce.'

*So. There you have it,* I thought to myself. *Not only is she a barmaid, but she's a smoker, a drinker, a thief, an adulteress and slovenly to boot, as well as a promiscuous home-wrecker.*

When she woke on Wednesday, Margery's head was thudding, like the noise Tyson's car radio made of a Saturday night, and the waterfall and roaring wind were there too. Yet outside, the trees drooped contentedly in the summer sun. Though the radio from next door barked, only the plasterers were at work, so the noise level was lower than usual.

Getting out of bed was disconcerting, an effort, but Margery managed to creep out to the lavatory. She was standing at the kitchen sink rinsing her bloomers when she thought she heard Walter's thongs come clicking down her passage. She turned and there he was, his suit over one arm and supermarket bag with some tools and a bunch of carnations in it over the other. 'Is it Sunday?' she asked.

'Wednesday,' Walter said and kissed her cheek. He hung his suit on the door, put his toolbox in the bathroom and the carnations in a jar of water.

'How are you, Walter dear?'

'One thousand and four days,' he said, rubbing his hands together. 'Job's right.'

'You look lovely, son.'

'Yep-see-dep-see.' Walter was wearing brand-new football shorts. He'd been shaved so close that his cheeks appeared varnished, and he'd been trimmed—hair, sideburns, eyebrows, nose and ears, throat, neck and shoulders. The kitchen filled with fumes—Old Spice.

'You've been to the barber,' Margery said, wringing the water out of her undies. She draped them over the tap and then lifted her breakfast dishes from the sink and left them to drain.

'And I never looked better.' In the bathroom he plugged his electric power drill into the outlet and revved it at the ceiling, bouncing on his toes. 'Got a date. With Anita.' He did a little to-fro on his toes. 'We're going to the pictures.'

Margery reached for the kitchen table and lowered herself cautiously onto the chair, keeping her eye on the windowsill for balance. Walter checked his forelock in the bathroom mirror. Satisfied, he straightened his left leg and pulled the hem of his shorts.

'What are you going to see?'

*'Pirates of the Caribbean,'* he said, and did a little duck and weave.

'My favourite film is—'

*'Mrs. Miniver,* I know, but Anita picked Pirates *of the Caribbean,'* Walter said, unpacking more tools from his bag, being very important. 'I'm meeting her here first.' He measured Margery's arm with a tape measure. 'Anita Potter is the best home help and carer you'll ever have. The kind of girl a bloke could marry.'

'"Caution is the eldest child of wisdom", Walter dear.'

Walter went back to the bathroom, humming as he unscrewed the handrails over the bath.

'At least she can make tea,' Margery said, glancing at her shining crystal cabinet and her gleaming doorknobs, 'though she's yet to show an interest in polishing.' She levered herself to her feet, flicked the kettle on then took a very long time to get two cups and saucers safely to the table.

Walter pointed at Margery with his electric drill. 'I'm going to replace the shower rose, install a hand-held one for you.'

'Thank you, dear.' Margery asked him how the food safety hygiene course was going.

'S for Smart Walter,' he said and winked as he wrenched the old shower rose off the pipe. Unfortunately, some residual water plopped out and dislodged his sculpted, careful forelock. He downed tools, whipped a small comb out of his shorts and resurrected his hair, carefully scraping as much as he could over his bald patch. He attached a rose on a pliable metal hose to the pipe and screwed the rose holder next to the taps. Then he changed the taps in Margery's kitchen. 'There you go,' he said, proudly.

'I won't have to use the shifting spanner to turn them now, will I?' Margery asked.

Anita came down the passage, singing, 'Anyone home?'

Walter put his finger to his lips, *sshhh,* and winked at Margery.

She arrived in the kitchen wearing shorts—very short—and a singlet cut off at her midriff. Walter was far too captivated by the fact that she was probably only wearing three (possibly two) items of clothing, plus her thongs, to notice that behind her was a brown-skinned little girl with a mass of wild, black, cork-screw hair. Anita put her bag on the kitchen table next to the teacups and said, 'How was the funeral?'

'Bail up, your money or your life,' Walter said from behind her, aiming the power drill and the shifting spanner at her like two six- shooters.

'Aren't you a wag,' she said and drew the little girl out from behind her. 'This is Ruby. Ruby, say hello to Mrs Blandon and Walter.'

'Hello.'

Finally, Walter shifted his gaze from Anita to the little girl, who was dressed in blue tights and a red, webbed T-shirt. 'Hello, Supergirl.'

'I'm Spider*man*,' Ruby said.

'Have you got a dolly at home?' Margery asked.

Ruby said, very patiently, 'No, Mrs Blandon. Spiderman doesn't have dolls.'

Anita opened a soy milk carob drink for Ruby and she sat up at the table next to Margery sucking through a straw. Margery was captivated by Ruby's curls, waving at her like kelp in a sea swell. She put one hand over one eye, but it didn't help—the walls still sagged, the floor still rose and fell, and the curls still spiralled.

Ruby told Margery matter-of-factly that she had a web that was fail-safe and eight eyes and that they were going to see *Pirates of the Caribbean.*

Margery mentioned she'd always admired Walter Pidgeon. 'He was very dependable, a good provider and a considerate husband. Loyal.' Since Walter was in the second bedroom changing into his suit, Margery told Anita, 'Walter's always been very loyal and dependable.'

'How do you get wrinkles?'

'Ruby!' Anita said and put her finger to her lips.

'You get them as you get older,' Margery said. 'For free.'

'You're just like a real grandma.'

'I am a real grandma.'

'My grandma drinks beer and smokes cigarettes.'

'There's nothing wrong with that,' said Anita.

'No,' she said, 'I know, but she hasn't got blue curls and sensible shoes like this old lady.' Then she crawled onto Margery's knee and Anita reminded her that Mrs Blandon had a sore shin, so Ruby asked how she'd fallen over.

Margery wrapped her arms around Ruby and gently explained how she got her shiners, so Ruby told her that her grandmother had fallen off her stilettos and broken her hip.

'That's a shame,' Margery said, but Anita quickly assured them Nanna was alright and would be coming out of rehabilitation soon.

Ruby poked her drinking straw through one of Margery's curls, 'We use to live with my Grandma but she had to move out because she set the flat alight.'

'Shush, Ruby,' Anita said.

'She got her own flat then, but she has to move out because she's set it alight twice and everyone else in the flats hates her now.'

'Nan's got lots of other friends,' Anita scolded.

'They're all dead.'

'Right. That's enough about Nanna.'

She cupped her sticky little hand over Margery's ear and said, 'Is your invisible friend here?'

'Mind your business!' Anita snapped, but Margery just said,

'She's here,' and tapped her heart.

Walter appeared, resplendent in his purple suit, and as he'd anticipated, the three girls in the kitchen looked up at him posing in the doorway, back-lit by the open front door, his purple silhouette fringed in rays of sparkling daylight.

'Oh, my,' Margery said proudly, so Walter fiddled with his gold boxing glove cufflinks.

Ruby said, 'Your suit's too small.'

'*Tsk,*' Anita said to her daughter, and Margery said, 'Walter's going to renovate my bathroom, all by himself.'

Walter said, 'I'll explain what I'm doing, Anita,' and headed for the bathroom.

'Tell me on the way,' Anita said, scooping up Ruby. 'Come on, Spiderman and Superman. Let's go see Jack Sparrow.'

As soon as Anita's loud car was out of sight, Margery shuffled back inside, sat down on the end of the bed in the spare room and sorted through the frames, threads, crewel needles and fabric in her sewing box. When she had a good-sized frame and suitable Aida cloth, she flipped through her frail, yellow pattern books until she found what she wanted. A pattern for a dolly.

# ROOM 4321

At the time, there were things I didn't pick up on, but I see them now, as I sit here going over things. I've made myself another cup of tea, and I ate the complimentary biscuits. They're tough. Cheap. They mean well here, but they skimp. Most people these days seem to be well-intentioned on the surface ... like that bloke called Ray, Anita's flatmate, whom I suspect has a shady past, like Anita. She said to me, 'I've organised a man called Ray to come around to install a modern telephone. It'll be free!'

Walter said, 'Consider it a gift from the tax payers and share-holders of the nation in partnership with our magnificent Prime Minister.' He said the job would be right and that Ray sounded like a top bloke.

Ray didn't look like a top bloke. In fact, I got a fright when he turned up the next day. For a start he was black from head to toe. Black tracksuit, some sort of Maori or Hawaiian or some-thing, and he was completely bald, the shiniest scalp you've ever seen with a helix tattooed on it. When he turned, it was like his skull whorled and lifted. He handed me a big box from the telephone shop and said he'd put the phone wire out through the side window. I explained I'd lost the key to the lock, but Ray didn't need the key. It was very evident that he had a substantial amount of agility and ability. He got that window unlocked with just a small piece of wire, and he climbed up onto the roof like a baby monkey, just used the wheelie bin and the drainpipe. When I made him a cup of tea—and here's the biggest surprise—it was also evident he possessed very nice table manners. He took the food to his mouth, not his mouth to the food, used his serviette and placed his knife and fork on his plate while he chewed ... with his mouth closed. The only issue I really had was that he dunked his Scotch Finger, but he did it in a very considerate way.

'If you want to know about people, watch them eat.' That's what Dad said the night Lance first came to tea. I taught my children table manners but Lance always sawed his food with his elbows out, gesticulated with his knife and leaned over his plate.

I said, 'You gave me a fright at first, Ray,' and he said, 'You look a bit of a fright yourself. How'd you get your shiners?'

I explained about the fall at the letterbox, and the one in the bath, and the other one at the telephone table, and the motorcycle incident.

'Met your new neighbours yet?'

'As a matter of fact, yes, I have met them.'

'Their alarms gone off yet?'

'Twice,' I said. The very night before, Wednesday night, I was telling Ray, the place lit up like cracker night. Then there were bells and wailing horns and sirens and flashing lights. Gave me a terrific fright! Then Tyson and his mates were running from the place, scattering left right and centre, dropping tools and boxes of things all over the front street. A security van arrived, rushing up the street with its lights flashing. Of course, Tyson and his mates were nowhere to be seen by then, but Kevin would have told them what happened because he was there, in the middle of the street, with a torch and his phone. The workmen didn't seem to be inconvenienced the next day. As sure as I'm alive, there they were again at six o'clock that morning, as usual, the whole army of immigrant men grinding, banging and hammering away.

Ray said he was familiar with Tony and his work. Anyrate, he screwed smoke detectors all over the house, and then he set about installing my phone. 'The old one's an antique,' he said. 'Worth a few quid.' Then he implanted the telephone numbers from my address book into the telephone. Phones remember things these days, Cecily, they've got a little TV screen on them that tells you who's ringing. It's all done by a thing called electric technologics. Mind you, most of the numbers in my address book are crossed out now. Really, I've only got Walter's and Judith's numbers left. Shirley as well, though I think she moved up to Queensland a long time ago, well before Lance died. It just seems wrong to cross her out when she could be still alive, somewhere. As you know, the rest of them—Clarry, Willy and Terrence—are dead ... from the drink, actually, if I'm absolutely honest with myself.

'Play that piano, do you, Mrs Blandon?'

'No, Raymond,' I said and explained that the louts from across the road threw rocks on my roof whenever I played. Mind you, it used to give me great pleasure to do scales at seven o'clock in the morning when Mrs Bist was at church after they'd kept me awake all night with their music going *boom boom boom* over and over. 'They're a nuisance, those boys,' I said, and I told him how they burned my fence to cook toast, how they stole my water and often ran an extension cord from the outlet where the sleep-out was to their place.

Ray said, 'I think you'll find your new neighbour, Tony, will sort them out, Mrs Blandon.'

And he did.

He was right, that Ray. That very night Tyson's house was raided, and it turns out it was Tony. Revenge, apparently, because Tyson tried to break into his cellar. Dreadful noises came out of Tyson's, though it was all over fairly quickly. Kevin's light went on and, not long after, I saw the police and then the ambulance come. The ambulance carried two of them off. I'm pretty sure one of them was Tyson.

Bonita was there first thing the next morning. I told her it sounded like someone was torturing cows in the middle of the night.

'What did you see, Mrs B? Was it Tony?'

'I really can't say,' I said. 'But you can always ask Kevin,' and so she went straight to his place.

I must say at this point, Cecily, that if what I heard at Mrs Parsons' wake was true, if Bonita Jarvis bet her house—the house her father built by hand—on Walter's last fight, well, no one asked her to. She did it on her own, and if Tyson's upset about it, there's no need to take it out on me by burning my fence. But he won't be doing that anymore.

I hardly heard a peep out of those boys after Tony raided their house that night.

I'm not sure Ray was very happy when he left my house that afternoon. It took him a long time to put the new wires in, and at one stage he was crawling around under the house. I could hear him swearing. I mentioned Lance had the telephone put on in about 1955.

'No bloody kiddin',' he said, but he found about fifteen old teaspoons that went missing years and years ago, and a green shoe I'd lost in 1948. It was still brand-new.

'You didn't find a cat?' I said. Pat's cat from across the road came over and died under our house. It stank for weeks.

'No dead cats,' he said and handed me dozens and dozens of buckled and dusty packets of Sudafed tablets. They were all empty. I wasn't sure what to make of them. 'Where were they?'

'Shoved down the gap between the verandah and the house. With the teaspoons.'

That was where the boys' bunk was. Walter was on the top bunk.

'You used to be able to crack these old tablets in half,' he said, 'get the amphetamines out in one tiny pill, but the pharmacists got smart and changed how they made them, if you know what I mean.'

I didn't. And I never found out. Walter said there was no point knowing things that didn't matter anymore.

It turned out to be a marvellous thing, that new telephone. The first phone call I got showed 'Private Caller' on the little screen. It was Julien from the green environment society, so I've just sent off the last cheque to save the whales. They're on their own now. But when the new phone rang that night, I didn't even have to get out of bed. I just reached over and picked up the handset from my bedside table. I looked at the little screen, pushed the 'talk' button and said, 'Hello, Judith.'

She hung up.

This was the time everything was starting to come together, Cecily, and you'll understand why I'm here.

I have no trouble remembering that Sunday because I felt very unwell, again, when I woke up, and also because of the copulaters. You know, Dad visited me here once when I was first married, and he was pleased when we went to the park to talk. 'Look, Margie,' he said, 'a place to sit where it's nice.' But he was appalled when he noticed the pub opposite, and that pub *has* ruined a lot of lives, not least of all mine, and as you know it ended Lance's life. *Boom*, just like that. Truth is stranger than fiction. That's a fact. But the pub has been entertaining, and you do learn how the other half lives.

Anyrate, that Saturday night when I looked out my bedroom window and saw the copulaters on my verandah I thought they were people wrestling, but then I recognised it was a white bottom, bobbing away. I saw who it was. It was that Russell from number two twenty-three, the chap who hit us on the motorbike and caused Mrs Parsons' death. He wasn't with the same lass, though.

As I say, I felt unwell around that time, but I usually felt better by lunchtime. In my mind I was resigned to the fact that I'd developed septicaemia of the shin, but it wasn't septicaemia. It was Judith. I'll admit that putting the tablets into my dosette back to front *could* have been a genuine mistake, I suppose. Goodness knows I've made one or two in my life ... so it seems.

Anyrate, I made myself get out of bed and get on with things because you've got to be stoic, and it was Sunday. On my way out to greet Walter I saw the used condom draped over my geranium, so I got the tongs and moved it before Walter came. Then down the street he came, thongs clicking, the biggest grin on his face you've ever seen.

'One thousand and eight days,' he said. 'And I've never been better.'

'You're a good boy.'

He kissed me at the gate and I put the frozen chook in the freezer for next week. That done, I turned the potatoes and pumpkin, and then he set the table and I turned the peas on. 'Did you enjoy the pictures, Walter?'

'Top job,' he said and winked at me.

'Did you ask her out again?'

'I don't want to overwhelm her.' He turned the page on his newspaper and said earnestly, 'Patience gets us to the object, hurry speeds us to ruin.' That was a proverb I embroidered and stuck to the wall above the boys' bunk.

By that time I'd accepted Anita, feeling that she couldn't help being born the way she was, especially having a mother like hers, and she seemed marginally better than some of those card tarts with their matted beehives and revealing outfits that followed Walter about.

I asked if the Boyles were coming that Sunday and Walter stopped buttering his bread, 'You do not have to go to a home. Understand?'

'Don't point with your knife, Walter.'

'Understand?'

'I understand. I do not have to go to a home. Thank you, Walter.'

'The job will be right. Anita's the best carer you've ever had.'

I believed he was on my side at the time. And he was, but for his own reasons.

Walter and I did the crossword, then Walter made the gravy and we said how sad it was without Mrs Parsons. Just as we sat down to eat, the Boyles arrived.

It turned out to be another dreadful Sunday. For one thing,

Kevin broke his ankle. At the time I felt Judith had spilled the fat so that I would slip on it. All I'd done was tell her she looked awful, because she did. Her rash was all up and down her arms and behind her knees, and she looked as withered as a Christmas balloon in June.

Kevin was only in hospital for a night, but a fall down those steps would have killed me.

When Judith started to cry, Barry said, 'Judith hasn't been herself lately, have you, old girl?'

'I'm not old.'

Pud muttered, 'You're almost fifty.'

Barry patted his weeping wife's shoulder. 'Don't get so upset. I'll buy you some pearls.'

'That's not the point,' Judith sobbed. 'I don't know why I even care, no one else ever did.'

Margery said, again, 'I want you to have the watch, Judith. It's yours anyway,' but her daughter was working up to something, she could tell, she was organising the words in her mind, battling to bring them to her lips, speak them through her tears, and then she finally blurted, 'I feel ... that you never really cared.'

Pud rolled her eyes. 'You should never have started that counsellor's course, Mum,' but Judith took a cross-stitched tea towel from the cupboard knob—*A tidy house is a tidy mind*—and stood in front of her mother, preparing, to recite the rest of the words she'd rehearsed. 'You cared about cross-stitch! Affection, connection and bonding begins at birth and must be present from the first moment.'

'You were in the humidicrib and I was unwell and—'

'Parenting practices, particularly low levels of warmth and affection, poor supervision and monitoring are strongly related to issues to do with self-esteem, criminal behaviour and lack of success in relationships.'

Margery put her cutlery down and clutched the table. She focussed on the windowsill, which seemed to be tipping sideways.

Pud said, 'Look, Mum, so Gran wasn't a perfect parent—'

'If you tell me I'm a not a loving, caring mother, DeeAndra, you may as well tear my heart from my chest right now and smash it into a million pieces on the ground—'

'Despite what Gran did or didn't do, you're an *excellent* mother, okay? Just look at me, I'm perfect, aren't I? Gran can't fix anything now. You're fifty. Get over it!'

Everyone remained still except Margery, who put one hand over her eye and shepherded some peas to the lip of her plate.

Judith gazed, open-mouthed at her daughter. Then she closed her mouth, blew her nose on the tea towel, threw it in the bin and plopped down in Mrs Parsons' chair.

Margery pushed her glass of sherry across the table to her daughter, and Walter started eating again. Pud got her grandmother another glass and Barry plonked the sherry bottle in front of her, saying, 'I, for one, am very glad Judith's said what she needed to say, and so now, Marge, you might feel a little more well-disposed towards your daughter and her wishes.' He rubbed his hands together, 'See, there's a vacant room at the retirement village, ready and waiting for you anytime you want over the next day or so. Beautiful room, air-conditioned, heated in winter. Got your own window, nice and secure, *safe.*' Margery remained focussed on shepherding peas onto her fork, so Barry pointed towards the almost-complete new home next door. 'Did you notice, Wally, that they've installed a very, very sophisticated security system?' He whistled and shook his head, 'Computerised. Surveillance cameras, alarms, intercom, sensor lights ... The area obviously requires a superior level of protection, *but,* we could provide that protection for your mother in our elderage facility.'

Pud said, 'You don't have to go to that retirement place, Gran.'

'She can't manage here on her own,' Judith said calmly, taking a roast potato from her mother's plate. 'It's clearly dangerous.'

'She's alright,' Pud said, refilling their sherry glasses.

Judith gestured at her mother's multicoloured, bloated face and said with a mouthful of potato, 'Call that alright?'

Margery hid her leg under the table.

'If her shin gets infected she will need a skin graft,' Walter declared, repeating Anita's wise words with great authority. 'And you're the one that's not alright, Judif.'

Judith turned on him. 'How would you know, Wally? You've been off in a *Wal-terior* universe ever since you were lying in the hospital with a dent in your skull and your eyes fixed and staring and the machine going *beep-beep-beep*. In fact, *nothing's* been alright for years.' She snatched one of Walter's roast potatoes. He put his spoonful of peas and gravy down next to his plate— *Calm like a canvas, Walter. Calm like an empty venue*—and said evenly, 'Anita says she can stay here and get services free from the council.'

'That's just plain irresponsible.' Judith got up, grabbed the baking dish and headed outside with it, picking the hard, oven-baked remnants of chicken and vegetables from the base of it.

Margery said she needed the dripping for next week, but Judith was already outside, pouring the fat down the gully trap.

Walter yelled, 'That'll block the drain and it's unhygienic,' but she just came back in licking her fingers and dumped the roasting dish into the sink.

Then Barry reached to take a roast spud from Walter's plate, and Walter stabbed him with his knife.

Barry squealed, grabbing his hand, blood oozing between his fingers. Pud rolled her eyes and went to get the first-aid kit from the bathroom, and then Kevin appeared in the kitchen with Fifi in his arms. 'Saw your car, Judith. How did the meeting with the new partners go?'

'They're not partners yet,' Pud said, sticking a bandaid to her father's hand.

Judith tore a strip of chicken from the carcass and shoved it in her mouth. 'Marge has to go, Walter, for the good of everyone. I can't keep ringing and calling in day after day to make sure she's not lying dead, or sick from a leg infection.' She grabbed Margery's leg and held it up. 'See? She should be in a hospital.'

Kevin said, 'You'll get septicaemia, Mrs B. It'll go to your heart and kill you.' Judith dropped her mother's leg and Margery bit her lip, her hand on her heart, the pain shooting up her leg.

Barry put his hand on Kevin's shoulder. 'Found out any more about Mrs Parsons' house?'

'We think her son will get it.'

Judith said, 'I reckon he'd be dead by now. He was taken away well before Marge got here,' and Walter said he seemed to remember hearing that there was something wrong with him, but Kevin said, 'It was *her,* it was Mrs Parsons. They took him away from her.'

'Think what you like about my neighbour,' Margery said, 'but when all is said and done, Mrs Parsons was respectable.'

Kevin stepped towards Margery, 'There was something wrong, though. Bonita Jarvis said her mother told her there definitely was a *Mr* Parsons, that he owned the house she lived in, then he was gone and so was the baby.'

'Gossip,' Margery said, but Pudding said, 'No, Gran, there's evidence,' and that's when Kevin, Judith and Barry decided they'd go next door to see the clothes in the drawer, and that's when Kevin slipped on the fat dripping all down the back steps. The sound was shocking, *bang bang bang* then *crack,* like someone snapped an enormous raw carrot. Fifi yelped and lay stunned where she landed, and Kevin bayed like a wounded mule, which brought the neighbours out. Miriana put her head over the fence and called, 'Ohmygawd, ohmygawdwhatishappenink?' and all the Ahmeds came out of their house to peer across the fence tops.

'Looks like it's broken,' Barry said. 'Better phone the ambulance, Pud,' and he continued towards Mrs Parsons' house, but it was locked and the key wasn't hanging behind the door.

Pudding looked at Kevin's skewed ankle, which was starting to look like jellied plums, and said, 'That's disgusting.' Then she turned on her mother, 'You spilled the fat, Sajida.'

'It was an accident,' Judith sighed.

Walter put a packet of frozen peas on Kevin's ankle, and Kevin started crying, 'I was training for the Great Victorian Bike Ride along the Great Ocean Road.'

Margery said, 'You can still see it on the telly.'

Later, when the sun had all but set, and knowing Kevin was unconscious in hospital, when the smell of burning satay chicken and char-grilled lean beef hung thick over the Brunswick barbecues, when the bins were overflowing with empty boutique beer and wine bottles, and dip containers rolled across the deserted park, Margery struggled, like an ant wading through detergent, across to Pat's. With her secateurs she decapitated the stabbing roses hanging from the arch over the gate and fought her way to Pat's precious Barronne Prévost rose bush, drooping and bountiful in the middle of the unkempt front lawn. She cut a dozen or so soft, fat blooms, gently up-ending them into a supermarket bag, and when the bag was bulging with perfumed stems, she made her way cautiously back across the narrow street.

# ROOM 4321

Everyone's gone home and left their lights on. There are lights on all over the place, for as far as I can see. A complete waste of electricity, but this bed, I must say, is very comfortable. The sheets are tight across my toes but it's very nice to lie in. When I was sick, it was, I found, better to sit up rather than lie down, and as the day wore on I felt better. The roaring in my head ceased.

I'm unaware of what exactly happened but Anita dropped in on her way to Mrs Razic's. I remember I was at home in Ascot Vale—at least, I dreamed I was. Mother was at the stove wearing that apron with the poodles, and there was the thud of Dad's bag on the back porch, so Shirley, Terrence, Clarry and Willy ran through the kitchen to meet him, and then there was the smell of steam and coal dust from Dad's wool suit, and you were there. It's hard to explain, but it was like the *feeling* of *being* there, of having you there alive and complete. That's how I'd best describe the sensation—complete. My instincts were alive, I could *feel* you, see you sitting there smiling at me, alive, and you said, 'Oh, sister, end my aching heart,' and I reached out for you. Such happiness! I was pleased and eager to go with you, be with you, and my soul cried and my heart turned over in my chest and I ached with the deepest longing, and I actually touched you, *felt* you, except it wasn't you. It was that ruddy Anita.

At this point I'll state truthfully that Anita did save my life, and I know I should be grateful she discovered that the tablets in the dosette were wrong that day, but that said, she was only doing her job. As I say, I'd come to terms with the fact that the shin septicaemia was making its way to my heart. So what was the point of doing anything about the other problem ... that Judith was trying to kill me?

It was a shame about Kevin's ankle, but he doesn't know how lucky he was. He could have been killed the very next Saturday. If Kevin had been able to drive to see Pat the next Saturday, we might have been killed, but Florence had moved in by then and we took the car out shopping. So it was us who had the accident, and it was, I believed, because Judith sabotaged the brakes.

In the end, that accident with Tony's red car turned out to be a fortuitous thing.

I'm beginning to see now that sometimes the worst things happen for the best. Like Lance and his floozy. Of course now I know Pat was right about Lance having an affair, but there's not much point telling her she was right since, as I've mentioned, she's got beer soup for brains now. Poor old Pat. After Lance and Bill died we gradually became friendly again. Not because we became widows together, but because I had a car, and she reminded me that despite our stand-off over the Public Scalping Incident followed by her revenge—'Your husband's having an affair'—that in the middle of it she was the one who came straight to tell me about that last fight. 'Sit down, Margery,' she said, and I did because I knew whatever had brought her all the way to my kitchen table must have been worth it, and then she went on to describe what happened, how the whole pub went dead quiet for fifteen minutes when he fell. Everyone saw it, except me.

I hated the fact that it was Pat who told me about Walter's fall, but she did come straightaway because she didn't want me to hear it on the wireless, and she wasn't gloating. She was weeping. 'It's a tragedy,' she kept saying. 'A tragedy.' As if I needed to be told. Well, naturally, for years after that, my main concern was Walter, but in hindsight I see now that the fall affected everyone.

Judith and Barry had just got married, actually. Morris was around a lot more in those successful times as well, and Lance was seeing the result of all that talk about making his boys 'into something'. Lance and Morris were heroes at that smelly pub, even Judith had friends at the time. We were all so proud. People in the neighbourhood actually stopped to speak to me. Even the pub people waved. They'd never talk but I know now that was because they were all holding a big, fat secret from me. At first Walter's success was the best thing that ever happened to everyone, I suppose the *only* thing that ever really happened. And the whole street—the whole of Brunswick, in fact—was joyous when he won the championship, but I know now some people, like Bonita Jarvis, lost an awful lot on that last fight.

The party was over.

Mind you, the Jarvis family were notorious scattergoods.

It's taken nearly forty years for Walter to get back to normal. Way back when it first happened, Lance only visited him once in the hospital, but he wasn't comfortable with all the tubes going in and out of Walter, then they told Lance he couldn't smoke in the ward, so he didn't come back. I stayed by his bed, urging him on, talking into his dear ear, directly into his poor bruised brain, while they kept him alive with the machine.

Sad they never had those machines for you. You could have been here now, and I wouldn't be sitting here thinking about throwing myself off the balcony, that's for sure.

When Pat said Walter was in hospital, I thought of you, Cecily. It all came back. So this time I stayed. I wasn't going to leave Walter.

To think that Mrs Parsons endured all that terrible pain as well. All those years I thought she was just reading, but she was pining, sitting there with a glass shard in her heart. Upset it, and it'll kill you.

Such a waste.

I suppose you could say we both lived lives according to circumstance, rather than to spite circumstance.

And I've ended up here, fleeing from my daughter and my husband's mistress ... and it seems it's all my fault. *Our* fault.

Pat once said, 'You gotta live life, Marge. You don't want to lie there in your grave all those centuries thinking about what you should have done, eh?'

Truth is, I never really did care.

Fate leads the willing, and drags along the reluctant.

I'm also aghast to say, Cecily, that at this point it very much looks as if Judith has a point, and, that said, I suppose if I do throw myself off the balcony she'll say, 'See, Barry? I told you she never cared about us!'

It's never occurred to me that there was anything wrong with my little family, but as I sit here in this room …

You could say that, in hindsight, the signs were all there.

They were never apparent, though.

Well, alright then, I just never saw them.

But I always did the right thing, was always pleasant and helpful, kept the children away from danger, taught them not to gollop their food, to use their manners … Lance generally clipped them over the ears if they squabbled or told lies.

But he was the biggest liar of everyone.

It was the next Sunday that the truth started to come out.

# DAY 30

Margery's screen door was snibbed, but when Anita reached through the torn flyscreen to turn the handle, the door did not give. It was shut tight. Through the window she could see Margery's empty bed and immediately pictured her spread like a fish fillet along the bottom of her big old bath, bleeding from the head, dead.

The gate at the side of the house was also jammed shut, so she eyed the window locks again, conscious of the painters next door, mindful of her probationary terms. The need to smoke a cigarette seeped up through her fingertips, her lungs clawed towards her mouth, her tastebuds stood up. She glanced down into her basket, but she patted the patch on her arm; 'Disneyland,' she said. She nudged Margery's front window with the heels of her hands, and the ancient lock, resting in rotted wood, gave and rose far enough for Anita to shove her basket through. She dived in after it before the window suddenly fell and paint, like dandruff, sprinkled onto the verandah.

Margery was snoring in her tapestry world, snug in her wise words and copied pictures, surrounded by fragments of the world as others saw it. Her cheeks drooped and her partial denture clung to her dry bottom lip. Succulent bunches of white Barronne Prévost roses in old preserving jars dotted the surfaces and the air was thick with their heady scent. Her hands lay idle in her lap, along with her cross-stitch frame—the outline of a golliwog, its hair like a sea anemone. From the little transistor radio on her imitation teak table, Frank Ifield sang, '*I remember you, you're the one who made my dreams come true, a few kisses ago ... I remember too the distant bells and the stars that fell, like the rain out of the blue ooh-ooh-ooh-hoo-hoo-hoo.*'

'Mrs Blandon? Margery Louise Blandon, are you there?' She

would not rouse. Anita took Margery's pulse. It was weak, urgent and her pallor was ashen, her breathing shallow and rapid. Anita started to feel panic rising, saw herself back at court answering a charge of neglect, failure of duty of care, murder ... But then Margery reached out and touched her, her eyes fluttering, so Anita took her hand. 'Come on, Mrs Blandon, wakey-wakey.' Margery coughed, sucked in her denture and squeezed Anita's hand.

'How do you feel?' Anita said.

Initially Margery looked pleased, beatific, but then she focussed on the cushion on the couch opposite and snapped, 'Obviously, I'm perfectly alright. Why are you here?'

'You're the colour of porridge. I'll put the kettle on, then I'll phone the ambulance.'

'I'm not going anywhere, especially to hospital! Judith will take me straight to a home if I go there.'

While the kettle boiled Anita checked the house, came back through with Margery's pot, which she obviously hadn't emptied for days. The colour rose in Margery's pasty cheeks and she called out, 'I'll do that,' but Anita emptied it, left it soaking in the laundry trough then poured Margery a cup of tea. Margery reached for it, missed the handle, knocked the cup and spilled tea, then lifted it and missed her mouth. 'I need new glasses,' she said, tea dripping over the rim. When the cup connected with her lips she drank greedily. 'Walter tells me the pirate film was very good.'

'Swashbuckling. Walter and Ruby loved it.' Anita looked around the kitchen. The Sunday dishes were still in the sink. 'Would you like a poached egg on toast, Mrs Blandon?'

Margery focussed on the cushion on the couch again. 'Only if it's not too much trouble, dear.'

Anita put a slice of toast on, filled a saucepan with water to boil and reached for the eggs, and that's when she noticed the dosette in the ice-cream container on top of the fridge. 'Who put these tablets in?'

'Judith.'

Anita sighed and gave Margery the lunchtime blood pressure and heart tablets she needed, rather than the diuretics she'd been taking incorrectly. 'You'll feel better soon, Mrs Blandon.'

While Margery chewed slowly on her egg on toast, Anita reorganised the tablets in the dosette according to breakfast, lunch and dinner rather than breakfast tablets at dinnertime and dinnertime tablets at breakfast.

'You been feeling sleepy during the day? Wobbly?'

'A bit.'

'Too wobbly to get yourself something to eat.'

'I don't get that hungry,' Margery said, scraping the plate clean with the crust of her toast.

Anita poured her another good, strong cup of tea and put two slices of buttered bread and jam on her saucer. 'You'll come good in a little while,' she said, patting Margery's shoulder. 'You've been taking your diuretics at night, no wonder you're tired.'

'It's obvious my own daughter's trying to kill me.'

'I'm sure she didn't mix up your tablets on purpose, and you don't have to go to a home.'

Suddenly, Margery said, 'I should never have gone to that dance.'

Anita put her hand on Margery's head. 'What dance was this, Mrs Blandon?'

'You know the one—Moonee Ponds Town Hall, 1945. Wall to wall returned soldiers. I thought I was in love when I got married. Well, you do, don't you, on your wedding day?'

'I guess some people do.'

'In my day, a marriage was a marriage. It would have been a disgrace if I'd got divorced, as bad as adultery. What about your husband?'

'Some of them were good,' she said.

'You know, they say you marry your father, but that's not true.'

'Apparently my father was just one of the blokes at the bar.'

'Well, that explains a lot,' Margery said.

Anita continued to gaze out into the backyard but said pointedly, 'I hear Mrs Parsons had a baby?'

'Yes, but Mrs Parsons wasn't the sort to have a baby out of wedlock.'

'Ever meet *Mr* Parsons?'

'Mrs Parsons was a person who just wouldn't have had a baby out of wedlock.'

'But if she had, you wouldn't hold it against her, would you?'

'Not Mrs Parsons, no.'

'I'm told her son was brought up by his father and grandmother.'

'Who told you that?'

'Mrs Razic. My grandmother brought me up, but my mother came every Wednesday for tea,' Anita said.

'You must have felt abandoned,' Margery said.

She stopped dressing Margery's wound and looked out to the backyard again. 'I could blame my mother for my shortcomings, but that'd make me an even lesser person than I am now. She did what she needed to do to survive and be happy. I knew I was the apple of her eye.'

'Have I got septicaemia?'

'No.' Anita put Margery's shoes back on and tied her laces.

'I'll survive then.'

'You'd survive better with a flatmate.'

'I've got Cecily,' Margery said.

'Cecily?'

'My twin sister, Cecily.'

Anita looked down the hall.

Margery put her hand on her heart and said, 'She lives here.'

'Oh,' Anita said, 'your invisible friend!' She bound Margery's wound and took her cup of tea to the back step, where she sat, dug into her work basket and found nail clippers. As she talked she trimmed Margery's toenails. 'Tragedy can have a ripple effect; it can go on down through all the generations.'

'That's true. My mother was never the same after Cecily died.'

'You looked like her, that must have been a comfort ... or maybe it wasn't.'

Margery shrugged. 'Anyrate, my father suggested it was best for me to move on. So I did.' She looked around the room. 'Just now, she was here, it felt like she was right here, beside me.'

'Mothers aren't perfect.'

'No, but she should never have died alone in a nursing home. I know that for sure now.' She sipped her tea. 'It's a shameful thing but my own dear, respectable, broken mother died alone in the middle of the night in a nursing home because I was stuck here with Haemorrhoid Face and two toddlers. What I should have done was gone to my own mother, taken her back home to Brisbane Street, stayed there to care for her and her sons, my brothers, lost and drunken sods that they were by then. Drink got them, too, if the truth be known. I'm not sure why, it was just the way things turned out, but it had started well. We were all so united ... Shirley was long gone by the time Mum got sick—she was the first to go after me—but our mother would have died herself rather than send anyone to die alone in the middle of the night in a ward full of snoring strangers and a male nurse reading a novel behind a glass wall.'

Anita stood up, patted the Nicorette patch on her arm and said, 'You're absolutely right, Mrs Blandon. Absolutely right. I'm going to see my mother this very minute.'

As she was leaving, Anita glanced around the room and said, 'I'll see you two girls next time.'

# ROOM 4321

The clock radio says it's 2.45 am. I'll give it another hour or so. The young things are still about at this time. I've watched Tyson and his mates leave the house at midnight to go out, so I'll just wait a bit until everyone gets to where they're going.

You know, if Anita hadn't roused me that Monday, my life could possibly have ended, and it would have passed without me knowing the painful truth of it. Part of me wants to blame Lance entirely for everything. Just think, alive for eighteen years and then, *bang!* Committed to a bloke for eternity. 'I s'pose it's about time we made it formal,' he said one day, and I just went along with it since it was what you did, move on with things. After a while it was like living with a boarder. He got up at the same time every morning and went to work, then after work he went to the boxing club, then to the pub, home for tea and back to the pub again, unless he fell asleep in his chair. On Saturday he went to the boxing club, the football and afterwards to the pub, and on Sunday it was sitting about reading the papers and yelling at the kids until pub time. It was supposed to be closed of a Sunday, but they'd all slip in through the back door. All I had to do was provide his meals and make his bed.

I wanted to go home, but that one time my father came here—I was just pregnant at the time—we sat in the park and he said, 'I have to agree with your mother that a marriage is a marriage, and you've got to do what's fair to everyone. Your mother's been through a lot.'

And so now I understand the truth of it; whenever Mother looked at me I suppose her heart broke a little bit more.

Perhaps if you hadn't died, or if you hadn't been born ...

My marriage was a mistake, but it was also a solution, and now, as I come to terms with that, my heart is breaking all over again.

You get used to things, and as the years passed I got used to Lance throbbing away beside me. It was a bit like sleeping with a warm dill pickle. He snored, too, but the kids quite liked him. Eventually he moved to the second bedroom with his possessions—his oxygen bottle, ashtray, cigarettes, the form guide and his transistor radio.

Pat and Bill had quite a good marriage. Similar interests, you see: the pub, horse racing, Legacy.

Lance once said, 'I thought I might find a pearl if I cracked your shell, Margery, but all I found was the oyster.'

It's apparent to me now that Lance was actually *very* happy. He had the best of both worlds.

This brings me to Florence. The very evening Anita saved me from a drug-induced death at my daughter's hands, I telephoned Walter, who I still trusted, fool that I am. I told him that he was a good boy and I'd be thinking about him studying for his food hygiene test. He was busy and couldn't talk at the time, but he said to me, 'I'll see you tomorrow, Mumsy We've got a surprise for you.'
A surprise.

I thought it was going to be Morris. I thought to myself, *I bet it's Morris,* and I even remember lying in bed that night saying to you, 'Morris is coming home and I can make amends.'
Then I decided Walter was marrying Anita, and I got up to check if the silverfish had got to the dress I wore to Judith's wedding.
It was one of the most sleepless nights I've ever had.

Some surprise it turned out to be. My poor old heart. Just thinking about it makes it pump hot blood around my body, trying to find a cool spot.

# DAY 31

There was a vacancy at a nursing home on the fringes of Melbourne, but Anita felt it was too far away, too foreign to her mother's sense of normalcy, and the place was bleak, dwelling in shadows cast by the walls of a damp valley for most of the day. She suspected the managers, Theo and his wife, Amanda, turned the heating on only during visiting hours—and she had seen the food. It was diabolical. But the hospital wanted Florence out, they needed her bed. There was nowhere she could go, and it was actually Margery's very own words, true words, that confirmed Anita's suspicions: to put her mother in that particular nursing home was to condemn her to hell, even if it was temporary.

From the back seat, Florence said, 'I've been here before,'

'You used to live just down the road opposite the park.'

'Of course I did,' Florence said, unconvinced. At times she struggled to align what she thought might be memories of actual events and what she suspected she'd liked to have done. Most of the time she remembered who Anita was, but there were times it took a while to place her, though she always knew Anita was special. And she loved Anita's little girl, or was it a boy? A pirate, anyway.

They helped her out of the car and led her towards Margery's house. 'Who lives here?'

'You may not have actually met Margery,' Anita said. 'She's not the drinking type.'

Ruby looked at her grandmother and said, 'She wears sensible shoes.'

'Fancy,' said Florence, wondering why they'd be bringing her to see someone who wore sensible shoes. She paused again at the front gate, or at least where the gate should have been, but its frame was lying on the worn square of grass, bordered by several trampled geraniums. The palings and rails from the fence were also missing, though the posts remained. The number on the letterbox was two fifty-three. The narrow workers' cottage with the peeling paint and slumped verandah looked familiar, as if she'd passed it before, and she felt she'd seen the busted cane divan on the verandah, though she was certain she'd never been inside. When she got to the lounge room, she stopped in her tracks. The small room, made oppressive by the walls and floor crowded with cross-stitchings—framed proverbs and scenic landscapes, floral placemats, antimacassars and doilies—was stuffy and conventional. An old lady's house. The trophies shining brilliantly in the crystal cabinet disoriented her, and she was wary of the old lady with the bruised face folded into the deep, vinyl chair. Then she noticed the photos on top of the television and her heart started to thud in her delicate, smoker's chest. Her legs started to buckle, and she reached to steady herself on the nearest chair—Lance's chair.

Margery didn't know who Florence was, though she recognised her, or rather, recognised her type. Pat's type.

Anita introduced the two elderly ladies. 'This is my mother, Florence Potter. And this is Mrs Margery Blandon.'

Florence looked at Margery, one side of her face bruised blue, yellow and black, and said, 'Had a bit of a fall, have ya, love?'

Margery's chin rose, her shoulders straightened and she pointed regally to the sunken couch, 'Do sit down,' but Florence felt her way into Lance's chair.

Anita said, 'I'll put the kettle on.'

Ruby kissed Margery on the cheek and Margery patted her knee, but Ruby declined the offer and went to her grandmother. She put her arm around Florence's shoulder. 'Nan is really called Flossy.'

'I see,' said Margery.

'They're pretty, those roses,' Florence said and nodded at Pat's flower on top of the television. 'Yes,' said Margery. 'Baronne

Prévost. They came from England in 1842.'

'Fancy,' Florence said and crossed her fine legs, drawing Margery's gaze to her open-toed slippers. Florence was a fine-boned woman, slender, like a pencil. Her calves were slim and her feet long and narrow below thin ankles. Her throat was impossibly narrow, her eyes huge blue ellipses above high, firm cheekbones that pressed against her ivory skin. Her hair was thick and white, swept back and tumbling, like Ava Gardner's. She was an old lady who didn't present as an old lady. Florence was what Lance would have called 'a real looker'.

Ruby looked from her grandmother to Margery, then back to her grandmother and back to Margery. She looked directly at Margery and said, 'You've got the most wrinkles.'

'Shh,' said Anita, putting a tray with cups, milk, a strainer and biscuits on the small table between Margery and Lance's chairs. 'See the cushion covers, Floss?' Anita said.

Florence looked around the room at the fussy cloth artwork. 'Like the cross-stitch, do ya, love?'

'I wouldn't do it unless I did, would I?'

Florence lifted the seat of her walking frame, reached into a little basket and drew out an old brussell sprout. She gave it to Ruby and said, 'Pop that in the bin for me willya, love.' She said she hated sprouts but the nurses were writing down what she ate. 'They wouldn't let me out of hospital unless I ate my vegies. I can't stand brussell sprouts.' She looked up at the photograph of the upside down Prime Minister above the kitchen door and said, 'I feel the same way about him too,' and laughed a throaty, well-used laugh.

'He's upside down because your daughter is disrespectful,' Margery said, which shut off Florence's laugh like a tap. In the quiet moment that followed, Ruby ran her hand along Margery's forearm and said, 'Do wrinkles hurt?'

Anita, who was making tea, told Ruby it was impolite to ask too many questions, then Florence looked directly at Margery and said, 'Been in this house a while, haven't ya, love?'

Margery said, 'It appears I won't be here for much longer, but yes, I've lived here since 1948. My children have all left home.'

'You don't say.'

The next ten minutes or so in the lounge room were largely silent, and then Walter appeared in the doorway while Anita was pouring the tea. Ruby jumped up and drew her sword, and Walter said, 'You'll never make me walk the plank!' They had a pretend sword fight and he caught her up in his arms and gave her a tickle, then he reached to give Anita a tickle but she stuck her hand out and said, 'Steady on, big boy,' and they laughed, loudly and nervously. Then Anita introduced Walter to Florence, and he said, 'It's a very, very great pleasure to meet you. Anita's told me a lot about you, and I can see where she gets her good looks.'

Florence said, 'Aw, get away with you,' and blushed.

He followed Anita to the kitchen, and Florence said, 'Seems like a lovely boy, your Walter.'

'He is,' Margery said, though he had failed to kiss her hello, which hurt, like a brick thrown at her chest. Then Florence uncrossed and crossed her legs and said, quite casually, 'Shame that last fight left him a screw short of the full meccano set.'

Margery smarted, opened her mouth to rebuke the rude interloper's accusation, but Walter arrived with his cup for tea, Anita behind him. Florence asked, 'I don't smoke anymore, do I?'

'You gave it up,' Anita said.

Little Ruby shook her head. 'You don't smoke because you set the flats alight.' Anita nudged her, but she flipped up her eye patch and explained to Margery, 'You used to risk your life at Nanna's place.' Florence laughed, and Margery nodded understandingly. It was then that she noticed she still had her slippers on, noted her corn-topped toes poking from the holes Anita had cut in the top of them, and also noted Florence's open-toed, slingback stilettos, her toes, polished the same colour red as Anita's hair. Margery excused herself, got out of her chair with as much grace as her old body would allow and went to change

into her shopping shoes. From her bedroom mirror, a plain and
bruised old lady with a tattered blue perm and a sallow complexion, wearing a practical cotton button-through, gazed back. She
took off her shopping shoes and put on her Sunday shoes. From
the lounge room, she heard Anita ask Florence if she thought
the house was nice.

'It's small,' Florence said, but Anita pointed out that it was
bigger than the flat Florence had lived in.

'This chair's got a bit of a dent in it,' she said. .

'It was my husband's chair. He's been dead for twenty years,'
Margery said, sitting down gracefully and crossing her knees.

'Twenty years, eh?' Florence said, reading the antimacassar
under her arm: *Errors, like straws, upon the surface flow.* Walter
pointed out that his father had the top spot for watching the
telly, and Florence nodded at the photo of Lance and said, 'Was
that taken just after the war?'

'Nineteen forty-five,' Margery said, and Florence pointed out
that he looked like 'a real charmer', so Margery changed the
subject. 'It's been warm, Florence.'

'It's summer. Call me Flossy, love.'

'And you can call me Margery. Not *love.*'

Walter leaned on the mantlepiece and crossed his feet,
rubbed his nose, changed feet, crossed his arms, straightened
his left leg and pulled the hem of his shorts, rubbed his nose
again and blurted, 'Since we're all here, we've been finking that
you and Flossy could be flatmates, Mumsy.'

'Temporarily,' Anita said, and Ruby nodded. 'Just until we
find somewhere else for her.'

'You don't have to go to a home, Mumsy, and it'd be a good,
kind thing to do to let Flossy stay, just until we find somewhere
else.'

Margery placed her teacup gently in its saucer, picked a
thread from her sleeve and picked up one of her many incom-
plete cross-stitches, *Deceit always returns to its ma ...*

Anita said, 'It's just we've got nowhere else to go.'

'They threw her out of the hospital,' Ruby said, 'and there wasn't even a fire,' and Anita's elbow shot out and knocked her pirate hat.

Margery looked at Walter. 'Why can't she live with her daughter?'

In the silence that followed, Anita's mouth opened, closed and opened again, then Ruby said, 'Because if she moves in we'll all get thrown out.'

Walter stepped from one foot to the other, rubbing his nose, saying, 'It's an in-between fing,' and Anita said, 'We're still looking for somewhere but it's hard; we'd appreciate your help.'

Margery said, 'I was under the impression you were helping me. It was all a scheme.'

Walter said, 'Don't be like that, Mumsy,' and tugged the hem of his shorts.

While Margery searched for ideas why she couldn't tolerate a flatmate, Florence kicked her red toenail in the direction of the piano and said, 'How about a tune, love?'

'I only play for certain people,' Margery said, so Anita said, 'Flossy sings.'

'And dances,' Ruby added.

Florence nodded, 'We should go to the Town Hall one Sat-dee night, they have a dance.'

'Be triffic,' Walter said, but his mother looked down the short hall to the bright street beyond the torn screen door.

'People die there,' she said.

'Good way to go,' Flossy said.

As if on cue, the green and pink of Judith's little van slid past, then reversed and braked, and Margery watched her daughter carefully reverse to park neatly against the kerb. The specials that week were Design and Application of Photographic and Remedial Camouflage Make-up.

Florence said, 'That's why I don't want to go to a home—you die there.'

In her car, Judith peeled wedges from a grapefruit, shoved

them into her mouth and chewed, wincing. Walter and Anita talked on, told Margery again it was only temporary, that it would save her from going to a home, the house would be fixed up ...

Judith wiped her mouth and checked her lipstick in the rear-vision mirror, then she got out of her van, pulling her loose top down over her tummy bulge, now flatter, drooping in soft rolls. Her chin, Margery noticed, was again a definite thing on her face.

Anita said, 'You said yourself, Mrs Blandon, that the cruellest thing that ever happened was that your brothers and sister put your mother in a home, that she would have died rather than send someone to that fate.'

Margery flushed with shame, her skin smarting up her neck and across her cheeks. She looked down at her shin, felt it throb under its clear dressing, took a deep breath and said, 'That's blackmail.'

Anita looked crushed, her eyes started to spill tears and she said, 'I'm so, so sorry, Mrs Blandon.'

'You're treacherous, both of you.'

'We're desperate,' Walter said, placing his arm around Anita.

As she stepped over the fallen gate, Judith stopped to shove her grapefruit peel through the slit in Margery's letterbox.

Margery said, 'Here's Judith,' and they went straight into what can only have been a planned strategy, or so Margery thought. Anita went to scrub out the bathroom, Walter sat reading an old newspaper, and Ruby ran to the front door.

'Un-snib the door, please,' Judith said. 'And just whose little girl might you be?'

Walter said, 'Judif!' as if he hadn't seen her for fifteen years, and went to let her in. She walked past him, straight out to the lav. When she eventually came back in, she ignored Anita and Walter and stood in front of her mother. She pointed to the welts of eczema crossing the bridge of her nose, eking down from her hairline. 'This rash is from stress, Marge, and you are giving me the stress. I've had enough. You have to go to the elder-age facility, there's a bed waiting. We've got a piano there, you know.'

'Margie's got a piana, 'avencha, Margie?'

Judith ignored Florence. 'You won't be alone anymore; you'll have company twenty-four hours a day.'

'I'm not alone.'

Judith said, 'You've always been alone.'

'That's not true.'

'You can go every week to the senior citizens' centre, Marge. You can do the planned activity program, like the weekly trivia competition, the musical get-togethers, nostalgia sessions, ball games, craft and cooking at the day centre.'

'I can do that here.'

'You can play cards or go to the dances or the sing-a-longs.'

'Don't want to.'

'What about swimming? You can ease your old bones in the nice, warm spa bath.'

'You wouldn't get me in one of them,' Florence said. 'Everyone over fifty leaks a bit.'

Judith looked at Florence. 'Who are you?'

Florence said, 'You look buggered, love. Have a seat.'

'Do I know you?'

Florence creased her eyebrows together and tried to think, and Margery said, 'This is Florence, my new flatmate.'

'Call me Flossy.'

It seemed the air evaporated from the lounge room. Walter started washing the dishes.

Judith stared at Margery, shifted her weight from one foot to the other. 'Flatmate?'

'So I won't have to go to the home,' Margery said.

'It'll be good for a while,' Anita said. 'Could be just the thing for Margery.'

Judith just nodded and said, 'Well, that's that,' and sat on the couch. 'Fate,' she said, looking across at her wedding photo on top of the television. 'I'll leave it all to fate.' She was a lovely bride, twenty years younger, slim and glowing with happiness.

Barry had hair, and she was nestled in the crook of his arm, his other arm above his head, fist clenched like a winner.

In the backyard, Anita tore off her Nicorette and lit a cigarette. 'I'll give it up next year.'

Ruby asked, 'What about Disneyland?'

'You can see it on the telly, for free.'

A bare bulb hung from the ceiling of the tiny second bedroom, the wardrobe was a half-sized kiddies' cupboard, its doors hanging ajar, the bedside table adequate, but the little room was mean despite the softening taint from the cross-stitch curtains and floor mat, the bedspread, pillow cases ... and the wall hanging: *Deceit always returns to its master.*

At the end of the bed was a large cardboard box filled with wooden embroidery frames, bunches of thread and cloth off-cuts. The corners of Florence's mouth turned down as she studied the thin bed. It was just an abused hammock slung between two bedheads really. 'That bed doesn't even look like it's fit to die in.'

As it happened, it was the place Norma Blandon, Margery's mother-in-law, had taken her final breath. One shuddering, thunderous Saturday night in 1950, with little Walter and Morris tucked up in bed and Lance at the pub, Margery shoved the last of the mashed potato and gravy into the limp, whisker-ringed orifice that was Norma's mouth and settled with her sewing by the gas stove to listen to the radio. While Margery hummed and lightning cracked in the boiling blue-black sky, a vegetable bolus broke from between Norma's gums and her slack cheek and slid to lodge in her trachea. Because she lacked a cough reflex due to an undiagnosed stroke, the old woman's eyes quietly bulged and cried; she turned red, crimson, purple then blue, and, finally, deathly white.

Before she went to bed, Margery switched off her mother-in-law's bedside lamp and noticed she was unusually peaceful, dead to the world, in fact. 'Bother,' she said, sighing. A roll of thunder passed overhead, and the rain stampeded across the roof. Margery pushed out onto her small front verandah, gathering in her dressing gown, and looked down towards the pub, but the storm swelled and her feet turned cold, her slippers made tight and heavy by lashing rain. She stepped into the sleep-out, noted the small mounds under the blankets in the bunks and knew she wouldn't go for help. How could she leave her two small sons huddled in their bunks while a storm pushed and sucked at their thin door and rattled the glass louvres in their window frames?

She slept six hours straight that night, knowing she didn't have to get up in the night to turn her mother-in-law and change sodden bedsheets, and at breakfast she refilled Lance's cup of tea and said, 'When I went in this morning your mother was dead.'

Little Walter, who was seven at the time, said, 'Can we sleep in her room? It's scary in the sleep-out.'

Anita came into the bedroom and looked at her mother, a fixed smile on her face. 'Won't take much to fix it up for you, Floss,' she said cheerfully, and Florence looked about the shabby little room and said shakily, 'I never imagined I'd end up here.'

As Walter was leaving, he looked wistfully at his mother's geranium bush, straightened his leg, pulled the hem of his shorts and said, 'Mumsy, I love Anita, she's easy to be around. Comfortable.'

Margery said, 'Love is like a mutton chop, sometimes cold and sometimes hot.'

'I'd like to marry her,' he said. 'Adopt Ruby.'

'You can have my wedding ring,' she said, 'though I'm not sure where it is.' She then went inside and picked up the cross-stitch basket cover she was sewing for Anita: *Great things are done when men and mountains meet.*

When Anita had pulled up with Florence in the back of her car, Bonita and Tyson were sitting on their couch in the ruined house opposite, watching Tony and Miriana supervise removalists lugging boxes and furniture into their new, almost-complete, architect-designed house. Tyson was still bandaged, nursing the effects of Tony's revenge attack some nights previously.

'That house went up real fast,' Bonita said.

'Tony and his missus are fascist tyrants.'

'I'm not believing what I'm seeing now, and I'm watching it happen,' Bonita said, flicking her ash onto the floor. Across the road, Ruby helped Florence out of the car while Anita carried her possessions—one medium-sized red, blue and white striped bag, a pillow and a sponge bag—into Margery's flaking little cottage.

'What?' Tyson asked, then winced, feeling his bruised ribs and dislocated fingers.

'I could tell you a story,' Bonita said, 'but I won't because secrets kill, and you'd tell Pudding.'

'No I won't, tell me.'

She dragged on her cigarette, exhaled. 'For a start, the skinny one, Flossy, was the most notorious publican west of Sydney Road, just *loved* a party. But she's a pyromaniac. Burned down two houses, as far as I know.'

'Yeah?' Tyson sat bolt upright, winced again, but his pain turned to pleasure picturing Margery's house aflame, the old lady crawling from the boiling inferno, her nose and mouth ringed in soot, her nightie melting and her hair burned on her grilled scalp, while Tony and Miriana banged noiselessly on their translucent windows as their electronic house filled with acrid chemical smoke under a smouldering roof.

'Don't start fantasising,' his mother said.

'No,' Tyson said, 'the Brunswick Bull lost ... the Brunswick Bullshitter.'

'I've told you, it was *me* who bet the house, me who lost the house, alright? It's not Mrs Blandon's fault, just get a life, alright?'

Tyson ignored her, stared over to Margery's house.

Bonita looked at the old, oval-faced, pink-gold watch on her wrist and asked, 'You sure Mrs Parsons threw this out?' though she had seen the initials—R.B.—engraved on the back.

'Yeah!' Tyson lied. 'It was in the bag with the kilt.'

His mother shrugged. Ruth Bist and Mrs Parsons were both gone anyway. 'Gotta go,' she said. 'Tracy's doing my roots.' She ambled up the middle of the street towards the commission flats, a plume of cigarette smoke billowing in the air behind her.

Later, when he saw Florence on the front verandah, a skinny old dear with bright red lips and motley legs, he crossed the road, leaned on the letterbox and lit a cigarette.

'You haven't got a smoke, have ya, love?'

He handed her a cigarette and brand-new box of matches.

# ROOM 4321

You must remember that, at this point, I had an infected shin and the possibility of hospital, and therefore death, ahead of me. My normally respectable appearance was besmirched by black eyes and abrasions, which were no fault of mine, and it had been impossible for me to get a wash, tint and set. My podiatrist had deserted me, I was facing eviction and a future in a home for incontinent lunatics, and I'd been goaded by real estate agents as well as my very own children. Then I found myself between a rock and a very hard place.

Incredibly, worse was to come.

When Judith was standing over me, saying, 'I've had enough,' and Florence was there imploring me with her homeless eyes, and Walter and Anita looking so fraught, well, I looked up and on my wall was a quote from Doctor Woods' desk calendar: *If I am not for myself, who will be for me? If I am not for others, what am I? And if not now, when?* When Mrs Miniver found the weakened enemy soldier in her garden, she remained calm. And when she was in her kitchen getting food for him, and he was, I might add, aiming a gun at her, she remained calm. You could see she even pitied the poor, starving beggar, despite the fact that her husband was out risking his life to fight the Germans somewhere in a sea of enemy submarines at that very moment. In the circumstances, assisting the enemy was the right thing to do. Inevitably, the enemy weakened and fell, and Mrs Miniver, being the type that she was, seized control. Grabbed his gun. Slapped his face ... beat him and won, thus saving herself, and others, from harm. Mrs Miniver did the right thing, and so I said to Judith, 'This is Florence, my new flatmate.'

'Job's right, then,' Walter said, but you could see the blood draining from Judith's face, leaving just her eczema, like dried jam. She just sort of melted onto my couch then, wiped the sweat from her face with one of my cross-stitched cushions, while Florence started a long explanation about how she'd been unwell, and while she was in hospital they put her rent up but she'd spent all her savings on her medical bills and her pension didn't cover what was left of them as well as her rent, so she was forced out of her flat, but Ruby interrupted to explain that that wasn't quite right—Florence actually got kicked out of her flat because even though she'd given up smoking she'd still managed to set it alight because she boiled her egg dry and set the smoke alarms off and other peoples lives were put at risk.

'The department wanted to put her away,' Walter said.

'The ACAT team!' Ruby leapt from the couch to stab the invisible ACAT team with her pirate sword.

Then Anita was in the doorway, a cloth soaked with bleach in her hand. She pinched a strand of hair in her fingers and ran the bleach cloth over it and watched it to see if it turned yellow. Judith used to do the same thing to her fringe as a teenager.

'It'll be good,' Anita said, 'could be just the thing Margery needs.'

'Could be,' Judith said, smiling.

I thought at the time, *Judith's seen the sense of it; she's decided it'd be foolish to put me in a home. At last! She's given up on the whole idea of buying into a nursing home,* then she said, 'But what if Florence wants to make a cup of tea or light the gas heater? She'll have to have matches.'

*No!* I thought. *It suits her! She wants Florence to set the house alight with us in it!*

It's reasonable then to imagine that when we had the so-called 'accident' with Tony's red car my suspicions about the unscrewed brake hose rose because it was Judith who urged us take the car out! 'It's Big Shop week, Marge, and there's two of you—you should go and buy everything you need, have a nice trip out together.'

'To the supermarket?' Florence said, as if Judith had suggested we go to Werribee Sewage Farm for the day. 'There's no need for me to go.'

I remember Judith said, 'You need to split the cost of the groceries.' Then she smiled, 'It's best if you go together.'

It's best if you *go together.*

So the very next day off we went, *together,* and we had the accident.

It just goes to show, even if you do something right you still get punched in the heart.

Judith could easily have sabotaged my car, but I can't be certain. And as I sit here now, it is conceivable to me that perhaps she thought she had good reason to harm me. No mother is perfect, after all.

After the accident I told Walter. I said, 'It was tampered with. Judith's trying to kill me.' He said that couldn't be true, but at the time I thought, *Walter's in on it! He and Anita have planted Florence here to upset me! They're trying to irritate me to death!* It was a reasonable conclusion. As I've told you earlier, those first few days Florence argued with me over everything—the dishes, drying the knives and forks, the toilet paper and the bin-liners—and she also broke my signed photo of the Honourable John Howard! You know, I asked and asked but that Anita never turned that photograph back up the right way. Anyrate, what happened was, Florence went out to the front verandah, left the door wide open behind her and, naturally, it slammed. *Bang, tinkle-tinkle,* and the photo of our Honourable ex-Prime Minister was in a hundred pieces all over my lounge room floor. I rushed out to tell her but she just said, 'Good riddance. He was a mean-spirited old wowser.' Then she looked right at me and said, 'And there's far too many of them around the place.'

I remember picking our distinguished ex-Prime Minister up off the floor and placing him gently on top of the television, but to be honest, at the time I didn't notice Lance was missing. The gap where his photo usually sat didn't actually catch my attention at that precise time.

Then, in the middle of that very night, Florence set the smoke detectors off because she was puffing away in her room! Kevin's light went on, but it was Tony from next door who came in and turned them off with a broom. We still didn't get much sleep though, because when he went back to his house, *his* alarms went off.

But getting back to the story. The argument we had that Thursday, Big Shop day, the day of the accident with Tony's car, started because it was recycling day as well, and my new flatmate failed to get up in time for the recycling truck. So, I knocked on her door and called, 'You have to put your stubbies in the recycling bin.' She didn't answer. I could hear the truck coming, so I knocked again. No response. Mrs Bist's and Mrs Parsons' deaths came to mind, so I opened the door and there she was, flat on her back in bed, dead, just like Lance's mother that stormy night, only Florence is thin, of course. At least I thought she was dead, lying there on her back with her cotton gloves, if you please, folded across her chest, her eyes covered by a sleeping mask like Zorro, and her face smothered in white cream. Why? I wondered. Why bother at her age? I poked her to make sure she really was dead, but she wasn't. She slid her eye mask back and pulled her earplugs out by the tassels, reached over to one of my best teacups on the bedside table and picked her teeth out of it, and that's when I saw the photograph. Lance, *my* husband, on *her* bedside table.

She just flicked the water off her dentures and said, 'I like a man in uniform,' and popped her teeth in.

Still, I didn't suspect a thing. For a start, I'm the first to admit Lance *was* very handsome in his uniform, and he wasn't damaged from the war like some of them who came back, poor things. He only got the oxygen bottle later because of the cigarettes. Pat's Bill from across the road had bad lungs as well, but his was from the brick dust. That's one thing Pat's never expressed gratitude for, the fact that Bill's life ended suddenly and unexpectedly. In fact, she once said to me, 'I hope you're happy now you've killed my husband,' and I said, 'Nonsense, Lance killed him, and anyrate, it's better than suffering through a slow, painful death from brick-dust poisoning.' Mind you, Bill smoked cigarettes as well and they never did establish which one of them struck the match that blew up the pub.

Anyrate, I took Lance's photo, put it back on top of the telly and emptied the stubbies. That afternoon, as I said earlier, off we went—the thieving adulteress and I—to do our Big Shop and Tony ran into us at the corner. Ruined Morris's car entirely. When he looked under the hood, Tony said right away that the little hose had come away from the brake fluid cylinder.

He asked if I had insurance.

'Not that I know of,' I said.

We were alright though. Florence got a bit of a bump on her head, and my nose hit the steering wheel. But it was definitely not my fault. I put my foot on the brake pedal and it went straight to the floor, and the low red sports car came floating along the road towards us like a magic carpet, and then *bang!* There was a crunch and Tony's car stopped dead in the middle of the road, glass sprinkled all over the bitumen, and we ended up in the hedge at the end of the lane.

Frightened the living daylights out of us.

Tony's car was Italian, which made it very, very expensive to fix, but that's his fault. Australian cars are perfectly adequate. After all, if these foreigners want to assimilate they should drive our cars.

Under that black tracksuit of his Tony was like boiling poison, but at the same time he was reluctant to phone the police, so Florence got him to phone Anita.

I appreciated her doing that.

When Anita and Walter got there, Tony said, 'I've got a grand-mother too, but we don't let her out.'

You get that sort of thing in Brunswick, different customs.

He had his finger right in Walter's face, 'Fifty thousand dollars *At least,* Bud. Start saving.'

Walter stayed calm, but his twitching fists have a mind of their own.

'Well,' I said, 'you've left red paint all over my bumper bar.'

Then Tony says to Walter, 'I know you. You were that boxer.'

*Now he'll back off,* I thought, *now that he knows he's got the Middleweight Champion of Victoria to contend with.*

Walter's fists clenched and he shifted his weight, but he just said, 'I know you too.'

'Then you'll know where you stand, eh?' Tony grinned. 'Shame about that last fight.' He wasn't sincere, though. I could tell.

Anyrate, Walter's fists came down then because it turned out he did know about this Tony. Fortunately, Anita was able to stem the flow of blood from Florence's head with a couple of butter-fly bandaids. It looked nastier than it actually was, the blood against her white hair. It wasn't until later, at home, that Anita concerned herself with my nose. My word it hurt, but I'm pleased to say my shin avoided any trauma. 'You got a mouse in your nose,' Walter said. That's a boxing word for a bump.

We were most concerned about Tony, who seemed rather threatening in his manner, but Walter said it was just 'hairy-chested bullshitting'.

But you could tell Anita wasn't convinced. She said she'd have a yarn to Ray, but I'm sure he couldn't lend me fifty thousand dollars. Such a lot of money for a bonnet, a couple of mudguards, a bumper bar and some lights.

'You could pay it off over time,' Florence said, but Anita said that she didn't think I'd live until I was five hundred and seven. You'd think Florence could have offered to help pay since she's the reason I was out driving in the first place.

Walter and Anita examined the little bracket that holds the hose to the brake fluid cylinder. 'Loosened,' Walter said.

Florence said, '*Tsk*,' and shook her head, 'Who woulda done a thing like that?'

Walter said it was old, but I pointed out the obvious: 'Someone good with a nailfile, or with strong fingernails.' From the way they looked at me, I could tell they were concerned too.

'You'll have to stick to the local shop for a while,' Anita said.

It was a shame. Toilet paper was on special that week.

The next day, Friday, I sat down to some cross-stitching. If I do something simple, like arrowhead stitch, it settles my nerves, and if I need to be distracted from something worrying, I do something more complicated, like double-herringbone, which is what I was doing that day. A placemat, one of a set I'd been working on for a couple of years—the six wives of Henry VIII. I was doing Kathryn Howard. Double-herringbone is very hard-wearing.

Florence liked to smoke to settle her nerves, so she sat out on the verandah to harass passers-by. She did very well that day because she looked like she'd had brain surgery with that big bandage around her head. Tyson gave her a packet of cigarettes and some beer. Goodness knows what the Ahmeds think of her. I heard her call out '*Shalom*', but they ignored her. According to Florence, *shalom* means 'hello' in Arab. It was in *Ali Baba and the Forty Thieves,* she claims, but I can't remember it.

Anyrate, I heard a man say, 'You're determined to raze the entire northern suburbs, aren't you?'

Florence said, 'Shit,' and came scurrying down the hall, trailing smoke, her frame going *tweetweetweet*. Hot on her heels was Ray. He had her packet of cigarettes and was crushing them up, one by one, like sawdust. Anita was behind him. You could hardly see her, even though she had on the highest heels I've ever seen. And that so-called skirt she wears is more like a bandage wrapped around her hips. Ruby had her trusty sword in her firm little fist. Ray was all dressed up in a lovely suit. Very well tailored, you could see. Fitted him like a glove. It was black with thin lapels and hugged his muscular legs, and his shirt was very white against his brown complexion. I could almost see my reflection in his polished shoes, and his tattoo whorl gyrated on his shiny scalp as he turned. Diamonds in his ears and on his mirror sunglasses, like Walter's, and he smelt lovely as well. He pointed at Flossy and said, 'Do not smoke, understand?'

'I've apologised,' she said. 'You got a new house, didn't you?'

Anita patted the arm of Ray's lovely suit, and he touched her hand reassuringly. Little Ruby kissed me and went to sit with Florence; she flipped her eye patch to her forehead and took her grandmother's hand. Anita sat on the arm of my chair, rubbing my shoulders, and explained that they'd had a discussion with the man in the red Ferrari and he wants sixty thousand dollars, then no one said anything for quite some time. Thoughts skipped along in my head like elm seeds on a breezy day.

Finally, Anita said, 'Mrs Blandon, you might have to sell your little house,' and there was another long silence, and into that silence came the cheery sound of Walter's thongs flipping up the passage. As ever, Walter arrived and filled the room with his big smile. Then he noticed Anita. 'You're here already!' he said and plonked a commode in the middle of the lounge room. 'There you go, Floss.'

Then he saw Ray.

I said, 'One thousand and thirteen days, Walter.'

Ruby raised her sword for a battle but changed her mind because Walter was captivated by the spectacle that was Ray, standing there glinting like Louis Armstrong in a spotlight.

'Walter,' Anita said, 'this is Ray.'

Ray put out his hand, but all you could see was confusion rushing about all over Walter's face.

Anita explained that Ray had a meeting with Tony, tried to sort things out. She was tense, I remember, but I know why now—like mother, like daughter.

'Ray,' Ray said, but Walter still didn't shake his hand, he just kept looking at Anita and back to Ray and then to little Ruby. 'Ruby tells me you're a good sword-fighter.'

At that moment I understood. Ray was Ruby's father.

Ray didn't blink, didn't show any sign of anything; he was just lovely to Walter, saying, 'I saw you fight. You're a champion, mate. You go to the Brunswick Club sometimes,' and, 'Ruby has told me a lot about you. She talks about you all the time.' Finally, Walter thawed and his manners returned. He shook hands with Ray and the tension eased. Ray unbuttoned his nice suit jacket and went on to explain that he knew Tony, 'as I'm sure you do, Walter,' and said that if I did have to sell, 'there'd be plenty left over to buy a nice unit somewhere.'

'Right,' Walter said, folding his arms in a commanding way. 'A nice little unit, Mumsy.'

All I could do was just sit there. Homeless.

Florence said, 'I'm happy to sleep on Margery's couch.'

Ray bent down to Florence and said loudly, 'Despite what your daughter wants, I'll see to it that you're placed in the safe care of a government institution, one with a sprinkler system.'

Florence just looked at Ruby and said, 'Get me a beer, willya, love?' and Anita passed her one from her handbag.

Ray patted Walter's shoulder. 'It was a Sunday punch, mate,' he said, but Walter was too emotional to speak. His lips went all stiff and he reached to the back pocket of his shorts and got his hanky just as a tear slid out from under his sunglasses and down his cheek.

Poor Walter. I know how he felt, Cecily, his heart torn apart, because I felt the same.

But what could I do?

It's not as if Tony looks like he needs sixty thousand dollars. I mean, you help people in need, but he doesn't look like he needs anything at all.

It's just a car. He could buy another one.

And of course Walter's wedding plans were over, finished.

I said, 'Who's going to tell Judith?'

'I will,' Ray said, and Walter handed him the little bracket thing that holds the brake tube in the little bottle of brake fluid in the engine.

Ray started by saying, 'There's been an accident, everyone's perfectly alright, but are you aware of any car insurance policy?' Everyone in the lounge could hear Judith wailing through the phone.

It didn't take them long to get to my house at all. Remarkably, Judith seemed quite calm, *resigned,* but Barry looked a bit like the first schoolboy in the polio vaccination line. Judith denied unscrewing the brake lead. 'Why would I do that?' she said to me. 'Why would I send you out in an uninsured car to have an accident? If I wanted you dead, I may as well get an insurance payout rather than spend my life paying for your damage and other people's hospital bills!'

She said I was demented and paranoid, said I shouldn't be driving. 'Your potential to ruin lives is all too bloody evident,' she said, but I wasn't sure about Judith, given the business with the mice and little Sylvia.

At the end of the day there was nothing anyone could do. It looked very much like I'd have to sell my house, pay for Tony's repairs and buy a flat somewhere.

Of course, then they realised the house wasn't insured either, so I had to follow Florence wherever she went and search for cigarettes and matches before bed. We were sitting out on the verandah that night; the sounds of the pub band were floating down the street, some sort of country and western song, I think it was, and she was tapping her foot, humming along.

'People don't sing properly these days,' I said.

'No,' she agreed. 'There should be more dancing.'

'I doubt you've ever taken life seriously, have you?'

She said, 'The worms don't care what you've done.'

At this stage I can see she had a point. I always tried to do the right thing, but most of my life I've felt like a bit of a nuisance. It could have been the effects of the trauma of the second accident, but when she said that, well, I went to bed knowing something hadn't been quite right.

Given the truth that came out the next day, it seems I had everything completely wrong. But it got worse. I've seen some colourful Saturday nights in my time, but that night was something else, and it turned out to be the end of my troubles with Tony. In fact, everything was all over by Sunday night.

# DAY 35

When Tony and Miriana moved into 251 Gold Street, Margery actually enjoyed the increase in traffic around her little house, so she was lying back that Saturday night, keeping an eye on the crowd heading to the pub but watching with great interest the people who came and went from her new neighbours. The place still swarmed with workers, but it was at lock-up stage, and Tony and Miriana were there a lot, not always for the whole night, but they were there. The visitors were mostly men, the type Margery thought swarthy. Some stayed a long time, some only a few minutes. Some used the front door, others used the side door. Miriana always answered the front door, Tony always answered the side door. Then the people from the pub started to visit, stepping furtively past Margery's house to knock on Tony's side door, emerging a few minutes later to return discreetly to the pub. From the car across the street, Tyson and his mates watched with envy, sitting low in their rotting car, music subdued to a dense throb. Margery had not seen Kevin's light go on, but a police car cruised slowly past, twice.

Florence was fast asleep in the dingy little second bedroom flat on her back, anointed with cold cream, her gloved hands folded across her abdomen, her lips, unsupported by her dentures, moving in and out with each breath—*pftt, pftt, pftt*. In her dreamy sleep she was leaving her bar, following a long, lean, lovesome man with a shock of thick, black hair through the rooms of her pub. He turned and looked down at her and she followed his warm, glad eyes to the stairs, her small hand in his firm grasp, and up they went, step by lovely soft step, towards the rooms upstairs. She felt a yearning, a willing ardour, and the insouciant expression on the tall, prepossessing man who loved her—and he *did* love her—gave way to a longing that sucked the breath from her, a lust in the pit of her being, and as she lay back in luxurious fog she felt the weight of him on her, felt herself give, swoon, then the windows started to jitter and the earth itself shuddered and the room filled with a booming noise, and she woke up.

Margery saw the figures flit past her window, like bats, and then the banging started, metal on wood, and the yelling. Soon sirens blared, screaming down the street, circles red and blue flashing across the fences and hedges, and there was the sound of windows breaking and a loud thudding in the sky above. Margery thought of war, films showing exploding trenches, crushing tanks, aeroplanes and the whistle of falling bombs.

Across the hall, Florence thought of explosions too and sat up in bed. 'The pub!' She turned the lamp on, decided there was a blackout, then remembered her eye mask. She wasn't upstairs in her pub at all. She tidied her hair with her fingers, pulled out her earplugs, popped her teeth in and then Margery was standing beside her bed, saying, 'Quick, Flossy, get out—the house is on fire!'

But in the passage it was clear the house wasn't on fire. Margery stood clutching a box containing photos and Walter's boxing scrapbook. Florence held tightly to Margery, cuddling her, her eyes wide. Around them, spotlights strobed.

'Is it the pub?'

'An earthquake,' Margery declared, just as two police cars screamed to a halt outside. They shuffled together to Margery's window, leaned into the strobing lights and were illuminated— two old ladies in nighties blasted by red and blue flashes. Then the helicopter rose and flew away and the thudding receded, but the wailing started. Someone was injured. It was Miriana, she was being bundled into an ambulance. 'The baby!' they said.

Florence moved towards the kitchen, steadying herself against the wall. 'Sherry?'

'I think I will,' Margery said.

While they sipped their second glass, Florence added sherry to the shared essentials shopping list.

Sunday morning, Florence sat languidly on the busted cane divan on the front verandah, smoking, while Margery lingered at
the letterbox. Eventually, the girl with the striped hair swung
her tall black box of a car into the kerb, a phone to her ear and
a cigarette between her fingers on the steering wheel.

As she passed, Margery said, 'A happy event in the night, I
gather?' and Florence added, 'Everything went according to
plan, I hope?'

The girl glanced at the two old ladies in their dressing gowns,
one battered with smashed glasses, the other wearing red stilettos and a bandage on her head. 'Youse are fucked,' she said and
went inside.

'Something's gone wrong with the baby,' Margery said, and
Florence agreed, 'Born spastic,' though Margery suspected it was
worse, given the visitor's grave expression. As the morning wore
on the two wise old women decided their conclusion was very
likely—more and more people arrived, sombre-looking people,
'ethnics in dark cars with flash wheels' Margery called them.

She went inside to stuff the chook and put it in the oven, then
did the vegetables and made Walter's caramel sinker. She picked
up her cross-stitch but soon abandoned it to join Florence on the
front verandah again. Strangers passed, pausing to stare at Tony's
place. Florence persuaded cigarettes from them, Tyson gave her
a can of beer. Margery saw people she hadn't seen in years: Mrs
Blunderstone leaning from her front gate, old Victor balancing
on walking sticks, Mrs Devlin in her wheelchair, and Mrs Razic,
also with a bandage on her head, clinging to her gatepost, all of
them craning down towards Tony's place.

'Everyone's aged so much,' Margery said.

Eventually, Walter appeared at the end of the street.

'Here he comes,' Margery called, and Florence joined her at the gate to wait.

'Walter's got a food hygiene examination coming up. He's under a lot of pressure, and on top of everything your daughter's broken his heart,' she said tersely. Florence shrugged and said, 'That's life for you.'

But Walter wasn't gloomy at all. He was grinning, a frozen chook under one arm and a supermarket bag in the other. 'One thousand and fifteen days,' he said.

'You're a strong boy,' Margery said, presenting her cheek for a kiss. 'How are you, son?'

'Never better.' Then he gave Florence a kiss.

They prepared the meal, as usual. Florence had a light beer, and Walter poured Margery a sherry, got a glacé cherry from the Christmas pudding fruit mix and dropped it in.

'You're very cheerful, Walter dear.'

'Mumsy,' he said and pinched her cheek, 'I've got some good news for youse two.'

He retrieved a newspaper from the supermarket bag and unfolded it. The headlines read, in bolder-than-necessary black ink: DRUG FACTORY RAID.

'That,' said Walter very importantly, 'is Tony.'

'From the red car?'

'From next door?'

'Yep-see-dep-see.'

'Well, that'll teach him,' Florence said.

Walter said, 'And now, girls, you can tear up that panelbeater's quote and throw it away.'

So they did. They tore it up and threw it in the bin. Florence had a second beer and Margery had another sherry. 'I could play a few tunes,' she said, and Walter found his Elvis Presley songbook.

When Barry pulled up outside, the Boyles could hear the piano amplified down the short passage and out into the street. Tyson's house was quiet, and as they walked towards Margery's lounge room the air swelled with full-bodied notes. In the small room, the soft acoustics provided by the thread wisdoms on every surface made the room thick with piano sounds. While Margery played, her fingers firm on the notes and her broken glasses fixed on the sheet music, Walter sang, eyes closed, one knee forward and his hand high, like a frozen discus thrower, the other hand holding an invisible microphone to his lips. He was a man immersed in song, brilliantly lit by a battery of spotlights, the back-up singers throwing his solid notes to the top of the stadium, the trumpets and drums thunderously loud, the audience roaring.

Judith stopped in the doorway, made her husband and daughter stay still. 'Watch,' she said, and they watched Walter sing, *This time, Lord, you gave me a mountain, a mountain you know I'llllll neverrrrr climb. It isn't just a hill any longer, you gave me a mountain this time.'*

They stayed still when the words came to an end and the notes still floated from the piano, even while Margery's hands were in her lap. Florence wiped her eyes and Walter started to come out of his dream. Judith and Pud clapped like true, mad fans, Barry smiling and applauding as well.

'Wally,' Judith said, shaking her head, 'that was absolutely fantastic.'

Pud threw her arms around her uncle. 'God, Wally, you're so cool.'

'Did you see the papers?'

'Yes!' cried Judith, smiling from ear to ear. She looked better than she had in weeks. 'Sing us another one, Wally, and we'll set the table.'

Margery shuffled through her sheet music and Judith set the table to the sound of 'In the Ghetto'. Then they crowded around the little table for Sunday lunch, reliving the events of the night before, piecing the story together. Judith tucked into a plate of roast chicken breast and peas, Barry and Pudding made do with roast potatoes and pumpkin, and Walter was pouring sherries all round when the daylight streaming in from the open front door faded and the floorboards started groaning, as if an elephant was making its way up the passage.

They turned, and there were Faye and Joye, hovering in the doorway, two morbidly obese women with small-sized heads and marquee-sized frocks, wheezing like hot-air balloons.

Florence tried to escape but was wedged in by hungry Blandons and her wheelie frame.

Judith glanced up. 'Hi, Aunty Faye, Aunty Joye, sorry about Uncle Ron,' then went back to her meal.

Faye said, 'I'm not sorry,' and tried to get through the door, but there wasn't really enough room in the kitchen. Pud stared pityingly at her huge great-aunts, their faces receded, their chins like small shells on large, pink sand dunes.

'We come for the will,' Faye said.

Walter was shepherding the last of his peas onto his spoon with his knife by now. The others were staring at them, speechless, and Florence was holding the newspaper high, pretending to read.

Faye started, 'We're moving back here,' and Joye finished, 'Ron's sister, Eunice, wants our house.'

Judith continued eating but Barry suddenly became alert. Margery dropped her knife and fork and Walter laughed.

'This'll be good,' Pudding said.

Lance's sisters were laying claim to the house, said Lance actually owned only one third of it. And now they wanted their share, their two thirds. They wanted to move back home, because Eunice—Faye's sister-in-law—was moving back to Ron's house ... where the sisters had lived for sixty years.

'You can't move back here,' Judith said, stealing Margery's last roast potato. 'There's not enough room for you.'

'There certainly isn't,' Pudding muttered.

Margery said, 'Judith gets the pearls, Morris gets the car and Walter gets the piano; the house is to go to the blood children of Lance Morris Blandon's loins.'

Joye said, 'This house was never Lance's to give away.'

'Anyway,' Faye said, 'Judith told us Marge was going into a home.'

'Well, she's not going into a home,' Judith said. 'She's got a flatmate now. And home help from the council, so they can both stay here until they die.'

Walter and Margery looked at her, thinking they'd misheard. Joye started to look around for somewhere to sit, but if she sat on the couch then she wouldn't be able to see into the kitchen, and there was nothing else she could fit into.

Faye held the doorjamb for support, 'Marge doesn't deserve this place anyway,' and raised her arm to wipe her sweaty forehead, like a walrus lifting a flipper.

'She does,' Judith said. 'She came here as a bride and worked to contribute.'

'And,' Walter said, 'she was a good wife and mother.'

Joye said, 'A good wife, my arse,' and Faye nodded. Under her, a floorboard cracked. 'Starved of love, Lance was.'

At this point, Florence dropped her newspaper. 'He bloody was not!'

# PART FOUR

*'Fall seven times, get up eight.'*

Japanese proverb

# ROOM 4321

If you think it's appalling to have someone else lay claim to your home, then stay tuned, Cecily. It gets much, much worse. If this was a novel the readers would probably say, 'I knew that. I guessed it was her.' But I hadn't. I hadn't even suspected.

Life is cruel. I feel like such a dill. Pat was right, and I suppose everyone in the whole suburb knew, except me.

Walter said he 'never knew a fing', though he confessed later that he got suspicious when he learned Florence had worked at the local pub. 'I knew the old man had a sort down there,' he said, 'but I never met her because I didn't condone their type of friendship.'

They recognised her when she spoke. 'Flossy!' Faye said. 'Haven't seen you since Lance's funeral.'

Yes, that's right. My husband had a mistress, for almost fifty years it turns out, and she was living in my second bedroom. I had provided the strumpet with refuge.

I said to her, 'Did you know who I was?' and she said, 'Got suspicious when we pulled up outside, was pretty convinced when we came through the gate, and knew for sure when I saw the photo of Lance on top of the telly. I'd only ever seen you peering out through the front window.'

On her way to and from Pat's, I suppose.

They were just looking at me, Faye and Joye, spite and glee in their eyes, though Joye was slowly bending under her own weight.

Now this is where it gets *really* interesting. Yes, that's right, you guessed it—Anita arrived, sailed down the passage calling, 'Yoo-hoo!' and then her red bushy head appeared between the shoulders of the fat sisters, bright as a button, 'Seen the papers?', but then her face dropped. 'What?'

Little Ruby squeezed between the zeppelins, gave me a big hug and climbed onto Flossy's lap. She looked at Faye and Joye and said, 'Gee, you're big.'

Then Ray came in, happy as Larry. 'Truth is stranger than fiction, isn't it, Wally?' he said to Walter, then he cottoned on that something was up. 'What?'

So there we all were.

The Blandon family and what was left of our roast chicken and vegies, and the fat sisters, sweating because there was nowhere to rest their bulk. In the middle, a small pirate with a cardboard sword. All of us, just there in that small house, everyone looking at each other, the pennies dropping one by one.

I'm just grateful Mrs Parsons missed the whole messy thing.

At least five heartbeats passed. I looked at Florence, but she just lifted her skinny little alcoholic's foot up and looked at her red stiletto—the ones I'd found in the letterbox.

'Florence,' said Judith tentatively, 'was Dad's mistress?'

'Cool,' Pud said, looking at Flossy with interest for the first time. 'This is *so*, like, not ordinary.'

Ray was just looking from one of us to the other, as if we were shells and there was a pea under one of us, and Anita said, 'I swear I didn't know, Mrs Blandon,' and started scraping about in her bag for a cigarette.

Sometimes I would look at Lance and actually feel a small warmth flow through me. He was very good-looking, and he was charming, funny and *manly,* but something was missing. We just never sort of clicked, I suppose. I'd have liked someone who wanted more from life than the pub, beer and boxing. But you don't know anything when you're eighteen. Such a waste.

As we all know now, I knew nothing.

I needed my wits about me, and I didn't have my wits about me.
Ever, it seems.

Judith said, 'God, Marge. How could you *not* know our father
was having an affair?'

Here it comes, Cecily, it's getting worse, because then Pudding
said, 'You don't really think Charmaine's just Dad's secretary, do
you?'

Judith just looked at her so-called husband, his dyed comb-
over looped and held fast behind his ear, his Buy and Sell
cufflinks glowing. She just sighed, stabbed her potato with her
fork and chewed it like it was made of tyre rubber. I was proud
of her at that moment, she was very contained, so I followed her
example and I am pleased to say I remained dignified throughout the whole sordid business.

Faye started to laugh, so Judith said, 'Well, you can't talk, your
husband left you,' and Joye said, 'We didn't mind, did we Faye-
zee-way-zee, love?'

Barry shook his head and just went to stare sadly at the back
step.

About then Joye started to stagger. She tottered back and
landed on the couch, and then poor old Faye was defeated by her
own bulk and staggered back as well, landing on the couch, the
air swooshing out from under her. A leg of the couch snapped
and shot out from under it, skimming across the lino and knocking the television. On my heart, I swear, the picture of Lance
toppled and crashed onto the floor, the glass scattering.

Makes me smile to remember it.

I should never have gone to that dance. I should never have left
the front gate of my childhood home. Ever.

Now, here's the very worst bit.

Suddenly Pud had a thought. She stood up straight and looked at Anita and said, 'Who's *your* father?'

There was another silence, and all eyes went to Flossy the Floozy.

Anita said, 'Well, Floss? *Mum*? Who is my father? Tell me, who should I call *Dad*?'

Well, Cecily, you've never seen anything like it in all your life. Florence was white as kidney fat, the newspaper in her hand shaking.

Walter took his sunglasses off and rubbed his eyes with the heels of his hands. Ray picked up the picture of Lance in his army uniform among the splintered glass, and all I can say is I was relieved my bladder was empty because, Cecily, I felt very loose, very lost for control of my vital functions. As I was looking at Anita, I saw him. I saw Lance in her. Her eyes were her mother's, ice-blue, but it was the way her face was put together, and her thick hair, and that square nose. The Blandon nose. Pudding saw it too, and she said, 'Cool, Gran, you've got another daughter,' and I heard poor Walter grunt, as if someone had trodden on his stomach. He got up and walked in a little circle, ran his hand through his hair, dislodging his careful curl.

Ray put his hand in Ruby's curls and said, 'And that also means you've got another grand-daughter.'

Little Ruby clapped her little brown hands together, 'Goody,' and jumped up and down, rattling the plates in the kitchen bureau.

Walter made a sort of strangled sob then, his face in his hands, leaning on the fridge.

Anita said, somewhat thinly, 'I'm happy to have a lovely new stepmother.'

Judith said, 'You got any bastard kids out there, Barry?' and Pud got excited. 'Have I got secret brothers and sisters?'

'You can move out, Barry,' Judith said. 'DeeAndra and I will keep the house.'

'Fine,' Barry said, still staring at the back step.

At this point I stood up, unbuttoned my frock at the front, unfastened the pearls looped around my waist and handed them to Judith.

'Goody,' she said, and Pud took off all Judith's gold chains straightaway and fastened the pearls in place for her—two strands of lustrous, cream Mikimotos around her neck. She had on a plain, boat-necked blouse, and I must say the pearls did look lovely on her.

'They look fantastic, Mum,' Pud said. 'Barry'll buy her matching earrings for her fiftieth, won't you, Dad?'

'Anything. I'll do anything.'

Pud said, 'I've just got to tell Tyson, he'll love this,' and ran down the hall, her strappy high heels banging on the lino. With that, Ray, Ruby and Anita came and stood with me and Florence and Walter, and looked through the kitchen door to Faye and Joye on the couch, like beached whales. Then Judith came and stood with us. 'Looks like you've got yourselves a flatmate called Eunice.'

Faye said, 'You'll be hearing from us,' and she and Joye hauled themselves up and waded off down the hall, the air behind them brightening as they went.

Anita made sweet black tea, and that's when I thought of it. I should have guessed. The tea. Lance had obviously taught Florence how to make tea properly, the way I made it.

Lance always said, 'If nothing else, Margery, you make the best pot of tea in Australia.'

I thought it was a compliment at the time, but now I see everything in an entirely new slant.

Anita said, 'I remember Lance, he sat at the end of the bar leaning against the wall.'

'The top spot,' Florence said, 'opposite the front door, between the telly and the pool table on the way to the men's toilet.'

'He gave me fifty cents once,' Anita said and started crying. Ruby patted her thigh.

'It was a long time ago,' Ray said.

I said, 'It doesn't feel like it at this precise moment, thank you, Raymond.'

Of course, the problem of what to do with Florence remained.

'She can go and stay with Walter,' I said. 'He deserves her. Betrayer.'

'I never betrayed you, Mumsy. I swear to God, I never knew, and I've got my hygiene test Tuesday.' Walter skipped, changing feet, so that one of the plates in my bureau fell and smashed. That crockery set was a wedding gift from my parents.

'Flossy the Floozy,' I said, and she shot back, quick as a flash, 'How do you think I feel? Having to live with the woman who wouldn't let Lance go so we could get married.'

'He never asked to be let go.'

'He did.'

'Didn't.'

'Did too.'

'He didn't. I'd have let him go.'

That shut her up for a second.

'He never asked?' she said.

'Never.'

'Lying bastard.'

It was too much for Walter. He went out to the clothesline, walked round and round.

The entire truth about everything came out that afternoon. Goodness gracious me … the things I didn't know …

In the end, they all slunk off and left us there, together.

Ruby gave us both a kiss and said she'd like to keep us both. 'And,' she said, 'it'd be convenient for me if you stayed in the same house.'

Anita wanted to take Florence with her, but Ray wouldn't have any of it. 'They may as well settle things now,' he said.

I settled it alright. 'Pack your bags.'

'All right then,' she sniffed, 'be like that.' Then she squeaked out the front.

I shut the door and left her there on the verandah, sitting on her wheelie frame with her blue and white striped bag and her fine legs crossed and her red painted nails, smoking a cigarette, like a tart at a bus stop.

I was gutted. Again. A little red devil in my heart was sawing big chunks off and chucking them down into my stomach.

The cross-stitched work basket cover—*Great things are done when men and mountains meet*—I used for a lavatory lid cover. It fitted, with a bit of adjusting. I'd just got back inside and sat down to watch the travel show with the sherry bottle when there was a knock at the door. I tried to ignore it. I knew it was something to do with *her,* but it just kept on and on, so in the end I opened it up and there they were—that blasted constable and Flossy the Floozy, holding a stubby of beer.

'Lock her up. She's an adulteress.'

'Adultery isn't a crime in this country, Mrs Blandon.'

It was a heartless thing to say if ever I heard one and, as you now see, the constable was a conspirator as well.

I said, 'She's a pyromaniac as well,' just as Tyson walked past. Flossy called out, 'Give us another cigarette, willya, love?'

I told Constable Morgan to go away and closed the door, but he simply showed up at my back door. 'I don't suppose I could trouble you for a cup of tea. Please?'

'You're an irritating, heartless boy.'

'I know. How are you going with the powdered milk?'

I ignored him because I knew that he could see the packet sitting on the table and the little jug I mixed it in. Mostly for Florence, actually.

'My grandmother did very well on it,' he said.

'You told me that. I'm not stupid, you know.'

He popped the kettle on and got out the cups and saucers. 'I can see that, so that's why I want you to settle your differences with your friend.'

'She's not my ruddy friend! She's a thief—she stole my husband.'

'Mrs Blandon, your husband died twenty years ago when his leaky oxygen cylinder blew up in the pub, triggering an explosion of the gas heating system.'

'They have a forty-year-old daughter together and she's still alive! And I'm sheltering the adulteress who gave birth to her! I'm living with the mother of my husband's illegitimate child, *and,* if it wasn't for that very same floozy, Walter wouldn't have got all upset and punched my son, Morris, and he wouldn't have gone to Thailand and ended up in jail!'

'Think of what the consequences could have been for other people's sons if he'd got to Australia with his suitcase,' he said. 'Some people don't care that they ruin other people's lives.'

That was a blow. I had used those very words to accuse someone else of ruining Morris's life by planting drugs in his suitcase.

I also understood then that the entire world, everyone on earth, knew truths that I had chosen not to believe.

'Have you got a hankie?' the constable said.

'Of course I have,' I said, reaching up into my sleeve.

He ran his hand over his short hair. 'Whatever the problem was way back then, at *this* point we can't just leave her sitting on the street. She's frail and thin enough to blow away.'

'There's no wind.'

He had no comeback for that, by gum, so while he was regrouping I complained about the helicopter. 'The police helicopter woke me last night, and it flies over at least three times a day—it's very, very loud. Louder than the others.'

'I'll mention it next time I see the "copter copper",' he said.

While I had him where I wanted him I also complained about Tyson stealing my water. You could see the look of weariness wash over his face. He said it was a matter for the water police, and went and got the floozy. He sat her at the table with me and left. Just left us there.

'Thanks, love,' said Flossy, and she sipped the tea he'd left on the table.

The rage I felt for that woman at that moment, sitting there, calmly drinking my tea ... I could taste the hate for everyone boiling up into my mouth, like acid reflux after too much cabbage.

As he closed the front door I said, 'If I throw myself from a tall building, sonny, you can tell my family they drove me to it.'

# DAY 37

I got up the next morning, it was Monday, and my muscles were sore from being tense. I didn't sleep a wink, just lay awake all night stewing, going over things, remembering. All those Christmas parties they had at the pub. All those years, and I never knew. All that time.

It's galling, that's what it is, like my first breakfast at Gold Street when Joye gave me a bowl of cereal and I found mouse droppings peeping at me from the milk and sugar at the bottom. They cackled about that for two years. 'Can't take a joke, eh?' they said.

What I imagined my life to have been was totally shattered, but things just seemed to go on as usual for everyone else.

Anita breezed in the next day as if everything was normal.

At this point I'll confess something, Cecily. You see, as it turns out, Morris has an illegitimate child. Of course, everyone knew except me. That Sunday afternoon I acquired an illegitimate stepdaughter and two illegitimate grandchildren. Pud said it doesn't make any difference these days if you're illegitimate, and Walter showed me a photo from his wallet of the poor child. Ruby was pleased to have another 'cousin', and Pud was pleased to have Ruby as a cousin too. On the back of the photo Morris has written 'May, 2004', so May could be her name, but then it could also be her date of birth. In the photo she's about five, though you can't tell with Asian-looking kiddies. She's a pretty little thing. In the past I've been accused of being racist, so I actually put the photo on the telly next to Pud—how can I be racist?

Anyrate, my new stepdaughter arrived and took over again, stripped the beds, put the washing machine on, swept and mopped the floor and sat on the back step while she had a smoke and a cup of tea. So I gave her a piece of my mind. I told her she was getting paid for sitting on a step doing nothing. 'It's my day off,' she said. 'I'm just here to stop the bloodshed.'

I reminded her that she was illegitimate because her mother committed adultery with my husband.

'Fair statement,' she said. 'But I'm not to blame, am I?'

Then Florence piped up and said, 'You never wanted Lance anyway. I've made mistakes, but I don't pretend to be perfect. And anyway, we haven't got a home because your husband blew it up.'

She swears it was Lance, not Bill, who struck the match.

Anita sighed and went to my linen press. She dug out a set of sheets at the bottom of the pile. 'Not those ones,' I said.

Lance's words rang in my ears; 'I thought I'd find a pearl when I cracked your shell, Margery, but all I found was the oyster.'

You see, when I found out I was pregnant with Judith, I packed and got ready to leave again, but he came home from the pub earlier than usual. At the time I was doing one last load of washing. I just happened to be poking the clothes down into the copper, so I had the copper stick in my hand when he came in and, well, his nose got broken.

I made it clear I'd done my duty. No more children. So I got the sewing machine out.

Anita was just standing there in the bathroom, by the linen press, holding the sheets up with her head to the side, two little creases between her eyes, like Lance looked when he pored over the form guide, his little transistor squeaking away beside him.

Florence cleared her throat and brushed something from her

lap, and I watched Anita's face change as it dawned on her that she was holding two double-bed sheets sewn together up the middle. I've told you my reasons for keeping Lance on the other side of the bed, but I wasn't going to explain why I sewed the sheets up the middle to those two, looking at me as if my head was melting.

If the truth be known, I never liked sexual intercourse. Once I got over how just plain rude the act was it seemed like a ludicrous thing to do.

Marriage wasn't like *Mrs. Miniver* at all, Cecily. Mrs Miniver couldn't have been the woman she was without a noble man like Walter Pidgeon. He came from New Brunswick in America, and of course Lance brought me home to Brunswick to live, but Lance certainly wasn't Walter Pidgeon. He wasn't any sort of Lancelot either.

Anyrate, as soon as Judith got married and moved out Lance took his ashtray and his oxygen apparatus and moved into the second bedroom. I took the sewn-up sheets off, and put them at the bottom of the linen press and moved into the middle of the bed.

So now I'm here. For one more hour I stayed in that house that was never actually mine, with my husband's mistress, but try as I might I couldn't reconcile harbouring her. As the mother of the rightful blood offspring of Lance's loins, and since Morris has sent word that Lance said, 'No child of mine's mother should be upset in any way,' She'll probably inherit the whole place until she dies. I don't care. I've had enough. For the last time I admired my lovely doorknobs and Walter's trophies reflecting the warped little house I've lived in for sixty years. Sixty years living a lie. I said goodbye to my life's work, my cross-stitching, and told Florence I was going.

'Hang on,' she said, 'I'll get me cardie and go with you.'

Pat always had to be part of everything as well.

In the six days that Margery and Florence lived together, Anita dropped in every day. While she dressed Margery's wound she'd attempt to solve any conflicts the two old ladies were having, then make sure they had an evening meal organised. She'd also search her mother's room, inspect the little basket under the seat of her wheelie frame and check her pockets for cigarettes or, more specifically, matches. On Tuesday, Anita breezed down the passage carrying groceries and cans of Home Brand light beer, Ruby trailing her, spearing her cardboard sword into invisible assailants. Florence was alone in the house, sitting in Lance's chair, the radio blaring, her red stilettos tapping on the cross-stitched mat—*You gain nothing by removing the laughing lunatic from the empty theatre except to deny him his happiness*—an opened stubbie in one hand and a cigarette in the other.

'How are ya, love?' her mother said.

Little Ruby turned the television down.

Anita said, 'Where did you get that cigarette and how did you light it?'

Florence looked at the cigarette in her hand as if she'd never seen it before.

'I suppose it was the same person who gave you that stubbie?' Anita said.

Mystified, Florence replied, 'I suppose it was.'

Anita went into the kitchen, dumped the shopping bags on the table then stood in the doorway, glaring down at her mother. 'Where's Margery?'

Florence looked around the room and peered down the passage. Then she stared past Anita into the cupboard-sized kitchen and said, 'Not in there, is she?'

Anita maintained her gaze, looking steadily into her mother's large blue eyes. 'Can't see her.'

'Tried the toilet?'

Ruby said she'd check and skipped out the back door. Anita packed the beer, eggs and milk into the empty fridge. 'Have you discussed the evening meal?'

'Who with?' Florence said, glancing at the empty chair next to her.

Ruby came back in and declared that Margery was not in the toilet. 'She's not in the car either, Mum,' she added, and they both stared accusingly at Florence.

Florence said, 'Get us another beer, wouldya, love?'

Anita took her mother's empty beer bottle then snatched her cigarette and dropped it down the neck. 'Ruby, check the park.'

Ruby ran to check the park, her pirate cape flapping behind her.

Anita searched all five rooms of the tiny, single-fronted workers' cottage. Then she checked the shed and the car boot. She went through Mrs Parsons' shed to her house, tried the front and back door and peered in all her windows. On her way back she popped her head over Tony's back fence, but no one was about so she went across the road and banged on Tyson's door. From somewhere deep in the dark, fungusy interior, someone called, 'Fuck off,' so she took a deep breath and went next door to Kevin's place.

Kevin answered the door eating corn kernels from a tin. He was wearing a knee-length, green reflector jumpsuit and one bicycle shoe because the other ankle was still in plaster. The plaster featured one signature—his own. He smiled broadly at Anita and said, 'I think I've placed you now.'

'Seen Margery?'

'She's lived over the road for sixty years,' he said and winked.

Anita sighed. 'Have you seen Margery *today*?'

'I rode past her on my way home from work. She was at the tram stop on Sydney Road, city-bound, in her hat and coat. I called out, but she was deep in conversation with herself.' He scooped another spoonful of corn into his mouth.

Anita turned to go back across the road and Kevin said, 'I know where I've seen you. At the pub, years ago. And there's something else, something you don't know, but everyone else does.' Anita was gone, gliding back over to Margery's house on her two fine, tea-coloured legs.

'Do you know who your father is?' Kevin called, but she ignored him.

Florence saw them marching down the passage towards her again.

She raised one finger, 'About that beer ...' but Anita went straight past her to the fridge. Florence was pleased when she took a can of beer out, confused when she held it tantalisingly in front of her. 'Flossy, try to remember. Think! When Margery left, where did she say she was going?'

Florence's eyebrows moved together and she bit her bottom lip. 'Margery,' she said, knowing she knew her but failing to conjure a memory that would show her exactly who Margery was.

'Your flatmate,' Ruby said.

'The old woman?'

'Yes,' said Anita, and Ruby added, 'You're no spring chicken yourself, Nan.'

Anita nudged her daughter. Florence creased her eyebrows together again, focussed on the couch opposite, trying to remember. She folded and unfolded her thin, alcoholic legs, then said brightly, 'To see a friend?'

Ruby said, 'She hasn't got any friends, besides us.'

'It's not a guessing game, Flossy. She's lost.' Anita leaned down, took her mother's chin in her hand and looked deeply into her eyes. 'Did Judith come today?'

'I would have remembered if *she'd* been here.'

Anita let her mother take the can of beer from her hand. 'So Margery hasn't gone with Judith?'

Florence said, 'Na,' looped her thin finger under the pull tab

and ripped it from the can. Ruby fetched the mobile phone from
her mother's basket and handed it to her.

'She said she was going to her sister's.'

# PART FIVE

*'Folly has raptures to give.'*

Robert Burns, 'The Raptures of Folly', 1793

'It's too late to jump now. Far too many people about.'

Margery sat on the edge of the queen-sized bed, which she had circumnavigated several times in order to make tidy again. 'Well, it could be said, Cecily, that you, my greatest comfort, have been my undoing. Twice.' She wiped her eyes with her hanky, and after some time she said, 'Actually, that's not fair. It's me. You couldn't help dying and Dad was right, I should have let go, then perhaps things wouldn't be the mess they appear to be.' She allowed herself to weep again for a short time. When she was composed again, she said, 'I suppose I'll have to admit, it does seem as if I may have let people down. *Three feet of ice does not come from one day of freezing weather,* as they say.' Then, in an effort to console herself, she added, 'At least Judith's finally got the pearls.'

She gathered her handbags and was heading to go down for breakfast when the receptionist arrived with a tray: tea, milk, juice, toast, jam, butter and fruit compote. 'You're Mr Boyle's mother-in-law, aren't you?'

'He's an adulterer as well.'

'Your family are on their way; they've been very worried about you.'

Margery said, 'That's nonsense. I've been a dam in the river of everyone's life forever.'

'I'm sure you haven't.'

'Well, you wouldn't know, would you? Why did you tell them I was here?'

The receptionist put the tray on the table and pulled out the chair for Margery to sit down. 'A policeman phoned your son-in-law when he arrived for a breakfast meeting. That's all I know. Sit down and have your breakfast.'

Margery sighed, sat down, turned the teapot three times and lifted the lid on the plate. 'Eggs. No point letting them go to waste.'

'No.' The receptionist stayed while Margery scoffed her breakfast down, and as she was pouring her second cup of tea, the Blandons arrived—Walter and Anita, Barry and Judith. The receptionist left, closing the door behind her.

Walter rushed to his mother and threw his arms around her. Her tea spilled into the saucer. 'You alright, Mumsy?'

Judith slapped her forehead with her palm. 'Jesus Christ, Marge. We've been frantic!' Anita checked Margery's shin and studied her swollen nose and black eyes. Then she sat back and looked at Margery, who poured her spilled tea back into her cup, refusing to look at anyone. 'Why did you come here?'

'I needed to get away.' Margery sipped her tea.

'Why not just go to the library, or the park?' Barry asked.

Margery slammed her cup into its saucer, spilling the tea again. 'All my life I've done the right thing—and look what's happened. My choice is my husband's mistress or a home for mad, incontinent old people.'

'You talk to yourself.'

'Shut up, Barry,' Judith said.

'It's not fair to blame Cecily. She's the best company I've got! It would have been better had I died along with her.' Margery looked defiantly at her children. 'If she'd stayed alive everything would have been much better.'

'You wouldn't have us, Mumsy, we've been very concerned—'

'Nor would I have had a husband who had a mistress for fifty years. Their illegitimate child is standing over there, and she's forty years old!'

'Thirty-nine,' Anita said.

Walter stood and, using a wise and reasonable tone, said, 'It is understandable that you don't want your husband's friend to live with you, but—'

'It's outrageous!'

Walter hung his head. 'Mumsy, I'm sorry.'

Margery glared at him then looked away.

Barry suggested that times had changed and went on to make the point that Florence wasn't a bad person, that Lance might have felt good knowing that she could find refuge at the house. 'After all,' he said, looking at Judith, 'everyone's entitled to a home.'

'She can have my room at your retirement village.'

Judith said, 'There is no village, Marge,' and Barry shook his head, 'There's nothing ...'

'Don't try to make yourself look good, Barry, just because you're giving me and DeeAndra the house.' The BlackBerry in Barry's hand buzzed and he silenced it immediately.

'Look, Marge,' Judith said, 'as it stands now, the thing is, you don't have to live with Flossy forever, but she's got nowhere to go so, just for the time being, can she stay with you? In the circumstances, it's the right thing to do.'

'Please,' Anita added.

Margery sipped her tea.

'Lance stuck by all of us, in his way,' Walter said. 'He didn't abandon you or Floss, he did the right fing.'

'He lied, betrayed me.'

'But you can't blame Flossy, Mrs Blandon. It's not right.'

Margery looked Anita in the eye. '"Right" is whatever anyone prefers "right" to be, it seems.'

Anita threw up her hands. 'Well, Mum lost her job and her home at the pub when Lance blew it up, and now she's homeless again.'

'As far as I'm concerned, what *she* did wasn't right.'

'In some people's eyes, yes, but two wrongs don't make a right, and all they did was be happy together, and Lance still did the right thing by you. He didn't throw you out, he didn't hurt you on purpose. You know what it's like to be lost and lonely, you found that out when you were fifteen.'

'How dare you! That's not fair.' Anita flinched and turned to look at the view. 'What I did was right. I stayed faithful to my husband because a marriage is a marriage.'

'That's only according to God,' Walter said, and looked at the view with Anita, but he could still feel her eyes on his back.

In the silence, Barry spoke, directing his words at Judith. 'And *was* it the right thing to do? For the kids, for your husband, for *you*?'

Judith said, 'Shut up, Barry,' so he held his hands up in surrender again and stood at the window with Anita and Walter.

'If Dad was feeling lost and lonely, then okay, he found compensation in the arms—'

'*Compensation?*' Anita cried.

'But imagine how Marge feels? Lost? Lonely? Lied to? Take it from me because I know what it's like to learn your husband prefers someone else, that whenever he looks at you he's lying to you, repulsed—'

'Now come on, Jude, that's not how I feel about you.'

Walter put his hand on Margery's shoulder. 'I feel like a bit of a dill myself.'

'We all do,' Judith said.

'I have morals I'm prepared to die for. He betrayed me, you all betrayed me—even you, Walter.'

Judith said, 'Walter knew less than I did, Marge. Bloody Morris is the one who knew everything.'

Anita added that all Walter ever does is try to help, and Margery shot back, 'He was trying to help *your* mother.'

'He was trying to help you too. And I'd like to point out that Floss could have easily marched across the street and told you the truth and broken up your home and family for the sake of her own happiness, and mine, but she didn't.'

'Well, two cheers for her,' Judith said.

Anita sighed. 'We don't want to put either of you in a home. We know now that you must have felt terrible putting your own poor mother into a home.'

The teacup and saucer slipped from Margery's hands,

bounced on the carpet splashing tea across the hibiscus and lyrebirds. Anita and Walter reached for the cup and saucer, and Margery put her hand out to Judith, indicating she needed to get to the bathroom quickly. Her legs buckled beneath her and she leaned heavily on Judith's arms, but they got there. Margery clutched the handbasin. 'Thank you, Judith. I'll be alright now.'

'You sure?'

'Yes, dear.'

Judith closed the door.

'Don't lock the door,' Anita called, but she did. It was like the day in the park; bells were echoing and her chest was thick with the weight of her labouring heart when it became clear that Cecily could not be found in a room or a street nearby. She put the toilet lid down and sat, taking deep breaths, her hand over her heart. When she felt she could, she raised her eyes and looked at her reflection, looked past the bruises and her swollen nose into her eyes. She removed her broken glasses, put them in her handbag, and confronted herself.

'Well,' she said, 'there it is. Nailed to my own principles with my own words, and at this very minute I'm feeling just how my mother felt when I put her in a home. *Let the punishment be equal with the offence.*'

Judith knocked at the door. 'Talk it over with us, Mum, your family, we're in the next room alive.'

Margery sat up straight, cleared her throat and said, 'Our parents brought us up to live by principles of right and wrong, but I know now that sometimes people can be wrong. They think what they're doing is right, but it turns out it isn't. You've got to be able to see things as they are, and then do what's best. And so here I am and, as I see it, I'm expected to go against all my long-held principles about what's decent and good, what's respon-sible and right, in order to do what all those other people out there think is morally correct. They're asking me to embrace my enemy for the sake of what's "right".'

She smoothed the wet handkerchief, folded it neatly and put

it in her handbag but had to reach for some toilet paper to stop the tears falling onto her lap. Through the door Walter said, 'Mumsy, you still in there?'

She rolled her eyes, '*Tsk*', and reached for the doorknob, but she made herself stop and look again. 'Go on, Margery, say it.' She reached for more toilet paper and muffled another sob. 'There's a lot I didn't know, but if I'm honest, I know now I have to look to myself to see why.' Her breakfast rose into her throat, but she swallowed it down and took a deep breath. The she powdered her tender nose, adjusted her hat and smoothed her coat. 'It all seems so clear now.'

They were relieved to see their mother, dry-eyed, standing as straight as her stoop would allow, her expression composed and somewhat preoccupied, as usual. Margery looked at her children. Usually they presented so well, but Walter's hair was stringy and dangling from his bald patch, and Judith was wearing a faded tracksuit. Anita was sitting on the bed, her aims and legs crossed tightly, her knees jigging. Margery realised it was the perfect opportunity to be what everyone needed her to be. 'What about your exam, Walter?'

Judith looked at her watch. 'It just started.'

I'm glad they prevented me from jumping off the balcony, because I met Mrs Parsons' son. He's a nice-looking man, olive-skinned, got the tight, curly hair. I'll say again that I'm not prejudice, but when he showed up at my door I assumed he was a God-botherer, so I held the screen door snib and was about to say, 'I'm Jewish'—it usually works—but he said, 'I'm Samuel. Are you Mrs Blandon?'

When I said, 'Yes,' he looked as if he was about to cry, so of course I asked, 'What's happened? Is it Morris?'

'No,' he said, 'it's Samuel. Sam Parsons. You were my mother's best friend.'

Well, you could have waved away a fly and I'd have toppled over. I had to take hold of the doorknob. 'I tied her laces,' I said. You know, Mrs Parsons always took an interest in my sewing when I showed her, always listened when I explained about the stitches and the different sorts of threads and linens. Of course, now I know I could have been more like a friend would have been—talked about the books she was interested in—but you live and learn. I gave Samuel Mrs Parsons' watch. He was reluctant to have it but I said, 'You should keep it, even though you can't wear it. I gave my daughter my watch, and my pearls, and your mother's watch ticked away on her wrist for all those years … just waiting until you came along for it.'

He started to cry when I said that.

Anyrate, Kevin gave him some photos of all the neighbours and the kids having fun in the street. There were swarms of kids playing in the street in those days. You don't see them nowadays. I saw photos of Melbourne Cup parties and pub parties with Lance and Florence there, and all the neighbourhood plays Kevin put on. Even Faye and Joye were in some photos. They were big even back then.

That reminds me, we never heard another thing from Faye or Joye. Not a thing.

I was in some photos with Mrs Parsons next to me, or just bits of us: a leg or a foot, the side of her beret, my cardigan. There was a lovely shot of her and me standing together at her front gate. On the back of the photo it said, in Pat's writing, 'Princess Margery and Squigglehead, 1956'. It was taken during the Olympics. 'The Friendly Games', they called them. Of course, none of us could afford to go so we had our own Gold Street Olympics right here in the park. The kids had brick-throwing competitions, high jump, foot races up and down the street, Olympic cricket ...

It was the life Samuel could have had.

'I just turned sixty-three a few days ago,' Samuel said. That would have been the card Mrs Parsons bought. He said he got a card from his mother every year.

That's when Kevin asked about the rumours. 'What was wrong with your mother; why did your father take you away?'

Samuel's expression turned very embarrassed and sad, and he couldn't look at us, but all he said was that it was family pressure. 'People had attitudes we don't find acceptable these days,' he said, but he hastened to make clear that his father supported Mrs Parsons all his life, right up until only weeks before he died. That'd be the hundred dollars every month, I'd say. I suppose Samuel was torn between his family wishes and his mother. It goes without saying that it's obviously a very real shame he left it for so long before he did something about it.

Anyrate, he's going to renovate Mrs Parsons house and move in, so he says. Kevin's volunteered to help him, though I don't know when he'll have the time because he's joined a rowing club of late and he's often up and away before sunrise.

Now that I've thought about things, Cecily, it's as clear as the nose on my face that poor Mrs Parsons was treated dreadfully, simply because some people didn't approve of her type.

Before Samuel left, he said, 'I'm glad you're still alive,' and I said, 'Probably only for a few more years.'

But, you know, I intend to enjoy them as best I can.

There's no point living for things we can't have because you don't get the life you could have.

Naturally, I've had to accept that Morris has made a life for himself overseas. He's got his own family. They say they might be able to come back one day, but Ray tells me it's tricky. I happened to overhear him chatting to Walter and Judith on the street one day, and they mentioned something about plastic surgery and second-hand passports.

I lament not having my wits about me for so long, but, Cecily, there are things to be said for not knowing the truth about some things. And since I'd been through it all again, told you everything, in the end I also came to this: basically, Florence Potter is a floozy and an adulteress, but she isn't evil, or bad. So if I deny her refuge, then I am doing something bad, some might say evil. It's the principle of the matter, so I've had to shelter my enemy for the sake of what's right.

It's like the death-penalty principle. If you agree with the death penalty then you'd have to agree to hang your own son, or let someone hang your nephew for doing something wrong. It makes you a killer.

I don't need God to tell me what the right thing to do is. I've always had the wise words from the calendar, and I've tried to do the right thing, and although I suspect Judith might have tried to kill me, I must believe her when she says she wouldn't want Charmaine killed, if you see the principle.

If the truth be known, I was never really fond of Barry, but Pud likes him, even though he's an adulterer, and he said Judith was never 'warm and tender'. Perhaps that's not entirely her fault, and I can't condemn Morris for having an illegitimate child any more than I can blame Anita for being one ...

There was talk of selling my little house and buying me and old Forgetful Florence a little flat each, but selling my home to furnish her is just far too generous, and anyway, she'd probably burn herself to death. They've got her on a list for a nice home somewhere, but I'm warned it could take some time. We'll see what winter brings. We've had some terrible flus these past years, and this house is draughty and damp when it rains, and she's got the bad chest, being a smoker.

Anyrate, Judith's used my house as security to get a loan for her gymnasium. Judith's much better. After Barry left she was terrible for a while, but she's come good. She looks marvellous, just marvellous, though the weight's come back on, of course, but she carries it well, and when all is said and done she's happier, and that's the important thing, isn't it? I still think it was all that grapefruit that gave her the rash, though she swears it was stress. I told her, 'You've got to be happy in the now, you can't just be happy in hindsight.'

Anyrate, there's a boom in Boxercise, apparently, and her gymnasium is in an old warehouse down near Sydney Road. Judith Boyle—Fitness, Health and All Your Beauty Needs (Ladies Only). Walter helps out, and it's wonderful for him as well. He failed the Basic Food Hygiene test—twice—but I'll take the blame for that, because even though I was driven to the balcony, I could have been more considerate about the timing and his exam. He's doing the course again.

The new couple living at Tony's have complained about the noise and the drunks from the pub. They're lobbying to have it closed. Florence wouldn't sign their petition, and I didn't either. How dare they move in and just think they can change things to suit themselves? Tyson upended their rubbish onto their car last night, which set their car alarm off, and then their house alarms went off. I see Tyson out there today, cutting down their new tree for his barbecue.

You should have seen the look on Pat's face when I turned up to see her with Florence! Florence was just standing there in the day room, looking about as if she was seeing an elephant for the first time, when Pat pointed at me and said, 'Did you come in her car?'

'You lied to me, Pat Cruickshank,' I said. 'Kept secrets, for fifty years.'

'It was the right thing,' Kevin said. 'Mum was in the middle. What you didn't know didn't hurt you, or Flossy, or the kids, or anyone.'

It's a flawed principle, if you ask me. Anyrate, Florence pipes up and says, 'You can't kill a whale for swimming past, can you?'

Well, I've never heard that proverb before but I imagine what she was trying to say was that Pat was doing what she had to do to keep everyone swimming along, for the greater good. I could easily have said, 'Shielding men from the effects of folly is to fill the world with fools,' but I didn't. You have to admit it did me no harm knowing nothing about Morris, did it?

Anyrate, Pat is the one in a nursing home now, and I'm still living in my own home, with her best friend! So ha-ha-har!

I just hope we don't burn to death in our beds.

It is a responsibility looking after Florence, and a bit like living with a praying mantis. Nothing seems out of the ordinary, then all of a sudden I notice there's a creature in the house. That said, we all know there were a lot of things ... I just never noticed them.

All along Kevin knew everything, of course. Absolutely amazed, he was, the day he came in and saw Florence sitting there in Lance's chair. Fifi hopped straight onto her lap, and Kevin shook his head and said, 'I'd never have imagined this in a million years, Mrs B, that you would end up living with Flossy Potter.'

I said, 'Never judge a book by its cover.'

# ACKNOWLEDGEMENTS

Thanks go to Jenny Darling and all at Random House. Also thanks to my honest and dedicated readers: Terry, Natalie Warren, Mercy O'Meara and Sue Maslin. For their inside knowledge, nurses Hannah May Ham and Alicia Ham, and for his expert advice, Morgan McLay, and as always, for love and support, lan McLay.

Thanks also to Vic Arts, and The Victorian Writers' Centre for the 'Writing @ Rosebank' fellowship

Rosalie Ham was borns and raised in Jerilderie, New South Wales. She completed her secondary education at St Margaret's School, Berwick, in 1972. After travelling and working at a variety of jobs (including aged care) for most of her twenties, Rosalie completed a Bachelor of Education majoring in Drama and Literature (Deakin University, 1989), and achieved a Master of Arts, Creative Writing (RMIT, Melbourne) in 2007. Her first novel, *The Dressmaker,* was published in 2000. Her second novel, *Summer at Mount Hope,* was published in 2005.

Rosalie has also had stories published in *Meanjin, The Age, The Bulletin* and *Invisible Ink.* When she is not writing, Rosalie teaches literature.

ligature *finest*

Made in the USA
Monee, IL
15 April 2022